Colin Falconer is the author of over thirty books of fiction and non-fiction, which have been published in Australia, UK and the USA and translated into sixteen languages. A former journalist, he was born in London and now lives in Western Australia. Colin Falconer writes contemporary fiction as Mark D'Arbanville.

ALSO BY COLIN FALCONER

Anastasia
Aztec
When We Were Gods
Harem
Death Watch
Venom
Fury
Opium
Triad
Dangerous
Disappeared
Rough Justice
The Certainty of Doing Evil

AS MARK D'ARBANVILLE

The Naked Husband
The Naked Heart

MY
BEAUTIFUL
SPY

COLIN FALCONER

BANTAM
SYDNEY • AUCKLAND • TORONTO • NEW YORK • LONDON

MY BEAUTIFUL SPY
A BANTAM BOOK

First published in Australia and New Zealand in 2005 by Bantam
This edition published in Australia and New Zealand in 2006 by Bantam

National Library of Australia
Cataloguing-in-Publication Entry

Falconer, Colin, 1953–. .
    My beautiful spy.

    ISBN 1 86325 506 0.

    1. World War, 1939–1945 – Secret service –
    Great Britain – Fiction. I. Title.

    A823.3

Transworld Publishers,
a division of Random House Australia Pty Ltd
20 Alfred Street, Milsons Point, NSW 2061
http://www.randomhouse.com.au

Random House New Zealand Limited
18 Poland Road, Glenfield, Auckland

Transworld Publishers,
a division of The Random House Group Ltd
61-63 Uxbridge Road, Ealing, London W5 5SA

Random House Inc.
1540 Broadway, New York, New York 10036

Cover design: Darian Causby/Highway 51 Design Works
Cover images: Getty Images
Typeset in Sabon 12/15.5pt by Midland Typesetters, Australia
Printed and bound by Griffin Press, Netley, South Australia

10 9 8 7 6 5 4 3 2 1

For my beautiful Karen-Maree

When love is not madness, it is not love.
— Pedro Calderon de la Barca

BOOK ONE

BOOK ONE

I.

Bucharest, September 1944

In other circumstances he should have been wary of venturing into the ruins of Bucharest after sunset. Six blocks from the hotel the city was a world of darkness and monstrous shadow, lit only by the blue flames of spirit stoves, refugees huddled in the wreckage of ruined apartment blocks.

Soon he was lost. He swore heavily under his breath. Christ. Even with the heavy revolver in his jacket pocket he was nervous. There were scavengers and deserters all over the city.

He turned a corner and bumped heavily into another man. It startled him and he reeled back, ready for an attack. But the man ignored him and walked on.

He was about to walk on, too, but some instinct made him turn around and follow him. He moved out of the shadows and saw him for just a moment, silhouetted in the moonlight: a broad and square face, flat and hard as a shovel, hair shaved short to his skull. He knew this was the man he had seen that afternoon, in Demischenko's office, standing expressionless behind his chief.

The man turned into an apartment block at the end of the street and went inside. This was it, this was her apartment.

He took out the revolver. He had practised on a shooting range but he had never fired in anger or in darkness or in a confined space. He heard the Russian's footsteps echo on the stairwell above him. He started to run up the stairs.

In the darkness, he tripped on some rubbish and fell headlong. His shinbone cracked on the concrete. He swore at the pain.

Already the Russian was kicking in the door. He shouted a warning, hoping to distract him, and ran blindly up the stairs.

The door to the apartment lay on the floor, ripped off its hinges.

A single candle burned on a table in the middle of the room. He called Daniela's name but there was no answer.

There were few places to hide and he had only a few seconds to decide. He could not wait there in the doorway. Holding the revolver in front of him, two-handed, he ran into the kitchen.

Empty.

'Daniela!'

He has to come for me first. I can't let anything happen to her.

He heard a noise behind him, from the bedroom. He turned, saw the Russian silhouetted in the doorway in the candlelight. He saw the pistol raised towards him and felt very calm. There was a sense of sudden and blissful peace. It was over. He knew what would happen and he took a split second to correct his aim, knowing it might make every difference to her, if not to him.

The pistol shot sounded like cannon fire in that confined space. He fired his own weapon at the same time. He did not feel the bullet. He did not even know he was hit. He concentrated on his aim, as if he was back on the practice range, and squeezed off two more shots before he went down. There was no pain.

2.

Nick Davis first saw Daniela Simonici in the American Bar of the Athenee Palace Hotel in Bucharest in the June of 1940. He couldn't take his eyes off her. The city was full of beautiful women, penniless countesses and fox-furred demimondaines looking to be rescued, and until that moment he had spared them only an appreciative glance, as a man does.

But this woman was different.

The crowd was mostly British and American journalists, and there were a handful of diplomats like Nick. She walked in with a German tourist – he was SD or working for the Abwehr, they all were – and he was already drunk. He was talking too loud and laughing too much, and everyone in the bar was staring. In the corner the knot of Germans from the legation on Strada Victor Emmanuel III didn't like what they were seeing either.

Her boyfriend was young, tall and blond, a fine example of Hitler's dream except that he couldn't stand unaided. His lips were shining and wet, his eyes unfocused. The delectable woman with him had reached a pitch of embarrassment; her eyes wandered the room and several times they returned to Nick, speculating.

German boys were much in demand. They had money

and they had just conquered Poland. It was an irresistible combination. That and the ice-blue eyes.

Bendix finished his gin and tonic and lit yet another cigarette. 'It's getting bad. Two ICI chaps got beaten up last week, right outside their houses. These people want us out, Davis.'

Nick wondered if Bendix was the right choice for the operation, if he could hold his nerve. He had warned Abrams about him, but there wasn't much alternative, in the circumstances.

'Just hold on for a little while longer,' Nick said.

'It's all right for you people, down here.'

Nick looked over at the woman. She had glanced up again. He caught her eye. Suddenly it was hard to concentrate. 'We need you to help us,' Nick said.

'We?'

'The government. We can't let the Germans walk in and take that oil.' The Ploesti oilfields were the largest oil reserves in Europe. Hitler needed oil for his armoured divisions. Before the war many British oil companies had won concessions there. The Germans had pressured the Romanian King to kick them out, and he had complied. He didn't have much choice.

'How are you going to stop them?'

'There are plans in place. But we need you, Bendix. You have the contacts up there, you know who we have to pay off.'

'Pay off? What are you planning to do, for God's sake?'

'We just need someone to make some payments to the right people. Think you can do that for us?'

Bendix smoothed down his moustache. He looked around the bar; his hands were shaking. He was a businessman, not a spy. MI6 had recruited a lot of the executives from British oil companies up there at Ploesti, but these days there were fewer and fewer of them to sweet talk.

7

'Not cut out for this cloak and dagger,' Bendix said. He finished his drink and stood up. 'All right. I'll hold up my end. You just tell me what you want me to do.'

Nick gave him his instructions as they walked outside. Bendix's driver was waiting in a dark Opel. 'Good luck, Bendix,' Nick said and they shook hands. Bendix climbed into the car and drove away.

Nick thought about catching a taxicab and changed his mind. It was only three blocks to his apartment. He crossed the square past the Atheneum, the city's opera house, ignoring the imprecations of the *trasura* drivers.

He heard a commotion under the portico of the hotel. It was the blond German and the girl he had seen at the bar. They were having an argument and the girl was screaming. Nick turned around and went back.

'Are you all right?' he said to her in French.

The German boy was trying to drag her towards a waiting taxicab. He had her by the arm and she was trying to pull herself free. The doorman was pointedly ignoring them, as was the taxicab driver.

'Go away, Englisher, this is not your business,' the blond man said.

The girl swore at the young man in French and kicked out at his shins. He yelped in pain and hit her across the cheek with the back of his hand.

Nick spun him around and hit him once, hard, in the stomach. He doubled over and went down.

As he lay on the ground, the woman kicked him in the ribs with her stilettos for good measure. She was about to kick him again, but Nick pulled her away.

'*Cul de vache!*' she shouted.

'A real charmer. Known him long?'

'Long enough.'

'Who is he?' he asked her.

'His name's Haller.'

8

'Is he your boyfriend?'

'Tonight he was my boyfriend. But he's not any more.'

'What was that all about?'

'He insisted I go home with him. I said no.'

'A lady's prerogative.'

'These German boys don't think so.'

Haller had crawled to the potted aspidistra outside the foyer and was noisily regurgitating the evening's alcohol. The doorman looked horrified.

'My name's Nick. Nick Davis. I'm with the British Legation.'

'Daniela Simonici.' She was loose limbed and tall, with long dark hair to her shoulders and golden eyes. Her clothes were expensive, purchased from one of the Paris salons along the Chaussée. A woman like this was not accustomed to walking anywhere.

'Well. As you no longer have a boyfriend, and the streets are not safe for a lady this time of night, would you allow an English gentleman to escort you home?'

A flicker of a smile. 'Are you?'

'English?'

'A gentleman.'

'Of course.'

'As long as you don't expect a goodnight kiss.'

'A Nazi salute and a promise to write would be fine.'

That look in her eyes: what did it mean?

'Let me get a *trasura*. Where do you live?' He nodded towards one of the horse-drawn carriages waiting outside the hotel, its owner staring truculently at them from its running board.

'Near Strada Lipscani.' The Strada Lipscani was in the Jewish Quarter, and he wondered if she was a Jew. That could be trouble. But he took her arm and led her over to the carriage. 'Let's go.'

The *trasuras* appeared romantic from the balcony of the

Athenee Palace but up close they just smelled of horse and the driver's peasant sweat. Nick could make out the horse's ribs through the bronzed skin of its flanks.

'Go out with Germans a lot?'

'He seemed like a nice boy. He is quite good-looking and he tells funny stories. But some men change when they get some drink in them. I don't know why.'

'What's he doing in Bucharest?' Nick said, the professional in him working round the clock.

'Something to do with oil, I think.'

Something to do with oil. The only reason the Germans were in Romania had something to do with oil; something to do with Hitler wanting all of it.

'I think he'll kick himself in the morning when he remembers how he behaved. I can't imagine why a man would prefer the company of a bottle to yours.'

'For myself, I'm glad he got drunk now. Now I am being rescued by a beautiful Englishman with blue eyes. I think everything has turned out very well.' She looked up at him and he was suddenly aware of how close she was sitting. And she was so beautiful.

As they got further from the hotel, the boulevard grew darker, empty. A dangerous night, and edgy. He could hear the greenshirts chanting in the squares and the churches, and occasionally they saw mobs of belligerent young men roaming the streets, singing and waving Romanian flags, celebrating the imminent fall of Paris. It was a carnival atmosphere, with an undercurrent of violence.

'You live alone?'

'You do not have to speak French to me any more,' she said, in perfect English.

'Where did you learn to speak English?'

'I learned Yiddish, French and English from my father. I learned German from my mother, she was born in

Timisoara. I can tell you're surprised. You think perhaps I am overqualified for my present position?'

'What is your present position?'

'I dance with Germans and I let them buy me drinks and silk stockings.'

He wanted to ask her if that was all she did. Bucharest was not London; women here did much as they wanted and, for a Romanian woman, sleeping with a lover was as fashionable as buying a new hat. So he was left to wonder.

They turned off the Calea Victoriei, the horse's hooves clipping on the cobblestones. The wide boulevards became streets; the streets became alleyways. At this time of night she would have been an inviting target if she had walked alone. Who would care in Bucharest these days if a Jewess was raped or murdered? It happened often enough at police headquarters.

'Where are your family?'

'My mother died just before the war. My father is an habitual criminal. He insists on being Jewish at every opportunity, so the police were forced to lock him up.'

'I see.'

'What about you, *monsieur*? You are a diplomat, *né*?'

'Does it show?'

'If I gave you money, could you get me three visas?'

It was a question he was asked all the time, but not so bluntly and not by a beautiful woman in the middle of the night. He hesitated and she took that for her answer.

'It doesn't matter.'

'You want to get out of Bucharest?'

'I'm Jewish. Of course I do.'

'Three visas?'

'I have . . . a brother. We are still trying to get my father out of prison and when we do, we want to get out of this awful country and away from the fascists as soon as we can.'

11

In Romania, visas were more valuable than gold; the British Government had instructed the legation to issue visas under only the most extenuating circumstance. They didn't want all these Jews flooding into Palestine and upsetting the Arabs. 'I'll see what I can do. But these days it's very difficult, the Foreign Office in London . . .'

'It's all right, I should not have asked.' She tapped the driver on the shoulder. 'Just here.'

They stopped outside a rundown apartment building; a single gas light burned above a green door, and the paint was cracked with age. The only other light came from a feeble street lamp further down the alley. The kind of place the greenshirts liked to dump a beaten Jew.

She saw the question in his eyes: A woman who knew four languages and wore expensive clothes from the Chaussée, what was she doing living in a rundown apartment in the Jewish commercial district?

'We used to live on Bratianu,' she said. 'Before the government took everything we had.' Her hand brushed against his. 'Thank you for your kindness.'

'Perhaps I will see you again.'

'I hope so, *monsieur . . .*'

He helped her down from the *trasura* onto the cobblestones.

'Wait,' he said. He took a card from his pocket and handed it to her, took out a fountain pen from inside his jacket. 'Write down the names. I'll see what I can do about the visas.'

She gave him a wry smile. She didn't believe him, of course.

And then she leaned across and kissed him. A long time since anyone had kissed him like that. She pulled away and he watched her disappear through the door. He got back into the carriage and the *trasura* driver flicked the reins. The horse plodded on again through the darkened streets.

And that was all. A chance meeting. An act of gallantry. A brief flirtation. He was married and she was probably too young. He imagined he would never see her again.

3.

But a week later he still could not stop thinking about her.

He watched his wife pour herself a drink from the decanter and knew he hated his marriage. They no longer had anything to talk about and their relations with each other were bloodless. It was as much his fault as hers; he had dedicated his life to his work, and having a decorative wife had been an essential part of it. But he supposed he had been a very suitable husband, if not a passionate one.

They were a habit with each other. But didn't most couples live this way? Most of his acquaintances endured it with equanimity, spiced boredom with an occasional discreet affair. Why should his life be different?

Divorce seemed unthinkable. Jennifer would be devastated. And how would the boys react? And yet the war had made him realise how precious life was, and he didn't want to waste any more of it on this stale marriage.

It had been easier when they had the boys with them, the emotional distance between them had not mattered as much. Now they were alone, he realised how empty their lives were with each other.

A light breeze came with twilight, stirring the deathly

hush of the afternoon. The leaves on the lime trees had curled to brown in the heat. A fireball sun turned the gold-leaf dome of the Byzantine church across the street to flame. As it fell down the sky, a rose blush appeared on the stark walls of the King's palace.

It was the hour of the Korso, when the bourgeoisie of Bucharest took their promenade along the Calea Victoriei. They were drab, the Romanian middle class, the women in Parisian black with such pearls and silver fox furs as they could afford. It was only peasants who wore bright colours, so a Romanian proclaimed his status in dreariness.

But tonight there was an added solemnity about the walkers. The shadow of war was inching closer.

For a year now the newspapers had scoffed at the Germans and their grandiose military pretensions; the fall of Poland and Norway and the Low Countries had been explained away in the press as blunders by ill-prepared generals.

But for middle class Bucharesti the fall of Paris was akin to the barbarians sacking ancient Rome. Didn't they call Bucharest 'Paris in a village'? The architecture and boule-vards were inspired by France, there was even an Arc de Triomphe for the fallen of the Great War. When the Germans jackbooted into Paris, it was the rape of culture and art and fashion; no-one loved the French like the Romanians, and with the centre of the civilised world under the swastika, all the old certainties were gone.

Nick had been in the country over a year now yet still did not have its pulse. He sometimes felt as if he had been thrown onto the set of a bad Italian opera. The King was a clown who spent his country's trade balance on refurbish-ing his palace and buying jewellery for his mistress, while the Germans and Russians intrigued for ways to possess Romania's wheat silos and oilfields. Meanwhile at the

15

legation, Nick and his colleagues argued about ways to sabotage the oil barges on the Danube, while at night they traded for second-hand secrets in the Athenee Palace Hotel.

The old Bucharest was slipping away; the previous summer you could buy caviar by the pound at Lucchiano's, French perfumes and silk gloves for your wife direct from Paris in the salons on the Calea Victoriei. Now the shops on the Chaussée were boarded up because of the fascists and there was talk of food shortages in winter.

He closed his eyes and thought again about Daniela Simonici, remembering the smell of her perfume.

'Penny for your thoughts,' Jennifer said. She came out onto the balcony holding a gin and tonic in each hand.

He took his drink from her. 'I was wondering where we'll be a year from now,' he said, which was not true, but sounded plausible.

'Still doing penance in this awful country, I expect.'

'I shouldn't think so. The Germans are in Paris, for God's sake. They'll be jackbooting along the Strand by the end of the year.'

'Oh, it won't come to that.'

Her complacency infuriated him. 'What's going to stop them?'

She sat down, crossed her legs. 'I'm worried about the boys.'

'So am I.'

'I think perhaps I should go home. I hear Hoare is thinking of evacuating families and all non-essential staff.'

He swallowed half the gin and lapsed into silence. Hoare was the Minister, Britain's chief representative in Bucharest, head of the legation. It was true, the danger to British nationals was growing daily, some British oil executives in Ploesti had recently been arrested and beaten up. The Romanian nationalists hated all foreigners except the Germans and soon even Bucharest might not be safe.

He didn't like the boys being so far away either. London was under heavy bombing every night from the Luftwaffe, and a thousand nightmare scenarios had played through his head, of Jamie not making the air raid shelter in time, of Richard asleep in his school dormitory when a stray bomb crashed through the roof. He wanted Jennifer to be there with them, as if the presence of their mother would somehow throw an aura of safety around them.

He had another, more selfish, motive. He would be able to discover how life would be without her.

'What's wrong, Nick? Or would that be breaking the Official Secrets Act?'

It was a sort of running joke between them; she never asked about what he did, or where he went when he left on 'embassy business'. Sometimes she did not hear from him for a week. She knew not to ask.

'Nick?'

'I'm sorry?'

'I asked you, about a million years ago, what is wrong.'

'Nothing. Just thinking.'

'About work?'

'I don't always think about work.'

She raised an eyebrow at that.

He studied her in the gathering darkness, her features highlighted by the table lamps. Still a very attractive woman, slim, straight-backed, her features classically beautiful, as they were when he first met her almost twenty years ago. He wondered, if it ever came to it, what she would do without him; he wondered what he would do without her. But he could not go on living inside this emotional vacuum. Once, he had been too obsessed with his own career to notice; now he was older and his ambitions no longer seemed as important as they once had.

He got up to pour himself another drink.

'You're drinking a lot.'

17

'Two gin and tonics is not alcoholism.'

Night fell suddenly. Their apartment was three blocks from the main square, and from the balcony window he could make out the King's palace. It was in darkness, except for a blaze of light on the third floor, where Carol was meeting with his council in an emergency session.

The world was closing in on the King, or Carol the Cad as his intimates called him. The languorous nights with his mistress on the Avenue Valpache were numbered. Now he was besieged by affairs of state, matters that he had not allowed to trouble him before. Silent crowds had gathered outside the gates, keeping vigil, staring up at the Venetian chandeliers on the third floor as if waiting for a divine miracle. Russia closing in from the north, the Germans flooding in down the Danube, the Hungarians and Bulgarians waiting like vultures for any tidbits. Hard to see what would save them all now. Carol was certainly not the man for such a crisis; he was as incompetent and corrupt a man as Nick had ever met.

'Oh my God,' Nick heard Jennifer say from the balcony. 'They're back.'

He took his drink outside and looked down into the street. A mob of around a hundred green-shirted young men were marching along the boulevard, shouting slogans. Some of them carried weapons. They were on their way to the main square and the palace.

'Iron Guard,' Nick said.

'Why don't the police arrest them?' Jennifer said.

'Some of them *are* policemen.'

'What's the King doing, then?'

'He'll be under the sheets with his girlfriend's thighs around his ears to block out the noise.'

'Don't be vulgar.'

'There's nothing can be done about them now, Jen. They're the future.'

'I'd have them all shot.'

'He tried that once. That didn't work either.' Just before the war thousands of cadres had been executed on Carol's orders. The joke was that the Guardists were like potatoes, the better part of them was underground. The rank and file had taken exile in Berlin; now the tide had turned and they were swarming back, more of them swaggering through the streets every day.

Nick sat down and watched the mob make its way up the boulevard towards the lights of the palace.

'Things may start to get a little uncomfortable soon,' he said.

'They won't harm us,' Jennifer said.

'Why not? Because we have diplomatic immunity? Because we're British? Because your father's distantly related to the Duke of Norfolk?'

She heard the testiness in his voice and frowned. 'Are you all right, Nick?'

'It's getting chill out here,' he said. He got up and went inside.

The truth was, that until recently, there had been few unguarded moments. It had always been a life of closely guarded secrets, privately and professionally. But he had grown tired of the secret life, of the secrets he had kept from others, of the secrets he had kept from himself.

4.

It seemed like a remote posting to some, and when he had first been sent to Bucharest he had realised his career inside the Secret Intelligence Service was blighted. But it was different now; he realised fortune had been kind to him. The war could be saved here: the key to Hitler's plans lay in the Ploesti oilfields.

No-one inside the legation knew Nick's real employers. He had never made close friends inside the building as a matter of policy. Only the Ambassador, Hoare, the military attaché and Nick's immediate superior in the Passport Control Office knew his real job. He set himself a little apart to disguise his secret life.

His office was small, cramped and draughty. There was no heating and just one small window; it was too cold in winter and too hot in summer. There was a clutter of filing cabinets around the walls and piles of dusty manila folders on his desk, none of which he ever opened. His real work was secured in a grey metal safe in a corner of the room and only Nick and the Ambassador knew the combination.

Up until a few weeks ago, he had had a Romanian secretary called Nadia to type correspondence he never sent out; his memos to Whitehall he coded himself and handed to the Ambassador to give personally to the cipher clerks in the basement.

Nadia was a peasant woman, with a bun of thick black hair and a large mole on her left cheek. One day she did not come to work. This surprised him, as she was always punctual. The next day he discovered she had been arrested by the police. He made a number of enquiries to the gendarmerie but he never heard of her again.

Her husband was a Jewish tailor. He had disappeared too.

The head of station was the Chief Passport Officer, Abrams, an aloof functionary of middle years who seemed too taciturn for the sort of work they were engaged in. The grey wings at his temples appeared so perfect they could have been painted on.

Abrams was one of those rarest of creatures, a Cambridge-educated Jew. Such a collision of ambition and religion had left its mark on him and he had made himself into a parody of an English gentleman. He drank endless cups of tea, and spoke reverentially of the King in the hushed whispers normally reserved for the deity. He talked solemnly of cricket and rugby union.

He would weigh strangers in a detached and steady gaze that those who did not know him found chilling. His features were unremarkable except for a jagged white scar on his forehead that gave him a slightly sinister appearance, the result of a fall down some stairs at his public school.

He was unmarried and most of the other staffers considered him remote. There was a rumour that he was homosexual.

The morning after the demonstration in the palace square, Nick was summoned to Abrams's office. Abrams indicated a chair on the other side of the desk and began to talk casually of the weather. He sipped his tea with the gentility of a country vicar while he complained about the heat. Nick fidgeted in his chair and waited for him to get down to business.

Abrams set down his teacup with an air of finality and some regret. 'We're almost ready,' he said.

'It's on?' Nick asked.

Abrams pushed a file across the desk. It was marked TOP SECRET in red stencil. Abrams settled in his chair to allow Nick time to read.

Nick opened the file, tried to contain his excitement. It was the blueprint of a plan to sabotage the oilfields at Ploesti. The Royal Engineers 54th Field Company had been sent to Istanbul from Egypt and were already secretly sequestered outside the city by the Turks, disguised as the Istanbul Number 1 Road Construction Unit. A British merchantman was waiting in the Bosphorus loaded with explosives and equipment.

It was a bold, almost reckless, plan. There would be a lot of lives lost. But without that oil, Hitler would be hamstrung, and it was on seemingly small tactical coups, such as the one they were planning here, that wars turned.

Nick looked up at Abrams, both eager and apprehensive. 'It's about time.'

'Whitehall are waiting for word from us when we have everything ready.'

'Ready?'

'The ship that is to carry these men and their equipment will landfall at Constanza. Elements of the Romanian Army are to provide transportation.'

'That's very kind of them,' Nick said.

'Considerable sums of money are about to change hands.'

Christ. So much that could go wrong. The pay-offs

would have to include Romanian army drivers, border guards, customs officials and not a few generals; perhaps too many people for such a plan to be successful. It was a scheme hatched in the cosy world of Whitehall, not Bucharest. But if they could make it work, it might yet win them time from Hitler's invasion plans and save Europe from disaster.

'Why are the Turks helping us?'

'Ankara believes Romanian oil will one day fuel an invasion of Turkey. They think it is in their interests to help us, while maintaining the illusion of neutrality.'

'Illusions are important.'

'Bendix will be paymaster. There's a suitcase waiting for you in the safe in the Ambassador's office with a considerable sum of sterling inside. You're to take it up to Ploesti when I give you the word and deliver it to him personally.'

'Yes, sir.'

'Make sure he understands what we need and the necessity for complete secrecy. That's all. Good luck.'

'Thank you, sir.' He got up to leave. 'By the way, I want to talk to you about some visas . . .'

'What visas?'

'They're friends of mine. Jews. Used to have money but the greenshirts have cleaned them out, taken everything.'

'Well, that's a familiar –'

'These are friends. I want to get them out of the country.'

'You know British policy on Romanian Jews, Davis.'

'There's only three of them.'

'Thin end of the wedge.'

'Or a drop in the ocean. Depends how you look at it.'

'Have they applied?'

'Not yet.'

Abrams's eyes were perfect mirrors. 'Well, give me the names. They'll have to come to the embassy and fill out the forms in the usual manner. I'll see what I can do.'

'I'd appreciate it,' Nick said, and Abrams went back to his paperwork.

He first met Jordon in a dusty corner office in the basement, came across him quite by accident. He had a screwdriver in his hand and a pipe clamped between his teeth, absorbed with the small metal device that lay on the desk in front of him.

'Who are you?' Nick said. 'What the hell are you doing with that?'

Jordon looked up and smiled, revealing a charming gap in his front teeth. 'Jordon. Section D.'

Section D – short for Dirty Tricks – was a branch of his own service, the SIS. No-one had even bothered to tell him Jordon was here.

'Davis,' he said. 'Nick Davis.'

'Oh, right. Heard of you.'

So much for security.

'What are you doing here?'

'You weren't told?'

'Apparently not.'

'Sorry. Thought someone would have mentioned it.'

'Is that a detonator?' Nick asked, knowing precisely what it was.

Jordon disarmed him with a grin. 'If you hear a bang, head for the nearest door and send someone down here with a paper bag for the bits.' He tamped some tobacco in his pipe. 'They sent me here from Cairo. There's talk about dynamiting a few barges at the Iron Gates on the Danube and blocking the channel.'

'Is there?'

'Whitehall sent some plastic explosive in the diplomatic pouch.'

'Nice of them.'

'It's in the safe there,' Jordon said, pointing to the squat grey metal cabinet in the corner of the room. The grin fell away. 'Have to stop Hitler getting his hands on that oil. Any means.'

'Any means,' Nick said.

Jordon went back to his detonator and his fiddling. What a surreal war, Nick thought. Abrams had not even seen fit to tell him Section D were in the building. He wondered what else he wasn't telling him.

5.

Something medieval about the Jewish Quarter, the narrow cobbled streets and the Orthodox Jews with their ringlets and long beards, the tailor shops selling horsehair and buckram and rolls of lining. Something medieval, too, about the hate these people fostered. Nothing like baiting a Jew to make a politician popular with the people.

He found the bookshop he was looking for just off the Strada Lipscani, a noisy and steamy market in the heart of the Quarter. It was dusty, cramped and narrow, religious books and commentaries crowding the shelves. He waited in the back of the shop giving little thought to pretence. He had not been followed.

A stocky Jew in a black fedora walked into the shop and their eyes met briefly. He pretended to look for a certain book, overplaying his hand, as amateurs will. Eventually he took a thick volume of religious commentary and slipped an envelope inside. He replaced it on the shelf and went out.

Nick found the book, took out the envelope and put it inside his jacket. The Jew was general manager of an

26

armaments factory; the envelope contained the production schedule for the last three months.

Nick slipped out into the sunshine, the candescence of the cobblestones burning through the soles of his shoes. He felt exhausted by heat and by futility; the production schedule would be filed away in some dusty cabinet in Whitehall and would make not a scrap of difference to the course of the war. If they could sabotage the Ploesti oilfields, he would feel he had performed his country a service, but he suspected the mandarins in London were stalling at upsetting a neutral government with such precipitous action, no matter what Jordon said.

And then he saw her, a glimpse of her face in the crowd, and his heart lurched in his chest. She roused him from his grim reflections like the slamming of a door; he saw her only briefly, a jade-green shawl bobbing among a sea of ringlets and black homburgs. She turned a corner into Strada Zarafi. He ran to catch up with her, but she was gone.

He stood there in the street, feeling foolish.

He climbed into the coach of a waiting *trasura* and told the coachman to take him back to the British Legation.

A flick of the reins and they moved off. The leather seat was scalding where the hood could not provide enough shade from the sun. He now just wanted to get back to the legation, away from the beggars, the noise and the crush. The city cooked in the furnace heat, the air gritty with dust and pale yellow like a smoke haze.

A motorbike and sidecar carrying three Guardists in green peasant shirts roared past, passed so close that the horse skittered and the coachman had to use his whip to bring the beast under control. A police car, bell clanging, roared past seconds later, the policeman behind the wheel shouting abuse at the coachman, who ignored him with the lumpen passivity of a sack of potatoes.

Instead the coachman directed his rage at the horse.

'Settle down, you stupid Jew!' he shouted and slapped her again with his whip.

Stupid Jew. Even the *trasura* drivers.

Nick felt his skin prickle. He twisted in his seat and watched the police car disappear into the twisted lanes off Lipscani. The smell of violence in the air. The horse shied and twitched. A premonition of death overtook him, bitter and overpowering.

It was Levi, walking ahead, who saw the motorbike and sidecar parked in the street outside their apartment. He shouted a warning. *Greenshirts.*

Simon grabbed Daniela's hand and they turned and ran. A black police car turned the corner behind them, blocking their escape. Two policemen jumped out. One of them was holding a wooden truncheon. The other had a whip.

'Run!' Simon shouted to Levi.

Levi slipped on the cobblestones and went down. The two policemen were on him immediately and started beating him. He screamed when he went down for the second time but that only seemed to encourage them.

Daniela couldn't move. She had retreated into a doorway and stood there with her hands to her face, screaming. Simon was already at the corner. Two greenshirts came out of the apartment, grabbed him and dragged him back up the street towards the police car. They bundled him in the back and the car drove away, the wheels bouncing on the cobblestones. Terrified passers-by threw themselves in doorways to get out of the way.

The two men who were beating Levi grew tired of their

game. There were flecks of blood on their faces and their shirts. Levi didn't look human any more; his hair was matted with black blood, his face unrecognisable. He lay like a bunch of rags on the cobbles.

The men looked up and saw her, and one of them gave a wolfish grin and winked at her. She knew what would happen now.

Someone grabbed her hand. Thinking she was about to be captured, she tried to twist free. But it wasn't a greenshirt, it was him, the stranger from the other night, the Englishman who had taken her home in the *trasura*. She gaped at him in astonishment.

He dragged her after him down an alleyway, bare brick walls crowding either side. There was a *trasura* waiting at the end, the driver throwing anxious glances over his shoulder. When he saw the greenshirts, he jerked at the reins and moments later he was gone.

'Bastard!' the Englishman shouted after him.

She looked behind them. The two greenshirts were almost on them.

She threw off her high-heeled shoes and, still clutching his hand, she followed him through the maze of streets, suddenly deserted now, fire burning in her lungs.

6.

The lobby of the Athenee Palace Hotel had been witness to many unusual entrées, but the appearance of a barefoot and beautiful woman with blood on her skirt, hand in hand with a dishevelled and sweating Englishman, created an immediate buzz of interest.

The American Bar, Nick decided, was too public. Instead he led her to a small courtyard at the back of the hotel, accessible only through the French doors in the breakfast room. A Romanian army officer and his paramour had come there for a clandestine meeting, and they looked up resentfully at this unwelcome intrusion.

Nick and Daniela sat down at a grey weathered table, under the limes. It was just on dusk.

'Wait here,' he said.

He went to the bar and brought back two glasses of *tsuica*. Daniela's hands were shaking so badly she could not hold the glass. Her skirt was torn, her face grey and streaked with sweat.

'I must look a mess,' she said.

He helped her drink the *tsuica*. She gasped as the strong brandy hit the back of her throat.

She took his hand; she had small hands, delicate and fragile and pale. 'Why did you do that?' she whispered.

'I don't know,' he said.

'You saved my life.'

'Who were those two men?'

'The one they threw in the car was my . . . he was my brother. Levi . . . Levi was a friend.'

'There was nothing you could have done.'

'I've got to find him.' She tried to finish the *tsuica* and spilled some of it on her skirt. He took it away from her. 'Where have they taken him?'

'Prefecture headquarters, I expect.' Poor bastard, he wanted to add. The Prefecture had a grim reputation and the police there did as they wanted with any unfortunate that fell into their power.

'I have to find him,' she repeated.

She was shaking uncontrollably now. He put his arms around her, and held her, and she wept. Her tears were wet on his shirt; he leaned towards her, smelled the fragrance of her hair.

'Why were the greenshirts after you?' he murmured.

She gasped out the story; her father had owned a bank, the Banque de Credit Bucaresti. Simon had been a director. He had been convicted *in absentia* of fraud, but it was an excuse to make it seem like the authorities had not stolen the bank from them. They had both been hiding from the police since their father had been arrested two months before.

The young Romanians on the other side of the court-yard were staring at them. We must look a strange sight, he thought. 'You can't go back to the apartment, they will be waiting for you. Have you somewhere to stay tonight?'

'I haven't any money. Everything I have is in the apartment.'

'Then we'll have to find you somewhere to sleep,' he said.

He stood in the middle of the room, one hand holding her wrist. She looked lost, like a little girl. He drew the drapes across the window and their eyes fell on the huge bed at the same time.

She had been transported in a few hours from a run-down apartment building in the Jewish Quarter to a minor salon in Versailles, heavy gold drapes on the windows, gilt Louis Seize chairs covered with rose brocade. The door to the balcony was ajar and the summer breeze brought with it the fragrance of roses from the garden below.

'What will happen to Simon?' she said.

He pushed back the fall of dark hair from her face. 'I'll see what I can do.'

Her eyes had the faraway look Nick had seen on the faces of soldiers returning from battle during the Civil War in Spain. He put his arms around her, held her, felt her move against him. He wanted to scoop her up in his arms and carry her to the bed. But some instinct stopped him; he knew she would submit as this was the only way she had to repay him, and he did not want to be repaid, did not want to sully what he had done, with casual sex. Besides, wasn't that what every other man wanted from her?

And he was not the kind of man to have casual affairs. Not his style at all.

'What's wrong?' she murmured.

'I have to go.'

Hard to decipher the look on her face.

'I'll come back in the morning and we'll see what we can do about your brother,' he said.

He stepped away from her and hated himself for being so bloody upright about this.

He went quickly to the door and left.

As the key turned in the lock, the door swung open and Jennifer threw herself in his arms. 'Where have you been? I called everyone at the legation.' Her eyes went wide. 'What happened?'

'I'm all right.'

'There's blood on your shirt.'

'It's all right. It's not mine.'

It's not mine. What did he mean by that? It's not my blood on me, so you needn't have worried? He wondered how the blood had got there; perhaps when Daniela had fallen as they were running from the greenshirts. It might have come from the graze on her hand.

He couldn't meet her eyes. 'I'm fine, Jen.' He disentangled himself and moved past her into the apartment. He badly needed a whisky. He went to the liquor cabinet and splashed three fingers into a tumbler.

Better.

'Are you going to tell me what happened?'

'The greenshirts decided to crack some heads in the Jewish Quarter. Got caught up in it.'

'Caught up in what? Whose blood is this?'

'I don't know.'

She was staring at him like he was a stranger who had just lurched through the door into her living room. Perhaps he was.

He caught a glimpse of himself in the hallway mirror. He looked like he had come from a bar fight. There were flecks of blood on his white shirt, and the eyes that stared back at him were cold and dangerous.

'Are you all right?' Jennifer said from the doorway.

'No. I nearly got myself killed.'

Jennifer accepted this news with equanimity. Perhaps another, more terrible, possibility had occurred to her.

'It's almost midnight, Nick. Where have you been?'

'Had a few drinks at the American Bar. Steady the nerves.'

'You didn't think of ringing me, letting me know you were all right?'

'You know what the telephones are like in this damned city.'

'It's only three streets away. You could have come home.' Her voice was rising, anger mixed with the tailings of worry. 'What the hell happened?'

'I was in Strada Lipscani. I saw some Jews being attacked by some greenshirts, and I helped one of them get away. That's all.'

He drained his glass. 'We should make plans to get you out of Bucharest,' he said. 'It's getting too dangerous here.'

He went back to the liquor cabinet and poured another whisky. All these years he had spent under cover, keeping the government's secrets. But now he wondered if he could keep pretending to be someone he never was, day in and day out, at work and at home, for King and country, heart and home.

7.

Daniela was getting ready to leave the hotel when reception called her room and told her that a Monsieur Davis was waiting for her in the lobby. She had not expected to see him again. She dressed quickly and went downstairs to meet him. He was standing by one of the pillars, a distinguished, handsome man in a charcoal suit with clear blue eyes and curly black hair. He smiled at her as she walked towards him. Most men smiled at her like wolves; but this one was different, and she did not know what to make of him.

He had a car waiting outside, a black Humber, and a driver from the legation. He held the door for her, then climbed into the back seat beside her.

'Did you sleep well?' he asked her, in English.

She had slept hardly at all, of course, crying and worrying over Simon. Just once she had fallen into a quick seamless sleep and had woken suddenly a few minutes later screaming, eyes wide, seeing Levi lying bloody and beaten in the street. But she told him, yes, she had slept well, for she thought to tell him otherwise would have seemed ungrateful.

'I didn't sleep at all,' he said. It sounded like a reproach and she wished she had told him the truth.

'You do not have to do this,' she said to him. 'You have already been too kind.'

35

'All part of the service, *mademoiselle*.'

She saw him toying with the wedding ring on his finger, slipping it on and off, on and off, staring distractedly out of the window.

'Did you get into trouble with your wife?'

He looked at her. 'No.'

She took his hand and kissed him tenderly on the cheek; the last thing he had ever expected her to do. 'Thank you,' she whispered.

They stopped at the Prefecture and he went inside and was gone for a long time. When he came out he was sombre. He got back into the car and shrugged his shoulders. There was nothing to say. Once, a visit from an official from His Majesty's Legation with a fistful of *lei* would have carried some weight with a Romanian policeman, but those days were long gone.

Daniela stared out of the window at the cold stone walls of the police headquarters and wondered what was happening to Simon in there.

She felt cold on this hot morning. She was breathing too fast and he put his arm around her, pulled her into his shoulder. She let him hold her, didn't want to believe she would never see Simon again. She would not let herself even think that.

They turned down Strada Zarafi, where they had fled from the greenshirts the day before. The bookstore windows were broken. It had been looted by the greenshirts, and torn and half-charred books lay scattered across the cobblestones. He felt a bump as the wheels rolled over them.

They stopped outside the ancient apartment block where she and Simon lived. The street was deserted. People were afraid to leave their houses this morning.

Nick stepped out of the car behind her. 'It was just you and Simon lived here?'

She nodded. 'I have one . . . other brother. His name is Amos. He ran away to the country when my father was arrested. I haven't seen him for weeks.'

'What about the other man you were with?'

'Levi?'

He nodded, thought about the young man lying like a bloody piece of meat in the street.

'He was hiding from the work gangs.'

The work gangs; if it was not so appalling, it would have been funny. The government had disallowed all Jews from military service, but in the newspapers they were vilified for refusing to fight for their country. Then all young Jewish men of fighting age were inducted into the service of the military as forced labour, digging trenches.

Her shoulders sagged in defeat as she looked up at the first-floor window.

'One night you're eating lobster at Capsa's, the next you're in a flat with no bathroom eating barley soup. Now my father is sitting in a basement cell in the Prefecture and I don't have enough money to get him out. Even if I did, where would we go?'

'I think I can get those visas for you.'

'It's too late now.'

'Not for you.'

She pushed open the door to the building and he followed her inside and up the stairs. The stairwell was dark and he had to grip tightly to the cold iron balustrade, feeling his way up to the landing.

The door to the apartment lay on the floor, splinters of the door frame clinging to the hinges. She went inside, stepping over broken furniture, glass crunching under her shoes. The greenshirts had been thorough, taken what they wanted, destroyed everything else.

The spirit seemed to go out of her. She fell to her knees and sobbed, her whole body shaking. He knelt down beside her, winced as a shard of broken glass pierced his knee. 'It's all right,' he whispered and tentatively slipped his arms around her. She allowed him to hold her for just a moment, then shook herself free.

He stood up, feeling quite helpless.

'Daniela . . .'

'Just go.'

'What will you do?'

'I'm staying here.'

'It's not safe.'

'I've nowhere else to go.'

'Perhaps I can find you somewhere.' He helped her to her feet, felt her sag against him, beaten. He helped her back down the stairs to where the car was waiting. He gave his driver an address on the Boulevard Bratianu. They sat in the back and he put his arm around her and held her, and to hell with whoever saw him.

He would not let her languish in that apartment alone. He would find her somewhere to stay. He knew just the man to help out.

8.

Ploesti was just thirty-seven miles north of Bucharest on the Danube plains. Europe's premier oil reserve was a sad, grey industrial town where oil sometimes seeped out of the ground and stuck to the shoes. Long before they reached the outskirts, Nick saw the lights of the gantries.

The brown leather suitcase lay beside him on the back seat. He laid a hand on it to reassure himself of its presence and stared at the back of his driver's head, fascinated by the fleshy folds of skin that fell in scallops over the collar of the man's shirt. Extraordinary. He had no neck.

His name was Ionescu, Ilie Ionescu, one of the drivers from the car pool at the legation. By his size and demeanour, Nick suspected he had other talents, and that was why he had been assigned to him for this little errand to Ploesti. A gorilla with car keys.

He stared out of the window at the darkness. If he and Abrams could pull this off, it would be one of the greatest coups in the history of the intelligence service. It might not stop the bombs that were falling on his country, but it might prevent that lunatic in Berlin from going ahead with any planned invasion.

Ionescu stopped at an army roadblock. The guards

stared with naked hostility at Nick's diplomatic passport until they found the banknotes that had been tucked inside. The money was quickly transferred to their uniform pockets and they were waved through.

Nick smiled to himself. They said the common language in Romania was French, but it wasn't; it was money. It gave him heart that the plan would work. If a few thousand *lei* could get him into Ploesti, a few million might get a squadron of engineers into the oilfields. But they had to do it now, before it was too late.

Bendix lived alone in a two-storey house near the Gara de Sud. As they drove up, Nick felt a prickle of apprehension. The house was in complete darkness. Ionescu stopped the car outside the house, turned off the engine and waited.

The street was dark and deserted. Nick waited and watched and listened, but the clicking of the cooling car engine was the only sound.

'Stay here,' Nick said to Ionescu. He picked up the suitcase and got out of the car, strode up the dark pathway with more confidence than he felt. He knocked at the door. No answer. He looked through all the windows at the front of the house but could see no movement inside.

He went back to the car. Ionescu looked nervous. 'It's dangerous just sitting here, Monsieur Nick,' he said in Romanian.

'There's a torch in the glovebox,' Nick said, and held out his hand.

Ionescu handed it to him.

'Give me five minutes.' Nick went around the side of the house. He tried the back door. It was open. Bad sign.

He hesitated, felt for the reassuring weight of the Webley revolver in his jacket pocket. 'Bendix?'

He flicked the light switch on. Nothing. Someone had turned off the mains power. He swung the torch beam around the room; there were shards of broken crockery on the floor, and the kitchen table had been upturned in a struggle. His finger tightened around the grip of the suitcase. Twenty thousand sterling, a fortune.

He felt his heart hammering against his ribs.

'Bendix?'

He took out the revolver, removed the safety and moved across the kitchen. He swung the torch through an adjoining doorway into the living room; the beam picked out an upholstered sofa, two low bookcases under the window, a lamp standard. Bendix lived simply; or rather, he had lived simply, for the lamp now lay on its side and rested on his prone body.

Nick knelt down beside him and felt for a pulse. He was still warm. As he withdrew his hand, he felt wetness on his fingers. Blood. There was a pool of it congealed like jelly around Bendix's head. The torch beam tracked pieces of scalp over the Bokhara rug.

He heard a noise from the kitchen, stood up and turned around. He had the presence of mind to switch off the torch so that he did not present an illuminated target.

German voices called to each other in the darkness, and he was blinded by two torches shining directly into his face. He raised the Webley in his right hand but knew he did not have time to fire. Instinctively, he threw himself to his right.

He heard gunshots so loud and so close it made his ears ring. He waited to die.

9.

'Why didn't you shoot, Monsieur Nick?' Ionescu shouted from the front seat. He was gesticulating wildly, one hand on the wheel. 'Why didn't you use your gun?'

Nick was slumped in the back seat, stunned, overtaken by a sense of unreality. He opened the case on the seat beside him, needlessly checking once again that the crisp bundles of sterling were still there. He locked it again.

Ionescu was driving too fast but with good reason. There were two Germans lying on Bendix's carpet, both shot once in the back, and they needed to be in Bucharest before the bodies were discovered by Moruzov's secret police.

'Why didn't you use your gun?' Ionescu said again.

If Ionescu had waited five minutes, as Nick had ordered him to, Nick would be dead; if Ionescu had not instead waited in the shadows, like the professional he was, if he had not followed the two Germans into the house, pistol ready, Nick knew that right now he would be lying face down on the Bokhara rug in a pool of his own blood, just like Bendix.

'I didn't have time,' he said to Ionescu. 'Concentrate on

the road. You just saved my life. Do you want to kill me with your driving?'

Ionescu shook his head and muttered something under his breath.

They drove wildly through the black night. Nick's mind was in chaos. They had been betrayed. Someone had informed the Abwehr, the plan leaked even before the Romanian military and customs had heard of it. The leak must have come from inside the legation.

His hands were shaking, the adrenalin coursing through his body. A cold reservoir of anger formed inside him. Before this, he had seen betrayal as somehow impersonal, a crime against his country.

But this was personal. Someone had nearly had him killed.

He undressed in the dark and slipped into bed beside his wife. Jennifer murmured in her sleep and rolled away. 'You're cold,' she mumbled.

He kissed the bare skin of her back, needing the comfort of another warm body. He had nearly died tonight and she would never know. For so long he had enjoyed his secrets. Tonight he just felt alone and afraid.

An hour earlier Abrams had met him at the door of his apartment on Bratianu in his dressing gown and slippers. Even woken from sleep he looked cool and distinguished and unruffled. His hair parting was still precise, undisturbed by his pillow. 'Davis? What happened?'

'Problem, sir. Have to talk to you.'

'You'd better come in.'

They had sat in armchairs in his living room, perfect

English gentlemen, except one of them had blood on his hands. Abrams had listened to Nick's account of what had happened in Ploesti with dismay.

'You're a very lucky man,' Abrams said when he had finished. 'The two men were no doubt Wehrmacht special forces.'

'They killed Bendix and then they waited for me. They knew I was coming.'

'So it would appear.'

'Who else knew?'

Abrams was silent for a long time. 'About Bendix? Clive Allen recruited him originally.'

Allen was the Bucharest correspondent for the *London Times*. He had been working for SIS for six years and his job at the *Times* – which was absolutely legitimate – provided perfect cover for his activities.

'Anyone else?'

He shook his head. 'Just the two people in this room.'

'Clive Allen? Why?'

'You never ask why, Davis. No-one ever understands these things. There's a hundred reasons.'

Abrams looked up at the ormolu clock on the sideboard. 'It's late. You should go home and try to get some sleep. There's nothing more we can do tonight. There'll be hell to pay at the legation tomorrow. We'll talk about this again in the morning.'

And so now he lay in his own bed, exhausted but unable to sleep, his mind churning over the night's events. His eyes felt gritty and fatigue had left him lightheaded.

There was a leeching of light in the eastern sky. Almost dawn.

If I had died tonight, he thought, would I be satisfied with my life? The question was asked again and again to the darkness, over the beating of his panicked heart.

If I had died, was any of it worth anything? Are there regrets?

Yes, there are regrets. I would like, before I die, to know what it is like to really love somebody.

He thought about Abrams, quintessentially correct and remote, and saw himself in a few years, if he survived this war. This was not who he wanted to be.

He thought about Daniela, of how she had kissed him in the *trasura*, and felt a stab of guilt for thinking of another woman while his wife lay sleeping there beside him.

Suddenly life seemed so much more precious, and there was less time to waste. As daylight inched into the room, he felt disoriented and confused. He realised with terrible clarity that he hated his life, his secrets, and his detachment from his own longings; long ago he had calculated the course of his life to the fraction of a degree, only to find now that his compass had been pointing south the whole time.

IO.

The Germans had set up a propaganda office downtown, the German Bureau. For months there had been a map of France in the window showing the pincer arrows of the Wehrmacht advance, its claws converging on Paris. Recently it had been replaced with a map of the British Isles, the major cities ringed with flame.

Should be in England tonight, Nick thought, instead of sitting here drinking coffees and *tsuica* in a warm hotel lobby, playing mind games with the enemy. In London they're crowded in tube stations every night, while the Luftwaffe turns the city into rubble.

Dropping bombs on his sons.

Hard to see these Germans every day and swallow down his hatred. So long since he had seen the boys; in normal times they would have come out to join them for the summer holidays, but that was not possible now. He knew there were soldiers fighting in Burma and the Malay peninsula who had not seen their families for perhaps as long, but at least they knew what they were doing and why. He was stuck here waging a phony war it now seemed no-one in Whitehall wanted him to fight.

He hurried across the square to the Athenee Palace. The hotel was as much a landmark of the city as the King's palace; it had been built in 1910, its architect drawing inspiration from the Maurice and Ritz hotels of Paris, though the original caryatides and turrets had now been removed. The facade had faded to a dirty yellow over the years and the shutters had been painted a bright blue, with unerring tastelessness.

The statue of Carol I, astride a bronze horse, gestured heroically towards his descendant's palace on the other side of the square. The gigantic red gladiolas in the Athenee forecourt flourished beside a meagre and parched square of lawn. The canopy above the entrance threw the narrowest of shadows.

He ran the gauntlet of the beggars camped outside the hotel, most of them professionals blinded or maimed by their parents in infancy. Opaque eyeballs and running sores and stumps were thrust into his face in the manner of street hawkers trying to tempt him with homemade pies.

'*Mi-e foame, foame, foame . . .*'

But the heat had even dissipated their energies and they did not pursue him with their usual enthusiasm. He pushed gratefully through the revolving door into the cool of the foyer.

It was gloomy inside even on the brightest summer day and the three rows of paired yellow marble pillars gave the hotel the appearance of a cathedral. The rust-coloured marble walls and the Bordeaux-red carpets added to the wintry atmosphere. The only light came from the electric chandeliers.

Max King was waiting for him in the American Bar. Max was the Reuters man in Bucharest, the epitome of English pipe-sucking masculinity in grey flannel trousers and tweed jacket with leather patches at the elbow. Most of the journalists spent every day in the bar. Their work came to them; this was where everyone in Bucharest headed if they had rumours or tattle to sell.

Their acquaintance had started professionally, for Max's

sources were better than his own. Nick never knew where he got his information but he always seemed to know what was going to happen inside the palace twenty-four hours before anyone at the legation. Over time he had become Nick's best friend and confidant.

Clive Allen was there too.

Max took out the pipe and grinned. 'Nick! My favourite spy!'

'For God's sake, Max.'

'Hell are you, old boy? Been telling Clive here about your little adventure the other night in Jewtown.'

Nick looked over at Clive. They had not spent much time in each other's company. He was not at all like Max; he laughed rarely and gave away little of himself. I should take you outside right now and get the truth out of you about Ploesti, Nick thought. But what if Abrams is wrong?

'Better if you tell the story,' Max said.

'I was in Strada Lipscani. Some greenshirts attacked these Jews right there in the street. The police were there too. They beat one poor bastard to death right in front of me. The other one was thrown into a police car and no-one's seen him since.'

Max shook his head. 'Goodbye to old Bucharest, I'm afraid. Things are going to get very unpleasant here. Especially after Carol goes.'

Everyone but the King himself knew he would have to go. It wasn't just that he was corrupt or that his avarice was legendary. Nick often entertained visitors with stories of how the King retained a monopoly on the manufacture of military uniforms and then charged his own soldiers exorbitant prices to buy them from him. He had once even spread rumours on the stock market to destabilise the national currency so that he could take profits on the black market. The truly astonishing thing was that most Romanians were neither shocked nor even surprised by his corruption.

It was the loss of national territory and national pride that had turned the people against him. The Russians had just annexed two of the northern provinces and the King had done nothing. Ironically, it was one of his few wise decisions, for it was a war Romania could not have won, but in his compliance the Bucaresti finally lost faith with Carol the Cad. The people were now looking to the nationalists for salvation, and to men like Horia Sima, the leader of the Iron Guard. In desperation, the King had tried to placate the mob by declaring an amnesty for Iron Guard members and had made Sima the Minister of Culture and the Arts. It had not been an outstanding success. From his new post Sima had directed the arrest, torture and execution of hundreds of Jews.

Turned it into an art form, in fact, was Max's grim joke.

And it had still done nothing to silence the voices raised against the King. There were demonstrations in the square every day, most of them organised by Horia Sima himself.

Clive had contributed little to the conversation. Now he finished his drink, made a polite but curt farewell, and left.

'Everything all right, old boy?' Max said after he had gone.

'Yes. Of course.'

'Did he upset you?'

'No. Why?'

'Just the way you were looking at him, old son. Poor old Clive. Whatever he's done, don't be too hard. Drinks more than is good for him,' Max added and ordered another round. It was eleven o'clock in the morning.

'How's Daniela?' Nick asked him, changing the subject.

'Don't worry about her. Trust Max. She's fine.' He patted him on the shoulder. For the last week Max had been sheltering Daniela at his apartment on Bratianu, keeping her out of harm's way. When Nick had appeared at his door that morning with a beautiful waif with tear-stained cheeks, he had asked no questions.

But he had made assumptions.

'Be discreet, Nick. You're a married man.'

'I don't know what you're talking about,' Nick said, startled to hear his secret desires so baldly stated.

'Women like Jennifer don't miss a thing.'

'Then you should hire her for Reuters.'

'Love to, but she doesn't look like she drinks enough.' He raised his glass. 'Good health,' he said, with his usual flair for inverted prophesy.

II.

They sat in the garden of Cina's restaurant in wicker armchairs, the evening sun dappled through the leaves of the lime trees that shaded the courtyard. Crowds had gathered in the square in front of the palace gates. Another demonstration against the King.

The strings of coloured lights that hung in the trees gave the garden a fairytale appearance. White-jacketed waiters scurried from table to table while patrons grabbed at their coat tails, demanding service.

Nick finally caught the attention of the waiter. Jennifer ordered asparagus with hollandaise sauce and fresh raspberries and cream for dessert; she had never had a large appetite.

'Are you going to be gloomy again?' she said. 'I do so hope you're going to be better company tonight, you haven't been yourself for weeks.'

He wondered how he was going to say this to her. Something had changed in him these last few years, much more than he realised.

They had met in the summer of 1924, at a ball in the Savoy Hotel in the Strand. He had come down from Oxford and was staying with his brother in Kensington.

She was beautiful, well travelled, educated at Roedean. Her father was a diplomat and Nick's own ambition to join the service had met with her wholehearted approval. He had needed a wife, it was almost required along with an Oxbridge classics degree. She was looking for a suitable husband and he supposed, looking back on it, that what had happened between them was inevitable. He must have been a very different man then. For her part she did not seem to him to have changed at all; it was the changes in him that had rocked their marriage. Looking back, it disturbed him that he could not remember how he had asked her to marry him, or if he had asked her at all. They made love for the first time a month before their wedding, in a beachfront hotel in Brighton. It was not all he had hoped, but he told himself it would get better.

Jennifer fell pregnant quickly with Jamie; two years later Richard was born. Life seemed straightforward then. He was consumed with work, and if anyone had asked him back then, he would have told them that a successful career and a stable home was all a man needed for contentment. He never considered otherwise.

They lived for three years in Buenos Aires, but very early in his career his ambitions within the diplomatic service had somehow been skewed to the more arcane pursuit of intelligence gathering. Soon there were postings to Lisbon and Madrid with the Passport Control Office.

When they had married, it had been for better or worse. He was twenty-three years old and had no idea what such words meant for him, or for her. He never imagined that he would one day feel as he did now.

Time was a trickster, it left you looking for beans under the wrong cup; had he never really loved her or had the love been lost so long ago that he just thought it had never been?

And now there was Bucharest; the world had slipped into war and he had entered his own conflict with himself. The storm clouds had gathered over Europe and over his own small world, and he did not know what the outcome of either struggle would be.

'Are you happy, Jen?'

'Whatever do you mean?'

'With me. With us.'

'Of course I am,' she said and he saw a flicker of apprehension in her eyes. For all her discontent, he realised that she had never considered doing anything but making the best of things.

A gypsy troupe in white blouses and velvet breeches were playing sad Oriental melodies in the Chinese kiosk in the centre of the garden. He hated gypsy music as a rule, found it too maudlin, but tonight it somehow matched his mood.

'Is this enough for you?'

Jennifer frowned at him. 'Enough?'

'Don't you wish there was . . . some passion in our lives? That we spent more time together? That I talked to you more?'

'I don't think I follow you, Nick. What is it you want to talk about?'

It hit him then. He was the unhappy one, not her. She had accepted the distances between them, his long silences, his long hours at work. And perhaps he had liked living this way once. When had he changed, how? Now he wanted to change the rulebook on her. Somehow it didn't seem fair.

It occurred to him for the first time that she was happy with their marriage, that for all her complaints over the years, she wanted very little of him. Without her acquiescence, it would be quite impossible to end it. He knew he couldn't be the one to walk away. He didn't have enough reasons, there was no infidelity, no blistering arguments. And what about the boys?

'I don't think I've ever felt so unhappy,' he said.

'There's a war on, as you're so fond of telling people, Nick. Tell that to the people in the air raid shelters back home.'

He took a deep breath and tried again. 'I'm unhappy – about things with you and me.'

He saw the terrible pain in her eyes and he had to look away.

'What are you saying?'

'I'm saying . . . I'm saying have you ever thought that we would be better apart?'

There was a sudden welling of tears in her eyes. 'No, Nick. No, I've never thought that.'

He realised he couldn't do this to her.

'Good Lord, what's that noise?' she said.

Over the sound of the gypsy violins, he heard the distant thunder of marching feet. There was a murmur around the square that grew to a low, insistent chant: '*Abdica . . . abdica . . .*'

Nick knew that the King's Prime Minister, General Antonescu, was in the palace at that moment, trying to persuade the King to abdicate in the best interests of Romania. It seemed others had decided to bring some additional pressure to bear.

'What's going on, Nick?'

'The usual nonsense,' he said. He didn't know why he didn't try to explain it to her; possibly because he was sick of Romanian politics, and he just wanted to forget about work for a while. Or perhaps dissembling had become a habit with him.

Soldiers were throwing up barricades around the square, guards rushing towards the palace gates. A shot rang out, then another. Other diners jumped up from their tables, spilling glasses and plates. Some ran to the low hedge to get a better view of what was happening. The more timorous ran inside.

A crowd of greenshirts had marched into the square, chanting 'Down with the King!' and singing their anthem, the *Capitanul*. A few minutes later a lorry drove into the square and soldiers leaped out, their boots hammering on the cobblestones. A tank, painted sky blue, rumbled into position in front of the palace.

'We're going to see some fun now,' Nick said.

'Let's just get home,' Jennifer said.

A military van with a loudspeaker mounted on the roof drove up to the palace gates. A metallic voice ordered everyone to clear the square and stay indoors. Anyone on the street in half an hour would be arrested. Nick took Jennifer's hand and led her out of the restaurant. They would skirt behind the Atheneum to avoid the mob.

'You were going to say something else to me,' Jennifer said.

'Saved by the Revolution,' Nick murmured under his breath and they started to run.

By four o'clock the next morning Carol was on his way to Constanza in a German diplomatic car with his mistress. Carol's eighteen-year-old son Michael was invested on the throne in his place, but the real power passed to Antonescu, who became Conducator. Green-shirted legionaries marched through the square singing, while the guards who had fired rifles over their heads the night before cheered and raised their arms in fascist salute.

When Antonescu named his government a few days later, half his cabinet were prominent fascists and Nazi sympathisers. Horia Sima was made Vice Premier and in the incense-blackened Romanian churches the patriarchs announced that they would canonise Iron Guard martyrs as saints.

More German soldiers had appeared on the streets. There were rumours that two infantry divisions had been sent to guard the oil wells at Ploesti from sabotage by the British.

And still we sit here twiddling our thumbs, Nick thought, waiting for Whitehall to give us the green light. He might as well be stationed in Chile, for all the good he was doing for the war.

A chill fell over the city. The cafés along the Chaussée took down their awnings and brought the tables and chairs in off the footpaths. The evening promenade had dwindled to almost nothing. Winter was on its way.

12.

Max opened the door in his dressing gown. He tied the cord at his waist and grinned. 'Sir Galahad,' he said.

'Can I come in?'

'Treat the place as your own. Everyone else does.'

Nick followed Max into the kitchen. Max put a pot of coffee on the stove and lit a cigarette. Immediately he collapsed into a paroxysm of coughing that lasted almost five minutes and left Nick thinking his friend was about to die, except that he had seen this performance before. Finally the coughing subsided and Max took a deep breath.

'That's better,' he said and took another deep draw on the cigarette. 'First one of the day. Clears the lungs out.'

From up close Nick could make out the grey roots in Max's hair. They had been friends a long time before he realised that he dyed his hair. His vanity was somehow unexpected.

'How's Daniela?' Nick asked him.

'Wonderful. Can't thank you enough. She can't keep her hands off me. But you mustn't let her stay here too long, she's wearing me out.'

'Very funny.'

Just then he heard a door open and Daniela came out of the spare bedroom, dressed, glowing, perfect.

'Coffee, darling?' Max called.

She smiled at Nick. 'Hello, Nick. Don't mind Max. He teases all the time.'

'I know.'

'So you saved me again,' she said to Nick.

'He did nothing of the sort,' Max said. 'It's my apartment.'

Max poured the coffees. 'Well, the slave has prepared breakfast. I'll go and get dressed now, if you don't mind.'

After he had gone they stared at each other a moment in silence. 'You look wonderful,' he said.

'I don't know how to thank you,' she said, and he decided she probably meant that in literal terms.

'I've been to the Prefecture again. No luck, I'm sorry.'

She stood too close and touched his hand with hers. He wished she would take it away, and at the same time wished she would move closer.

'I can't stay here for ever.'

'Max loves having you here. Everyone thinks you're his mistress. His reputation in Bucharest with other women has soared.'

'What about my reputation?' she said, and he realised he had assumed too much about her. Just because every other woman in Bucharest was sleeping with the Germans.

'You're safe here.'

'I'm a Jew, Nick. We're not safe anywhere.'

'Safer here than in the Jewish Quarter.'

She nodded, conceding that point at least. 'Why are you doing this? Why are you helping me?'

'Does everyone have to get something in return?'

She took her hand away from his. 'Usually.'

'For the good of my soul, then.'

'What's going to happen to Simon?'

He shrugged his shoulders. He could make a guess but he didn't want to tell her what the chances were of her ever seeing her brother again.

'You are so kind. You're the kindest man I've ever known.'

Nick wondered if Jennifer would agree. He looked at his watch. 'I have to go to work. Stay here as long as you want. It's okay.' He was about to go, hesitated. Sometimes she looked indestructible, but other times, like now, she looked like a small and wounded bird.

She reached out a hand to touch his cheek but he smiled and moved away. He knew if she had touched him again he might not be able to control what he did next and that wouldn't do at all. Least of all in Max's kitchen.

Later that morning Abrams walked into Nick's office and dropped into the chair on the other side of the desk. He rarely left his own office to venture this far into the building, so Nick knew this had to be important.

'I want you to search Clive Allen's flat.'

'What am I looking for, sir?'

'I don't know. But he was behind Bendix's death. I'm sure of it.'

'We have proof?'

'There is no-one else, Davis.'

Abrams drew invisible patterns on the polished walnut of the desk with an index finger.

'He betrayed us. He betrayed his country.' Abrams hesitated, was about to say more, then got up and left as abruptly and unexpectedly as he had arrived.

Nick had never trusted Clive Allen; there was something about him he had never quite liked, in his eyes, but he had never thought him a traitor. The Ploesti plan had been their one chance to affect the course of the war from inside

Romania, but now that the Germans had moved two regiments of the Brandenburg division into Ploesti, any sabotage would be impossible.

Clive Allen.

Nick put on his jacket and went down to get a car, and to get Ionescu.

Clive lived in an apartment near the Carlton building on Bratianu. Gaining entry was not difficult. Ionescu found the caretaker and, after some haggling in Romanian, a sum of *lei* changed hands, and a key was produced.

Once inside, Nick made a quick inspection of the flat. Clive was a closet drinker; the apartment was full of empty bottles, on the floor, even in the sink. Hard stuff too, whisky and *tsuica*. Not a good sign.

Ionescu watched the door; Nick was quick and expert. In half an hour he found what he was looking for in a false drawer in the dresser in Clive's bedroom. It was a brown paper envelope, stuffed with pounds sterling, and on the back was a telephone number. Nick used the telephone in the living room to ring the number; a voice answered in German.

He wrote down the number, replaced the envelope in the dresser and went out again, locking the door behind him.

13.

Abrams was at his desk in the Passport Control Office. His secretary showed Nick into the room. A dusty portrait of King George V, looking as solemn as God, hung above Abrams's head.

Abrams did not look up from his papers. 'What did you find, Davis?'

Nick told him about the envelope and the telephone number scrawled on the back.

'You rang the number?'

'It's the German Legation on the Strada Victor Emmanuel.'

'I see. Have you drawn any conclusions?'

'There's only one conclusion I can draw.'

'I agree. Thank you, Davis. That will be all.'

'There's one other thing.'

'Make it quick. I actually have visa applications to process here. It's getting in the way of my work but the Foreign Office won't extend my budget for more staff.'

'I have a plan to stop Romanian oil getting through to Germany.'

'We've been through this. Whitehall won't sanction it now. The Ploesti fiasco has scared them off.'

'This won't involve British nationals. We use the Haganah, the Jewish defence forces. We offer to exchange them for Jewish women and children here in Romania, smuggle them into the country and issue an equal number of visas for the Jews coming out. In return, the Haganah men remain behind as guerrilla fighters to sabotage the rail and river links up the Danube.'

Abrams stared at him for a long time. It was a brilliant idea and Nick knew it. This way the Zionists got Jews out of Romania, and his own government could truthfully say they were not increasing the intake of immigrants into Palestine. And it would disrupt the flow of oil to Hitler.

Abrams shrugged. 'What do you want to do?'

'I want to go to Istanbul to speak to Ben-Arazi, the Zionist representative there.'

'Very well. I'll pass on a coded message to London.'

Nick got up to leave. He turned around.

'What about Clive Allen?'

'That will be all,' Abrams said and returned his attention to the weight of paperwork in front of him.

It was a bright day in autumn when the Germans came to Bucharest. All morning squadrons of Messerschmitts and Heinkels flew low over the rooftops, letting the Bucharesti know the Luftwaffe had come to play.

Antonescu had invited the Germans to send a military mission into Romania, though he hardly had a choice in the matter. An alliance suited Romania better than invasion, and, besides, who else would save them from the depredations of the Russian army to the north? Every Romanian Nick spoke to told him that Hitler would help them reclaim Bessarabia and Bucovina from the Russians, some feat of mental gymnastics allowing them to forget that it was Hitler who had supported Stalin's claims to those territories just six months before.

For the arrival of their new friends, the management of the Athenee Palace hung a swastika from the façade, the massive red and black flag dropping three storeys to the awnings over the main entrance. Nick had never seen so many people in the lobby for the *aperitif*. They had all come to be a part of this little turn of history's wheel; the diplomats and oil men and journalists and, of course, the women in their fox furs. There was a palpable air of apprehension, and among the Romanian women, yes, excitement. The nervous tension built through the morning, like a mistress waiting for her handsome but brutal lover.

Nick joined Max in the lobby to watch the show.

'How's Daniela?' Nick said.

'Gone,' Max said.

Nick looked around at him, startled. 'Gone? Gone where?'

'Don't know, old boy. Came home yesterday evening and there she was, not there. She left some money on the table for the food she'd eaten and a note saying thank you very much. There was this for you.'

He handed Nick a letter.

'Going to open it?'

Nick stared at the envelope.

Max bought another round of drinks. He raised his glass and murmured '*Naroc*'. Nick ripped open the letter and read the few words she had written in French.

Cher Nicholas, you have been so kind. But there are many things you do not know about me, and I cannot rely on your kindness, and the kindnesses of your friends, any more. I am going to stay for a while with some friends of my father. I am sure we will see each other again in the Athenee Palace. All of Bucharest meets there, sooner or later. Thank you again, for saving my life, and for trying to help, monsieur blue eyes. Daniela.

There was a buzz as the first of the Mercedes saloons pulled up outside. Moments later high-ranking Wehrmacht men flooded into the lobby, resplendent in stiff grey uniforms with red lacquered collars and red piping on their trousers, many wearing the Iron Cross first class.

The sound of their boots on the marble echoed around the foyer. They gave full-blooded Nazi salutes to the German diplomats and Romanian army officers there to greet them. This was not the casual flick of the hand favoured by Gestapo men and even Hitler himself; these men were aristocrats and they clicked their heels together with a sound like a gun blast and shot their arms straight out in front of their eyes.

Max turned to Nick and raised an eyebrow. 'There goes the neighbourhood,' he said.

It was one of Max's jokes but neither of them laughed. They both knew that Romania was no longer just a rather quirky place to be in the middle of a European war. Suddenly Bucharest was very, very dangerous.

Daniela looked down into the cramped cobbled streets of the Jewish Quarter. She knew that Nick Davis would never know how much he meant to her. He was that rarest of treasures, a man who treated her kindly and wanted nothing from her. He had saved her twice, and found her places to stay when she had nowhere else to go, and had not demanded sexual favours. From the moment she had seen him she knew she could trust him. Was that what they called love at first sight? He had the bluest, gentlest eyes she had ever seen on any man, and whenever she saw him it felt like there was a nest of puppies squirming in her stomach.

Yes, she supposed she was falling in love with him, her most unlikely of heroes.

But she was no good for him. He was married and soon he would be leaving Bucharest. Men like Nick Davis did not have affairs and she was not going to take him away from his wife. And there was so much he did not know about her, that she had not told him, that made anything between them quite impossible.

She had lied to him about so much, but those lies would never hurt him, because this could never amount to anything. Perhaps another time and another place, another life, there would be another chance.

But this one could be too cruel.

14.

Two days later Clive Allen was at the Piatsa Universitatea, reporting on an Iron Guard demonstration. A gang of young students chased him, because he was a foreigner. They cornered him in an alleyway off the boulevard and beat him with fists and iron bars. Another journalist from Havas, a French agency, managed to get away and drove back to the Athenee Palace to get help.

When Max and a handful of other journalists went back to the square in Max's Humber, they found Clive lying face down on the pavement, his head in a pool of blood. A crowd had gathered around him.

He had been so badly beaten one of his eyeballs had removed from its socket and all his teeth were broken. He was mercifully unconscious. His head was so swollen that Max only recognised him from his suit.

They picked him up and took him to the nearest hospital, where a Romanian doctor left him lying on a gurney for two hours. The next day Hoare, the Minister, arranged for him to be evacuated on a ship back to England but he died halfway between Constanza and Istanbul.

Nick never mentioned the incident to Abrams. But he often wondered about it. In his experience, there were few accidents or coincidences in his profession.

That same evening Nick saw Daniela Simonici in the American Bar.

She was surrounded by three Wehrmacht officers. The broken and dishevelled girl he remembered from the last time he had seen her in these surroundings was gone. The transformation was astonishing.

She must have sensed his gaze, for her eyes moved from her companions to him, and when she saw him, the dazzling smile dropped away.

One of the Wehrmacht officers saw Nick staring. He put a proprietorial hand around Daniela's shoulders and smiled through a wreath of smoke. First Paris, then Dunkirk; they got everything they wanted.

Haller was watching with naked jealousy from a corner table. He was not as drunk as the night Nick had first seen him; he was able to sit unsupported, a significant improvement.

'Do you have a light?' a voice said in German.

Nick turned around. The man was short and stocky, with greying hair. He had a Nazi lapel pin. Nick produced a lighter and lit his cigarette for him.

'You are an Englisher.'

'What gave me away?'

'You do not have a girl with you,' he said with a low chuckle. 'Siegfried Maier. At your service.' He gave a slight bow and clicked his heels in the Prussian manner.

'Nick. Nicholas Davis. I'm with the British Legation.'

'Ah, a diplomat. I have never met so many diplomats since I have been here in Bucharest.'

'It's a place that requires a lot of diplomacy. What do you do, Herr Maier?'

'I have business interests,' he said easily.

Nick could imagine what those interests were. For months now the government had been closing down Jewish-run businesses and installing Guardist commissars, who knew nothing of commerce, in their place. Or else Guardist police descended at night, taking Jewish businessmen to the Prefecture on falsified charges, where they languished under the tender mercies of their gaolers until they agreed to sign over their holdings. Now German and Italian businessmen were rushing to Romania to buy banks and department stores and newspapers for almost nothing.

'How long have you been in Romania, Herr Davis?' Maier asked.

'About a year.'

'Do you like it very much?'

'It's wonderful, if you like *tsuica* and fascists.'

'Personally, I have developed a taste for *tsuica*. But you should not grow too fond of the city. You will not be here for very long.'

'A shame. The fascists were starting to grow on me.'

'Of course, we may all be friends again very soon. The war will be over quickly, and by next Christmas everyone will have forgotten all about it. It may be better for everyone in the end. Still, a pity for you if you have to leave. The women here are very beautiful.'

'I hadn't noticed.'

'I suppose it's just as well, they seem to prefer German boys. Anyway, I am sure we will meet again sometime in the course of our duties. For as long as you remain.'

'I shall anticipate that pleasure.'

A soft smile and he moved off. Nick looked around for Daniela. She had disentangled herself from the Panzer division that had been following her around the bar and had gone out to the lobby. He followed her, saw her walk into the breakfast room, and then out through the French windows into the little courtyard where he had taken her after he had helped her escape from the greenshirts.

He stood for a moment in the doorway, watching her. She was staring up at the night sky. Suddenly she looked around and saw him standing there. She slipped on her smile as easily as slipping on a cardigan against the chill. 'I think I've drunk too much vermouth,' she said.

'You should slow down,' he said. 'It's only early.'

'I try but the boys keep filling up my glass.'

'The boys? You mean the Nazis.'

She made a face. 'You're in a bad mood. Perhaps I should leave you alone.'

'Haller's been watching you all evening.'

'Haller?'

'The young man who vomited in the aspidistra.'

'I don't remember that part. All I remember is that I met this beautiful blue-eyed Englishman and he was very gallant and took me home. I think I might have kissed him in the *trasura*.'

'He must be a very lucky man.' He took off his jacket and wrapped it around her shoulders.

'I don't think so. If he knew all about me, he would have run away as fast as he could.'

'What were you thinking about when I came out?'

'I was thinking that life can be a strange thing. A year ago I was living on the Boulevard Bratianu and everything seemed simple and I had the next ten years planned perfectly. Now look.'

'What was in your plan?'

'Oh, you know. The usual things. Someone who loved me and treated me well. Children. All those things you already have, *monsieur*.' And she gave him a look that he could have construed as reproach.

'I never planned it, Daniela. It just happened. Another

funny thing that life does. I feel like I've been sleepwalking through my life until now.'

Their eyes met and locked. So much they already understood about each other.

'Where are you living now?'

'An apartment. Close to where I was before.'

'I've been looking for you. I think I can get you those visas.'

'The visas?'

'I imagine you'll just be wanting one now.'

A flicker of pain in her eyes.

'You can go to Palestine. Perhaps even Britain.'

'But I can't, not without . . . Simon. He's still in prison.'

Dead by now, Nick thought.

'Come to the embassy, make a proper application, bring a photograph. I can organise everything.'

She shook her head. 'Thank you. But I can't. Not now.'

He wanted to say to her: Just think of yourself, you won't see Simon again. He couldn't bring himself to do it.

She was shivering. A breath of winter in the air.

'It's cold out here,' she said. She was standing too close. Big eyes, a crooked smile. He found her closeness unnerving but he made no effort to move away.

'I remember the first time I saw you in the bar,' she said. 'I felt something for you the very moment I saw you: I knew you were different.' She handed him back his jacket. 'Thank you, *monsieur*. Did I tell you that you look very handsome tonight?'

'I thought you preferred men in uniform.'

'Compared to a man with such wonderful blue eyes and a cream tussore jacket? Never.' And she reached up unexpectedly and kissed him on the lips. He tried to pull her towards him but she squirmed away, laughing.

What am I doing? he thought. I am still a married man, and this girl can only compromise me privately and professionally.

'I'll never forget you,' she said, then turned away from him and went back inside. He stared after her, wished he had met her a long time ago. But then he would not have been the man he was now and she would have been too young. Perhaps this was the perfect time, though time alone would tell if anything would come of it.

Haller was waiting in the lobby. He was drunk, for it was nearly ten o'clock and he found it indecent to be sober after eight. Nick wished all the Germans were like Haller: the Panzers would have driven into ditches and trees before they left the Rhineland.

'What were you doing out there?' Haller said, in heavily accented English.

'Go away.' Nick tried to push past him but Haller grabbed his shoulder.

'We're going to kick you out of Bucharest.'

Nick wasn't in the mood for this. He could smell the drink on Haller's breath. People around the lobby were staring. This was the kind of floorshow they came to the Athenee Palace for and he didn't want to be a part of it.

'You're drunk.'

Haller pulled back his fist and hit Nick on the jaw, cutting his lip with a wild, drunken swing. Nick saw it coming but was too astonished to duck out of the way.

He immediately sat Haller on the seat of his pants. It took only a single punch and afterwards he regretted it, for Haller could have vomited on his polished Oxfords.

Suddenly Maier appeared. He grabbed Haller by the arm, stood him up and hissed something in his ear. Haller stumbled away.

Maier turned to Nick with a slight bow of the head. 'My apologies, Herr Davis.'

'Don't apologise. I won.'

'A new experience for an Englishman. Your lip's bleeding.'

'It's nothing.'

Nick saw Daniela watching from the door of the American Bar. The expression on her face caused his sense of triumph to evaporate. His little victory had impressed her not at all. He left, a little ashamed, the taste of his own blood salty in his mouth.

15.

Jennifer was waiting up for him when he got home. She was in her nightgown, sitting in her favourite chair, reading a book. The lamp threw a yellow pool of light on the pages.

She looked up at him over the top of her reading glasses. 'You're bleeding.'

'I started a second front.'

'In the hotel?'

'It's our bridgehead into the Balkans.'

'Tell me you're joking.'

'Some young Nazi hothead took a swing at me.'

'Why?'

'Why do you think? We're at war.'

'In Europe. Not in the lobby of the Athenee Palace.'

'He forgot where he was.'

'Now you're being flippant.'

'He was drunk.'

She closed her book with a snap. 'How many more times are you going to come home covered in blood, Nick? You're supposed to be a diplomat.'

'I suppose I just haven't been very diplomatic lately.'

She waited for him to say something else, but he didn't. 'Has something happened?'

73

'What do you mean?'

'I don't know. You're not the same any more.' He stared at her. Had she heard a single thing he had said to her in Cina's? 'Is there another woman, Nick?'

He felt something tighten in his chest. 'No, of course not,' he said and it was true, there was no other woman, because he would never sleep with Daniela Simonici. But in his head he had made love to her a thousand times already, so perhaps even this truth was not as clear as it might have been. If he ever did find the courage and moral conviction to leave, he didn't want this to be about another woman.

'I'm going to bed,' he said.

Jennifer came to bed a little later. He pretended to be asleep.

They lay with their backs to each other. He stared at the yellow light that spilled through a gap in the curtains, knew it came from the Athenee Palace Hotel, where Daniela Simonici was laughing and flirting with drunken German officers.

Jennifer rolled over, slipped an arm around him, nestling her body against his. She kissed his shoulder.

'I'm sorry,' he said. 'I'm just tired.'

He turned over onto his back. She slid her hand down his body, in what was a familiar routine to him now. When he was ready, she pulled him towards her and urged him into her.

He made love to her with a fierce passion, imagined it was Daniela beneath him, her dark hair fanned across the pillow, her head thrown back, a dew of sweat on her forehead, soft pulse beating at her throat. He imagined they were her thighs wrapped around him, her voice in his ear whispering to him and urging him to love her. And when he reached the moment, he cried out, something he had never done before, and almost said her name.

'Darling,' Jennifer whispered afterwards and cradled his head against her shoulder as he fought for his breath. He knew he had betrayed himself. 'Darling. Are you all right?'

'I love you,' he whispered, but he was still thinking of Daniela. Why had he said that? Was it only from a sense of guilt, because it was what she expected to hear?

'I love you too,' she said, and he winced, wishing he could feel something he did not. 'That was . . . intense. I thought you were tired.'

'I'm sorry. Did I hurt you?'

'No,' she whispered. 'No, you didn't hurt me.'

Because he didn't want to hurt her. That was the truth of it. He didn't want to hurt her, he just wanted his freedom back.

16.

Everyone in Bucharest was a spy; and if they weren't spies, they were diplomats and military attachés who wanted everyone to think they were. There were British and French oil engineers on their way out of the country, and German and Italian oil men on their way in; there were mink-wrapped Austrian blondes in the pay of the Gestapo hoping to seduce information from the Romanians, and Romanian girls on the arm of German Legation staff for the same reason.

They were all drawn to the Athenee Palace Hotel because this was where Bucharest came to be seen and to trade secrets.

Everyone who worked in the hotel also worked for Moruzov's secret police: the valets, the porters, the woman in the white apron in the lavatory, even the pink-cheeked pageboys with their little monkey caps strapped around their chins. You went there in the evening and by next morning someone in the palace across the square would know who you dined with and where, what you ate, when you got back to the hotel and who you slept with.

Nick knew who worked for whom, that was his job: the bearded tobacco merchant in the corner reading a Greek newspaper was paid by the Germans; the pretty dark-eyed woman sitting at the bar drinking vermouth worked for the French. The sharp-eyed fat man in the white suit with the grey goatee worked for everyone, but he was sleeping with a German asset – a nice young boy from Stuttgart – so he was no longer considered reliable even as a double agent.

The large table in the lobby was a barometer of the war. All the foreign newspapers were laid out there: the *Voelkische Beobachter* and *Boersenzeitung* were yesterday's; while the headline on the battered copy of the London *Times* reported the French retreat across the Marne on June 12, and was so limp and worn it was impossible to hold it upright. For a casual guest of the hotel, the dates and condition of the newspapers would have told them all they needed to know about who had the upper hand.

The Germans were well invested in Romania now. Officially, the German presence was a military training mission; in the American Bar the journalists laughed aloud and wondered what a country the size of Romania could do with two hundred thousand rifle instructors. The Germans had also taken over the Athenee Palace Hotel. On the day of their arrival the management had cleared guests from several floors for the exclusive use of Wehrmacht officers. Many staff from the British Legation had been sent home and most of the foreign journalists had left too; Max King was among the few who had decided to stay.

There was a hush about the hotel on a Sunday morning, knots of men and women whispering about their assignations of the night before or talking politics and bartering prices for secrets real and imagined. It was so quiet that shoes squeaking on the parquet floors between the wine-red runners sounded like the screech of hydraulic brakes.

Nick and Max sat together in a salon just off the lobby, on one of the plush cherry-red settees, drinking *tsuica* and searing Turkish coffee. A gold-framed portrait of Antonescu had been propped against the French windows on an easel where an oil painting of King Carol had rested a few weeks before.

The King is dead. Long live the King.

Nick studied his friend; Max had the air of the dilettante. At a distance his thick black hair and long lean physique gave him the look of a forty-year-old, when in fact he was nearer to sixty, and a closer inspection revealed a spiderweb of capillaries on his nose and cheeks from too much heavy drinking and too many late nights. He had a wife and family in Hampstead that he rarely spoke of. Other journalists deferred to him; he had had bylines from some of the world's most infamous cities, had interviewed Hitler and Lenin, and covered the Chinese civil war, and the massacres in Shanghai.

He leaned in, his elbows resting on his knees, his voice low. Their complicity was reflected in the gilt mirrors along the walls.

'There's talk the Germans are preparing to march into Greece,' Max said, fishing for news. 'They're going to launch the invasion from here.'

'I wouldn't know about that,' Nick said. 'I'm just the assistant military attaché.'

'Of course, I forgot.' Max put three spoons of sugar in his cup. 'I suppose you wouldn't know about the other story I heard either.'

'What story was that?'

'That there were plans to send in a regiment of Royal Engineers to sabotage the Ploesti oilfields.'

'That would be committing an act of war in a friendly country. It would violate Romania's sovereignty.'

Max liked that. His belly laugh attracted stares from

around the room. 'Better to lose the war than have the King of Romania think you were impolite.'

Nick gave him a look of forbearance. How did he know about the engineers? Clive Allen, perhaps. It didn't matter now; with Bendix dead, the operation had been compromised and the 54th Field Company had decamped and quietly sailed back to Egypt. Jordon had disappeared from the dingy office in the basement as mysteriously as he had arrived.

'Well, it's too late now,' said Max. 'We missed our chance. The Germans aren't going to let us anywhere near Ploesti now. When they attack Russia, they'll need that oil for their tanks.'

'I only carry out government policy, Max, I don't make it.'

'Well, at least I struck a blow for the cause last night,' Max said.

'Tell me.'

'Every night the Krauts leave their shoes outside their doors for polishing. So I got up at four this morning and switched them all around. When the Wehrmacht got out of bed, none of them could get their shoes on. You know how the Teutonic mind hates disorder.'

It was a childish trick but Nick laughed. He wished he had been there to see it. It was more than they had done to frustrate the Germans in the last six months.

He sipped his coffee, Turkish, very bitter and very strong. The small handle-less cups left little rings on the marble-topped table.

'You know Romania has to get into bed with the Germans,' Max said. 'They don't have a choice. Do they realise that in Whitehall? If Chamberlain was in Downing Street he might have made a similar accommodation himself.'

'It won't happen with Churchill there. He likes a fight.'

'The Channel's saved us, of course.'

Max turned around and smacked several kisses into the air, in the local custom of calling the waiter. The man hurried from the bar with two more *amalfi*, the copper-coloured cocktails of vermouth mixed with *tsuica*.

As the drinks were set down on the table, Nick felt a stab of guilt. Last spring he had eaten caviar at Cina's, his conscience assuaged by the knowledge that, in a country as arable-rich as Romania, even the poorest could afford the staples of life and would not starve. Now, less than a year later, Russia's invasion of Bessarabia had swollen the city with refugees, inflation was out of control and there was a shortage of butter and eggs. Outside the hotel doors people were dying while he sat in a plush armchair drinking cocktails.

'*Naroc*,' Max said and raised his glass in a toast to the future.

'*Naroc*.'

Max grew suddenly serious. 'Got a cut on your lip.'

'Cut myself shaving.'

Finally: 'What's going on, Nick?'

'What do you mean?'

'I've known you nearly a year now. Not like you to get into a fight. Must have been hell to pay with the Minister.'

'The other fellow was drunk. I tried to get out of it, he hit me first.'

'Everyone's been talking about it.'

'And what have they been saying?'

'That it was over a woman.'

Nick sighed. 'It's not true.'

'Does Jennifer know it's not true?'

Nick chewed on his lip. 'You think I should tell her?'

'Take it from me, sport. If you do, wait for the right time.'

'There's a right time?'

'Of course there is. That's why they invented the deathbed.'

'Nothing happened.'

A shadow moved behind Max's eyes. 'Something always happens.'

Nick took a breath. Christ, he had to talk to someone. 'I'm just flirting, Max. Thought I'd forgotten how. I know I'm acting like a fool. You don't have to remind me.'

'Just be discreet, old boy. That's all. Going to have an affair, use a little tact, little panache. Not fist fight in the lobby. Duelling at dawn, next. Good Lord.'

'Not what you think.'

'What about you and Jennifer?'

Nick shook his head. 'She loves me. What am I supposed to do?'

'Do you love her?'

'We've been together a long time. Don't want to hurt her, Max.'

Max laughed at that.

Nick felt a flaring of anger. 'It's not funny,' he said. But then, thinking about what he had just said, he realised it probably was.

'No such thing as an amicable divorce, old boy. Oxymoron. Like a peaceful war. Friendly fist fight. Military intelligence. Contradiction in terms.'

Nick rubbed his face with his hands. These things were simple if you weren't involved. 'Just shoot me,' he said. It was a joke, but then he remembered Bendix and Clive Allen. Careful what you wish for, especially in a war.

'Sort out one mess before you start another,' Max said.

At that moment, there was a sickening motion underfoot, cups and glasses crashed to the floor, as if they were in the carriage of a train that had slammed to a halt suddenly in the shunting yard. Women screamed and for a moment there was a hushed silence. Then everyone started to laugh. Tremors were common enough in Bucharest these days. It was part of life, like the Guardists and the Nazis and the beggars at the front porch.

'One day there's going to be a real earthquake,' Max said, with his usual prescience.

17.

Istanbul

They met in a restaurant off Istiklal Boulevard, rode an ancient elevator to the fifth floor. They sat at a corner table overlooking the Bosphorus and the lights on the Asian side. It was dark, a rendezvous for lovers.

But Nick did not think that he and Ben-Arazi would be holding hands over the *meze*.

The conversation was stilted. He had picked Ben Arazi as an arrogant bastard from the first. But he couldn't let his personal feelings about the man get in the way of business. Over dinner they discussed the weather, Istanbul and, of course, the war. Ben-Arazi lectured him all through the main course on Palestinian politics and British perfidy.

While they waited for the coffee, there was a difficult silence. Ben-Arazi drummed a tattoo on the table with his fingertips.

'The Arabs have a saying,' he said finally. ' "The enemy of my enemy is my friend." I don't like the British. Nothing personal, Mr Davis, but I don't like you either. But you are the enemy of my enemy.'

'I want your help. In return, I may be able to help you.'

Ben-Arazi was coldly silent.

'If you can't destroy the oilfields, you have to close the Iron Gates if you want to deny the Germans the oil from Ploesti.'

The Iron Gates – the Portile de Fier – were near the Hungarian border, a narrow defile where the Danube passed through steep cliffs on either side. Only one barge could pass through at one time and then only with a specially trained pilot on board. Romanian oil from the Ploesti oilfields had to pass through the Gates on the way upriver to Germany. It had long been suggested that the judicious use of explosives could bring down the cliffs and close the Danube for weeks or even months.

'What do you have in mind?'

Nick leaned forward. 'Eight hundred Haganah soldiers. We bring them in to Romania in exchange for eight hundred Jewish refugees. We give the refugees visas for Palestine and help you get them out.'

'And what will these eight hundred soldiers do?'

'Your people are trained in guerrilla warfare. They will remain to ensure the Iron Gates stay closed.'

'Can you do this?'

'Can *you* do it?'

Ben-Arazi raised his eyebrows. 'Perhaps. Is this your idea or does it come from London?'

'From me. I have to know if it's possible before I commit this to London.'

Ben-Arazi shook his head. 'You think you can persuade them?'

Nick bridled at this. 'We're all on the same side here.'

'Mr Davis, if you think there are just two sides in this conflict, you are badly mistaken. The war has layers, like a good *halwa*. Perhaps *you* are fighting the Germans. Others have different ideas.'

'Meaning?'

'Oh, you will find that out in good time.' He finished his glass of *raki*. 'I take it the British Government will pay the bill for dinner.'

Nick watched him walk away, a small man with a short man's swagger. He didn't like him. But as Ben-Arazi himself had said, he was the enemy of an enemy, and right now Nick and the service he worked for wanted him as a friend.

He wasn't going to sit in this God-forsaken city doing nothing. He was going to serve his country faithfully and well, no matter what his countrymen did to try to stop him.

If the train had not been delayed for five hours by a derailment on the other side of the border, Nick would have been in his Bucharest apartment at three o'clock that morning when the earthquake struck the city. Instead he found himself sitting in a frigid railway carriage dozing and fretting, occasionally getting up to stamp his feet in the corridor to try to keep warm.

The train crawled into the Bucharest suburbs just as a filthy grey dawn broke over the city. It was like a curtain lifting on an apocalyptic stage; greasy skeins of smoke rose from burst gas mains, and there was rubble in the streets where houses and apartment blocks had crumbled like sandcastles.

A woman staggered down the middle of a street, covered in dust, blood caked onto her face. He saw a bedroom exposed, half the wall and floor gone, the bed and dresser still in place; he was afforded a glimpse of a framed wedding photograph on the wall.

An earthquake. Those tremors they had felt for months, that they had joked about, had been the harbingers of disaster.

The wheels screeched as the train came to a stop. They waited for what seemed like an eternity; after a time, he saw other passengers jumping down onto the tracks. He realised the rails must be damaged.

He pulled his suitcase down from the rack, opened the carriage door and jumped down onto the mud, where he slipped and jarred his knee, felt a cold stab of pain as he stood up.

It was bitterly cold, the sky dark as pewter, and a vicious wind buffeted him, carrying with it the smell of leaked gas, concrete dust and death. And another smell, pervading everything, the smell of open fires; all round the city smoke drifted from a thousand cooking-fires, the people of Bucharest afraid to go back inside their houses, carrying on with their lives this morning on the streets.

He had no idea where he was, except that he was somewhere in the suburbs of Bucharest, so he set off along the tracks, knowing they would lead him to the main railway station and from there it was perhaps a few minutes' walk to his apartment. He wanted to run but his knee felt as if someone was stabbing into the joint with a needle.

He passed a knot of his fellow passengers stumbling through the mud beside the stalled train with their suitcases and small children. Across the city he could hear the shrill bells of fire engines and ambulances.

On either side of the tracks he saw piles of rubble where homes had once stood. Six-storey apartment blocks swayed drunkenly over the street.

He wondered what he would find when he got home.

The *piatsa* outside the Gara de Nord was normally packed with *trasuras* and taxicabs and trams, and he would have had to fight his way through a clamour of beggars and ragged children who would have crowded around him the moment they recognised a foreigner. Today the square in front of the train station was eerily deserted; there were just two cars in the empty piatsa, one of them a grey-black Humber. He felt a flood of relief when he saw a familiar face.

'Max, what are you doing here?' he shouted.

'Came looking for you, sport. Christ, the state of you. You're limping. Hurt your leg?'

'Brilliant, you should have been a detective. It's nothing. I've got to find Jen.'

'We'll find her. I'm sure she's all right.'

His knee was throbbing. He threw his valise in the back of the Humber and got in, rolled up his trouser leg. His knee was swollen and he could feel the fluid building up under the skin, stretching it taut. Christ.

'What happened, Max?'

'Three o'clock this morning, woke up, felt the whole bloody room swaying, like being blown about in a gale.'

'Is the hotel still up?' Nick asked.

'Hardly a crack. God does a lot of terrible things but He wouldn't take away the only place in this bloody awful city where a man can get a decent drink. They weren't so lucky at the Carlton. Came down like a pack of cards.'

The Carlton was the tallest apartment block in the city. There would have been hundreds sleeping inside. But Nick couldn't worry for hundreds; grief is personal.

Max steered around a pile of cobblestones that had erupted on the street as if a giant fist had punched its way through.

'Can't you drive any faster?'

'Doing my best.'

There were fire trucks and abandoned cars everywhere, people milling in the street, afraid to go back inside their houses and flats. Others were digging desperately at the rubble and the broken masonry of fallen buildings with their bare hands, no-one to help them.

Nick felt as if there was a weight sitting on his chest as they turned into his street. He couldn't lose her this way. There was still too much unsaid, too much unfinished business between them. He would never forgive himself.

The apartment was down.

The west wing of the top two storeys had crumbled, caved in on itself, and only half the building was left standing. The rest was a twisted pile of plaster and tortured stone and wirework. What struck him was the quiet. There had to be a hundred people buried under the building and yet there was not a sound. A crowd had gathered to watch as brigades of German soldiers set about methodically clearing the rubble. German staff officers in long black leather coats stood silently watching the work.

Staring up at what was left of the apartment block, he could see their living room, a blue upholstered armchair balanced crazily over the lip of the shattered balcony. The bedroom, where Jennifer would have been sleeping, was gone.

He got out of the car. People were wandering around, dazed. A man shouted at him, a stranger with blood on his face, crazy with grief or fear; an old woman crouched in the middle of the street, cradling a jar of pickles in her arms.

He heard moaning from somewhere in the rubble. He climbed up the mess of bricks and iron and started scrabbling blindly at the shattered concrete and dust with his bare hands.

Soon his fingers were torn and bleeding and the rubble

gave way beneath him, took a long strip of skin from his shin.

He should have loved her more.

'Nick.' He turned, saw her standing with Max beside the battered grey Humber. Her face was chalky with plaster dust and her hand was bleeding.

'I'm all right, Nick, I'm all right.'

'Jen,' he said.

He clambered down from the rubble and wrapped her in his arms.

'Nick,' she whispered and he felt her sobbing against his shoulder.

'It's all right,' he said. 'It's all right.'

'I fell asleep in the armchair, waiting for you to come home,' she said. 'If I hadn't fallen asleep . . .'

He held her, crying too, totally unprepared for what hit him next. It was not relief, but disappointment. He did not want her to die; but a part of him, for just one shameful moment, had thought that he was free.

18.

They had taken rooms at the Athenee Palace. Nick peered through the curtains, down at the square. The city was blacked out and shrouded in fog. Armed men were running across the snow-hushed cobbles towards the palace. Gunfire echoed over the rooftops.

It was frigid in the room. They sat in their overcoats, huddled around the guttering candles that were the only illumination. The power was out again, the heating too. Jennifer's breath formed little clouds in the air.

She looked sad and the sadness lent her face a stark beauty that he had not seen in her for a long time.

'We have to get you out of here, Jen.'

She said nothing.

'It's too dangerous now. We don't want our boys left without a mother.'

Like thousands of other schoolchildren, the boys had been evacuated to the west coast, and had gone to stay with Jennifer's mother in Weston-super-Mare.

'You have to go. We have to think about Richard and Jamie.'

'I'm scared that if I leave I won't ever see you again.'

'All the other wives have left. It's best you go too. It's more dangerous here every day. There could be another coup.' She was silent. 'Do you hear that, Jen? It's gunfire.'

She shivered and blew on her hands to try to warm them.

'I'd feel better if I knew you were there with them.'

She gave him a look he could not decipher. She had always been a rather remote mother. Even when they were babies, she had preferred to hand them over to their nannies. In that respect, he imagined being a diplomat's wife had suited her well, because the boys had both, by necessity, been sent to boarding schools in England at a young age. He wondered if she regretted that lost time now; he knew he did.

He supposed this damned war was his one chance to make it all count for something.

'Do you still love me, Nick?' she whispered.

'Of course,' he said, and wished he had the strength to tell her the truth.

He went downstairs to the bar. Even in the candlelit dark, the scheming went on. An official from the Romanian Ministry of Defence was trying to sell transcripts of wire-taps from Antonescu's office. They might have been genuine. Nick passed on them. The man wanted too much and, anyway, what did it matter now?

He met Max in the American Bar. They had the place to themselves. The Nazis disappeared into their rooms at ten o'clock and most of the German military mission had moved to the Ambassador Hotel and only came back to the Athenee Palace when they wanted to sleep with a girl.

By midnight the corridors and stairs were lit only by a few sparse violet bulbs. Max went home. As Nick crossed the foyer, heading back to his room, he had the eerie feeling he was being watched. A grim-faced Gestapo man sat by the stairs pretending to read newspapers. The Nazis were wary of assassins taking advantage of their own blackout.

He heard laughter in the foyer behind him, a German bringing his girlfriend back for the night. In the cavernous gloom of the foyer, he saw a mane of long dark hair and he knew it was her, and he felt as if he had been stabbed in the heart.

He should have gone straight up to his room but for some insane reason he stopped and waited on the stairs. Maier saw him and grinned wolfishly. 'My Englisher friend!' he shouted.

Daniela. For almost a week he had worried over her, wondered if she might be languishing in some hospital, or lying among the piles of blackened corpses being hurriedly buried in unmarked graves all around the city.

She would not meet his eyes.

'Still awake, Herr Davis?' Maier said.

'Stayed up for a nightcap,' he managed.

'You don't conquer Europe with a hangover,' Maier said laughing. 'Goodnight!'

Nick watched them go up the stairs, transfixed by the perfect sway of her hips. She turned once and their eyes met. In the violet dark he thought he saw a movement of her lips and he wondered what it was she might have wanted to say to him.

He had no claim to her, but his longing was such that he tossed and turned all that night and could not sleep, his own torturer. He tried not to imagine Maier's possession of her, but of course, as he lay in bed, sleepless, he conjured every detail of their joining in all its exquisite agony.

Was it fear or jealousy that kept him from sleep? He and Jennifer lay like the entombed kings and queens in Westminster Abbey, on their backs, side by side, silent and cold.

He swung his legs out of bed and paced the room, spoiling for a fight. He wanted Jennifer to be awake but she only murmured in her sleep and rolled onto her side. So instead he put on his silk dressing gown – one of the few possessions they had rescued from their apartment – and went down to the lobby, feeling his way in the violet gloom of the lamps.

The lobby was cold, like a catacomb. Shadows moved about the entrance, German sentries on patrol. The Gestapo man dozed in his chair under the stairs. The reception clerk slept with his head on the desk.

He paced for the sake of pacing, tried to walk off his agitation, as if this razor edge of confusion could somehow be blunted with movement.

'You look like a tiger trapped in a cage,' a voice said.

He knew her voice, though he could not see her, just a silhouette in a chair set against one of the pillars.

For a moment he was too surprised to speak. 'What are you doing down here?'

'The same as you. I couldn't sleep.'

'Maier will wonder where you are,' he said, the pleasure of finding her fading as quickly as it took for his jealousy to reaffirm itself.

'He's snoring like a bulldog.' She hesitated. 'Why don't you sit down for a while?'

He found a hard-backed chair. What a strange life, he thought, the two of us sitting here while my wife and Daniela's lover sleep alone upstairs.

Daniela was wearing a fox fur coat that Maier had no doubt bought for her. She shivered inside it.

'I saw you earlier, here in the lobby. I don't think you saw me. Was that your wife?'

'I have women everywhere. What did she look like?'

The joke fell flat. 'She's very beautiful,' she said. 'Do you love her, Nick?'

'That's a good question and one I don't think I can answer right now.'

'Is that why you're so unhappy?'

'Does it show?'

'Yes.'

A long silence. 'Why Maier?' he asked her, finally.

'I don't know,' she said hopelessly. 'He helped get my father away from the Iron Guard, persuaded them to release him.'

So, Maier was her protector now. 'Is he all right?'

A shadow passed across her face. 'He's very sick.'

It surprised him, not that Maier had persuaded the Romanians to let the old man go, but that he had survived six months in a Romanian prison. He knew how they treated Jewish prisoners, especially the wealthy ones.

'Siggi's kind to me.'

Maier: Siggi. 'Well, that's important.'

'And I can pretend to like him. I'm a good actress. I always have been.'

'What's he like?'

'He reminds me of . . .' But she never finished whatever it was she was about to say. He wondered about it afterwards.

'It wasn't always like this,' she said. 'When we lived on Bratianu, I never thought I would be doing the things I do now. God likes to trip us up, if we get too proud.'

'You don't have to be proud. He does it to everyone.' He thought about that day he had seen her in the street wearing her green shawl, the afternoon the greenshirts had chased them. 'Does Maier think he can help you get your brother out of prison?'

'There are some things even Siggi cannot arrange.'

'That's a comforting thought.'

Their eyes locked.

'Aren't you afraid?' she said, after a while.

'Of the Iron Guard? Of course.'

'Isn't it strange? The greenshirts would kill you too, if they could. Only these Germans stand between you and a massacre.'

'I have thought about that, and well, in the circumstances – Heil Hitler.'

She laughed and her laughter fell into the silence like breaking glass. The Gestapo man, having briefly returned to his dozing, looked up sharply, as if they were whisperers in a public library.

'How long since you have been home?' she asked.

'Eighteen months now. A long time. Wars tend to disrupt your life.'

'What is England like?'

'We drink a lot of tea.' He wondered how you explained a country to someone who had never been there. 'The people are colder somehow. There's no passion in them. We have a saying: "keep a stiff upper lip". It means that no matter what you're feeling, you don't let it show.'

'Is that what you're like?'

'I suppose. For most of my life.'

'And now?'

'And now?' He was silent for a moment, then he took a deep breath. 'I want to sit up all night here talking to you, I want to hold you all night and never let you go. I have never felt this way about anyone before and certainly never spoken this way. But I have a wife and I have two sons and I cannot abandon them, and I feel sick to my stomach when I realise what a sham it has all been for so long. There. That's not exactly stiff upper lip, and it's not exactly Latin passion, but it's the best I can do right now.'

She took his hand in both of hers, held it like an injured

bird. Then she pulled him towards her and kissed him softly on the lips. For the first time he allowed himself to believe that she might feel the same way.

'I wish that . . .' she began, but she never finished and he never did discover what it was that she wished.

'*Liebling*,' a voice said from the stairs. 'There you are, I was worried about you. What are you doing down here?' Nick was surprised by the tenderness in Maier's voice.

Daniela snatched her hand away as if she had been caught picking someone's pocket.

'Siggi. You're awake. Sorry. I couldn't sleep.'

Maier strode across the lobby, stopped when he saw Nick. 'My Englisher friend. What are you doing here?'

'Insomnia. It's contagious.'

Maier looked stricken. 'Come back to bed, *liebling*,' he said to Daniela.

She sighed and stood up, obeying. 'Goodnight,' she murmured softly and followed Maier up the stairs. Nick thought he saw her look back once with longing, but how could he possibly have discerned such an expression in the darkness?

He must have been mistaken.

19.

At the end of World War One, MI6 had taken over responsibility for issuing visas to foreign nationals overseas. Someone in the Foreign Office had thought it a good idea to use the passport control system as a cover for the ministry's intelligence gathering activities. The PCOs were only loosely connected to the diplomatic corps but did not enjoy full diplomatic status; if necessary, the local ambassador could deny all responsibility for their activities.

But the PCO cover was thin disguise. Any hostile government could quickly discover the identity of the MI6 station head by applying for a British visa.

The cover role also turned out to be an onerous duty. One of the functions of the Chief Passport Control Officer was to issue visas to Jews wishing to emigrate to Palestine. In Bucharest the trickle of applications had become a flood and Abrams was overrun with desperate Romanian Jews seeking visas to escape the Jew-baiting and the pogroms that followed the resurrection of the Iron Guard.

This morning Abrams appeared fractious. His budget did not extend to employing more local officials, and although few of the applications on his desk would be successful, they were required to be processed. As usual he spent ten minutes complaining to Nick on the futile nature of his cover before he finally subsided.

'But this particular problem is not the reason I wished to see you,' he said. 'It's about this proposition you made to the Haganah agent.'

'You've heard from Whitehall?' Nick said, eagerly.

Abrams shook his head.

'But why?'

'We do what we're told, Davis. There are wiser and cooler heads in Whitehall.'

'Wiser?'

Abrams shrugged. 'While Romania remains neutral, the British Government is unwilling to violate the sovereignty of a friendly government.'

'Really? We've been doing it to France and Spain for centuries.'

'That's a very cynical point of view, Davis. Let me also remind you that I am responsible for the issuing of visas to foreign nationals, and the question of Jewish immigration into Palestine is a particularly difficult one right now.'

'What do I tell Ben-Arazi?'

'You tell him the truth, if it suits you.'

Nick could barely contain himself. But it wasn't Abrams's fault, of course. This was a Foreign Office decision. But, for God's sake. Germany was dropping thousands of bombs on their cities every night and Whitehall was worried about upsetting the Romanians. The MI6 in Bucharest had no money, no resources, so they just sat here watching the Germans do as they pleased, men like Maier laughing at them.

He would rather be in one of the armed services. At least if he had a gun in his hand he would feel he was doing something.

'These stupid bastards in Whitehall are costing us the war,' Nick said.

Abrams stared at him. He disapproved of strong language. There was a long silence. 'I want to talk to you about Maier,' he said, finally.

Nick stared back in confusion. 'Maier?'

'And this other woman you've been seeing.'

It took Nick off balance. His mind was still on the Ploesti oilfields. 'Woman?'

'If you're going to repeat everything I say, Davis, I'm going to lose my temper. You know who I'm talking about. Her name's Daniela Simonici, correct?'

'Nothing improper has occurred.'

'I'm really not concerned about that, Davis. But she's the consort of some very high-ranking German officers and your conduct might be called into question in Whitehall if not in heaven.'

Whitehall be damned, Nick thought. 'Are you asking me not to see her any more?'

'Of course not. Quite the opposite.'

'Sir?'

'Siegfried Maier is a colonel in the Abwehr,' Abrams said.

The Abwehr was the Wehrmacht's counter espionage service. Unlike the Gestapo, they were unconcerned with ideology – it was an intelligence service, the same as Nick's own SIS.

'Moreover,' Abrams went on, 'there are certain aspects of his background that make him of particular interest to us. If she is his mistress, as seems apparent, she may become a very valuable commodity.'

'What aspects?'

'I can't tell you that. But men like Maier could have a significant impact on the future of western Europe, in the light of last year's events.'

Nick stared at him. He had never known Abrams to overstate a case or fabricate melodrama. 'I don't think I follow you.'

'You don't have to follow this, Davis. Just do what you can. This man could be very important to us. So this woman could be important too. Find out if she's willing to work with us.'

'I'll do my best.'

'Be discreet, Davis. But don't let her get away.'

Don't let her get away. Right.

Nick got up to leave. He hesitated at the door. 'What you said about Maier, the future of Western Europe?'

Abrams pulled his in-tray towards him. More visa applications. He didn't look up. 'Need to know, Davis, need to know. Good morning.'

Ben-Arazi looked around the office at the grey filing cabinets, the grey metal desk, the dusty portrait of King George on the wall. 'Very impressive,' he said.

'I had to take down the Vermeers and the Rubenses. They clashed with my Ming vases.'

Not even a smile.

'Tea?'

Ben-Arazi shook his head. 'Let's get down to business.'

Rain wept down the grime on the window.

Nick had been dreading this. The bastard had been right all along. It didn't matter that Nick felt just as outraged by his government's timidity. Ben-Arazi had told him what would happen and the man's arrogance would be insufferable now.

'Well?' he repeated.

Nick shook his head.

The expression on Ben-Arazi's face betrayed contempt but not surprise. 'May I ask why?'

'We cannot be complicit in violating the sovereignty of a friendly government.'

'Romania? Friendly? They are as friendly to the British Government as a Bedouin. Three days of hospitality and then they cut your throat.' He stared at the ceiling in despair. 'You people are unbelievable. Why did you waste my time with this?'

'I'm sorry. This was not my decision. The question of visas to Palestine for Jewish refugees is a difficult one.'

'The shame of it is that you are not only wasting my time, you are wasting lives as well. But they're Jewish lives, so why should you care?' He leaned in. 'Personally, I don't give a damn about the Iron Gates. I care about the eight hundred Jews I want to save. What's going to happen to all these people after you British run away?'

Nick had no answer for him.

'I despise you,' he said. He got up and walked out.

Nick threw his pen against the wall. For God's sake.

It was now certain that the Romanian oil reserves were in Hitler's pocket. Nick had been convinced ever since that night in Ploesti that there was someone in Bucharest or in Whitehall who was sabotaging their efforts, and it had nothing to do with Romania's supposed neutrality or even any moral aversion to helping the Jews. Someone *wanted* the Germans to have that oil.

That was why Bendix had died. Nick would have died too, if he had got in the way.

He wondered how much Abrams was telling him.

And he wondered why this Maier – a colonel in the Abwehr no less – was so damned important. He sat there for a long time, thinking. Then he stood up and, with one arc of his hand, he swept everything off his desk and onto the floor. He picked up his chair and hurled it across the room at the wall.

The door opened and his new secretary tentatively put her head into the room. 'Is everything all right?' she asked. 'Fine,' Nick said, and went out.

20.

The young woman wept, her whole body shaking with the force of her grief; the man in the army greatcoat held her as if he was drowning. Nick never found out who they were, where they were from, never discovered if they were ever reunited; he liked to think that they were. When he wrote their story in his mind, the soldier always came home whole and safe and she was there waiting for him.

Their parting was replayed up and down the station that night. The platform was crowded, people shouting and pushing, porters shouldering their way through the crowds with trolleys of luggage, a bedlam of leave-taking and hurried farewells. Others slept among their meagre bundles of possessions, the bits of furniture and rolls of carpet. Refugees cooked cornmeal porridge over tiny spirit stoves, faces drawn and hopeless.

Nick and Jennifer stared at each other across the chasm that lay between them and finally he reached out with awkward arms and held her. He somehow felt cheated. He wanted to be the man in the army greatcoat, to hold his wife as that young soldier held his.

'Give Jamie and Rich my love,' he said.

'Of course. I imagine I won't recognise them.' A brittle laugh. 'You will be careful, Nick.'

103

'Of course.'

'If anything should happen to you, I don't know what I'd do.'

This declaration surprised him a little. He had always thought that Jennifer would be perfectly fine without him. 'You'll be okay.'

She held him. He felt her crying and patted her shoulder. 'It's okay, darling,' he said. A long time since he had called her that.

'Take care.'

'I'll be all right. No bombs falling here.'

'Not yet.'

The train would take her as far as Constanza on the Black Sea. A Turkish destroyer was waiting to take British nationals to Istanbul where a Royal Navy convoy would escort them on the dangerous crossing back to England.

They could not know if this was the last time they would see each other.

Jennifer reached up and touched his face tenderly with a gloved hand. He couldn't quite meet her eyes. She kissed him and hugged him quickly around the neck, and then she was gone. He watched her disappear through the crowd.

She climbed aboard the train, a slim woman in a tan raincoat, her silhouette blurred and indistinct. He waved as the train pulled away, lost among the clouds of steam, and he stared after her as she leaned from the compartment window. He watched her until she was out of sight, a memory to store away in his mind, like a photograph hidden in a secret drawer, to be taken out with private regret at some future time when they were no longer husband and wife.

The apartment was cluttered and small. Daniela peered out from behind the door, looking pale and frightened. Without make-up she appeared younger, and fragile.

'Nick.'

'Hello, Daniela.'

'How did you find me?'

'I had you followed,' he said and she thought he was joking.

'Come in.'

She made coffee in a pot on the stove in the tiny kitchen. She was nervous.

'What are you doing here?'

'I needed to see you.'

He saw the look on her face. She thought he was there for sex. Well, there was nothing to stop him asking, if that was what he really wanted.

'Do you live here alone?'

She didn't answer.

'You should get out while you still can.'

There was chicken soup bubbling on the stove.

She poured some of the broth into a bowl and covered it with a cloth. He heard someone cough in the bedroom and followed her out of the kitchen and down the dark and narrow passageway.

An old man lay on the bed, his breath rasping in his chest. The room smelled vile, of sweat and human waste.

'My father,' she said. 'See what they've done to him? He was a strong and handsome man when they arrested him.'

Daniela propped him up in the bed and started to feed him the soup. It leaked down the old man's chin, following a crease in the stubbled jaw. She dabbed at it with a napkin. A side of his temptress Nick had never seen.

'So why are you here?' she asked him.

'It's a delicate matter.'

Their eyes locked.

'You want to sleep with me?'

Her directness took him off balance. 'It's about Maier.'

'You want to sleep with Maier?' she said, breaking the tension.

'Not my type.'

'Too short?'

'Too blond.'

She smiled for just a moment, then spooned more broth to the old man, who was yet to open his eyes.

'I would like to pay you for certain information.'

'You want me to spy for you? After Siggi helped me get my father out of the Prefecture?'

'Did he?'

She shrugged her shoulders. 'In a way. But it cost me a lot of money. He said it was for the chief of police.'

'Well, that was probably true.'

'Are you a spy?'

'Do I look like a spy?'

The old man turned his head away from her. She said something to him in Yiddish but he shook his head. She sighed and put down the spoon.

'What sort of information do you want?' she said.

'You just have to keep your ears open. I'm not asking for secrets. My government needs to know what men like Maier are thinking, what they're saying about the war.'

'He's just a businessman.'

He smiled at that, and so did she.

'You'll do it?'

She tucked the old man up into the bed, kissed him gently on the forehead and put the cloth over the bowl. She stood up.

'I can't make you a promise like this.'

He followed her out of the room. She put the bowl on the kitchen bench and turned, her hands resting behind her on the stove, a challenge in her eyes. 'Do you want to stay?' she said, and there was a message for him in her eyes.

'I should be going.' I'm falling in love with this woman, he thought. Is this what I want? An easy, convenient affair now that my wife's gone? It just seemed too shabby. 'I have to go,' he repeated.

He hesitated, then hurried away, before he changed his mind.

Daniela watched him from the window as he walked back up the cobbled street. In a way, she was pleased he had not accepted her invitation, it made him different from other men. But there was a part of her that was sad; how many times did he have to prove himself to her? She had never had quite this feeling with a man before and just for once in her life she wanted to take what she wanted, have the moment and the man to herself. Just this one time.

She heard her father coughing in the other room and went in to him. He was dying, of the lung rot. When they brought him from the prison, she had barely recognised him. He was still a fine man when he went in; he had come out a ravaged skeleton.

She never remembered him holding her or cuddling her when she was small; when she got older he had called her a slut. And now, too late, he needed her. She could have taken the visa that Nick had offered her and gone to Palestine and escaped from this hell. But if her father had never loved her, at least now she could show him that she loved him, and even if he never opened his eyes and said the words she so longed to hear from him, she hoped he would know that in the end she had been a good daughter.

21.

Cold inside the car. Ionescu turned up the heater, the fan drowning out the rumble of the engine. They turned down a cobbled street near the old Hanul Manoc Inn and drove at walking pace. A man emerged from a nearby doorway and jumped into the back.

Jan Romanescu came from one of the aristocratic families of Bucharest and had been educated at the Sorbonne in Paris. His appearance belied this; his long greasy hair trailed over his collar and he had a long, unkempt beard. He smelled. But Romanescu was a confidant of Horia Sima himself and was therefore one of Nick's most important agents, the station's highest placed contact inside the Iron Guard. He was also a committed Bolshevik and Nick suspected – or rather, assumed – that he worked for the Russian military intelligence, the GRU.

'How are you, Jan?' Nick said.

But Romanescu was not a man for small talk. Too bourgeois, Nick supposed. 'Sima wants a showdown,' he said. 'There was a meeting at the palace last night. In the Council Room. Antonescu beat his fist on the table and Sima shouted back at him that he was finished, that he would see him hanging from the palace gates.'

Romanescu's coat was wet from the rain and the damp wool stink was worse than his body odour.

If there was a confrontation between Antonescu and the Guardists, and if the Germans supported the Guard, Horia Sima would take power, and there would be wholesale massacres. It would be anarchy. Even the British diplomatic staff might be in danger of their lives.

Some of the remaining legation staff wanted to evacuate now.

'Do you know what the Germans are going to do?' Nick said.

'Sima is convinced they'll support him. He's had assurances from von Killinger, the new minister.'

'From Hitler?'

'He says from Hitler. Sima believes him.'

'It's not in Hitler's interests to support the Iron Guard.'

'Sima says he's had a meeting with von Killinger at the German Legation. The Germans want Antonescu out.'

Nick shook his head. It was hard to imagine that it served the German interest to have Bucharest in the hands of the nationalists.

'What are you going to do?'

'There's nothing we can do,' Nick said.

'You should get out. The greenshirts are crazy.'

The windscreen wipers laboured against another heavy shower of rain. 'I'll be in touch when I can,' Romanescu said. 'But things will be a little difficult from now on.' He tapped the driver's seat and Ionescu stopped the car. Romanescu jumped out. 'Good luck, *mon ami*,' he whispered, then he slammed the door and ran off into the dark.

The smell of him lingered in the car, a pungent brew of damp wool and body odour. Despite the rain and cold, Nick wound down the window. He heard the sound of gunfire somewhere in the city, death out there stalking the dark.

Just a battle for survival now. They were no longer trying to defeat or even frustrate the Germans; the enemy was their saviour, their lifeline. If the Germans joined with the Romanian fascists in this fight, then the life of every British and American national in Bucharest was in danger. It was up to him now to tell Abrams what to do, whether to stay or leave. Those lives were his responsibility now.

We should get out, he thought. He did not know why Whitehall wanted them here. It was his own stubborn pride that told him they should stay. That, and his longing for Daniela Simonici.

22.

Winter took Bucharest by the throat. There was a dusting of white on the cupolas of the Cretulescu church, and except for the boulevards, where the streetcars were busy with wooden blades, the snow was left in crisp and virgin drifts about the city. To the north, the mountains appeared freshly washed each morning, the glaciers veined and blue.

Snow boots and rubber galoshes were left in pools of melted ice in the cloakrooms of hotels and in the waiting room at the legation. Ordinary Romanians took to wearing hats of black and grey astrakhan; the refugees and gypsies made do with old newspapers.

A new sound impressed itself on the consciousness when he stepped out of the hotel: the jangle of sleigh bells.

German troops continued to pour into the country. The square outside the hotel looked like a field camp, with row upon row of dull grey military lorries parked there. It was clear the Germans were staging for a campaign. Whether they wanted it or not, the Romanians were going to war with Russia.

A freezing doorway, hands thrust deep into the pockets of his coat. She was muffled against the cold, and looked up and down the street before joining him in the doorway, as if they were two lovers on a secret tryst. Two German soldiers in heavy greatcoats went past, boxes of chocolates under their arms, bought for a few coins in the *chocolaterie* on the Chaussée. They were laughing at some joke.

The city was living on the edge. Every night squads of greenshirt fanatics in leather coats and high fur caps roared off on their motorcycles to raid Jewish houses, to loot and terrorise. Guardist thugs from the countryside patrolled the streets in gangs, doing as they pleased.

The country had been sliding towards anarchy for months. Antonescu had fired the Director and Prefect of Police, both Guardists, and issued a decree effectively removing all the commissars from their lucrative posts. Overnight he had taken away the nationalists' power and the nationalists' money. The challenge had been thrown down.

'I wrote down everything I remember,' she said. 'Names of Germans sympathetic to the Guard, SS men who have been supplying the greenshirts with weapons.'

She produced an envelope from under her coat and he transferred it quickly to his back pocket.

'What does Maier think will happen?'

'I heard him tell one of his Wehrmacht friends that Killinger promised Sima he will support him against Antonescu. It was a lie. They want to see the Guard destroyed. All they care about is the oil, and the greenshirts are too crazy, even for the Nazis.'

'You believe him?'

'The Germans aren't squeamish. It's just politics for them.'

'Killinger has set them up?'

'Of course.'

Nick sighed. For God's sake. They said intelligence gathering was like a blind man searching in a dark room for a black cat that wasn't there. Did he believe Romanescu, an intimate of Horia Sima, or the mistress of his own counterpart in the Abwehr? Were they both wrong? Or was one of them – or both of them – deliberately feeding him lies? All he could do was report on what was said and heard and let someone else make the decision. He just wished so many lives, including his own, didn't depend on the outcome.

Could he trust her?

Her face was turned up towards him. And then suddenly he was kissing her. This time it was not impulse, he wanted her, all reticence gone. Her face was cold, her mouth warm. She responded immediately, her body pressed against him. Then she pulled away and was gone.

Afterwards he waited there a long time, overwhelmed. For the first time in his life he felt truly alive.

Abrams stared at the reports scattered across his desk; lies, rumours, half-truths, contradictions. In the end, it was all guesswork and logic.

'What do you think, sir?'

'I don't know, Davis. It makes sense that von Killinger is playing a double game.' He rubbed his forehead. 'Do we ignore the highest placed agent we have inside the Iron Guard?'

'You asked me to recruit her, sir.'

Abrams sighed. 'The Minister wants to know if we should evacuate the remaining staff.'

'I think we should believe Miss Simonici. The Germans would never let Sima have Bucharest.'

'You trust her?'

'More than that. It makes sense.'

Abrams nodded. 'I hope to God you're right. Or this time next week we'll all be dead.'

23.

Now, a week later, Nick stood at the Legation window and watched as black smoke spiralled into the sky from the Jewish Quarter.

A burst of machine gun fire echoed across the city, rattling the windows. 'It's finally started,' Nick said.

They left the office and went down to the basement. Everyone had crowded into the signals room. The receiver was tuned to the government radio station, and one of the interpreters gave a running commentary to the handful of staffers who still remained. The station had been taken over by the Iron Guard and there were repeated calls for legionaries to report to Legion headquarters for duty.

There was a thick fug of smoke in the room. Everyone was chain-smoking.

'What do you think Jerry will do?' someone said.

Nick looked at Abrams. He supposed they would all find out soon enough.

24.

The Athenee Palace Hotel remained one of the safest places in that blighted city. The Germans had set up a cordon around the hotel to protect their own and there was a machine gun post on the porch. The streets were dangerous now and Nick had been unable to leave the hotel to go to the legation for two days. He had no idea what was happening to the rest of the British staffers. A strange war, their safety and survival secured by their enemy.

He found O'Leary, from the *Chicago Herald Tribune*, in the bar. Most of the other journalists had been ordered out of the city long before. Only Max and O'Leary had stayed behind.

'Where's Max?' Nick said.

'Haven't seen him since this started. Don't worry. He'll be all right. He knows his way around.'

Nick didn't feel as confident as O'Leary. Max lived in an apartment on Bratianu, two blocks from the hotel. There had been some heavy fighting around there the previous afternoon.

So far the Wehrmacht had sat on their hands and done nothing, as Daniela's reports had indicated.

Out in the lobby, men and women were whispering in

little groups while Wehrmacht officers strode about in their polished boots, laughing and shouting to each other as if it was all a great game. And to them no doubt it was; they could have crushed either side at any time. They were like school prefects watching two small boys fight in the schoolyard for their own amusement.

The crackle of gunfire from the street added to the apocalyptic gloom; Nick felt as if they were waiting in the lobby of hell for the end of the world. If that was true, it was a fitting cast of characters; they were all there, the princesses-for-hire and the armaments bosses and the Gestapo agents and erring husbands.

A tank cannon fired close by and the walls shook, the windows rattled. Several women screamed. 'Christ,' Nick said aloud and saw his own fear reflected in other faces in the foyer. Even the bellhops and the waiters stopped what they were doing and waited, holding their breath.

'People say Antonescu's dead,' O'Leary said.

'If they're still fighting,' Nick said, 'then he's still alive.'

Daniela was out there somewhere. There were stories of Guardists rounding up all the Jews. This morning he couldn't keep still. Perhaps she was with Maier. Surely he wouldn't let his mistress die out there.

He had to know where she was. He had to know she was all right.

A neighbour ran in to warn her of what was happening. There had been gunfire echoing round the city all morning, but for the last hour it had been eerily quiet. 'The green-shirts are coming!' the neighbour shrieked at her and then Daniela heard her running down the stairs.

Daniela went to the window. The greenshirts were dragging whole families into the street and herding them into trucks. The street was blockaded at both ends. There was no way out.

She ran into the bedroom where her father was sleeping. His breath was sawing in his chest. He would be gone soon. If she was on her own she might find a way to get away.

'Oh papa,' she murmured. The sheets smelled of sweat and rotting. She put her arms under him and lifted him easily off the bed, just skin and bones now. 'It's all right, papa,' she whispered. 'Everything will be all right.'

She heard a woman screaming in the street, and the brute voices of the greenshirts. 'It will be all right, papa,' she repeated and stood in the middle of the apartment with her dying father in her arms, limp as a child, while the heavy boots of the soldiers echoed on the cobblestones. She did not know what to do.

25.

A crowd had gathered in the lobby around the front doors. Nick went over to see what had drawn such an audience. There was a man in a brown overcoat running towards the hotel across the empty square. He slipped once on the ice and his hat fell off but in his panic he got straight up and kept running and made no effort to retrieve it.

From the other side of the square a Guardist legionary shouted at him and raised his rifle.

'Who is it?' a Brazilian diplomat asked.

'It's Max King,' Nick said. 'He's a journalist with Reuters.'

'He's crazy,' the diplomat said.

They all heard the crack as the legionary fired his rifle. Max kept running. The two German soldiers at the machine gun emplacement outside the doors decided the bullet had come too close to them and they fired a burst from the machine gun over the legionary's head. The sniper ducked and ran for cover.

Max leaped over a drift of dirty brown snow and threw himself on the hotel porch. The other guests cheered.

The German soldiers cheered too, laughing at his escape in the way they might enjoy seeing a bedraggled cat escape a pack of dogs. They patted him on the back and hauled him to his feet, propelling him through the doors where several of the other guests helped Nick drag him to one of the sofas.

Max was not of a mind to join the general air of celebration. He was wheezing like an asthmatic and now his legs had carried him to sanctuary they would no longer support him. The onlookers parted to let him through and Nick dumped him unceremoniously onto a cherry-red sofa where he was immediately surrounded by the bored and the inquisitive.

'Are you all right?'

It took a while for him to get his breath back. 'Those people are animals,' he gasped.

Until this moment Max had for ever been the laconic Englishman; now he was shaking with fright and his face was a pasty shade of grey.

Someone ran to fetch him a reviving shot of *tsuica*.

'What happened?'

'Tank started shelling the apartment. Figured it was time to move, old boy. Until then I was just too fucking scared.'

Nick helped him get the *tsuica* down.

'You just won't fucking believe what's happening out there.'

Nick thought about Daniela, stripped, raped, beaten. He saw Maier walking into the American Bar with two Wehrmacht officers. He called out to him. Maier turned around, surprised.

'My Englisher friend. I am glad to see you safe and sound. What can I do for you?'

'Having a good war?'

'This is not a war. That's just a dogfight out there.'

'How many dogs can drive a tank?'

Maier looked uneasy. 'What's wrong, Herr Davis?'

'Where's your girlfriend?'

120

'Miss Simonici? I have no idea. Is this any business of yours?'

'Your friends in the green shirts may have her right now. Doesn't that worry you?'

'This is not my concern.'

Nick took a step closer. 'You know she's Jewish?'

'Keep your voice down!'

'You have to help her!'

'I do not have to do anything.' Maier looked frightened. He glanced over his shoulder at the two Wehrmacht officers, who were watching the exchange with interest. 'Now I must say good morning to you, Herr Davis. Please do not approach me this way again!'

He walked away.

Nick went back to Max. A few solicitous spectators had crowded in again, from boredom, Nick decided, rather than genuine concern. He pushed them aside. Max was still shaking, his eyes fixed on the carpet.

Nick sat down beside him. 'I need your help, Max.'

'What?'

'Got to help me find her.'

'Who?'

'You know who I'm talking about.'

'You go out there, you'll get yourself killed.'

'Better than sitting around here watching the Germans laugh at us.'

'You do remember you're married, Nick?'

'Just need your car, Max.'

There was colour in Max's face again. He sighed. 'Hell with it. Let me have a cigarette and I'll come with you.'

26.

The Germans at the machine gun post stared in astonishment as they ran past. Nick felt the rutted snow
through the thin soles of his shoes. The bitter wind slapped
his face. If he had run naked across the square he could not
have felt more vulnerable, or more alone. Small arms fire
echoed over the rooftops. His blood pounded in his ears.

Max slipped on the ice and went down. Nick hauled
him to his feet and they ran side by side along the Strada
Episcopiei before throwing themselves in the doorway of
the nearest salon. Once, it sold the latest Paris fashion,
but the windows and doors were boarded up now. There
would be no winter collection this year.

They were both breathing hard. The dirty white wedding cake of the Athenee Palace already seemed hopelessly
remote.

Max couldn't get his breath. His usual morning exercise
consisted of propping up the American Bar before lighting
a cigarette. Saliva leaked from his mouth as he dragged
himself to his feet. He stumbled out of the doorway, hug-
ging the wall. Nick followed.

Cars and buses had been abandoned along the boulevards. Nick saw a corpse sprawled across the driver's seat
of a taxi, blood congealed in thick clots on the upholstery.

The city smelled of burning, and black smoke hung over the rooftops like a pall. The streets were empty. He and Max were the only ones out on the street in this city full of snipers and madmen.

Everything was blurred by fear. Nick did not remember running down Bratianu. It felt as if there was cold fat in his stomach.

Max's apartment was just two blocks from the hotel, a six-storey building in the Parisian style. The Humber was parked outside in the street. There were burnt-out cars behind it and in front of it but for some random and inexplicable reason it had been spared during the previous day's violence.

They crawled inside the car and Max fumbled with the keys but his hands were shaking so badly he couldn't find the ignition. Nick snatched them away from him.

'Get out of the way, Max.'

'I can do it, sport.'

'No, you can't.'

Max crawled across the seat and cowered in the floor-well on the passenger side. Nick tried the ignition. The engine was too cold to start. He hoped the water in the radiator hadn't frozen over.

There was a starter handle. He got out of the car and bent down in front of the bonnet, his back an inviting target for every sniper in Bucharest. The engine coughed and coughed again, and then the handle kicked back and almost smashed his wrist. 'Start, you bastard!' he shouted.

It stuttered into life.

The windscreen was caked with ice. He scraped it off with his gloves and then crawled behind the wheel. 'Going to get us killed, old boy,' Max said.

Nick drove at walking pace through the deserted streets, crouched down over the wheel, waiting for a bullet to shatter the windscreen at any moment. Max was still crouched

123

on the floor, his head on the passenger seat. 'Don't know how I let you talk me into this,' he said.

'Sorry.'

'Fucking should be, sport.'

They drove almost five blocks, past bodies frozen in bizarre attitudes of death. The walls of the buildings were pocked with bullet holes. They didn't see another soul.

They reached the outskirts of the Jewish Quarter. Nick stopped the car. He was panting with fear, and his breath left clouds of vapour in the air.

'We'll go on foot from here.'

He got out, and crouched down beside the front wheels. Max crawled across the driver's seat and slid out beside him.

'We're going to die, old sport. You know that?'

A crack of rifle fire from the next street. Too close. Any moment a squadron of Guard legionaries would come around the corner and they would be finished. The sweet stench of death made Nick retch. Or was it just his own fear?

When he was done, Nick wiped his mouth with the back of his hand. 'Let's get going,' he said.

They heard the screams from a block away. Instinctively, they dropped on their bellies in the wet snow.

'Christ,' Max said, 'think I've pissed myself.'

Nick turned around. Max's face was a mask of humiliation and naked terror.

'Wait here,' he told him.

He crawled to the corner. There were perhaps half a dozen greenshirts in the street and they had found a Jew to play with. The man looked like a student, a Hassid with a shaved head and long curls around his ears. He was wearing a long black coat stained with all manner of filth from his hiding place.

One of the greenshirts aimed his rifle at the man's feet, and fired. The bullet sparked off the cobblestones and his terrified prisoner screamed and danced. One of the others had a can of petrol and threw the contents over the man, who screamed again. Realising what was about to happen, he tried again to escape, but one of his tormentors knocked him down with the butt of his rifle.

The man with the petrol can threw a lighted match and the poor wretch erupted into a writhing ball of flame.

Nick crawled back to where Max lay face down in the slush of wet snow. He hauled him into a nearby doorway by his collar. 'Don't move, just keep quiet!'

The screaming went on and on. Not all the greenshirts stayed to watch the fun. Three of them passed within a few feet of where Nick and Max lay, heading west towards the square. A few minutes later the others hurried after them.

Nick imagined what would happen to Daniela if these bastards found her. He would not even let himself think he might yet be too late.

The stink of roasted meat was overpowering. When the greenshirts were out of sight, they started to run. Nick spared a glance for the blackened corpse lying in the middle of the cross street but it had mercifully stopped screaming and now lay quite still, like a bundle of charred rags.

The Jewish Quarter was deserted. Frozen bodies lay in the street like litter. Daniela's building had been looted and burned, blistered wood still smouldered among the blackened shell of the walls.

Nick heard sniper fire in the next street. He pressed his back against a wall. It was still warm. He closed his eyes.

'We're too late,' Max said.

They huddled side by side, watching their breath form into white vapour. 'Nick, we're too late! You did your best. Let's get out of here.'

'Not yet.'

Nick ran across the street, leaping over broken armchairs and torn books, the pages printed in Hebrew turning in the wind. He almost slipped on a trampled prayer shawl lying in a pool of black congealed blood.

The fire had collapsed the roof and it lay in a blackened rubble around the stairwell. A brass menora lay under a piece of twisted tin. It was still scalding hot to the touch.

He was about to turn away when he heard a noise close by. It sounded like someone coughing. He saw a cement staircase leading down to a basement beneath the skeleton of the metal stairwell.

'Is there anyone there?'

He climbed over the tangle of beams and tin to the foot of the stairwell. Dried blood had smeared on the concrete, where it had mixed with the melting ice.

He heard it again, the sound of someone coughing. He kicked open the basement door. There was someone in there, in the darkness, he could hear the sound of someone breathing, a dry sound like sandpaper scraping on wood.

'Hello?' he called and then in French: '*N'avez pas peur. Je suis Anglais. Je veux vous aider*. Don't be afraid. I am English. I want to help you.'

'. . . Nick?'

Someone struck a match and lit a candle. It was Daniela, crouched in the corner, her hair matted, eyes wild. She was squatting down beside her father, who lay wheezing on the floor, unconscious.

'Daniela?'

The old man coughed again, and there was a pink froth on his lips. 'He's dying,' she said.

He knelt down beside her. She slumped against him and started to cry. He held her. Finally, she pushed herself away, wiping her face angrily with the back of her arm, almost as if she was ashamed.

'When the greenshirts came, we hid down here,' she said. 'I carried him. Like he carried me when I was a child.'

He's going to die anyway, Nick thought. They both knew that. The old man's breath smelled like the grave.

'We have to get you out of here,' he said.

He could feel the bones of her shoulder through her coat, which was fox fur, French fashion. He remembered it from that night in the hotel foyer. Now, encrusted with filth, it was not fashion at all, but was at last doing the job for which nature intended, keeping a body warm and alive through winter nights.

He helped her to her feet.

'What about papa?' she said.

An exercise in futility. Whatever happened, this time tomorrow the old man would be dead. He was unconscious and didn't know what was happening anyway. It looked to Nick like heart failure or perhaps lung rot.

But they couldn't leave him.

He scooped him up in his arms. It was like picking up a bundle of dried twigs.

'What are you doing here?' she asked him.

'I came looking for you.'

'Why?'

Why. A good question. He didn't have an answer for her, any more than he had the answer for Max. 'Let's get out of here,' he said.

He carried the old man up the stairs, Daniela following him. He ran across the street, where Max was still waiting, crouched behind a burnt-out van.

'Jesus Christ,' Max said.

'I found her.'

'Fuck is that, old son? Moses? He's dead, for Christ's sake, put him down.'

'He's still alive.'

'Could have fooled me.' Max looked at Daniela and shook his head in astonishment. 'Don't believe it. He said he'd find you. This bastard's mad.'

Daniela was too exhausted to answer.

'Must get your story for the paper,' Max said and his mad laughter echoed along the street, over the bones of the burned and newly dead.

They started running towards the boulevard, saw the Humber on the other side of the intersection. Max was leading the way, but as soon as he reached the end of the *strada*, he swore and ducked back behind the wall.

There was a government tank, painted sky blue, parked on the boulevard not a hundred yards away. Nick sagged against the wall, the cold air burning in his lungs.

'Now what do we do?' Max said.

'We can't sit here. If a Legion patrol comes along, we're dead.'

Nick heard a metallic whirring as the tank turret started to turn. The barrel of the cannon was pointing up at the surrounding apartment blocks, searching for targets. 'Now,' he said and pushed Max and Daniela ahead of him. He hefted the old man in his arms and started after them.

From the corner of his eye he saw the tank's gun swivel around towards him. He braced himself for the inevitable burst of machine gun fire and wondered what it would be like to die, hoped only that it would be quick. Time slowed down. It was as if there were sandbags on his feet.

Daniela and Max had reached the corner. They were watching him, urging him to hurry, but they were so far away.

Too far away.

He staggered, turned, saw the machine gun in the tank turret pointing straight at him. But the gunners did not open fire; and afterwards he wondered why. Perhaps the mechanism in the gun jammed; or perhaps there was some other, arcane reason. Men kill senselessly and sometimes they show mercy in the same irrational and arbitrary way.

He had expected to die when he left the hotel; instead he reached the other side of the street and was shocked to find himself still alive.

27.

He didn't know where the boy came from; there were no battle lines to cross. The chaos in the city was absolute, and it threw up in the flotsam this boy, this child, in a green Iron Guard shirt, holding a rifle. He was no more than fourteen years old. When Nick saw him, it was not the rifle in his left hand that shocked him, it was the look of sheer joy on the kid's face.

Joy at finding something to kill.

He let out a whoop and brought the rifle to his shoulder. Nick heard the crack of the rifle, or perhaps the echo of it, a moment after he felt the sting of brick fragments on his face as the bullet hit the wall a few inches from his head.

Max and Daniela were ten paces ahead of him; the boy had not even seen them. There was nothing Nick could do, he still had the old man in his arms, and there was nowhere to run. He saw Max and Daniela turn at the sound of the rifle shot, saw their expressions of horror over the boy's shoulder.

The boy loped towards him, working the bolt action on the rifle. He was limping; an old injury by the look of it, or perhaps a defect from birth.

He fired again. But he was too excited to aim properly, and the bullet ricocheted off the cobblestones.

The boy aimed the gun again, at Nick's chest, then lowered it to the level of Nick's legs. Let's have some fun first, his eyes were saying. I'll make you lame like me. Fourteen years old. What could have happened to someone so young to fill him with such hate?

He is the same age as my youngest son, Nick thought.

Max and Daniela screamed at him to run, and the boy heard the shouts and turned around. He hesitated. Who to kill first?

Nick felt as if his legs were frozen to the ground. He was cold, and exhausted from carrying Daniela's father; just too tired to save himself. He shouted to Max to get Daniela off the street.

The boy was distracted with choice. And Nick saw his chance.

He let the old man slide to the ground and launched himself at the boy, who brought up the rifle just as Nick hit him with the full weight of his body. The boy fired off a single round. Nick had no idea if the bullet had hit him. He had heard of men who had been shot in battle and did not realise they were wounded until much later. It was adrenalin that made heroes.

The boy slammed backwards and his skull hit the frozen cobblestones with a sickening crack. The rifle clattered onto the ground. The boy convulsed underneath him and his eyes turned upwards into his head.

Nick stood up, his legs shaking. Killer or not, he was, after all, just a boy. Nick stared, a wave of nausea and revulsion sweeping over him.

'Is he dead?' Max said.

There was no need to feel for a pulse. He nodded.

'Jesus.'

He saw Daniela staring at him. It did not matter that

this was not the first time he had killed; or that on this occasion he had not intended for it to happen. This would haunt him for ever.

'Let's get off the street,' he said.

He turned to pick up the old man. The wrinkled face stared back at him, with that curious half-lidded expression of the recently dead. The boy's bullet had taken him through the heart. In death their young friend had found what he had been lusting for: a likely victim.

28.

The crack of small arms fire and the dull boom of tank cannon had been replaced by the sound of church bells tolling for the dead.

Antonescu had won. It had been inevitable; he had only stayed his hand to save even greater destruction to a city that already lay in ruins after the earthquake. Daniela's intelligence had been correct; the Iron Guard thought the Germans would help them and when they discovered the lie, it was too late. It was a mismatch after all; a few thousand green-shirted fanatics with rifles were no match for Romanian tanks and artillery.

But in those three days of chaos the legionaries had taken out their frustrations in an orgy of violence against the Jews. What they had done was unspeakable. Thousands had suffered deaths terrible beyond imagining. If not for her own instincts and fortitude – and Nick's recklessness – their fate would have been Daniela's also.

'Hell made you do it?' Max said. They were sitting in the American Bar, returned to the womb, as Max called it. Max was drunk; had hardly been sober for two days. He was propped at the end of the bar, cigarette burning to ash in one hand, a vermouth in the other. Ten in the morning and there were smears of grey cigarette ash on his jacket sleeves, and his eyes were puffy and red from too much alcohol and too little sleep.

'I don't know,' Nick said.

'Rescued her twice. Cash in your chips at the door. Good for six months rogering and no questions asked. Day or night. If you ask me.'

'Thanks, Max. I'm sure it's good advice.'

'Love's a form of madness, you know. Well, Plato said it, not me. Didn't want to intimidate you with my know-ledge of the classics.'

Nick shook his head, finished his drink and left the bar.

There was no power for the electric chandeliers and the lobby was grim and cold. A dismal world now beyond the doors of the hotel also, hell frozen over; stained and rutted snow, hunched soldiers in greatcoats rounding up prisoners, survivors stumbling dazed through a city bereft of mercy.

He saw Daniela sitting alone by one of the yellow marble pillars, slumped in a chair like a coat carelessly tossed aside by its owner.

He stood there watching her. He did not think she had seen him, for she did not look up, but then she said: 'Have you seen what they did?'

'I've been no further than the legation.'

The legation; another pitiful scene. He had reached his office by the back stairs, for the front door was besieged by hundreds of Jews who had survived the Guardist excesses and were now clamouring for visas to escape this terrible city. But the Passport Office in London would not allow visas to be issued out of Bucharest, and when the legation finally left Romania, these people would be abandoned to the Germans and their puppet prince.

'You heard what happened at the abattoir?' she said.

He nodded. Everyone in the city was talking about it. The Guardists had dragged six hundred Jewish men and women to the slaughterhouse where they put them through exactly the same process as the hogs; then they hung up the cleaned and gutted carcasses on steel hooks with signs that said: 'Kosher Meat'.

Even that fate was kinder than that meted out to those Jews arrested on the day of the revolt and taken to the cellars below the Prefecture. Wives and daughters were raped in front of their husbands and fathers; those that were spared this treatment were forced to watch as their men were put to death in such terrible ways that, when Antonescu's men reclaimed the police headquarters three days later, some of the women had literally gone insane with grief and terror.

They were still finding more bodies in the Baneasa Woods.

'How can people do this to each other?' she asked him.

It was a question philosophers had been debating for centuries and he certainly had no answer for her, for anyone. Killing another human being can be an act of fear or necessity, but cutting off their ears and noses first had always struck Nick as perverse. But then he was just an incurable romantic.

'I think sometimes it's the cocktail parties and polite conversations at dinner that are the aberration,' he said.

She shook her head, as if trying to clear her mind of the day's disturbing visions.

'I wanted to thank you again,' she said. 'For what you did. My guardian angel.'

What could he say to her? He had saved her from the Jewish Quarter and brought her back to the Athenee

Palace and allowed Maier to reclaim her. Perhaps it really was an act of nobility performed to assuage his sense of guilt over the queue of Jews at the door of the legation, and perhaps he'd let her go because he didn't want to fall any further in love with her, or because Maier could offer protection that he could not in the coming weeks and months.

But now he regretted it.

'You don't have to stay with Maier,' he said.

'What else should I do?'

'I can get you a visa. Get you out of Bucharest.'

'I can't,' she said.

'Why not?'

She would not answer.

'What are you going to do, then?'

'I don't know.'

'You have somewhere to go?'

'Oh, I think I'll survive.' And the way she said it stoked the smouldering embers of his jealousy. 'There are times I wish you hadn't been there that day the greenshirts came. There are times I wish I could have died with Levi.'

'You don't mean that.'

She didn't answer.

He saw Maier return through the revolving door. She stood up and leaned over him, kissed him tenderly on the cheek. 'I'll never forget you,' she said.

'Why won't you leave?' he said to her.

She shook her head. He never did understand until much later, and by then it was too late.

Antonescu insisted that the British leave at night. In the Athenee Palace the hotel porters brought down Nick's luggage and loaded it into an embassy car; there wasn't much to pack, most of his and Jennifer's possessions lay under the rubble of their apartment.

As he came down the stairs, everyone in the lobby stopped talking and stared. Some of the Germans were smirking, several even raised their glasses in mock salute; others, like Maier, had the dignity to turn away. His former associates, the little community of spies and aristocratic conmen and prostitutes, fought with other emotions: some regret, some anger.

The British were finally leaving Bucharest.

He saw her through the crowd, the dark mane of hair and golden eyes, standing among a crowd of grey German uniforms outside the American Bar. She looked up and their eyes met briefly. For a moment the smile vanished.

It was a short drive to the Gara de Nord through black and deserted streets, past walls scarred with bullet holes. At the station he joined the rest of his colleagues from the legation. The train would take them to Constanza where a Turkish destroyer was waiting to take them across the Black Sea to Istanbul.

As the train left the station, snow drifted from a starless sky. The whole world was going to hell and all Nick could think of was that he would never see Daniela Simonici again.

BOOK TWO

BOOK TWO

29.

Orient–Simplon Express, Sofia–Istanbul, February 1941

When Nick arrived in Istanbul, he was immediately seconded to the British Consulate with the same cover he had employed in Bucharest. He was briefed by the military attaché, Donaldson; the British Government now considered that it was only a matter of time before Bulgaria joined the Axis and they would have to evacuate the consulate in Sofia. The consulate's archives, Donaldson said, had been placed in a large packing case and Nick was to escort them back to Istanbul. He was given a ticket for the next train to Sofia and told to report to the envoy there.

The German tourists who had come sightseeing in Romania were now flooding across the Danube on the ferries for yet another vacation. When they opened their suitcases for Bulgarian customs officials, their vacation items included Wehrmacht uniforms and small arms. The Bulgarians smiled and waved them through.

In the lobby of his hotel in Sofia, Nick constantly heard cries of 'Heil Hitler' as the Nazis brazenly saluted each other. All pretence of neutrality had disappeared. Hitler had taken another mistress in the Balkans without having to marry her. Meanwhile columns of railroad cars rumbled into the rail sidings carrying armaments for the Bulgarian army, while rolling stock headed in the other direction laden with butter, vegetable oil and sugar.

One of the richest farming countries in the Balkans and most people couldn't get enough to eat. He bet they were doing just fine in Frankfurt and Heidelberg though.

It was a cold, dismal evening, a mist of rain drifting across the station lights. He was huddled in his overcoat, overseeing the loading of the crates from the consulate. A trickle of freezing rain worked its way down the back of his neck. He shuddered. The black dog had been on his back since Bucharest; and he was haunted by the spectre of defeat, for his country, for himself.

The Consul shook his hand. 'No doubt I will be seeing you in Istanbul very soon,' he murmured.

A brown-uniformed conductor hurried along the platform. '*En voiture, messieurs et 'dames, en voiture!*'

'Good luck, Davis,' the Consul said as Nick climbed aboard the train.

'Thank you, sir,' he said and went to find his compartment.

The corridors were crowded with people. He showed his ticket to the wagon-lit conductor and went to his compartment. He swung his case onto the luggage rack and hung his coat on the back of the door, where it leaked rainwater onto the floor.

He heard the guard's whistle as the train lurched out of the station. He was relieved to be getting out of Sofia. It reminded him too much of Bucharest in the last days, Germans everywhere, singing too loud and talking too loud, spilling out of every restaurant, every bar. They owned the bloody world now.

He tried to read a three-week-old copy of the *Times* he had brought with him from Istanbul but he could not concentrate, kept reading the same paragraph over and over. He tossed it aside and stared at the rain-smeared window.

He heard the attendant ringing the bell in the corridor. '*Premier service, 'dames et messieurs, le diner est servi, premier diner!*'

He wasn't hungry but it would be something to occupy his mind. He stood up and made his way down the corridor.

There was a salon car with two separate drawing rooms and the dining car was on the other side of it. It was his first time on the Orient-Simplon Express and he was impressed; it was lavish. The salon and dining cars had mahogany and teak panelling inlaid with rosewood, and there were original watercolours by Delacroix and Seymour. The chairs were covered with red embossed leather and the settings were suitably expensive, solid silver cutlery and Sèvres porcelain dinnerware. The glasses were Baccarat crystal.

A white-jacketed waiter took his order in French; bisque, a pilaf of quails and a '37 burgundy. Why not? he thought. I'm not paying.

He sat back and stared at his fellow dining companions. He was eating with the enemy. The train was used mainly these days by Nazi party bosses travelling between Berlin and the Balkans on diplomatic missions to puppet states like Bulgaria and Romania. The head of the Abwehr, Admiral Canaris, and von Papen, Germany's Ambassador to Turkey, were frequent passengers.

He tried to imagine who his fellow diners were and what they were doing on the train. The fat Austrian with the ginger goatee had to be a banker; the three Germans talking and laughing at the next table must be Abwehr; the Turk with the red carnation in his buttonhole and the fat gold ring on his pinkie looked too prosperous to be honest. He imagined him in his godown in the spice bazaar, trading opium, cardamom and government secrets over endless cups of thick black coffee and bitter Turkish cigarettes.

And then she walked in. He could not have been more shocked if the waiter had hurled a glass of ice cold water in his face.

She was with Maier. He was in uniform; she wasn't: a black sheer dress, dark hair radiant, scarlet-lacquered fingernails and lips moist with fresh lipstick. He felt sick with desire.

Maier saw him. He beamed as if he had seen an old friend. '*Liebling*, look, it is the Englisher! What an unexpected pleasure!'

He stood up. 'Well, it is unexpected, Herr Maier.'

'You remember Miss Simonici, of course.'

He gave a slight bow of the head in her direction. 'Miss Simonici.'

Her face was blank. He tried to read something in her eyes.

'Would you care to join me?'

'Just for a moment,' Maier said, and they sat down. 'So, Herr Davis, what have you been doing in Sofia?'

'Embassy business. You?'

'Tourism. Sofia is a very beautiful city.'

Nick hadn't thought so, but said he did.

'Still, it's best not to get too fond of a place, I find. You were fond of Bucharest as well, I remember.'

Nick did not rise to the bait. 'You're going to Istanbul?'

'For a short time.'

'More tourism? The war has been good to you. So many vacations.'

A smile. Maier enjoyed this fencing. 'Business this time, I'm afraid.'

'You're staying long?'

'I have no firm plans. Perhaps we will see each other from time to time.'

Daniela appeared bored by the exchange. He was acutely aware of her, and wished he could be alone with her, to talk with her, if just for a few minutes. She carefully avoided his eyes.

The bisque arrived and Maier got to his feet. 'But we are disturbing you. We should leave you to dine in peace.'

He stood up. 'Herr Maier. Miss Simonici.'

'Enjoy your dinner,' she said, the only words she spoke to him.

Maier escorted her to a table at the other end of the dining car. She took a seat facing away from him. He watched them talking, heard her torchy laugh, a sound that took him back immediately to the dimly lit foyer of the Athenee Palace Hotel. So, she was still Maier's mistress. She had told him that night in the lobby that she was a good actress, and he wondered if she was acting now. Was she happy? Impossible to tell.

But jealousy is a bad dinner companion. He had lost his appetite. He pushed his soup away untouched and decided to go back to his compartment. When he passed Maier's table, he did not look around at her.

Once, he had been contentedly numb; now he only felt

an acute sense that somewhere in his life he had missed something very important. He had never felt for a woman what he felt for Daniela; it was as if he had lived half a life.

Daniela tried to concentrate on what Maier was saying but in her mind she had followed Nick down the corridor to his compartment and was trying to explain everything to him so that he would not be hurt. Maier was talking politics to her, so fascinated with his own cleverness and intoxicated by his country's eminence in the world, and by extension, of course, his own.

He bored her.

Now he was explaining to her the merits of the Kavaklidere, a rich burgundy he had ordered for their dinner. But all she could think about was the tall Englishman in the tussore suit, with the sad blue eyes and comma of dark hair falling across his forehead who had inexplicably taken up residence in her heart.

30.

The attendant turned down the bed. When he had gone, Nick undressed and turned out the light. He lay there in the dark, watching freezing rain weep down the windows. He wondered what Jennifer was doing, thought about his sons, growing up in England without him.

Most of all he thought about Daniela, sleeping just a few compartments away.

He didn't remember falling asleep, lulled by the melancholy screech of the steam whistle, the clatter of the rails, the creak of the wooden panelling. He was disturbed in the early hours by a soft tapping on the door. Always a light sleeper, he was immediately awake. He got out of bed and put on his dressing gown. 'Who is it?'

No answer.

He took the revolver from the pocket of his coat hanging on the back of the door. He held it out of sight and inched open the compartment door.

He recognised her perfume first.

'Daniela?'

He checked the corridor. It was empty except for the attendant dozing in the chair.

Suddenly she was pressed against him, and she kissed him with a passion that left him weak. He realised he was still holding the revolver in his right hand and that the safety was off. Christ.

He slipped the gun under the mattress. It was dark in the compartment and he couldn't see her face.

'What are you doing here?'

'I needed to see you alone.'

'What about Maier?'

'I told him I couldn't sleep. He thinks I'm in the salon.'

'What if he comes looking for you?'

A crooked and unexpected smile. 'He won't find me,' she said. 'I'm not there.'

He pulled her down beside him on the bed. 'I never thought I'd see you again.'

'When Siggi packed his suitcase in Bucharest, he decided to take me with him. I suppose if you remember to bring everything with you, you don't have to buy the same things all over again in a new city. Things like a hairbrush, winter suits, mistress.'

'What are you doing here?' he asked her again.

'I came to warn you,' she whispered.

'Warn me?'

'I heard Maier talking to a German colonel at the station. They saw you getting on the train and the officer was telling him about you. They think you're a spy. He told Siggi that the Bulgarian police are going to take you off the train at the border, they're going to arrest you.'

He almost said: They wouldn't dare. But who knew what anyone would dare in the Balkans? Europe had gone mad; once, an Englishman could count on his country's power and reputation for safe passage in the world, but not any more. If they took him before they reached the border, he would simply disappear, apologies would be made, investigations would be launched and meanwhile he would be in some safe house in a Bulgarian backwater being tortured by experts for the names of all his intelligence contacts inside Romania and the Near East.

He felt a cold grease of fear erupt on his skin.

He switched on the lamp beside the bed. Almost two in the morning. They would be at the border in less than an hour.

'Why are you telling me this?'

'Why do you think?'

'I don't know,' he said. Was it because he had saved her life, and she felt she owed him a debt? Or was there another reason?

'I have to go now,' she said.

She leaned over him and kissed him again on the mouth. She took his hand and placed it on her heart and held it there for just a moment, then stood up.

'Wait,' he said to her. 'I need your help.'

'What do you want me to do?'

'The attendant at the end of the corridor. I need you to get him out of the way.'

'Leave it to me.' One last lingering kiss. 'I'll see you in Istanbul,' she said, and with that elusive promise, she was gone.

He left the door ajar, watched as she woke the attendant and whispered something to him. He never discovered what fool's errand she invented for him, but a beautiful woman soliciting help for any damned fool thing will always get what she needs, while a man may get no more than a helpless shrug and a gruff refusal. The attendant, still groggy with sleep, followed her out of the carriage and through the adjoining door.

Nick already knew what he was going to do.

He dressed and put the revolver in his pocket. He cut the sash to the blind with a pocketknife and slipped it into his other pocket. Then he threw open the window. The icy wind was like a slap in the face and needles of rain soaked the pillow on the bed. He slipped on his overcoat and quickly made sure he had his passport in his pocket.

With luck, the Bulgarian police would think he had fled through the window. He gave one last look around the room. Satisfied with his preparations, he slipped out into the empty corridor.

As he opened the connecting door to the dining car, the clatter of the wheels was deafening. He took a deep breath in front of the glass door in the vestibule, prayed there was no-one up and awake at this hour.

Empty.

He walked quickly past the kitchen. He heard two of the cooks arguing, already preparing breakfast.

The next door connected the dining car to the freight wagon.

He took out his revolver, but left the safety on. He had no intention of using it; it was for intimidation only.

The guard was asleep. He was snoring and had a rather endearing trickle of saliva leaking from the corner of his mouth onto the sleeve of his uniform.

If this had been the pictures, if he had been Robert Coleman or Errol Flynn, he would have knocked the guard over the head with the butt of the gun and the man would have conveniently fallen unconscious to the floor. In real life Nick's experience had been that if you didn't hit the man hard enough, he either yelled or got very angry, and if you hit him too hard, you broke his skull and killed him or else he fell so deeply unconscious he stopped breathing or choked on his own vomit.

He would not risk doing such a thing to some poor

Frenchman doing an honest if rather boring job, a man with perhaps a wife and a family at home. Most of the railroad employees didn't like the Nazis any more than he did, and some of them were even on the SIS payroll.

The man woke up when he heard Nick remove the safety from the revolver right next to his ear.

Nick told him in French what he wanted him to do. The man was groggy from sleep and shaking so violently with terror he could barely stand up. Nick felt sorry for him.

The man stripped off his clothes and stood there in his underwear. He was not an appetising sight. Nick made him unlock the freight car and pushed him inside. He tied his hands behind his back with the sash cord that he had cut from the blinds in his compartment and stuffed a gag in his mouth, using a strip of red cloth cut from a signal flag.

When it was done, he quickly took off his own clothes. The guard's eyes went wide. He thinks I'm going to get Bulgarian with him, Nick thought, with disgust. Even an old Etonian would have chosen a more tempting prospect.

Nick repeated that he had no intention of harming him and then he put on the discarded uniform. It was too small in the leg and too large around the middle. He had to cinch the belt to the last notch to keep his trousers up. He left the guard crouched on the floor next to the crate containing the consulate archives. When he got back to the guard's compartment, he felt the train start to slow. They were almost at the border.

31.

He sat at the guard's desk staring at the door that led from the dining car. He heard shouts on the platform. His heart was beating too fast. He thought about what Daniela had said: *I will see you in Istanbul.*

He knew it was foolish; a man who worries about losing a woman when he might shortly lose his life must be a little mad. What was it Max had said? Love is divine madness. Was that what it was? Was he in love with her?

He felt a slick of sweat on his palm and he wiped it onto the trousers of the uniform. He held the revolver out of sight under the desk.

They weren't going to take him, whatever happened. Death was easier to contemplate than torture. He wondered what Jennifer would say if he didn't come back. He thought also about his two boys and hoped that one day they would be proud of him.

He thought about Daniela and he thought about his wife. He thought about what dying might be like and wondered why the proximity of death could make a man feel so alive.

Concentrate Nick, keep your head clear.

Outside, grey sheets of rain were falling on some deserted Balkan backwater, and ugly men in drab uniforms sheltered scowling from the weather; but he was desired and in danger and the world had never been as luminous. He hated this damned war and he didn't want it ever to end.

Nick heard footfall in the dining car. They were coming.

There were three of them, in dirty brown uniforms with frayed sleeves and sweat-rimmed collars. They had stubble on their chins and bad moustaches; peasants trying to look like generals. One of them said something to him in Bulgarian and he replied, as the real guard would have done, in French. They stared at each other in mutual incomprehension. He knew from Daniela that they were looking for a passenger named Peter Box, the false identity he had been travelling under; *non monsieur*, he answered, respectfully, no gentleman of that name or any other has been through here.

The policeman bit his lip, uncertain. His hesitation convinced Nick that his ploy was going to work, and he relaxed, slipped the revolver back into his pocket.

One of the other policemen shoved past his colleague and headed for the freight van but Nick jumped to his feet and stood in his way. The policeman puffed out his chest, his black eyes just inches from Nick's face. His breath was foul.

Nick wondered what he would do.

32.

The policeman hesitated.

They stood there, nose to nose. But finally, to Nick's relief, the other man backed down. He turned and walked out of the van, waving the others after him. Nick slumped down into the guard's chair. His legs started to shake uncontrollably. Adrenalin.

The train lurched out of the siding. Nick went to the back of the van where there was a small window. They stopped again on the Turkish side of the border but no-one came into the freight car and finally they were waved through.

He was safe.

He put his own clothes back on and went through the dining and salon cars back to his compartment. When he appeared from the salon, the attendant stared at him in astonishment. Nick smiled and wished him a good morning.

It was frigid inside his compartment. The window was still open. He closed it and looked around. The Bulgarian police had upended everything from his suitcase onto the floor. Frustration rather than efficiency. He scooped up his clothes and shoved them back into his valise.

The bed was soaked with rain. It didn't really matter because he knew he couldn't sleep, not now.

He stared out of the window. The night was black and he saw in the glass the reflection of a gaunt Englishman cradling a Webley revolver in his lap. He listened to the rhythm of the iron wheels on the tracks, remembered Daniela's kiss, remembered she had just saved his life and remembered, too, her parting promise: *I'll see you in Istanbul.*

His reflection began to fade as light leeched into the sky. He found himself staring instead at a cold Istanbul dawn, at the dirty yellow ruins of Byzantium looming from the black cypresses. The train traced the decaying sea walls.

For a moment the lighthouse illuminated the dreary hovels still in shadow near the railway line. They lumbered past Süleyman's grand harem and the Topkapi palace, past the niches in the walls where the heads of the sultan's enemies had once fed the crows.

Istanbul could appear as a filthy ruin or a grand testament to history, depending on one's mood. This morning it inspired him to hope, a dangerous emotion indeed.

Donaldson was waiting for him on the platform at Sirkeçi station; Abrams, who had been seconded under cover to the staff of Istanbul's Passport Control Office, was with him.

When he stepped down from the carriage, he immediately took them to one side and told them what had happened.

'You'd better get away from here right away,' Donaldson said. He seemed neither surprised nor impressed by his escape, much to Nick's annoyance. He had a porter fetch his luggage and Nick headed for the exit.

He was already in a taxicab heading across the Galata Bridge to Pera when the freight car was unlocked by station officials and the guard was discovered trussed and gagged in his underwear behind a large crate. An immediate search was undertaken for the passenger in compartment B without success.

She saw him among the press of people and porters on the platform, before he disappeared through the gates, a tall Englishman in a cream suit, distinctive among the smaller Turks. As she lost sight of him, she felt a stab of guilt and pain. Life could be cruel.

Maier put his hands on her shoulders. She turned around and gave him a reassuring smile.

The archives were loaded onto a truck and removed to the consulate where the leader of the Bulgarian Peasant Party, until very recently the head of the resistance movement in his country, emerged from the crate hungry, exhausted, but otherwise unharmed. Having survived the journey with nothing more than two oranges to sustain him, he was given a hearty breakfast and congratulated on his escape from certain imprisonment and probable death. A pitiless Abrams debriefed him for five hours before allowing him to finally fall into an exhausted sleep.

Enquiries made to the Consul by Turkish police about an Englishman named Peter Box were politely rebuffed. He regretted that no-one of that name was known to anyone at the consulate.

The matter was quickly buried under a mass of paper-work in an office somewhere in Beyoglu and was never raised again.

33.

The consulate had arranged temporary rooms for Nick and the rest of the Bucharest staffers at the Pera Palas Hotel. Nick had the porter bring up his valise and after he left he went out onto the balcony and lit a cigarette. The icy wind took his breath away, revived him.

Out on the Horn a mist of rain swept across the water, and the fishing boats and ferries disappeared from view. The wind was salty, and cold enough to make the bones ache.

It had snowed the week before and dirty lumps remained like foam, clinging to the roofs of the houses and piled in drifts in the gutters.

He ran a hand across his face; he needed a shave. The night's events seemed suddenly unreal.

I'll see you in Istanbul.

She was out there somewhere. He knew he had to see her again.

Istanbul was not one city but three: old Istanbul clung to Seraglio Point, the conservative quarter, its mosques and harems lending the city its famous silhouettes; on the other side of the Golden Horn was another world of bars and nightclubs and restaurants around Taksim Square, the European quarter of Pera; and on the far side of the Bosphorus was Scutari, in Asia.

It was Byzantium to the Romans, and later Constantinople, where Justinian built the great church of Sancta Sophia, a masterpiece in stone that still dominated the old quarter fifteen hundred years later. Its Ottoman conquerors had transformed the city, and the skyline paid testimony to the sultans and pashas who had lived there, the great mosques of Süleyman and Rustem and Bayezid soaring above the clutter of houses on the south side of the Horn, while the elegant Tower of Justice rose from the cypresses on Seraglio Point where the sultans had once kept their harems.

It was Atatürk who had renamed it just a few years before, but to many old European families it was still Constantinople, and only the newest maps referred to it as Istanbul.

Nick remembered when he had first arrived from Constanza. As they passed the dark shadow of the Rumeli fortress, the city had been a blaze of light. Coming from Bucharest, a city held in the grip of winter and fear and food shortages, it was like being set free from a prison.

Turkey had so far succeeded where Romania had failed and had stayed out of the war, despite the best efforts of London and Berlin to drag them in. Hitler wanted Turkey as a base from which to attack Russia and the Middle East, and the British wanted Turkey to help them dislodge the Germans from the Balkans. But even the Lion and the Eagle were newcomers to such Ottoman lust compared to the Russians; for the past century they had wanted control of the Dardanelles and unhindered access to the Mediterranean. The war now offered them that chance.

But the Turkish President, Inönü, had so far kept his nerve and kept Turkey out of it. The Great War twenty years before had been disastrous for the country, and he was determined that they would not be dragged into another one. The economy was a shambles, and the military was too small and too ill equipped to defend the country. The army was thirty years out of date, there was no armour, no air force, no anti-aircraft weapons. Siding with either the Allies or the Germans could only end in catastrophe. Instead Inönü signed friendship pacts with all the big players and tried to appease each of them.

But Istanbul's neutrality made the city a magnet for desperate refugees from Bulgaria, Greece, Hungary, Yugoslavia, and Romania. These refugees had swollen the city's population by a hundred thousand souls, adding a new burden to a country where many were already suffering from hunger and poverty.

Neutrality attracted another type of resident also. As in Bucharest, countless foreign agents and spies now operated from the consulates, restaurants and hotels. By Nick's count, seventeen foreign intelligence services were operating there when he arrived, transforming the city into a covert battleground where elegant manners and polite language concealed baser motives.

And he supposed he was one of them.

The British Consulate was in Pera, a vast Victorian edifice off Istiklal Boulevard. It was in the European quarter of the city, which dated from the Middle Ages when Pera was an Italian settlement. Unlike the old city, the skyline was featureless except for the Genoese Tower, first built as a fortress, then used as a fire lookout and now principally employed as a giant neon advertising hoarding.

The dark cobbled streets of the quarter were home to banks, offices and merchant houses, clanging trams making their way up and down the Istiklal Boulevard, the city's equivalent of Oxford Street.

Nick got to his office at 9.30, went up via the back stairs, for the grand main entrance was reserved for regular diplomats. He had two offices, another room for files, and a secretary, on the same floor as the code room and the security officer.

As assistant military attaché, he was expected to interview men and women of every nationality who called on the Consul on their way through Istanbul. They were refugees, businessmen, diplomats, and bureaucrats and politicians ousted from their positions by the war. Nick debriefed them all, and often gleaned valuable intelligence; sometimes he was able to recruit them as agents.

It was explained to his consular colleagues that he was helping relieve the burden on the military attaché, but only Donaldson, the Consul, and Abrams knew his real paymaster. In Nick's experience, in every consulate and embassy he had been posted, everyone believed themselves to be so discreet they should know everything, but that was seldom the case. He had to be as careful with what he said to his colleagues in the consulate as he did in the most crowded café in Istanbul.

He went straight up to Donaldson's office. Abrams was there with him, and Nick briefed them on what had happened the previous night on the train from Sofia. Donaldson congratulated him on the success of his mission and his escape from the Bulgarian police.

'But why did this woman help you?' Donaldson asked him.

'I recruited her in Bucharest, under instruction from Mr Abrams here,' he said. A subtle inversion of the truth. How diligent he sounded. 'Her brother was imprisoned and probably murdered by the Iron Guard, and her family lost their bank and family home to the fascists. They threw her father in prison.'

'Why?'

'She's Jewish.'

'Jewish?'

Donaldson glanced at Abrams. A look passed between them.

'And she's Maier's mistress?' Donaldson said.

'Yes.'

'He knows she's Jewish?'

'I don't think he shares the Aryan view of racial purity. Besides, Daniela Simonici is a very beautiful woman.'

'And she's helping us because she hates the Germans?'

'There is a certain friendship between us. I helped her a couple of times in Bucharest.'

'Really,' Donaldson said.

Nick wondered what Donaldson was thinking. Abrams rested his teacup in its saucer and said: 'We should actively pursue her as a potential agent. The information she supplied to us in Bucharest ultimately proved quite valuable.'

'Do you think this is possible, Davis?' Donaldson asked.

Nick stared out of the window, the sweep of roofs and wooden houses crowding to the Horn. 'Yes. It's possible.'

'Can you contact her?'

'I don't know where she is.'

'Perhaps she'll contact you,' Abrams said.

'I hope so.'

There was a beat. Donaldson looked pained. 'Well, keep us informed,' he said.

Nick's first task was to re-establish the network he had start-ed to build in Bucharest. His most effective sources had not been the Daniela Simonicis of the world, but ordinary railway workers. When it became clear that they would leave Bucharest, he had started to build up a network inside Romania; already he had two sleeping car attendants from the Orient-Simplon Express on his payroll, as well as a brakeman and a conductor who travelled regularly on Turkish Railways to Sofia and Bucharest. While Turkey remained neutral, trains still travelled freely to all the occupied capitals in the Balkans and railway employees were able to smuggle money and documents across borders; and to gather intelligence, they didn't need bulky radios because they returned frequently to Istanbul and could make their reports in person.

The brakeman had proved especially valuable. He had a sharp eye and a keen memory. He had submitted regular reports on German troop movements and potential bombing targets inside Romania and Bulgaria.

Their main goal now was to try to anticipate Hitler's next move in the Balkans. Would he move against Russia or against Turkey? He could not strike at both. Would he invade Greece or Yugoslavia? Nick pored through endless reports, trying to see patterns, but it was like piecing together the pieces of a jigsaw that consisted almost entirely of sky.

The editorial in Istanbul's leading daily newspaper, *Cumhurriyet*, had no doubts: *For Germany a long drawn out war means defeat. Hitler's real target is the British Empire so he will not come towards Turkey.*

He imagined President Inönü hoped so. Their own intelligence assessment calculated that a committed German offensive would take Istanbul within forty-eight hours. Already many *instanbolu* were flooding out of the city; you couldn't get a seat on a train or a boat these days.

Abrams's own forecast was gloomy. 'Month at the outside,' he had said. 'I'd keep your suitcases packed. We'll be moving again soon.'

An air raid siren wailed across the city, interrupting his thoughts. Another drill.

The telephone rang. 'Davis.'

'It's me,' a voice said.

'Daniela?'

'We need to meet.'

'Is everything okay?'

'I can't talk now. Askatliyan's. Two o'clock.' And she hung up.

Askatliyan's Hotel was at the lower end of Istiklal, a grand Victorian hotel of faded glories. From the decaying lobby Nick saw waiters in once-white jackets shuffling among the handful of diners in a vast and dimly lit dining room of scrolled pillars and peeling gilt. The bedrooms here were more famous for the bed bugs than their luxury.

Nick pushed through the heavy mahogany doors into the bar. He sat two vodka vermouths on the marble counter and waited. She was fifteen minutes late. When she did arrive, he didn't recognise her; she wore no make-up and she had on sunglasses and wore a jade-green silk scarf over her hair.

She sat down. 'So. You got away from the Bulgarian police,' she said.

He felt suddenly breathless, as he always did around her. He wanted to hold her so much. 'Where's Maier?'

'He is off doing business somewhere.' She looked at him over the top of her sunglasses, an unnecessary and extravagant accessory. It was dark in the bar even at this hour of the day, yellow sunlight filtering through gaps in the faded silk curtains. 'You made quite a stir at the border. The police were running up and down the corridors, shouting and running in and out of the compartments. The rumour went round that someone had jumped from the train.'

'What did Maier say about that?'

'Siggi didn't say anything. I never know what he's thinking.'

'He didn't suspect you had anything to do with it?'

She looked genuinely shocked. 'Why would he think that?'

It was incomprehensible to her that he might suspect her. Was she that good a liar?

'You know, I wasn't sure until we got to Istanbul that you were all right. You're very clever.'

He was pleased that she worried for him and flattered that she thought he was clever. 'Thank you.'

She sipped her vodka-vermouth. 'Is your wife here in Istanbul?'

'No. She went back to England.'

She put a small pale hand on his, an act of such tenderness and intimacy that for a moment he couldn't think of a thing to say. There was a long and aching silence between them. Even now, with her eyes hidden behind the sunglasses and her hair covered by the scarf, she looked wonderful. But then he imagined he would have desired her even if she was dressed in a sack.

'So, you're still Maier's mistress?' he said.

'He treats me well enough.'

'But don't you hate these people? They put your father in prison and took your house and your businesses.'

'Hating Maier doesn't change what happened to my life and to Bucharest. Anyway, it was Siggi who helped get my father released. He's been kind to me.'

'Will he be as kind if he finds out you've been here?'

'He told me to come.'

It took Nick a few moments to understand what she

meant by this. Then, when he understood, it seemed so obvious he wondered why he had not suspected it immediately. 'He wants you to seduce me and then spy for him.'

'He doesn't know I saw you in your compartment on the train.'

'Why are you telling me this?'

'You know he's not a businessman. Not really.'

He nodded.

'No, he's a colonel in the Abwehr,' she said bluntly. And then, even more frankly: 'Which means I could spy for you instead.'

My God. The prospect had dazzled him ever since Donaldson had brought it out to the light. Not only might it be an intelligence coup, it would give him reason and opportunity to see her again. And now, here she was suggesting this very thing herself.

'It's dangerous,' he said.

'You asked me if I hated the fascists. Hating Maier doesn't get the Germans out of my country. But helping you, that is something I can do for all the ones who died, isn't it?'

'Why does he want you to spy on me?'

'He thinks you work for the British secret service.'

He stared at her. She stared right back.

'You would spy for us instead?'

She nodded.

'How?'

'He leaves papers lying around. I've seen them. Official papers.'

'Do you read German?'

'Of course. But I could copy them for you.'

'No. We'd have to get you a camera.'

'I will leave that to you. You must tell me how it can be done. Remember, it must seem that I am really spying on you, so you must give me something I can take back

166

to him.' She finished her drink. 'I have to go now. We'll talk soon.'

And she leaned forward and kissed him, left him with the taste of her lips and the rich scent of her perfume, aching for more.

The barman looked over at him; lucky Britisher bastard, he was thinking.

If only you knew, Nick thought. A dangerous game we are playing here. And I'm not sure I know all the rules.

34.

Dear Nick,
   How are you? I think about you all the time and wonder if you are all right.

England is very grim. There is still talk of an invasion and all the men not fit enough for the army are in the Home Guard and parade up and down the high street with ancient World War One rifles. Even Uncle Ernest has joined and he was too old for the last lot. I don't think the Germans would have a chance if they landed here – they'd die laughing.

You would not recognise the boys, they have grown so much. James is already taller than I and doing very well at school. Richard has become quite a studious boy, if a little shy. I'm sure he'll grow out of it.

The air raid sirens sound every night. Everywhere you go you see the rubble where houses have been bombed. We have our own shelter in the back garden and when the sirens go off, we rush out and climb in. There is a gas lamp in there so we can read and play games and it is quite cosy. The boys think it is all a huge lark. James wants the war to go on long enough so that he can be a fighter pilot one day.

Darling, keep safe. Please write when you can.
Jennifer.

They met again two nights later at Askatliyan's. Once again she was late. He waited anxiously in the bar, a sick feeling in the pit of his stomach when he thought she might not come. She finally appeared in a scarf and long overcoat, which she did not take off. It was cold in the bar, cold as the tomb.

Nick guided her to a corner alcove, and handed her the gift-wrapped box he had brought for her. He took off the lid and showed her the *lokum* and other confectionery inside. 'The camera's under the top layer of the box,' he said. 'If he's suspicious when you bring this home, you can show him there's real sweets in there.'

'Why would he be suspicious?'

He shrugged. He supposed he did not really understand her relationship with Maier. There was a part of him now that was eager to begin, the MI6 professional who wanted to know the secrets of one of the most important Abwehr agents in the Balkans. Yet another part of him did not want to expose Daniela to this danger. Using her this way had never been his intention when he had first seen her that night in Bucharest.

'You know how to use a camera?' he said.

'I can learn.'

'You have to get the distance just right. Because of the focus.'

She nodded impatiently. He sensed she was not listening to him. When she picked up her vodka-vermouth, her hands were shaking. She looked at him over the rim of the glass and there was a message for him in her eyes.

The look on her face was almost savage in its intensity.

'You're the most beautiful woman I've ever seen,' he heard himself say. 'When I'm with you, I can't think of anything else.'

'I'm not who you think I am,' she said.

'I don't care,' he said. 'I just want you to stay.'

She leaned close to him and he could feel her breath on his cheek. 'Yes,' she whispered. He took her hand and led her out of the bar.

She stood with her back towards him, looking out of the window at the mulberry sky. The song of the muezzin, calling the faithful to evening prayers, rolled across the roofs of the ancient city. She was silhouetted against the dark grandeur of the Sülemaniye mosque on the other side of the Horn, a velvet dusk hastening.

She stood that way for a long time and did not turn around until he touched her gently on her shoulder. He saw the track of a single tear on her cheek.

'I don't know if we should do this,' she said.

He took her face in his hands and kissed her softly on the lips.

Allahu Akbar, Allahu Akbar. God is great, God is great. Come to prayer.

He raised his hand to her cheek. She took it in both her hands and kissed his fingers.

He was surprised and confused by the salt of her tears. He did not understand why she was crying. Yet this did not feel wrong, not to him.

'Don't cry,' he whispered.

He unfastened the buttons on her dress, his eyes never leaving her face. He slipped the top of her dress from her shoulders, felt the press of her delicate breasts against his hands. She trembled at his touch.

He lowered his head to kiss the long line of her neck. 'Please,' she whispered.

He breathed in the fragrance of her, the silky softness of

her skin. He kissed her again, felt her body straining desperately against him. She moaned as his tongue traced the contours of her breasts.

The moan turned to a sob; the sob to tears; and then she started to cry. She buckled beneath him and he had to help her to the bed.

'Daniela,' he whispered.

She couldn't tell him how tired and sick she was of men using her, how disgusted she was at herself for the endless nights she had given herself away to faceless men in return for survival and a little kindness. And now here was a man she really felt something for and she couldn't do with him what she did with all the others.

She just wanted him to hold her.

And he did. He carried her to the bed and let her curl into him as she wept, and he kissed her forehead and stroked her hair and let her cry herself out, wondering at this beautiful and enigmatic creature that had entered his life and threatened now to turn it upside-down.

Her eyes blinked open. 'I'm sorry.'

'It's okay. Please. Stay here for a while.'

'I've disappointed you.'

He brushed a stray lock of hair from her face. 'It's okay. We don't have to if you don't want to.'

She kissed him, her face sticky with her dried tears. The moment seemed unreal. 'Baby,' she whispered. 'Baby.' He breathed in the scent of her hair, the scent of another woman, felt the soft pulsing at her throat as he kissed her neck.

It was the tenderness he had not expected. She cupped

his face in her hands and let him kiss her and did not close her eyes.

He did not fumble in the darkness as he had done for so much of his life as a married man. His eyes looked into hers, and it was this intimacy that shocked and surprised him more than the strangeness of her scent and the unfamiliar body beside him in the bed. What had he done with his life that he had never felt this way before?

It was the gentleness that touched him. He whispered to her how beautiful she was, and she sighed and smiled at him as if they were lifelong lovers. She ran her fingers through his hair and when he entered her, she did not take her eyes from his face. They stayed that way for what seemed an eternity, not moving, and the sadness and regret in her eyes moved him.

It was her sweetness he had not prepared for. He had wanted her desperately, yet he took her gently and slowly and she whispered to him in her own language, words he did not understand, but that he knew by the longing in her voice.

It was her surrender he had not expected. He was patient and when the moment came for her, he felt her nails tear his back and she started to cry.

She caught her breath and they stayed still for a very long time; he watched her eyes and she watched his, waiting, their bodies hardly moving, until the waiting became unbearable, and then they waited more. Finally, one almost imperceptible movement of her hips took him over the edge. It happened as he was staring into her eyes and she watched him with such sweet amazement, as if she had never seen a man do this before.

A guilty moment stolen from the gods. She was another man's mistress; he was another woman's husband.

She got out of bed and searched on the floor for her clothes. Watching her preparing to leave, he reminded himself that this was just a moment's madness, an adventure, nothing more. But even as a part of him retreated from her, another voice in him wondered how he could persuade her to stay a little longer.

'So what now?' he said. He felt as if he had swallowed a stone.

'I'll do what I can. Don't expect anything straight away. I will have to wait for the right opportunity.'

'I didn't mean about the camera. I mean about us.'

She turned and gave him a bittersweet smile. 'We'll see each other again soon.'

'How can I contact you?'

She rolled up her stockings. 'You can't. I will call you.'

She stood up and smoothed out her dress, then leaned over the bed and kissed him. She went out without another word. He picked up his shirt from the floor. It had her scent on it. He was missing her already.

Daniela found a cab outside the hotel on Istiklal Boulevard, and climbed in. This was wrong, everything was wrong, this was not what she wanted. Nothing could come to any good from this.

Her life so disgusted her she sometimes thought of jumping from the Galata Bridge. She had survived, but perhaps the only truly lucky ones were Levi and the others because it was over for them and they didn't have to struggle with this dismal life any more.

But there was Nick; the things he said to her were wonderful, things she had longed to hear for so long. She had finally found a man she wanted and who wanted more from her than just one night, but perhaps she had found him too late.

35.

He had moved to an Ottoman rowhouse near the great Sülemaniye mosque. There was a balcony overlooking the Horn. It was near the fruit market, among a warren of crumbling courtyards and narrow, cobbled streets overhung by wooden houses, blistered and rotting, the timbers blackened with age.

The house was full of dark mahogany furniture and smelled of the strong Turkish tobacco the previous owner had favoured. There were crimson Bokhara rugs on the wooden floors, and the walls were hung with silk kilims. There were hidden alcoves and ledges, where his servant's cats took up residence, always finding the sun at the right time of the day. There was a tiny rose garden at the back of the house with a single Judas tree. They said it was from a tree like this that Judas had hung himself after he received his thirty pieces of silver for betraying Christ.

Another poor bastard who couldn't live with the consequences of what had seemed like a good idea at the time.

The garden was surrounded by a high brick wall.

He waited by the back gate, looked at his watch; past ten o'clock. He moved into the shadows. No stars tonight, a mist of rain falling, as he anxiously paced this dark and secret garden.

He heard the click of her heels in the alleyway outside. He unlocked the door in the wall and she slipped through.

They went through the French windows into his study. He had left a desk lamp burning. He took her coat and hung it up for her. When he turned around, she was holding out her hand. There was a roll of film. He took it.

'Wait here,' he said. 'Do you want a drink?'

She shook her head. She sat down, crossed her long legs; he heard the rustle of silk stockings. Maier was looking after her well.

He went down to the basement, where he had arranged for one of the code clerks from the consulate to set up a temporary dark room. His name was Sanderson, and he immediately went to work under the safe lights.

It was a double play. Daniela had told him that Maier was paying her well for the information she brought him. But he didn't believe for a moment that she was doing it for the money.

After ten minutes Sanderson opened the first tank, put the spool in the running basin and then into the fixing bath.

A deadly game, this. It was Daniela who would pay if it backfired. He wished he had not allowed her to do this. What if Maier discovered her?

Sanderson held one end of film against the viewing box. Nick could make out the typescript on the negatives, felt his heart race.

The photographer put the strips in the washing tank and then pegged the wet films on the line, backlit by a hundred-watt bulb. Nick held the magnifying glass to the wet strip. He read, in German:

TOP SECRET. ABWEHR HQ BERLIN TO VON PAPEN, ANKARA.

'Finish these,' he said to Sanderson and went back upstairs to the study.

She was sitting in the winged armchair by the window across from the desk, her eyes closed. He thought she was asleep but as he walked back in she looked up and smiled.

'How did you do it?' he said.

'A man takes his trousers off. Sometimes he leaves his keys in them.'

'You stole his keys?'

'He left the trousers out for his valet to take to the laundry. His keys were in the pocket.'

'He'll find out.'

'No, he won't. He trusts me. He thinks I'm spying on you. And he's careless.'

'What about the keys?'

'He went out for a meeting and while he was gone I opened the safe and took photographs of any papers I could find. Then I put the papers back in the safe just the way I found them and then I put the keys back in his trousers. It was very simple.'

She sounded confident in her own abilities. But then everyone was confident until things started going wrong.

'I see.'

'Is that all? I see?'

'It makes me nervous.'

'It's what you asked me to do.'

'Yes, I know.'

'Was there anything there that might be important?'

'Perhaps.'

She stood up and her eyes were liquid. 'He's not expecting me back until after midnight.'

'You can stay?' he whispered.

'Yes,' she said. 'Of course.'

Just before midnight he walked her through the garden. A sliver of moon appeared between a rent in the overcast, a cool wind rustled in the leaves of the Judas tree.

'Be careful,' he whispered but she had already slipped away. Her perfume lingered for a moment before it was carried away on the breeze. He locked the door and went back to work.

Maier was sitting in bed waiting for her when she got back. The bedside lamp was on. As she walked in, he looked up from the papers he was reading. He said nothing to her and she found his silence unnerving.

She started to undress. He watched her. For a time, this had meant nothing to her, it was just a body. Now she felt sullied, going from one man's arms to another's.

She laid her dress neatly on a chair. She felt his eyes on her.

'I thought you would be asleep.'

'I decided to wait up for you.'

Through the window she could see the lights of the old city across the Horn. She wondered which light was his, for he would surely still be working. Why can't it be you here now? She was just a convenient affair, he would go back to his wife in England as soon as the war was over. He told her to be careful, yet he had been willing to let her spy for him, put herself in danger. She wanted to believe he loved her, but she knew he didn't, knew they all loved the illusion of her, but none of them really knew her.

This was the trouble with being a great actress: you dazzled everyone with your charm and make-up but in the end you could not trust that they loved you. How could they? She did not even know what was real inside her any more, didn't know who she was. She had become the performance.

She felt a deep ache inside her as she turned away from the window. She took off her underwear and quickly got into bed.

He put down his papers and turned off the light. She let him hold her, tried to relax as she felt the hardness of his penis against her thigh. His hand moved to her breast. She tried to surrender herself to his usual ways and the familiar taste and smell of him.

But there was only despair.

'*Liebling*, I want you,' he whispered.

'I want you too,' she said.

She knew she was dry and she did not want the intimacy of him inside her. Somehow, tonight, the violation would be too overwhelming. Instead she started to kiss his chest, then his belly, as signal of her intention, and his hand on her head encouraged her.

She took him in her mouth, heard him groan, felt a deep sense of relief that perhaps this was all he would expect of her.

What an actress I am, she thought. I wonder if I will ever really know myself, who I am, or even this woman I am playing to the world.

36.

The next morning, with twenty-six developed negatives in a brown manila envelope under his arm, Nick knocked on the door of Abrams's office. He had not shaved, had hardly slept. Abrams stared at him in mild disapproval.

'Davis. You look terrible. What's happened?'

'Something I want you to see.'

Nick put the envelope on his desk. Abrams frowned and picked it up.

He spread the glossy black and white prints on the desktop and studied them. Nick handed him a magnifying glass. Abrams was quiet for a very long time, examining each of the prints in turn.

'Some of it appears to be routine traffic between Berlin and Istanbul,' Nick said. 'But there are copies of two top secret dispatches from Canaris to von Papen in Ankara. I'll have them properly translated but this one appears to be detailed plans of German ground forces in Bulgaria, and this one is from von Papen describing his efforts to pressure Ankara into allowing military advisers into the country.' He picked up another of the prints. 'This one has the name of a Turkish national at the Ministry of Defence who has been supplying the Abwehr with classified information from the Minister's Office.'

Abrams leaned back in his chair and regarded Nick down the length of the fine patrician nose. 'This is very impressive. How did you come by this material?'

'Daniela Simonici. You were right. She's a gold mine.'

'She'll need some coaching. Some of the photographs are blurred.'

Nick swallowed down a flash of temper. Daniela had taken terrible risks to get this for them and Abrams's first instinct was to complain that he couldn't read all of them. 'Not bad for her first attempt, though.'

'How did she come by them?'

'She stole them from Maier's safe.'

Abrams was silent for a long time, considering the implications. Finally, he returned his attention to the photographs. 'We should give your new agent a code name.'

'I've given it some thought. What about Trojan?'

Abrams mused on this. As a history scholar, with an honours degree from Oxford university, it perhaps seemed a little too obvious. 'The Trojan horse. The prize Maier brings into his own house, not knowing he has invited the enemy. Very good, Davis.' He nodded. 'I appreciate you've probably been up all night with this but perhaps now you should look the part of the assistant military attaché and go home and have a shave and a bath.'

'Yes, sir,' Nick said and got up to leave.

'And Davis,' Abrams said.

'Yes, sir.'

'Be careful,' he said and for a moment the expression on his face was almost human.

37.

Every garden had a Judas tree, and with spring the Asiatic side at Scutari was a blaze of red against the black cypress trees of the vast cemeteries. Cherries appeared in the fruit market and cockchafers swarmed in the treetops. Belgrade and Athens fell to the Germans, while on one terrible night in May the Luftwaffe dropped one hundred incendiaries on London in just a few hours.

While Nick shopped for melons and apricots and peaches in the nearby markets, the Germans launched a massive invasion of Russia. The oil at Ploesti fuelled the Panzer divisions as they rolled through Minsk. Nick thought about Bendix, and how every attempt they made to close down the oilfields was blocked by some faceless mandarin in Whitehall.

With autumn there were figs and grapes, and polite conversation at cocktail parties in Pera, with mussels fried in batter, caviar, and savoury lobster patties. Meanwhile they starved in Stalingrad.

As 1941 rolled away and the rain swept across the grey waters of the Horn, far away on the other side of the world the Japanese attacked Pearl Harbor and finally brought the Americans into the war that had convulsed the rest of the world.

Nineteen ships of the Amercian navy went down that

December morning, but it was the fate of a rusting hulk called the *Struma* that consumed Nick's attention that grim winter.

38.

Nick crossed the lobby of the Pera Palas, and ran up the marble steps to the domed foyer. It smelled of cigarettes and age, a curious mixture of the Orient and Victoriana, the red plush and mahogany at odds with the fretted and arched windows of the mezzanine.

He found Max drinking gin and tonics in the bar, swaying dangerously on one of the high stools. He had been drinking heavily since Bucharest; the dash through the snow and the encounter with the young legionary had ruined his nerves.

Max had been reassigned to the Reuters office in Istanbul. But he was changed somehow; the difference was subtle and perhaps only his friends could see it, evidenced by a shadow behind his eyes and the slightest tremor in his hands.

'You look like death,' he said to Nick as he walked in. 'Hell you been up to, sport?'

'Just tired.'

'If you say so. Drink?'

'Why not?'

Max ordered two more gin and tonics. 'Have you heard about this ship that's docking here tomorrow? The *Struma*, out of Constanza. Some rust bucket packed with Jewish refugees that no-one wants. The Ancient Mariner all over again. Or the Ancient Meshuggah in this case,' he said and gave a braying laugh. Good old Max. No sensitivity at all for anyone.

'Nothing we can do for her here.'

'Of course not. We're British. We don't do things for other people, against our religion.'

'You have a point, Max?' Nick said, irritated.

'Have you heard the rumours, old chum? About what's happening in our old stamping grounds? Never liked gypsies and Jews, couldn't trust 'em, but I've heard the Germans are loading them in cattle trucks in their thousands and they're just disappearing. There's been massacres in Kishev. You saw for yourself what the greenshirts are capable of.'

Nick of course knew about the massacre in Kishev and the mass deportation of Jews and gypsies from Bessarabia and Bucovina. He had compiled endless reports that he had passed on to Whitehall. So far there had been no response to either issue.

'So what are they saying at the consulate, old chum? Are we going to see Panzers rolling across the Galata Bridge next week?'

'Your guess is as good as mine.'

'Come on. Just a whisper. Won't print it. Mother's life.'

'We don't know, Max. That's the truth. I don't think even Hitler knows what he's going to do next. But he's not going to attack Turkey while he's got his hands full in Russia.'

Max finished his drink and ordered another. 'Sometimes I have this nightmare about the Luftwaffe dropping incendiaries on Istanbul. All these wooden houses, it would burn for a week. They'd see the glow in Dusseldorf.'

Nick had had the same terrible dreams; he turned away, and in the reflection of one of the mirrored pillars, he saw a Turk in a brown suit smoking and drinking *raki*, pretending to read a copy of the *Cumhurriyet*. He was being watched. Emniyet, the Turkish intelligence service, he supposed.

'Guess who I saw the other day?' Max said.

From Max's expression, Nick knew where this was going.

'That chap Maier. Remember him? Spent the longest two hours of my life with you trying to get his mistress out of the shit for him.'

'Is he in Istanbul?' Nick said.

'What do you think he's doing here? Wonder if he still has that girl with him?'

'I've no idea.'

Max gave him a wry smile and leaned in. 'Careful, old love. Don't get caught up again.'

'No idea what you mean,' Nick said, and let the matter drop.

Abrams sat in the back of the Bentley, regarding the bustle along the docks at Eminönü with a look of utter disdain. The windows were up but his nose wrinkled at the smell of fish.

Nick had known Abrams now for over two years and was still not sure what to make of him. He was an austere man, never given to laughter or anger. Some people called him a cold fish but Nick wondered if they had misjudged him. He could be passionate about ideas and philosophy; he struck Nick as the sort of man who truly loved humanity, but just didn't like people very much.

'Well, there she is,' Abrams murmured.

The *Struma* was docked opposite the Tophane ferry landing, three hundred yards from the shore on the Asian side. They got out of the car and walked to the quay for a better view. The morning air was bitter and Nick could see his breath. The gulls cut the air with their screeching.

A rusted, overcrowded hulk, you could smell it from the docks. Tugboats and Turkish navy gunboats beetled around it, and there were soldiers patrolling the wharves, in case some misguided refugee tried to swim for the piers. Crowds of Turks had come down to stare, but their expressions were hostile. They were Jews out there, and they didn't want them in Turkey.

The *Struma* had left Constanza three days before, loaded with Jewish refugees fleeing Romania. At the mouth of the Bosphorus the engine had failed and the ship had started to drift towards a minefield, but was rescued by a Turkish navy tugboat and had been towed the last eighteen miles to Istanbul.

'The captain has told the port authorities that the engine needs repairs but they're suspicious. It's going to take about a week to fix the problem but no-one wants to pay the five thousand US dollars. They're not allowing any of the crew or the passengers off the ship while it's done.'

There were shadows of rain drifting towards them on the pearly water. They hurried back to the car.

'Can't we do something?'

Abrams gave him a disbelieving look. 'Why?'

'For the sake of decency. Out of Christian charity.'

'What would they want with Christian charity? They're Jews. Besides, Whitehall suspects there are Nazi agents among the refugees.'

'What possible reason do they have to think that?'

'Romania is on the side of Germany now. These people are all from an enemy country. So we have to be diligent, Davis. There are reports that the Germans have set up a school in Prague to train German agents to act as Jews. They learn to speak Yiddish and how to pray.'

'I suppose they have themselves circumcised as well.' They got back into the car. 'With all due respect, sir, that's utterly ridiculous.'

'I know that and so do you, but it's government policy and it's our job to implement it. What may not be so ridiculous is the idea that the Nazis are deliberately flooding us with Jewish refugees in order to anger the Arabs in Palestine and bring them into the Axis camp.'

Nick shook his head. He nodded in the direction of the *Struma*. 'But what's going to happen to them?'

'That's not the concern of the British Government. We have enough problems of our own.'

They drove back across the Galata Bridge. Nick felt sick to his stomach. He imagined it might be Daniela out there on that ship. Politics was a simpler matter when people were just numbers. It was when they had faces that it became a little more complicated.

39.

When they got back to the consulate, Nick's secretary told them their presence was required in the attaché's office. Donaldson was an enigma; he was short, stout and bespectacled, with the most beautiful wife any man on staff had ever seen. Without her he might have become a figure of fun, for he was the most bland and supercilious man Nick had ever met. But his wife's charm and beauty conferred a certain cachet. There was not a man or woman in the consulate who did not look at Donaldson and speculate on his secret, and treat him with added respect, or, in the case of the younger men on the staff, with a kind of mystified awe.

They were shown through to his office by his secretary. It was a large office, uncluttered, with tall windows and a commanding and airy view. It proclaimed his status immediately.

Donaldson was waiting behind his desk, fingers steepled. On the other side of the desk sat Nick's old friend from the Haganah, David Ben-Arazi. The atmosphere in the room was icy.

After the introductions were made, Donaldson offered Ben-Arazi a cup of tea.

'No, I don't want any tea. I want you to do something for those people on that boat.'

Donaldson asked his secretary to bring a pot of tea anyway.

'Have you seen the *Struma*?' Ben-Arazi said.

Donaldson looked at Abrams. 'Davis and I have just driven up from the docks,' Abrams said.

'There are over seven hundred people on that ship, more than three hundred are women and children. It was designed to carry one hundred passengers.'

'Yes. I understand.'

'Do you, Mr Abrams? Do you understand what it is like to be a Jew in any country other than your own? Do you know that before they left Constanza these people had their money and their jewels stolen from them on the docks? Do you know what it is like for a Jew in Romania since the Germans arrived?'

'Mr Davis here was one of the last members of our legation in Bucharest to leave Romania,' Donaldson said. 'I am sure he understands better than any of us.'

Ben-Arazi looked at Nick. As if a non-Jew could possibly understand, he was thinking. 'These people want to go to Palestine but your government won't give them visas.'

'There's nothing we can do about it,' Abrams said. 'We have our instructions from Whitehall. Have you thought about putting them on the train?'

'You know as well as I do that the Turks won't allow them to land, because you have told them your government would consider it an unfriendly act. You have bullied and harangued them into this and now you want to blame them for this situation.'

Abrams spread his hands. 'I wish I could help you.'

'Have you seen this ship? The Turkish authorities will not give me permission to go aboard but I have spoken with the captain. The vessel is overcrowded and food is running low. They cannot even cook the food they do have properly because the Germans in Constanza stole all their pots and pans.' He looked around at the three men in the room. 'What is going to happen to them?' he said, and his deep voice was suddenly choked with emotion.

'Personally, I wish them the best, of course,' Abrams said, 'but we can't change our government's policy.'

'Is it British Government policy for them all to drown?' Ben-Arazi was losing control of his temper. 'The engine broke down even before they left Constanza. She had to be towed out to sea by the Romanians.' He slammed his fist on Donaldson's desk. 'Do you know about this ship? She was registered in 1830, for the love of God. She was used as a cattle barge on the Danube when this war started, was declared unfit for sea travel! She's a death trap. I wouldn't trust her to get me to the other side of the Bosphorus.'

When Abrams did not answer, Ben-Arazi jumped to his feet. 'You're a Jew, aren't you? How can you work for a government that can do this to your own people?'

'I may have been born a Jew but England is my country.'

'Well, that is nothing to be proud of,' Ben-Arazi said and he turned and left the room, nearly knocking over Abrams's secretary and spilling the tea tray she was holding.

There was silence after he'd gone.

'Well, that went well,' Nick said.

Donaldson grunted, embarrassed. He stood up and went over to the window.

'Why don't we help them?' Nick said.

'You know as well as I that we need Arab support in Palestine against the Germans,' Abrams said. 'We won't get that by helping the Jews colonise the country.'

'If that's the only reason, we're not getting much value for our money from the mullahs. I hear they're practically reading from *Mein Kampf* in the mosques.'

'It would open the floodgates,' Donaldson said, sweetly reasonable. 'Thin end of the wedge.'

The thin end of the wedge. Politics by platitude. Nick knew that Churchill was sympathetic to the Jewish immigration, but there were men in the Foreign Office who didn't share his views. Men like Donaldson and Abrams. He had read a top secret report that had even floated the idea of sinking ships carrying Jewish migrants to Istanbul. It had concluded: *This is the only way in which the traffic can with certainty be stopped. It is, however, a step which, for obvious reasons, His Majesty's Government would hardly be prepared in any circumstances to authorise.*

Instead ships that broke the Palestinian blockade were seized, the immigrants deported and the crews arrested. The soft option.

'The Arabs will never be friends of ours,' Nick said.

Donaldson shrugged. 'That may be true but we cannot afford to inflame the situation further. That's official government policy.'

Nick got up to leave. 'Well, as long as it's just policy. Those people on the *Struma* should hate to drown because we meant it.'

He was almost out of the door when Abrams called him back. 'Davis,' he said, 'don't forget you're in the diplomatic service. Be diplomatic. Compassion has no place in politics. This is a consulate, not an orphanage.'

'Yes, sir,' Nick said and walked out.

40.

She came when she could; stayed as long as she dared. He would wait for the black telephone on his desk to ring, wondering what she was doing and where she was. She often came at night, slipping dark and silent as a shadow through the gate in the garden wall.

But tonight she seemed distracted, and there was no envelope for him. He tried to kiss her but she did not respond. He made them vodka-vermouths and she took her drink and went to the window. The *Struma* was out there in the darkness, he could see searchlights sweeping the water from the tugboats that guarded her.

He thought about the Jewish Quarter, the day of the attack by the Iron Guard. He thought that many people did not understand what it was to be a refugee, as if people would leave their homes and their whole lives on a whim. He remembered the Jew he had seen burned alive in the street, and Levi, lying like bloody rags on the cobble-stones. He felt suddenly and deeply ashamed of his own country. What was it Abrams had said? *Compassion has no place in politics.*

'They're Jews on that ship, just like me,' Daniela said.

'I wish I could do something.'

'What good are the British in this war? You couldn't help us in Bucharest, you can't help us now!'

He held out his hands in a gesture of despair. She was right.

'If you could help me, Nick, would you do it?'

'You know I would.'

There was that look on her face.

'Daniela?'

'I do need your help now.'

'Come here. Sit down.'

He sat on a divan by the little tiled stove where it was warm. She came to join him. She sat hunched over with her elbows on her knees as if she had been punched in the stomach. 'What's wrong?'

'That ship out there. I think my brother's on board.'

'Your brother?'

'Amos. He wrote to me a few weeks ago to say he had a ticket for a boat called the *Struma* and he was going to try to escape to Palestine.'

'He wrote to you? How did he know where you were?'

'After my father was arrested he escaped from Bucharest and went to the country. He thought it would be safer. But he wrote to me every week at the Athenee Palace. Even when I came here I wrote back to him, though I was never sure he got my letters. Until now.'

She stared across the black water.

'What's going to happen to them, Nick? I heard that the captain plans to run the British blockade and put her aground on the beach.'

'You've seen the state of the ship. Even if they get to open sea, they'll never make the crossing.'

'Is no-one going to help them?'

'My government is concerned that these people don't reach Palestine. They are trying to pressure the Turks to send them back to the Black Sea.'

'I know he's on there,' she said.

'What do you want me to do?'

194

'Can you get him off that death trap and get him to Palestine some other way?'

'I don't know.'

'I have helped you, haven't I? That must count for something with your government.'

She was avoiding his eyes. It made him uneasy. 'Is there anything you're not telling me?'

'Whatever happens, I don't want you to hate me.'

He frowned. 'Why would I hate you?'

She started to say something and stopped herself. Of course later he understood what she was afraid of; it was what she thought her brother might tell him that made her so afraid. But at the time he could only stare at her mystified and wonder what it was she meant.

41.

Neman Konic kept them waiting for half an hour in the anteroom of his office at the Ministry of Defence before seeing them. His personal secretary, a young man with an effusive black moustache, showed them into his office. Konic greeted them expansively and three glasses of apple tea were brought. The weather was discussed – it had been one of the coldest winters anyone could remember – and the progress of the war, which was just as bleak. Rommel's Afrika Corps were threatening Egypt, and in the Pacific the Japanese had taken Rabaul.

Konic offered them cigarettes. He lit his own and his head was immediately wreathed in a thick fug of smoke. 'Now then, gentlemen,' he said, in excellent if heavily accented English, 'what can I do for you?'

'It's a rather delicate matter,' Abrams said. 'It concerns the *Struma*.'

The ship's name fell into the room like a curse. Konic stared but said nothing.

'There's someone on board of great interest to us. We want to get him off.'

Konic raised an eyebrow. 'Your government has so far been most insistent that we do not allow any of these refugees asylum or free passage.'

'This matter is considered classified. It does not indicate a shift in government policy.'

'Would you care to tell me what this is about?'

'It concerns a certain individual on board who is in a position to help His Majesty's Government.'

Konic seemed to relax. His eyes sparkled with amusement. 'I see. Well, perhaps something can be arranged. It will have to be handled with some discretion, of course. What is this person's name?'

Nick leaned forward. 'His name is Amos Simonici. He is twenty-four years old, a Jew from Bucharest.'

'Why do you want him?'

'As I have indicated, it's an intelligence matter,' Abrams said.

'What will you do with him if we take him off the boat?'

'We will arrange a visa for him,' Nick said. 'Then we'll put him on a train through Syria to Haifa.'

Konic nodded, and put three teaspoonfuls of sugar in the little glass of apple tea. 'If we agree to help you with this, then perhaps you might assist us with an intelligence matter also.'

'Of course. If we can.'

'We think someone inside this office is providing the Germans with copies of cables between Istanbul and Ankara. We want his name.'

Nick looked at Abrams. Daniela had already provided them with that information. His name was Saffet Diker, and he was Konic's own private secretary, the man with the moustache who had just shown them into Konic's office. Nick had already approached him and blackmailed him into working for the SIS. Copies of cables intended for Konic now came first to Nick's desk at the British Consulate. This fact might prove embarrassing if the man was interrogated by the Emniyet.

'Why do you think we could provide you with that sort of information?' Abrams asked.

'One of your officers is meeting regularly with the mistress of an Abwehr colonel. Either the Abwehr is getting information from you or you are getting information from them. I suspect it is the latter.'

So, Nick thought, I was right, the Emniyet has been watching me.

'We'll see what we can do,' Abrams said.

When they left his office and were walking to the car, Abrams said, 'I hope this is going to be worth all the time and trouble.'

'If it's not, we can at least sleep well knowing we've done the decent thing.'

'I always sleep well, Davis,' Abrams said and got into the waiting embassy car. 'There's nothing on my conscience. What about you?'

A clear sky with ice-blue stars. The wind made his cheeks burn. He stood at the bow of the police launch as it cut through the water towards the black silhouette of the *Struma*. The lights of the city sparkled in the cold, clean air and a searchlight played across the dark water.

The ship was riding at anchor, still about three hundred yards from the shore. It appeared abandoned at first, but as they got closer, Nick saw crowds of people lining the ship's rails. They stood silently, like mourners at a funeral.

Up close the *Struma* looked even more pitiful. He wondered how she had got as far even as Istanbul; he would not have trusted her to cross the Horn.

The wooden hull was rotting, and rusted steel plates had been clamped to the sides to hold the vessel together. A crude wooden superstructure had been jerry-built on the deck, no doubt as quarters for additional paying passengers on the already overcrowded ship. He couldn't see any life preservers or lifeboats. They were hoping to reach Palestine in this rust bucket? She was the most miserable vessel Nick had seen in his life.

A yellow flag hung limp from the stern, to indicate the ship was in quarantine.

Nick looked up and saw people peering down at him, the pale and haunted faces of the damned. The launch pulled up alongside and a rope ladder was thrown down to them. Two of the policemen started climbing up, and Nick followed.

It was the stench he noticed first, the pervading taint of human waste. The ship was in darkness, but Nick glimpsed a pale human face in the light of a candle before the flame was extinguished by another gust of wind.

The police had torches, and they shone them around the deck, at the huddles of frightened, shivering people clustered together in little groups.

'Welcome to the rat trap,' a voice said, in French. 'My name is Garabetenko. I am the captain of this wretched ship. How can we assist you, *monsieur*?'

'My name is Davis. I'm from the British Legation.'

'You people finally want to help these poor bastards?'

'I wish we could.'

He ran a hand across his face. 'I didn't think so. What do you want?'

'I'm looking for someone. His name is Amos Simonici.'

'Why?'

'I want to get him off this ship.'

'You have a visa for him?'

'Possibly.'

'A visa. A visa! *Monsieur*, what is it like to be God?' He took a deep breath. 'One man among seven hundred. What has he done to be so fortunate?'

'Is he on board?'

199

They were buffeted by another icy blast of wind. The captain ran his hand across his face again and Nick heard the rasp of stubble on his chin. 'I don't have passenger rolls, *monsieur*. The bastard who owns this ship didn't give me a passenger list.'

'I need to find this man.'

'How old is this Simonici?'

'He's twenty-four years old and he's from Bucharest.'

'How do you know he's on board?'

'He wrote to his sister before he left Constanza.'

'His sister,' he said and he studied Nick's face, speculating. 'Well. We'll go and see if we can find him. You might find it interesting, while you're here.'

He followed Garabetenko down three flights into the bowels of the ship. Once he slipped and put out a hand to steady himself, and a section of plating came away in his hand, eaten through with rust.

As he went below, Nick gasped. The acrid stench of urine and sweat and human waste made it almost impossible to breathe. He turned his own torch and shone it around the berths. Men, women and children were stacked in wooden bunks to the ceiling, layers of them, four or five on each bunk. The only sound was the quiet sobbing of children and the troubled sleep of the sick.

Human cattle.

'Some of the children have fever,' Garabatenko said. 'We have thirty doctors on the boat and not a single aspirin.'

'I can get you medicine.'

'That would be kind. As you can see, there's no space to sleep but at least they're a little warmer down here. We can't allow more than a hundred people up on deck at any one time or this bitch will capsize.'

'I wish I could help you.'

'Of course you do, *monsieur*. Of course you do.' He put his hands on his hips. 'Is there an Amos Simonici down here?'

200

There was shuffling among the crush of miserable humanity. But no-one spoke.

Garabatenko squeezed through the press of people, clambering over battered suitcases and cheap boxes, shouting Amos's name.

'Who wants him?' someone yelled from the darkness.

'Are you Amos Simonici?'

'It depends.'

'Are you or not?'

'Why do you want him?'

'Show me your papers!' When the man wouldn't do it, Garabatenko gave up in disgust. He came back down the aisle between the bunks, shaking his head. 'You see, *monsieur*?'

'He has to be here.'

Garabatenko stood there, hands on hips. 'If I tell them you have a visa, everyone will say they are Amos Simonici. What does he look like anyway?'

Nick relayed what Daniela had told him: tall, dark curly hair, spoke English, twenty-four years old.

Garabatenko shook his head. 'Are you sure he's on board?'

'No.'

'Well, we'll keep trying. Perhaps he's on deck.'

They went back up the ladder. When he got back on deck, Nick thought he was going to retch. He went to the windward rail and took deep lungfuls of air.

'Six weeks we've been sitting here,' Garabetenko said. 'Why won't anyone help us?'

'Politics.'

'Politics!' He spat over the side. 'Wait here. I'll see if I can find this Amos Simonici for you. But I can't promise anything.'

A short while later, though, he reappeared and had with him a tall, gaunt young man in a shabby suit encrusted with the filth of six weeks of sleeping on the deck of the *Struma*.

'Are you Amos Simonici?' Nick said.

The young man looked terrified. He looked at Garabatenko, then at the police, then back to Nick. 'Yes.'

'You have a sister, Daniela?'

He nodded again.

'She's been worried about you.' Nick moved closer. The young man stank. 'Your sister's been looking for you. We may be able to get you off here.'

'Get me off?' He looked at Garabatenko, then back at Nick. He looked as if he was about to cry.

'Are you all right?'

'He's been very sick,' Garabatenko said. 'You can see that.'

The Turkish police sergeant was grumbling. They had been on the boat almost an hour and he wanted to leave.

Nick put a hand on Amos's shoulder. 'Have you heard from Simon?'

A shake of the head.

'It will be all right,' he said. 'We'll get you off.'

Amos said nothing.

The Turkish police sergeant demanded that they leave. 'Everything's going to be all right,' Nick said, and he turned and followed the police down the ladder to the launch.

As their boat pulled away, several of the passengers stretched out their hands and cried out, calling to him in Romanian and German.

That night he tossed in his bed, unable to sleep. Whenever he closed his eyes he saw the faces of those racks of human cattle in the stinking hold of the *Struma*, and all the demons of hell were pointing at him to accuse. He shouted back that he was innocent, but no-one listened.

42.

He could not meet Daniela at his house unless Maier knew of the rendezvous in advance and thought there was some professional reason for her going there, so today they arranged to meet behind the Sülemaniye mosque. He waited for her down an alley, stamping his feet against the cold as a light snow spiralled from a pewter sky. Istanbul was a tableau of mist and fractured, dark walls.

She appeared suddenly, her face hidden under a green scarf, her hands thrust deep into the pockets of her overcoat. She stood close, her breath freezing on the air.

She looked up and kissed him softly on the lips. 'Nick, darling.'

'I have news,' he said and held her closer against him.

'You have found him?'

'I went on the *Struma* last night. I found him.'

'Oh my God. How does he look?'

'Thin. He has been sick.'

'You can get him off?'

'I will do my best. I can get him an emergency visa for Palestine. We are still waiting for final word from the Turkish Government.'

'Did he say anything to you?'

Nick shook his head. 'He needs a doctor.'

She gripped his hand fiercely and kissed him again. 'You have to know how much this means to me. I will repay you. You'll see.'

'You don't have to do anything.'

She kissed him on the cheek. 'Don't ever hate me, Nick,' she whispered and then she slipped away, an elusive shadow in a grey and frozen world.

Abrams had betrayed Saffet Diker to the Turks for this. He was glad Abrams still slept well in his bed at night. He didn't.

43.

He was working late in his study. The jarring ring of the black telephone on his desk startled him. He looked at his wristwatch. Nine o'clock.

He picked up the telephone. 'Davis.'

'Nick. I have to see you.'

'What's wrong?'

'Liman's in Gate of the Thumb Street. Half an hour.'
And she hung up.

Nick left the taxi two blocks away on Istiklal and made his way towards Gate of the Thumb. A biting wind funnelled down the boulevard, but even on such a cold night there were strollers making their way between the bars and restaurants: German staff officers with Hungarian girl-friends; Turkish businessmen laughing and smoking; and British diplomatic staff with their wives, several of whom he knew and acknowledged with a nod of the head. In the cafés men and women were chatting in Italian and French and Spanish and Romanian.

He stopped on the corner opposite Gate of the Thumb as an apple-green tram rattled past. Whoever had followed her was either careless or overconfident; he saw the glow of their cigarette in the doorway at the bottom of the street. It was easier to follow a target in summer; there were outdoor café tables at which to sit and read the newspaper and look inconspicuous.

Now he knew where the watcher was, he felt more assured. He crossed the street and made his way to Liman's. He did not look over his shoulder, confident that their watcher would still be there when he left.

She was sitting at a table at the back of the restaurant, wearing a green silk scarf. There were just a handful of customers, most of them men. He sat down and asked the waiter to bring a bottle of *raki* and two glasses.

She was pale. He thought he had never seen her this frightened, not since that day in Bucharest when she had run from the greenshirts.

'What's happened?' he said.

There was a manila envelope lying on the tabletop. She handed it to him.

It was unsealed. He took out a thin sheaf of typed papers. 'What is this?'

'Read them.'

'They're originals. How did you get these? Out of his safe?'

'I have to get them back before he gets home.'

'Which is when?'

She tried to smile and it came off as a grimace. 'He might be home already.' Christ. This was insane.

'He was away for almost a month before Christmas. In Berlin.'

He read it through as quickly as he could. 'Jesus,' he murmured when he had finished.

'He's never talked about this. But there's phone calls, late at night. He has many secrets, Nick.'

'You have to get this back into his safe right now. Why did you do this?'

'You helped me find Amos. I wanted to do something for you.'

'A bottle of scotch might have covered it.'

She looked wounded. She took the memorandum from him and put it back into the envelope. When she stood up to leave, he reached out and grabbed her arm.

'Were you followed?' he said.

She shook her head. 'No.'

'Let me ask the question another way. You were followed.'

She looked over his shoulder. 'How do you know?'

'It's my business to know.'

She slumped back into her seat. She started to shake. 'Oh God.'

'I'll take care of it.'

'How?'

He put some money on the table for the *raki*. The waiter stared at him reproachfully; he had hoped the well-dressed foreigner would have dinner as well and leave a big tip.

'I'm going to leave now,' he told her. 'I want you to wait five minutes, then walk up the street and turn left.'

'It's dark that way, there are no street lamps.'

'It's all right, I'll be watching you.'

'What are you going to do?'

'There's a restaurant called Rumeli at the end of the alley. You turn down the alley on the opposite side of the street and walk right to the end and go into the nearest doorway and wait there.'

She hesitated.

'Just do as I say and everything will be okay.'

He got up and walked out. Ice shimmered on the cobblestones. He did not look back.

He went two blocks before doubling back, turned up a dark sidestreet and made his way back to Gate of the Thumb, where he turned into a doorway, deep in shadow, and waited.

He shivered even through the heavy woollen overcoat. Christ, it was cold. He heard the muted wail of Arabic music from an upstairs restaurant. The wind shuffled snow along the street. There were still strollers on Istiklal, but here, a block south, it was deserted.

Why had Daniela put herself in danger? And now someone had to die to save her. This attack of conscience would not have troubled other men, he knew; after all, there were thousands dying every day right across Europe, and the man who had followed them was the enemy, yet Nick had never quite managed that insouciance to killing that came easily to some.

He saw Daniela come out of the restaurant, saw her hesitate.

'Come on, just do as I told you,' he murmured under his breath.

She started up the street towards him, reached the corner less than ten yards from where he stood but did not see him.

He held his breath.

Yes, there he was, walking quickly, hands in his pockets, a fedora pulled down over his ears, head down against the wind.

Daniela's heels echoed on the cobblestones.

The man turned the corner and set off down the dark street after her. He was walking too fast, perhaps worried he would lose her in the darkness. Nick waited until he was almost out of sight and then set off after him.

He did not hurry, stayed in the shadows, out of sight. A splash of yellow light fell on the cobblestones from the Rumeli. He saw Maier's agent hesitate, probably asking himself why Daniela had chosen to walk alone so far from

Istiklal. But he had no choice but to follow. They would have been his orders.

Nick walked faster.

He swallowed down a wave of nausea. He knew what he had to do and he dreaded it. But for him also there was no choice.

Dark tenement doorways crowded in either side. The sound of Daniela's heels echoed off the walls. She turned into a doorway, as he had told her, and it was suddenly quiet.

Maier's agent hesitated. Nick could just make out his silhouette in the darkened alley; he must have guessed something was wrong.

It was over very quickly.

The man did not see the hand that crushed his windpipe. He went down clutching at his throat and died quickly. The Luger automatic that he had drawn from his jacket clattered onto the cobblestones. He had not even had time to remove the safety from the weapon.

When it was over, Nick took a lighter from his pocket and shone it on the man's face. He felt for a pulse to make sure he was dead.

Jesus. It was Haller.

He extinguished the light before Daniela could see who it was. He picked up the Luger and put it into his jacket pocket. Then he went to the gutter and vomited the *raki* and whatever remained of his supper.

'You killed him,' Daniela said, her voice flat.

He didn't answer. He was angry with her, wished she had not put herself in such danger that he had been forced to do this. He straightened and wiped his mouth with the back of his hand.

Nick dragged Haller into a doorway, propped him there. No-one would disturb the body until the morning. By then he would have arranged for it to disappear.

'Let's get out of here,' he said.

Knowing how to kill a man was one thing; doing it, and doing it at close hand, instead of through the bomb sight of an aeroplane, or through a periscope, or even through the sight of a rifle, was something utterly different.

He wondered what she thought of him now, if she was repelled or frightened. This was not the first time she had seen him standing over a dead body; but that day in the Jewish Quarter he had not killed intentionally.

He led her by the arm and within minutes they were back on Istiklal, where there was laughter and music coming from the restaurants and bars, and lovers strolled arm in arm on their way to warm beds and undisturbed sleep.

He knew he would not sleep at all that night, or for many nights to come.

They did not speak until they reached Taksim Square. Finally, he said, 'What will you do if he's there?'

'I will have to go in.'

'That's suicide. I won't let you do that.'

'There's no choice.'

'He'll kill you. He'll have no choice either.'

'I'll find a way to get these papers back without him seeing.'

'No,' he said. They walked faster. Maier's apartment was just two blocks from the German Consulate. He looked at his watch. Close to eleven.

'This was my fault,' she said.

'It was no-one's fault.'

They reached Maier's townhouse. There was no sign of his dark blue Mercedes saloon outside and Nick felt a flood of disappointment. He did not want her to go back. This was her opportunity to get away, and if she wanted to take it, he knew he would help her, and to hell with Abrams and the rest of SIS, to hell with the war.

She started to cross the street but he held tight to her

hand. 'Don't go back. I'll get you a visa. I'll protect you.'

'Why?' she said.

If only Abrams could hear him, he thought. He would turn blue with apoplexy. Daniela was a coup, one of the most promising agents they had in Istanbul. And what she had shown him tonight was political dynamite.

And here he was trying to end her career before it had really started.

'I can't,' she said when he did not answer. She pulled free and he watched her run across the street. She turned down a laneway at the side of the house. She would let herself in through a gate in the back garden and go up the back stairs, so the servants did not see her.

He knew he would not rest until her next phone call, until he knew she was all right.

But first he had to do something about Haller.

44.

'You look awful,' Abrams said.

Nick sat down. He hadn't slept, and he had been unable also to keep his breakfast down. He looked out of the window, at the grey city sweeping down Pera to the Horn. Flurries of snow settled on the windowsill. The coldest winter Istanbul had seen in years. The porcelain stove in the corner of the office laboured hopelessly against the chill. Abrams blew on his hands to warm them.

'I heard what happened.'

Nick shrugged.

'I'm sure it had to be done. What did Trojan want with you at that hour of the night?'

'She took some typed papers from Maier's safe. She wasn't able to photograph them.'

'And?'

He took a breath. 'It was a blueprint for the assumption of the German Government from the National Socialists. It assumed Hitler's death and the arrest of all of Hitler's high party officials. It also outlined terms for a negotiated peace settlement with Britain. It was basically a briefing document, unsigned and unattributed.'

Abrams just stared at him.

'As you said in Bucharest, Herr Maier is a very interesting man.'

'You think the document was genuine?'

Nick shrugged. 'I don't know,' he said.

For a long time neither man spoke.

'What are we going to do?' Nick asked, finally. 'Will we pass this information along to Whitehall?'

Abrams shook his head. 'Nothing they can do with it. And it just puts Maier in danger when he might be useful to us later.'

'You said in Bucharest that you had a particular interest in Maier.'

Abrams considered, then appeared to make up his mind. 'His father is a close family friend of the head of the Abwehr, Admiral Canaris. Canaris is from one of Germany's foremost aristocratic families and he hates the Nazis. He won't recruit fascists into any of his intelligence units. Naturally, Maier is of great interest to us. This war does not necessarily have to be resolved by military means, Davis. There are men in London and in Berlin who think there might be another way.'

'So you do think the document was genuine?'

'There have been whispers that certain members of the German elite want to eliminate Hitler and end this war. For the time being we can only wait and see.' He drummed on the desk with his fingers. 'What happened to Haller's body?'

'I came back here and called someone at Special Operations. I thought they'd know what to do. Apparently it went over the side of a fishing boat in the Marmara Sea just before dawn. It was well weighted and it won't resurface to embarrass us. Maier will assume he's dead, but he won't know why or how.'

'Won't it throw suspicion on Trojan anyway?'

'I know a Hungarian dancer in one of the clubs off Taksim. I've arranged for her to tell her fellow workers how she took Haller back to her apartment last night but he was drunk and started hitting her, so she threw him out. The story will get around Taksim pretty fast. That will confuse things enough without making it sound like too neat a story. Maier will think Haller went whoring and drinking, instead of doing his job. He might have suspicions but he won't ever be able to discover the truth either way.'

'I hope you're right,' Abrams said.

So do I, Nick thought. But he didn't say so.

They waited in his study while Daniela nervously sipped her orange tea and Nick got drunk on gin and tonic. They spoke little. He tried several times to start a conversation with her but she was too distracted and so they lapsed into silence.

Around nine Nick heard a car pull up outside. He went to the window and looked down into the street. It was the police. An officer opened the back door and a thin angular young man in a crumpled suit got out, clutching a battered cardboard suitcase.

'He's here,' he said.

She stood up, smoothed down her dress.

'Well,' he said. 'Shall we go down and meet him?'

'Nick?'

He turned.

'Forgive me.'

'Forgive you for what?'

The police were knocking outside. He went downstairs and threw open the door. A Turkish police captain saluted him and the young man with the suitcase stepped out of the shadows. He was tall, pale and gaunt, and he looked plainly terrified.

'Amos,' Nick said. '*Bienvenu*. Welcome. Come in.'

Nick thanked the police captain and the officer saluted again, got back into the car and drove away.

The young man stood just inside the door, switching the suitcase from one hand to the other and looking around him with quick, nervous movements.

Daniela came down the steps and they stared at each other. Nick waited for them to embrace.

'Who's this?' Daniela said.

45.

The young man gratefully accepted Nick's offer of food and wolfed down several plates of eggs and cheese. Now he held the tumbler of *raki* Nick had given him as if it was a Fabergé egg. 'The night you came on the *Struma*, I was curled up asleep in the cabin on the deck.' He spoke in a low monotone, unable to look Nick in the eye. 'The captain woke me up, asked me how old I was. He told me to stand up and then he asked me if I could speak English. I said I could. He asked me if I wanted to get off the *Struma*. I said of course I did. He said I was the luckiest Jew in the world. He told me that if anyone asked me, I was to say my name was Amos Simonici.'

'He said that?'

'He said I just had to say I was Amos Simonici until I got to the shore and after that I should hope for the best.' He looked up at Nick. 'You're not going to send me back to that boat, are you?'

Nick looked at Daniela but she had turned away. She was staring out of the window at the distant lights of Pera. She was crying, quietly.

He knew what the captain had done. He wanted to save one of his passengers, and if he could not save the real Amos Simonici, then he would create one.

'What's your name?' Nick asked him. 'Your real name?'

'Solomon. Solomon Leibovici.'

'Well, Solomon. Tomorrow I'm going to put you on a train to Haifa. The captain was right. You are the luckiest Jew in the world right now.'

He stood up and went over to Daniela, put his hands on her shoulders.

'Why isn't he on the *Struma*?' she whispered.

'Perhaps he tore up his ticket,' Solomon said. 'A lot of my friends tore up theirs when they saw the state of the ship. Maybe he's in Constanza waiting for another boat.'

Daniela shivered and hugged herself, rubbing her bare arms. 'Thank you, Nick,' she whispered. 'Thank you for trying. Thank you for everything.'

'I'm sorry.'

She turned and kissed him tenderly on the cheek. 'Perhaps he'll write again,' she said.

But he never did. She never heard from Amos again.

217

46.

He stood on the docks, watched the red and white tug-boat tow the *Struma* away from her berth, past the Rumeli fortress towards the Black Sea. The Turks had given them no warning and when it happened the British Ambassador was still negotiating for the children to be removed from the boat.

The seven hundred souls packed on board never did see the dirty brown coasts of Palestine. The tug cut the rope to the *Struma* on calm waters twelve miles off the Black Sea coast. The lifeless engine was useless and the *Struma* started to drift. The next day, just before dawn, she erupted into a ball of flame. Although she was flying a Panamanian flag, it was suggested that she had been torpedoed by a Russian submarine.

It was winter. Those that did not die in the initial blast soon succumbed to hypothermia in the icy waters of the Black Sea.

There was only one survivor.

BOOK THREE

47.

Istanbul, August 1943

She came sometimes late at night, a shadowed figure moving along the cobbled street. She would knock on the wooden door, two short taps and a longer one. He would be waiting for her, and she would slip inside in a rush of perfume.

It was a Byzantine game they played, for to maintain the deception that she was spying on him, as Maier had asked her to do, it was necessary to manufacture disinformation that she could take with her, to justify her late night visits.

Nick and Abrams were meticulous in planning what they would do and how they would do it, for it had to appear that Daniela had come by the material in some plausible way. At first they gave her false documents that she copied in her own careful, spidery writing. He would time her with his wristwatch, and she would never have more than half an hour to copy down whatever she wished, at random. She told Maier that Nick sometimes brought papers home with him from the consulate, which was actually true, though it was strictly against protocols. She would tell him she copied them while Nick was asleep.

And while she became his spy, Daniela Simonici also became his mistress.

He had come to know exactly the shape of her hips so that just by holding out his arms he could remember her; he could close his eyes and instantly summon the feel of her long dark hair on his cheek as she leaned over in bed to kiss him. He soon knew her so intimately that he knew how she slept, one arm tossed carelessly above her head, her face petulant in sleep as a fractious child. He knew how she tossed and kicked at night, tortured by her dreams. He knew the sweet and distinctive scent of her, and when they were together he inhaled the sweet musk of her skin like perfume.

After she was gone, the illusion of their intimacy would shatter and jealousy built in him like toothache. He envied Maier; although they were deceiving him, he had her with him when he woke in the mornings and she was a part of his life each day. It was this Nick wanted most of all.

He was never sure what went on behind those enigmatic golden eyes. He wondered about Maier and thought about what lies she told him. I can't get there with Siggi, she had told him once after they made love.

He asked her: So what do you do? Do you pretend?

Of course, she said, and all his insecurities glowed like hot coals, and he wondered then if she ever pretended with him. How would he ever know?

Often he would dream about her, wake with a sense of real pain when he reached for her and found she was not there beside him. He was working against himself; a part of him wanted to find a way to take her away from Maier, while his profession and his duty demanded that he do everything possible to keep her under Maier's roof and in Maier's good graces.

Nick was working late in his study, reading through a file he had brought home from the consulate. Tonight he would see Daniela again, the first time in almost four weeks, and every few minutes he listened for the sound of her footfall on the cobblestones outside.

Operation Cicero was the subject of the file, and it was Nick's own plan. Jan Romanescu had survived the demise of the Iron Guard and had made contact again through a Turkish businessman called Omar Kalmaz. His former Guardist double agent now operated a communist cell in Dobruja and had asked Nick if the British would supply him with a radio and explosives. Special Operations in Cairo had sent a sabotage expert called Jordon – Nick had last met him in the basement of the Bucharest legation – and Nick had formulated a plan to land him and a radio, together with a trained operator, south of Constanza, so they could link up with Romanescu's cell.

He heard Daniela's footfall in the alleyway, abandoned his papers and went out into the garden to unlock the door. As soon as she was inside, they threw themselves at each other. He carried her up the stairs to the bedroom and they fell onto the bed.

They made love quickly, urgently, the separation and its unbearable physical longing overpowering them both.

It always felt like coming home.

He looked like a little boy when he slept. She stroked his face with her hand, overcome with a wave of sadness. They had now, this moment, and this was all they could ever have. Whatever happened, she thought, these moments together would be with her always, no-one could ever take her memories from her.

But why can't I have more? she wondered. Does it have to be this way?

She kissed him gently on the forehead and stood up, felt the wetness of him run between her thighs. She wished one day it would be a part of him growing inside her. But she knew that could never happen.

She angrily brushed the tears from her eyes, put on one of his shirts and slipped out of the room.

He opened his eyes, wondered how long he had slept. He remembered they had talked quietly in the darkness after their lovemaking, but he did not remember falling asleep.

'Daniela?'

A few moments later she appeared at the doorway of the bedroom. 'Nick.'

'Where were you?'

'I went to get you a drink,' she said and handed him a glass of water. She sat down on the edge of the bed.

She lit the candle on the bedside table. She was wearing one of his shirts; the sleeves were too long and they reached below the tips of her fingers, the shirttails almost to her knees. She looked adorable.

She climbed onto the bed and sat astride him, the fingers of one hand curled among the hairs on his chest.

'I didn't know where you were. Was I asleep long?'

'Just a few minutes.'

'I'm sorry.'

'Don't be silly.'

They started to talk, as they always did. Sometimes they

talked for hours. She had endless questions about England; Guildford, where he lived, was as exotic to her as Bucharest was to him.

Their lives could not have been more different. She had gone to school each day down narrow cobbled lanes where she learned Hebrew and the Talmud, and greybeards chanted the Torah from dusty schoolrooms, and local Romanian boys jeered and threw rocks at them from the other side of the street.

Nick had endured a public school upbringing of canes and cold showers and muddy football fields, coming home only for Christmas and summer holidays.

The look on her face when he told her about his boarding school; she was incredulous, could not imagine it. Nick himself had thought it quite normal until later, when he grew up and met people who had been inseparable from their families all their lives. It seemed as outrageous to her as her own upbringing seemed to him, a world where you could be beaten for having another religion.

'My family lived in the same house in the Jewish Quarter for over a hundred years. My father broke the tradition when we moved to the Boulevard Bratianu when I was seven. It was a big family scandal.'

'Your family were Orthodox?'

'I remember Jewish holidays when I was a child, my uncles wearing kaftans with white stockings and fur-rimmed hats. My father was the first to change.' She smiled at another memory. 'Do you have roasted chestnuts in England?'

He nodded. 'You can buy them from street sellers in the autumn.'

'When I was a little girl, my father bought them for me from a man who roasted them in the street in a rusty red urn.'

'I can't imagine you as a little girl.'

'I was as skinny as a pole and I had big teeth.'

'I bet all the boys were crazy about you.'

'There was only one.'

'I don't believe you.'

'He was the first boy I ever kissed. I was fifteen years old and he took me into the doorway of a little bookshop on the way home from school. I remember I hated it. I did it because I wanted him to like me.'

'What happened to him?'

She shrugged. 'I don't know. He moved away.'

'How long did you know him?'

'I don't want to talk about it,' she said. 'I want to forget all about Romania tonight. Let's talk about something else. Tell me about London. Tell me about the Houses of Parliament. I've seen pictures. There's a big clock.'

'Big Ben.'

'Can you see it from all over London?'

'It's not that big.'

'And you have red pillar boxes. People put letters in them. I've read about it. I've often imagined what it would be like to go there. My father went to the Sorbonne in Paris. He promised to take me with him to France and London but . . . perhaps I will still go. One day.'

'When this is over –'

'This war will never be over. It will go on for ever.'

'I told you, Daniela, I can get you a passport and a visa, I can get them for you now if you want.'

'You can get them for me but not for all those people on the *Struma*, and God knows how many since then.' Her face softened and she took his hand in both of hers. 'Don't ever regret meeting me, will you?'

'Why would I do that?'

'Things happen.'

What did she mean? He thought sometimes that loving Daniela was like being in a room full of mirrors. She loved him but did not want to be with him, and would never talk about the future.

'I have to go,' she said.

He hated those words. For hours the spell the war held over them would keep the world at bay, and he could imagine they were lovers without the countries and complications that stood between them. He would imagine waking with her in the morning, pretend that tonight she did not have to leave. But then she would say those words he dreaded and the ephemeral nature of their love affair would plunge him back into the frustration and loneliness that had become his everyday life. Each time he felt a profound sense of grief, never knew if this might be the last time they would ever be together.

'Do you have to go?'

He heard her slip into her clothes in the darkness. 'Siggi will be furious if I stay out all night.'

'You're only doing your job,' he said, bitterly.

'If I sleep with you, I'm doing my job. If I don't get back until morning, he may think I've fallen in love with you.'

'Have you?' he said and held his breath.

She did not answer. Instead she leaned over the bed and kissed him on the mouth. He reached up and held her around the waist, tried to pull her back down onto the bed. She laughed and pulled away, replacing the strap of her brassiere over her shoulder.

She still had not answered his question.

'I really have to go.'

'Stay,' he said, and the way he said it, she could not make a joke of it. She pulled on her silk stockings.

'I can't.'

'You don't have to go back.'

'And then who will spy on the Abwehr for you?'

She stood up, slipped out of the moonshadow, the silver phosphorescence revealing his mistress in her underwear

227

and silk stockings. She looked so achingly beautiful. He wanted to preserve this moment, keep it indelibly in his memory for those times when it was over.

'Does he think you have me completely fooled?'

'He says that women are your weakness,' she said. She looked into his eyes and there was a moment when either of them could have spoken but instead they kept silent and wondered.

He sighed at the sinuous line of her spine as she shrugged her dress over her head. Watching her dress was both an erotic and a depressing experience, for each time it was a small departure, a rehearsal for the final goodbye.

'Be careful,' he said.

'He doesn't suspect.'

'If he ever finds out you are spying on him, he'll hurt you.' He couldn't bring himself to say: He'll kill you. He could not bear the thought of anything happening to her.

She tossed her mane of hair, and rolled her eyes, smiling. 'I'm always careful.' That smile, it dazzled a man, disarmed him, it was her most potent weapon. It deceived the world into thinking she was confident, and content with her life, even if tears were just a moment away.

'What if he comes home one day and the safe's open and you haven't had time to put away his papers?'

'I can hear his car drive up outside. I always have time to put things away.'

'What if one of the servants walks in?'

'I lock the door.'

He shook his head, unconvinced. He didn't like the risks, yet these were the risks he asked of her.

In the past two years he had come to know a great deal about Maier. He knew, for instance, that his various business interests in the Balkans – the department store in Bucharest, the hotel in Sofia, the spice warehouse here in

Istanbul – were genuine businesses, for Maier came from a wealthy Prussian family.

Before the war he had served in the navy under Canaris, and he held a doctorate in Balkan studies from Heidelberg university. He had been sent to Istanbul under cover by Canaris himself as a hemp buyer.

It was the best kind of cover, to have a paying job and to be seen doing it. But Maier did not look like a hemp buyer. Those patrician features, the grey wings of hair at his temples, the ice-blue eyes; they made him look every inch what he was, an aristocrat, a man accustomed to wealth and power.

Nick knew he travelled frequently between Berlin and Istanbul, taking sensitive documents by hand to Canaris himself at Abwehr headquarters. He knew, also, that he had safe houses in Taksim and Istiklal, and agents in Bulgaria, Istanbul, Ankara, Baghdad, Palestine and Damascus.

But of Siegfried Maier himself he had learned very little. Daniela would not talk about him. 'It does not help the war,' she said, 'and it will only hurt you.' He learned nothing of their life together. He knew that Maier had a birthmark on his right hip, that he liked to drink beer with his dinner and that he preferred Turkish cigarettes to German; but what they talked about, how they lived, if they ever laughed together, she kept from him.

'What's it like?' he had asked her once. 'With him.'

'I've told you that. Why do you ask me these questions? What do you want from me?'

'You never talk about him.'

'What do you want me to say? It only upsets you. Why do you want to torture yourself?'

'I just want to know, that's all.'

'He's kind to me. He's gentle, though I know you won't believe it. Of course I feel something for him. What do you think I am?'

'Does he ever ask about me?'

'Of course.'

'And what do you tell him?'

'I tell him you love me.'

'And what does he say to that? Does he ever suspect you're playing a double game?'

'Whatever lies you're making up for him in those envelopes are too good.' And then she had kissed him, as she always did when she wanted to distract him.

Now through the windows a crescent moon, Mohammed's moon, floated in a cold star-bright sky. He wanted to hold on to the moment, and never let go. But she was dressed and waiting for him. The night had passed too quickly; there was never a way to hold back the night.

He walked with her down the hill towards the station. Soon the fruit market would come alive; the vendors were setting up their stalls in the darkness, and a lorry passed, piled high with melons, its headlights flickering on the walls as it bounced over the cobblestones. *Hamals* bent double under towers of wicker panniers, headed for another long day of back-breaking labour, before the sun was even in the sky.

He heard the boom of a horn from the docks as the ancient city came awake. A lemon dawn. She walked beside him, straight-backed, the dark hair covered with a green silk scarf, a woman of grace and poise. An enigma. A woman he should never have fallen in love with, even though he supposed now that he had been looking for her all his life.

He found her a taxi outside the spice market. The driver was asleep on the front seat. He leaned in and shook him by the shoulder to wake him, gave him the address in Taksim.

'When will I see you again?'

'Soon.'

She got into the taxi. Going home to another man.

He leaned in the window. 'Be careful.'

'I love you,' she said and then she kissed him. It shook him, left him staring after the red tail lights long after they had disappeared over the Galata Bridge. It was the first time she had ever said that to him.

He walked back up the hill, the mosque of Süleyman crouching atop the hill like a great beast. The scent of her stayed on his clothes all day.

48.

The fishing boats bucked and rolled next to the quay, but the fishermen never lost their balance, shouting up to passers-by, their catch arranged on wooden trays on the deck. If there were not enough customers, Constantin would put a live fish in a tin can and throw it on the deck of the boat where it bounced and clanged, causing a little crowd of onlookers to gather at the rails, laughing and pointing. Passers-by would shout down their orders and the coins would be thrown down into the boat, then, after the money was counted, a bag containing the fish would be flung up to the buyers.

Constantin saw Nick and hauled on a rope to bring the boat closer to the quay. He leaped onto the dock.

He was a grizzled salt with three days' stubble and a sad moustache that gave him a perpetually downcast look. His long lank hair was thinning and was swept across his bald head like guitar strings.

Nick offered him a cigarette, and lit it for him. Up close he saw that the fisherman's fingernails were rimmed with oil from the engine and his teeth were bad.

'Dobruja,' Nick said.

Constantin smiled. He had been born and lived almost his entire life in a village ten miles south-east of there. 'I could find my way there with a blindfold.'

'We need three men dropped off, usual rates.'

'I don't care about money. When?'

'I'll be in touch.'

Constantin jumped back in the boat, rejoining the two crewmen who were Jews like himself, from his village in Dobruja.

The old fisherman threw another can on the deck, and some schoolchildren squealed with delight. He tossed them a small bluefish. His grandchildren would have been that age, if they were still alive.

49.

The sabotage of an enemy's installations and infrastructure had once been the purview of Section D of the British Secret Intelligence Service, but early in the war Churchill had formed a separate organisation, the Special Operations Executive, to take over those responsibilities. They were the mavericks, the renegades of the service. The errant sons. The SOE became more abhorrent to the Foreign Office mandarins than the Gestapo.

There were good reasons that Nick could see for separating the two organisations; SOE agents were trained for a single act of sabotage, while officers like himself were involved with long-term intelligence gathering that required plausible cover, good security and a great deal of patience. Different kind of chap altogether, he had heard SIS colleagues saying among themselves; they were chess players, but the SOE, well, they were just cowboys.

This particular cowboy had arrived on their doorstep from SOE Cairo. Patrick Jordon was tall and rangy and handsome in a public school sort of way, an affable, loose-limbed Oxford man with blues in rowing and rugby and a pipe forever clenched between his teeth but rarely properly alight.

Nick remembered him playing with the detonator in the basement of the Bucharest legation.

Now he, Abrams and Nick stood in the briefing room at SOE's Istanbul office, staring at a map of Romania that was spread out on the polished oak table. Jordon, wearing a navy-blue polo neck jumper and baggy khaki pants, regarded the map with scholarly interest.

The office was an eighteenth-century house close to the Park Hotel and the German Consulate. Nick glanced out of the window, saw von Papen, the German Ambassador, smoking and laughing with consulate staff in the leafy garden on the other side of the wall.

The enemy.

'The boat will land us here, ten miles south of Dobruja,' Nick said, returning to the map. 'The captain, Constantin, will anchor in the bay here and you and your radio operator will be taken ashore in a boat. The leader of the local resistance, Romanescu, will be waiting on the beach. He'll signal with a torch, two long flashes and a short one.'

Jordon nodded, looking very relaxed for a man about to go to war. 'This Constantin is reliable?' he asked.

'Completely.'

'You're coming with us?' Jordon asked.

Nick nodded. 'I want to talk to Romanescu. I'll stay overnight and come back with Constantin the next day.'

'By the way, the group you're going to spend the next six months with are all Marxists,' Abrams said.

Jordon looked up. 'Does it matter?'

'It may, later on. After the war.'

'I'm sure they want to see the Germans out of Romania as much as we do.'

'Perhaps. But they're going to be a headache for all of us when it's over.'

'First we have to win the war.'

'Oh, I don't think there's any doubt about who will win,' Abrams said. 'To be honest, Stalin worries me more than Hitler. I just hope we're not helping to turn Romania into another Russia.'

Jordon looked at Nick for support. 'The Russians are our allies, sir,' he said.

'They don't think about the consequences in London when they make these decisions. But the war won't last for ever, and then politicals like Nick and I have to sort out their mess. Want to see Romania annexed to Russia, do you, Jordon?'

'I believe everyone has a right to self-determination.'

'I don't think Stalin would agree with you there.'

Abrams went to the window. It was open and they could hear von Papen laughing at some joke. A strange war.

'Look at him,' Abrams said. 'Devious. Egotistical. Ambitious. There's a man we could have done business with.'

Nick saw the look on Jordon's face. Not many people liked Abrams; he wasn't sure that Jordon did.

Later, as they drove down Istiklal in the back of a Chancery saloon, Abrams turned to him and said, 'Queer duck, that Jordon. Not sure I care for him.'

'No, sir.'

'But that's the SOE. Spent their childhoods making bombs from castor sugar and benzine, I suppose. And pulling the wings off flies. Ever pull the wings off a fly, Davis?'

'No, sir.'

'There you are. That's why you work for us. How's the wife?'

The sudden turn in the conversation startled him. He wondered who had been talking; or perhaps everyone had. 'She's having a hard time of it over there, I think.'

'She must miss you.'

'It's hard raising children on your own, I imagine.'

'Of course. Still, it's important to have a constant wife, Davis. If you're ambitious. Speaks well, dresses well, that sort of thing. Remember that, won't you?'

They drove through the gates of the consulate. That was all Abrams said, all he needed to say.

Abrams may not have cared for Jordon but Nick thought Jordon appealing company, and that evening they arranged to go for a drink in Taksim, to toast the success of their mission. They walked up the dark cobbled street to Istiklal under a leaden sky, past the rows of bootblacks with their little stools and bottles of burnished brass. Nick and Jordon crossed Taksim Square dodging buses and clanging trams. The trams were bulging with people, some clinging to the sides, and the bells rang frantically as they bumped over the tramlines, scattering dawdling pedestrians. There was a large grey monument in the centre of the square commemorating the dead of the war of independence. The Turks had seen enough of wars in their history; Nick understood why they wanted no part of this one.

'How long have you worked with Abrams?' Jordon asked him.

'About three years now.'

'Odd, isn't he? All due respect and all that.'

'I suppose he is, a little. Always on his high horse about the Russians.'

'Jewboy?'

Nick nodded.

'Well, he'll learn to get along one day.' He grinned, the pipe still clenched between his front teeth. 'God, I could drain a lake right now. Call me daft, but war makes me nervous.'

There was a neon sign above a door that said ARIZONA. From inside the building came the wail of

Turkish music. Nick led Jordon down a flight of narrow steps into a dimly lit bar, with tawdry gilt walls, and mirrors so dirty they were almost opaque. It was hot and stank of tobacco and the sour taint of sweat.

There was just one other patron in the club, a Turk in a dark western suit who was slowly drinking himself into oblivion in the corner. There were a few rickety tables and chairs set up in front of a low stage where a bored and overweight Syrian girl was performing a belly dance.

Nick ordered a bottle of *raki* and two glasses. The first drink was to ease the tension in the shoulders and take away the pain behind the eyes; the second, to make the belly dancer appear more beautiful than she really was; the third, to make the world a friendly and benevolent place.

'Are you scared?' he asked Jordon, when they had broken the barriers of their reserve with strong spirit.

'I try not to think about it.' The pipe danced between his teeth. 'The thing you worry about most is betrayal. You never know when it's coming and often it's someone you trust, someone close to you. Have you ever been betrayed, Nick?'

Now there's a question to ask, Nick thought.

Often it's someone you trust.

Jordon reached into his trouser pocket and pulled out his wallet. He showed him a photograph of a young and pretty woman and two young girls, sepia smiles grinning out at the world, behind them the backdrop of a Scottish glen in some London photographer's studio.

'This is a single man's game, really,' he said. 'But you can die just as easily in the army or the air force.'

He brushed a forefinger lovingly over the three people in the photograph. 'Are you married, Nick?'

Nick produced his own photograph, smaller, pinched and tattered at the edges, taken some five years before. He had not looked at it in months. Too painful. 'The boys are grown now,' he said. 'It seems for ever since they were that young.'

'Kids have a habit of doing that.'

'My wife and I . . . well, things aren't that good between us.'

'Oh. I'm sorry.'

He doesn't know what to say, Nick thought. People never did. 'My own fault. I went and had an affair.'

Jordon drained his glass. Nick poured two more.

'You silly bugger.'

Nick laughed. He was relieved, he supposed, that Jordon seemed neither embarrassed nor appalled by his admission.

'I suppose I am. But I was in love with this woman. Still am.'

Jordon examined his pipe thoughtfully, as if he understood. 'That was bad luck.'

Bad luck: I could really like this fellow, Nick thought. 'Depends how you look at it.'

'Only one way to look at it. You fucked up.'

The obscenity dropped into the silence like shattered glass. Then Nick laughed. He's right, he thought, I fucked up.

'Well, I can't say I'm sorry. I loved her. I still love her.'

'How long's it been going on?'

'More than two years.'

The belly dancer plumped off the stage. The drunken Turk in the corner applauded enthusiastically.

'What are you going to do about it?'

'I don't know. It's complicated. You see, she's also working on our side.'

'So you're doing this to help the war effort?' he said, deadpan.

'Yes,' Nick said, 'it's my contribution to defeating Hitler.'

'Well, I'm sure you'll be mentioned in dispatches,' he said, and Nick smiled at that. 'Well, be careful,' he added, which was strange advice, Nick thought, for a man about to go of his own free will behind enemy lines, facing certain torture and death if he was caught.

They finished the bottle of *raki* and staggered back to the consulate in the early hours of the next morning. Nick rang the night porter and demanded someone take them both home.

50.

Back home, alone, Nick slumped into an armchair and thought about Jennifer, thought about the boys, the last time he had seen them. He had gone back to England the previous year, the Ambassador had found him a place on a Royal Navy destroyer.

Jennifer met him at the dock in Portsmouth, she had two strapping youths with her, and it took him some moments to realise they were his sons, almost grown to men.

He and Jennifer embraced as strangers. With James and Richard he shook hands.

The house in Guildford seemed somehow smaller, changed in some indefinable way. It belonged to another life. There was now an air raid shelter in the middle of the back garden and houses he remembered from childhood were rubble now, courtesy of the Luftwaffe.

That night he and Jennifer made love for the first time since she had left Bucharest. It was a disaster. He could think only of Daniela; Jennifer must have felt as if she was alone.

But afterwards she stroked his hair and whispered, 'You've learned some new tricks.'

He had not thought himself so transparent. He lay there in the darkness and listened to the beating of his heart, the branches of an apple tree scratching against the bedroom windows. He waited to hear himself speak but found instead that he was holding his breath, waiting for Jennifer to ask him the next and inevitable question.

'Is there another woman?' she whispered.

He waited to hear himself deny it, to see if he would still try to save their marriage. Or was it just plain deceit? If he did deny it, he suspected Jennifer would accept the deception and their lives would go on. She was accustomed to his secret life; this would be just one more secret, after all. And so he waited for the lie to come, but it didn't, and instead he heard himself say: 'Yes.'

She got out of bed and went into the bathroom. He heard her running the tap in the basin so that he would not hear her crying. He stood in the doorway, wanting to hold her, another part of himself drawing away.

'I'm sorry,' he said.

She ran some cold water on her face. 'You think I didn't know?'

No, he didn't think that. Two years was a long time for the strongest marriage to survive, and theirs had not been strong.

'We can get through this,' she said.

He didn't answer.

'It happens all the time,' she said.

It was true. It did happen. Men had affairs and their wives forgave them. But these were men who wanted their marriages to somehow survive, no matter how devalued and dishonest they had become.

'I'm sorry, Jen,' he repeated. 'I didn't plan for it to happen.'

'I don't want to know the details.'

'I think we should at least talk about it.'

'I don't think I want to.'

She went back to bed. He climbed in beside her and they lay on opposite sides of the bed, and neither of them slept. The sheets were cold; outside, a crescent moon raced between dark clouds, and he wondered if she could see this same moon now from the Galata Bridge.

After so long his boys were strangers to him. He realised he would have to get to know them over again and there wasn't time. By the time they accepted him as their father once more, it would be time to return to the war.

They were, of course, no longer interested in doing with him the things they had done before the war imposed itself between them. They were too old for games of checkers and hide and seek, and too young to come with him to a public house for a beer. And they had changed, not only physically, but in their characters. The malleable stuff of youth had begun to solidify into the traits of adulthood.

Richard, now fifteen, had become something of a book-worm, which disappointed Nick as much as it impressed Jennifer, who had plans for him to become a doctor; James was now an inch or two taller than his father and Nick's attempts to play football with his son were met with a sort of tender contempt, for Jamie was by now far more skilful.

He took them for tea and cakes in town. The conversation was difficult and stilted. James did most of the talking, asking him about Istanbul and the mosques and the things people wore, but mostly he wanted to know if his father had seen any fighting, and seemed disappointed when he told him that Turkey was a neutral country and all they saw of the war were stray bombers that sometimes appeared overhead.

He could not even tell the truth about himself to his own sons.

James asked what he did and Nick told him he worked in an office in the consulate. His son's disappointment was obvious. Every son wants his father to be a hero and heroes are not found behind desks. Perhaps one day he could tell him the truth.

'When are you coming back?' Richard asked suddenly. He had been pushing his teacake around his plate, converting it to a pile of crumbs.

'I don't know. When the war's over.'

Richard stared at the tablecloth. 'Mum was crying all the time when she came back from Bucharest.'

'It went on for months,' James said.

'I imagine she was missing me.'

'Are you missing her?' Richard said. Nick knew from the look on his face that he couldn't treat him as a child any more.

'Of course.'

'She's better now,' James said, 'she goes out a lot.'

A look passed between the two boys, a challenge of some kind. Richard's glasses caught the light as he moved his head. There was a long silence.

'What's the matter with you two?' Nick asked.

'Mum's got a new friend,' James said and Richard tried to kick his shins under the table.

'Stop it, Richard,' Nick said and immediately felt guilty for scolding him. The boy was taking his side, after all. He turned to James. 'Who is this friend?'

'He's an air force major,' James said.

'He's a spiv,' Richard said.

'He takes mum to the pictures.'

'He never did. Don't listen to him.'

'I'm sure it's fine,' Nick said. 'Your mum must get lonely. I don't mind.' He smiled to let them know it was okay, but they weren't fooled. He felt a bitter stab of jealousy. He had never wanted Jen to be unhappy, had even hoped she would find someone who would love her again. But another part of him had supposed she would stay faithful to him for ever, and his own possessiveness took him by surprise.

He wondered if he would ask Jennifer about this air force major later, or if, like her, he would be better off not knowing.

England was a different place to the one Nick had left four summers before. It was grimmer and perhaps less optimistic, too many widows and too many mothers who had lost sons. It was an England of ration cards and powdered eggs and gas masks carried over the shoulder in a cardboard box and under-the-counter sausages from the butcher.

Once, they went into London for tea in a Lyons coffee shop. He saw for himself what German bombs had done to the city and felt a stab of guilt for having not shared the miseries of his countrymen. While they had endured the Blitz, he had been starting an affair at a grand hotel in Bucharest.

He experienced a curious sense of dislocation. His body was in England but his mind and spirit were in Istanbul, his mind's eye following an elegant woman with a green scarf over her dark hair as she walked along a cobbled street of ancient Ottoman rowhouses below the Sülemaniye. In his vision she stopped at a house with a green-painted door and looked up at the balcony; there was an expression on her face that a stranger might have interpreted as longing.

They had not spoken about Istanbul since that first night. Once, he came home and heard her crying in the bathroom, and when he called to her, she locked the door.

It was a week later that she felt strong enough to re-examine the wound. They were sitting in deckchairs in the garden, reading the Sunday papers. It was a domestic routine he once would have enjoyed; now the very docility left him restless and irritable.

'What's wrong?'

'We need to talk, Jen.'

She folded the newspaper. 'I'm listening.'

And they sat there in silence. He didn't want to hurt her, but his choice, it seemed, was between leaving her or living a monstrous lie.

Jennifer broke the long silence. 'I knew you'd slept with another woman. It started in Bucharest, didn't it?'

'It started then. But I didn't sleep with her.'

'Don't lie to me.'

'It's true.'

'Did you think I didn't know?'

'I don't know what you thought.'

A tight, bitter smile. 'In some ways your transparency's a virtue, Nick. I can read you like a book.'

'Not a very good book.'

'Please. Spare me the mea culpas. Is it still going on?'

'The boys said you're seeing someone new,' he said.

She gave him a look of pure venom. 'So we're even, is that it? You'd like that, wouldn't you? Your conscience feel better?'

'Jen, that's not it at all.'

'He's just a friend. I wouldn't do that to you, Nick.'

But you did it to me, was the implication. He took a deep breath. 'Who is he?'

'You've got a nerve,' she said, then she stood up and went back inside the house.

He took the boys to the pictures, then played a desultory game of football with them on the common, but Richard wasn't that interested and James seemed to find his attempts to dribble the football around him laughable.

Afterwards Nick sat down on the grass, out of breath. Richard took out a book, while Jamie bounced the ball up and down on his right foot, showing off.

'I heard Mum crying again last night,' James said.

Richard looked up from his history book. 'Are you getting a divorce?'

'I don't know.'

'You are,' James said.

'Mum said you have a lady friend,' Richard said.

Nick stared at him. He couldn't believe Jennifer would say such a thing to the boys.

'Why don't you just tell us?'

'Because I don't think you'd understand.'

'Because you lied to us!'

'I haven't lied to you.'

'You're lying to us now.'

James was right. He was lying to them by not telling them everything. But he still thought they were too young to understand. 'We'll talk about this later,' he said.

The boys looked at each other. Richard reached up under his glasses with a finger and sniffed away a tear, pretended he just had an itchy nose.

Jamie kept bouncing the ball up and down on his foot. Suddenly he let it drop onto the ground and kicked it as hard as he could. It sailed into the air and bounced across the road next to the common, forcing the baker's lorry to swerve to miss it.

'That was a stupid thing to do,' Nick said. 'Go and get that.'

'I don't want to,' James said.

It was the first time Jamie had ever defied him. The battle lines had been drawn. They were just boys, and the world had only two colours, black and white, there were no shades of grey.

He felt miserable for what he was doing to them and to Jen.

He stood up and went to get the ball himself, then they walked back home across the common. The boys walked on ahead and no-one had anything more to say.

The last day he stood in the kitchen as she made him a special breakfast. She had somehow got six pork sausages from the butcher, and he watched as she fried them in the pan. She would not look at him.

'Sausages,' he said. 'Clever girl.'

'I got them under the counter.'

'What did you do to get those?'

'You're hardly one to ask me questions like that.'

'Did you get eggs as well?'

'Just count your blessings. Will she be waiting for you at the docks?'

'You can't get eggs in Turkey either.'

'You must be suffering. Do you want a divorce?'

The fat spat on her apron. They stared at each other.

'I've missed sausages. You don't get sausages in Istanbul. I'm getting quite tired of lamb with everything.'

'What's she like?'

'Tell me about this air force major.'

'There's nothing to tell.'

'No?'

'When we got married, it was for better or worse,' she said.

'I thought the priest meant the weather.' Lame joke. She put the sausages on a plate. They looked at each other again. 'I know what we said. But I was young and I thought I was never going to change and neither were you. I didn't know anything about life and even less about loving someone. I don't know what went wrong, Jen,' he said.

'You had an affair.'

'It's not as simple as that.'

'Isn't it?'

'You've been as unhappy as I have.'

'I think you're wrong there. The fact is, you're a selfish conniving bastard and you always have been.'

'Then why are you still married to me?'

'I don't have the foggiest idea. I might as well have been married to this . . . frying pan.'

'What's so hard about letting go of a frying pan, Jen? What's so much to hang on to?'

'We had a perfectly happy marriage until you picked up that tart.'

'You had a perfectly happy marriage.'

'I don't know you any more.'

'You never knew me. But that was my fault. I never told you anything.' And it was his fault. He had married her for all the wrong reasons, because she thought he was handsome and brilliant, because she made the perfect wife, because she was beautiful. He had stayed married for all the wrong reasons and because he never told her anything. How could she possibly understand him now?

'You make me sick.'

'Look. We can't go on like this.'

'I haven't even started yet,' she said and gave the sausages to the dog.

And two hours later they set out for Portsmouth.

Jennifer clung to him with a passion that day at the docks, and she did something he had never seen her do before in front of her sons: she wept.

'Please come back,' she whispered.

He couldn't make himself say the words.

'Please, Nick!' He tried to put his arms around her but she pushed him away. 'Promise me you'll come back!'

Richard hugged his mother. 'Of course he'll come back. You're coming back, aren't you, Dad?'

He looked at James and saw the hatred on his face. Jennifer looked up at him, her eyes bright with hate. 'I'll never let you go, Nick,' she said.

It was her benediction and her curse. And it echoed in his ears later as he leaned on the rail of the destroyer, the bitter winds of the North Atlantic howling at him, when all he wished for was a Nazi submarine to take away all his choices and absolve him of the guilt that had eaten at his soul. Because whether Daniela was still waiting in Istanbul or not, he knew he could not go back.

51.

Nick ate a breakfast of thick yellow yogurt and green figs and strong black coffee then he went out onto the patio to feed the birds. Every morning sparrows came to peck at the crumbs he left for them, specks of bread, morsels of fig. They were quick, nervous birds but one was a little more daring than the others. She would spend several minutes hovering and flapping in the bushes, working up her courage, and then she would come to peck a few crumbs from his fingertips, darting towards him, then as quickly retreating.

She reminded him of Daniela.

She sometimes complained to him that no man could ever understand her; at the same time she made herself so remote that no man ever could. It seemed to him that her self-imposed loneliness was a way of keeping the world at one remove from her. She would dash forward, peck hungrily at the crumbs of affection offered her, then as quickly fly away again.

That morning he waited longer than usual on the patio but the sparrow did not come. He wondered what had happened to her. It was a dangerous world beyond the garden walls, there were cats all over the city, looking for a quick and easy meal. Or perhaps she had simply flown away.

His brave sparrow never returned and he could only guess her fate.

An embassy driver came to pick him up in a black Humber, and he sat in the back seat, distracted by his own thoughts. The roads were choked with traffic; just ahead of them a silver-grey Rolls Royce of some rich spice merchant battled at the intersection with a pony cart, the farmer sitting on the running board, ignoring the urgent klaxon blare of the automobile horns around him. A donkey brayed and bucked and stamped while its owner slashed at it with his cane. Through the chaos, *hamals* laboured with handcarts loaded with sacks of coriander and turmeric and cumin for the bazaar.

Nick let the din wash over him, left the bedlam of Istanbul to his driver.

He stared at the soaring domes and minarets beyond the spice bazaar. His gaze settled on a woman walking arm in arm with a tall fair-haired man, scattering the pigeons gathered around the steps of the mosque. Her hair was hidden beneath a jade-green silk headscarf. He could not mistake that walk, that certain poise.

Twisting around in the seat, he saw them hurry past the blind and the beggared, ignoring the imprecations to buy razor blades and cigarettes. They disappeared into the warren of streets behind the *han*.

He shouted at his driver to stop the car and jumped out. The air was rich with the smell of spice from the Misir Carsisi. He caught another glimpse of her and started to run, pushing his way through the early morning crush, attracting the curses of beggars and sack-laden *hamals*.

Turks stared in wonderment at the wide-eyed English-man running through the souk shouting a woman's name. Didn't he know that the day was long and there were hours enough for the busiest of men?

He stood breathless in the crowded street, staring at a thousand bobbing heads, searching for the jade-green headscarf. The wail of the muezzin began calling the faithful to morning prayer. Beggars pulled at his sleeve. He could not see her. She was gone.

52.

The whole city lay breathless and steaming under the August sun. On his way to Max's Taksim apartment at midday, Nick clung to the shade of buildings like a man evading snipers. The heat had drained the city of its energy. Tempers were short.

Max was drinking more than was good for him. He sat in his shirtsleeves on the balcony drinking *raki*, and in the harsh summer light Nick noticed the spiderweb of broken capillaries on his nose and cheeks.

They talked about the war. The tide had turned after the German rout at Stalingrad just after Christmas. In recent weeks Allied troops had landed in Sicily and had captured Palermo. There were no more editorials in *Cumhurriyet* speculating on Germany's intentions towards Turkey.

'How's life on your side of the fence, old sport?'

'I'm okay.'

'Don't look it. Look bloody miserable.'

'Got a lot on my mind.'

'Cloak and dagger or matters of the heart?'

Nick added water to his *raki*. 'I can't talk to you about the cloak and dagger, Max.'

'Better talk to me about the other, then. Heard from Jennifer?'

Nick nodded. 'She's okay.'

'Forgiven you?'

'I didn't ask her to. It's finished, Max.'

'Don't be too hasty, sport. Just a bit of fun. If you can't have fun during a war, what can you do?'

'Who said infidelity was fun?'

'Not sure, probably a man, I imagine.' He grinned. It was common knowledge he had been having an affair with a Hungarian nightclub singer called Adrienne Varga for the last six months.

'I'm trying to keep this whole thing quiet, Max.'

'Of course. Understand completely. But it's a bit late, I'm afraid. Shutting the stable door after a dozen squadrons of cavalry have bolted and all the horses have died of old age.' He downed his *raki* and poured himself another. 'Spying for you, is she?'

'What do you think?'

'Hell yes, she's spying for you. Keep that to myself. Cross my heart. Naturally. Don't want to hurt the war effort. Absolutely.'

Nick said nothing.

'Hitler's finished, of course.'

'Not yet.'

'Writing's on the wall in bloody big capital letters. Stalingrad was what did it. Russians did for Napoleon, they'll do for him.'

'He'll keep fighting till the end, Max.'

'But will his generals?'

Well, that was the question, Nick thought. And if they didn't fight, what would happen? It was something he was hoping Daniela would find out for him.

'How's your love life?' Nick said.

'Thing about women, sport, is not to fall in love with them. That's the ticket. Word of warning for you there, old son. Fall in love and you just make a fool of yourself, no

255

good for anyone. Max King's first law of romance.'

'Thanks,' he said.

'Advice is free round here. How is the lovely Daniela, by the way?'

'I love her but I don't know if I can trust her.'

'Well, sport, you've just summed up the history of men and women in one sentence. Well done. Another drink?'

Cats scuttled from his approach as he trod warily on steep stairs, his nostrils quivering at the taint of sewage and rotting fruit. The hill led down to the docks and the fisherman's quarter, age-blackened stone tenements and rotting wooden houses leaning drunkenly into the street. He stepped over rags and melon rinds, even a severed donkey's leg.

He found a grim doorway and stepped inside, taking a deep breath against the stink of garbage from under the stairwell. He waited for his eyes to grow accustomed to the gloom and then climbed the stairs to the second-floor landing. He knocked on the door to one of the apartments.

He stood there waiting for Constantin to answer his knock, then hammered on the door a second time.

'Constantin! It's me! Open the door!'

When Constantin finally appeared, Nick was assailed by the smell of liquor on his breath. He doubted he had shaved or bathed for days.

'You'd better come in,' Constantin said and stood aside.

A squalid flat, one room and a kitchen. Nick's foot kicked an empty *raki* bottle that lay on the bare floor, and it rolled away under the table.

'When is it?' Constantin said.

'Friday.'

'Dobruja, yes?'

'Dobruja.'

'Dobruja,' he repeated.

Constantin had been born in Dobruja, had fished there all his life. He had fled in 1941, after the Germans came. He had been at sea when the Germans rounded up all the Jews in his village and machine gunned them in a field. He fled to Turkey in his fishing boat, the *Natalia*, and was sheltered by a cousin who lived in Galata.

It was two months later that Constantin discovered that his wife and sons had survived and were hiding in the woods outside his village. Constantin was preparing to sail his boat back to Dobruja and get them when his best friend from the village found him down at the quay at Galata. They had cried and hugged each other right there on the docks, and after they embraced, his friend told him he had some bad news, the worst news. His family had been captured and sent to a concentration camp in Poland.

Ever since, Constantin had been tormented with self-reproach. He was one of Nick's first and easiest recruits; all he wanted, all he lived for, was to do something, anything, to help beat the Nazis.

Nick gave Constantin some money for his expenses and for his trouble, knowing he would only use it to buy *raki*. Constantin needed something to dull the pain.

'Till Friday, then.' Nick said.

'Friday,' Constantin said and shut the door behind him.

Nick hurried away. He did not like to be around Constantin. Guilt clings to those who survive, he thought, it stains like blood. Constantin had snatched too quickly at his own salvation, only to find it a bitter gift indeed. Now all he desired was what he had once feared above anything: his own death.

Omar Kalmaz had the wasted look of the opium habitué; each time Nick saw him, he seemed to have fallen a little further into the wastrel's hell. His cheeks had hollowed and there was a rheumy vacancy about the eyes.

He was not much older than Nick but his bush of hair had already gone to grey and he had a sad walrus moustache that obscured much of the lower half of his face. His cheeks were so deeply lined that Nick sometimes imagined he could see dust settled in the creases. But he could still appear a handsome, even an imposing man, when he was away from the pipe.

There was something sad and discomfiting about addiction; and Omar's addiction had him by the throat. An opium addict was perhaps not the best or brightest choice for recruitment as an agent; Nick had inherited him from his predecessor in Istanbul. At first Omar had proved valuable, and even until recently had been able to keep the demon of his addiction under control. His contacts inside the Turkish Defence Ministry and the Emniyet, the Turkish secret police, were impeccable. Abrams even suspected the Emniyet may have planted him to feed information they could not pass on through normal diplomatic channels.

Omar had fallen naturally into the hands of his spymasters; his business interests often took him to Bucharest, where he exported carpets, copperware and leather. He met routinely with a Romanian trade official from the Interior Ministry who also happened to be the nephew of Ion Popescu, the leader of the liberal opposition in Romania and still an influential voice in the government.

As one of Antonescu's senior ministers, Popescu received regular reports from the Romanian Ambassador in Vichy France, including reports on troop movements and armaments factories there. For the last year Popescu had been passing copies of these to Nick through Omar, who brought them back to Istanbul in the false bottom of his briefcase. These reports found their way, along with Daniela's, to Air Marshall Harris and British Bomber Command.

Omar passed him a brown manila envelope, and Nick exchanged it for another, containing a considerable amount of money in pounds sterling.

'I have a message for you,' he said. 'Popescu Bey asked me to pass this on to you, and to you only.'

'Go on.'

'He wishes to start a dialogue. About the possibility of a truce.'

Well. The writing was indeed on the wall, and in bloody big capital letters, as Max had said. Hard to believe that just two summers before, the Nazis had seemed irresistible.

'There is something else. Popescu Bey is unhappy. He says you are supporting the communists. This fellow Romanescu.'

'It's one of the few resistance movements inside the country. Their politics don't matter to us for now.'

'He says the communists want to take over the country.'

'They are eager to help us defeat the Germans. That's our first priority.'

'I think he is willing to work with you. But these Bolsheviks make him nervous.'

'When do you return to Bucharest?'

'Within the month.'

'I'll try and get an answer by then.'

'Go with God, *effendim*.'

'And you also, Omar Bey.'

As he returned to the consulate, he closed his eyes, tried to shut out the din of hawkers and taxis on the Galata Bridge, and wondered if those pompous bastards in Whitehall might yet listen to reason, save not only themselves but the Romanians and, yes, the Germans as well, from Hitler and Stalin and the rest of this bloody madness.

Perhaps Abrams was right. It was Stalin they should be worrying about now.

53.

A hawk wheeled and dipped on the wind like a scrap of paper, watching the tiny specks below play out the dramas of their short lives. Through the shadow of a golden eye it saw Nick turn down an alleyway and go into the coffee house.

As it circled, it saw, too, the woman in the jade-green silk scarf who had followed him down the *soguk*. The golden eyes blinked again and then with a delicate tip of its wings it soared away, its eye attuned to other lives, other small dramas of the great city.

The wailing lament of the Turkish music on the radio irritated Nick today more than it ever had. The black dog on him again. He stood up as she entered and held her chair for her. She sat down and he helped her light her cigarette.

A waiter brought two small cups of Turkish coffee, the colour and consistency of steaming mud.

'What's wrong?' she asked him finally.

He did not answer.

'You might as well tell me. I know there's something. It's on your face.'

He took a breath. 'I saw you yesterday. Outside the spice market.' When she did not respond, he said: 'You were with a man.'

'What were you doing there?' she said, as if he was the one who should explain.

'I was on my way to work.'

'You don't often go that way.'

'You don't often walk arm in arm with other men. Do you?'

She stared hard at him, eyes ablaze. 'How dare you?' she whispered. 'Don't you still have a wife and children? Didn't you make love to her when you went back to England? Did you hold her, kiss her? Have I made any promises to you that make you think you own me?'

He leaned in. 'Just tell me who he is.'

A long silence. Then: 'His name's Grigoriev.'

'Who is he?'

'He works for the NKVD. For the Russians.'

Nick felt the blood drain out of his face.

'Don't look at me like that. You don't know what it's like for me, Nick. You don't live in my world.'

'Did you sleep with him?'

'No. I didn't sleep with him.'

'What were you doing?'

'Siggi asked me to be nice to him.'

'Like you were nice to me?'

She didn't answer.

'Did you sleep with him?' he asked her again.

She wanted to scream at him. How could any man be so blind?

'No.' She could see that he did not believe her. She leaned forward, her voice no more than a whisper. 'I've never lied to you. Everything I've said to you is true. Everything.'

What to make of this? There were so many women

inside Daniela Simonici. It was why she was the perfect spy, he thought; she could be so many people and make them all real and keep them separate.

'If you don't believe me, there's nothing I can do.'

He shrugged his shoulders, genuinely bewildered. She stubbed out the cigarette and left the café without saying another word.

When she turned the corner, she stopped and leaned against the wall. The grief welled up from some place deep in her soul. She started to shake. It was as if someone was shaking her by the shoulders and wouldn't stop. He would never understand her, no-one would ever understand her. She was alone and she always would be.

He found her leaning against the wall, sobbing. He put his arms around her, tried to hold her and she beat at him with her fists. He let her. 'I'm sorry,' he said. 'I'm sorry.'

A tram went past, the cobblestones vibrating with a continuous groan as it battled up the hill. Faces stared at them in astonishment from the windows.

'What is wrong with you?' she said.

'I don't know. I didn't mean to hurt you.'

'Get away from me!' she shouted again but instead of running away she fell against him.

A mist of rain spiralled from an indifferent sky. Finally, she subsided, and he stood there, holding her, found himself staring at the crumbling faience on the wall of a nearby mosque, the beautiful and ancient script a cipher, like a code that had the answers for him if only he knew how to read it.

She turned her face up to him and kissed him, her cheeks wet with tears.

He works for the NKVD. For the Russians. Siggi asked me to seduce him.

A room full of mirrors. Each time he turned, there was a different reflection, the truth never constant.

54.

The coast was a thin dark line, sensed rather than seen. The sea like steel. Constantin cut the engines and let the tide bring the *Natalia* into shore. He knew this stretch of coast from memory and from some seaman's sense that divined depth and distance without charts or lead line. Nick heard the rattle of the anchor, felt the pull of the tide as the *Natalia* swung around on the swell.

'There,' Constantin said. A torch flashed on and off three times on the beach. It was the signal.

They loaded the radio and the explosives into the rubber boat they had towed from Istanbul. Constantin's two deckhands clambered down into the boat, Jordon followed, then Deakin the radio operator, then Nick.

They started to row towards the shore.

'Something's wrong,' Jordon whispered.

The only sound was the rhythmic beat of the surf, a phosphorescent strip in the darkness.

'What is it?'

'I don't know,' Jordon whispered. 'Just a feeling in my bones.'

They jumped out into a heavy surf, there were treacherous rocks underfoot, and Nick went down. He came up choking, then helped Jordon drag the boat up the shore.

Deakin and one of the deckhands carried the precious radio up the beach, making sure it stayed dry, while his companion held the boat steady in the surf.

A dark and silent beach. They looked for the torches. Nothing. Where was Romanescu? Jordon had a Sten strapped across his shoulder. He unslung it, and loaded a magazine.

'What are you doing?'

'Getting ready for trouble,' he said and at that moment a searchlight snapped on and blinded them both.

Jordon was first to react, fired off a burst from the Sten that shattered the searchlight – Nick guessed it was mounted on the back of a truck parked near the beach road – and they were plunged again into darkness. There was an answering stutter of small arms fire from further up the beach. Nick heard bullets zip past, inches from his face, and he dropped onto the wet sand, his guts turned to water.

Jordon gave a strangled cry. Nick reached out a hand, found Jordon's head, or what was left of it, just warm porridge now. He heard Deakin screaming but he could not see him or the others in the dark, his night vision ruined by the searchlight. He crawled back into the sea.

He couldn't see the rubber boat, but the *Natalia* was silhouetted against a velveteen sky. He started to swim, struck out through the surf, arms windmilling desperately.

He was aware only of the pounding surf and the sound of his own breathing. Panic owned him.

'Give me your hand!' Constantin shouted. The old fisherman grabbed Nick's wrist and helped him haul himself up the rope ladder at the stern, where he threw himself on the deck, coughing, gasping in air. He could hear it again now, gunfire coming from the beach, heard the susurration of the bullets as they zipped overhead, the crack of splintering wood as another volley slammed into the wheelhouse timbers.

'Where are the others?' Constantin shouted.

'I don't know,' Nick gasped. 'Jordon's dead.'

Nick hauled himself to his knees, saw the winking of gunfire in the darkness. The windows shattered in the wheelhouse and Constantin cried out in pain.

'Constantin?'

'I'm all right!' The engine stuttered to life and he turned the stern around, throttling towards the open sea.

Another volley of machine gun fire, and the radio mast splintered like a match, then the wheelhouse seemed to explode. Nick gasped as wood splinters embedded themselves in his cheek and eye.

Exhausted from the swim, he dragged himself forward on his knees. Constantin was hunched over the wheel but Nick could not see how badly he was wounded. He felt his own blood leaking off his chin.

'Are you all right?' he said but Constantin did not answer.

Clouds black as ink loomed in the north, the last stars fading. Constantin lay slumped in a corner of the wheelhouse, bled out an hour ago.

Nick stood at the wheel and steered for the Black Sea shore, knowing he could not navigate the minefields at the mouth of the Bosphorus. He would find anchorage at a fishing village perhaps, or at worst, if he beached her, he could swim for the near shore. Constantin looked peaceful in death; back with his family, his dearest wish. And so Nick was alone in that last hour before he ran her onto the beach; alone to contemplate how he had been betrayed.

55.

'You're recovered from your ordeal?' Abrams said. Nick gingerly touched the cuts on his face above his eye where the wood splinters from the wheelhouse had embedded themselves. 'No damage,' he said. Once again he had cheated his death. Constantin, Jordon, Deakin, and two men who had gone into battle with him and whose names he did not even know, were now dead on the beach in Dobruja. A Turkish patrol boat had rescued him from the Black Sea village where he had beached the *Natalia*.

'The Germans must have been tipped off,' Donaldson said. 'We have to assume Romanescu's entire cell is either dead or under arrest.'

There was a long and embarrassed silence.

Abrams was frowning as if he had found an unmentionable stain on one of the carpets. He was a chess player, not a gladiator, he enjoyed the mental combats, the cerebral challenges of the game they played. The spilling of actual blood upset him.

'What about this Constantin?'

Nick shook his head. 'His whole family were murdered by the Germans, for Christ's sake.'

That sounded testy and not a little insubordinate.

Donaldson fidgeted in his chair. Abrams's cheeks flushed bronze.

'I'm sorry, sir, but he really is beyond suspicion in my book.'

'What about the crewmen?'

'He didn't tell either of his crew where he was going until they were in deep waters.'

Donaldson sighed. 'Well, the only other people who knew about this operation are sitting in this room.'

'Has to be a local problem,' Abrams said.

'That's what I told de Chastelain,' Donaldson said, 'one of Romanescu's people. But there's no way we can find out now.'

Nick felt a stab of unease. Sometimes he took files home to read at night, despite the breach of security protocols, and now he remembered that the maps and paperwork for Operation Cicero were on his desk one night when he had fallen asleep and Daniela had been there, free for God knows how long to wander around his house and look at whatever she pleased.

Abrams's gaze was unsettling. It was as if he knew; Nick battled with himself. Had she betrayed him? Had Daniela Simonici cost Jordon and Constantin and the others their lives?

Had she been willing to send him to his death?

A part of him refused to believe it. And yet.

How could he ever be sure?

He thought about the family photograph that Jordon had showed him in Taksim, remembered the gap-toothed smile, the unlit pipe clenched between his teeth, how he had talked so frankly of betrayal.

If I tell Abrams my suspicions, my career is over. And what will it achieve if Abrams is right, if the operation was betrayed by one of Romanescu's own people? I cannot believe she would do this.

'You know Jordon's the only real loss here,' Abrams said. 'Those Romanian guerrillas would have been a thorn in our side after this war is over. We're better off in the long run without them. We're going to win this war anyway. What we're fighting for is the peace.'

Nick wondered what they would think of Abrams's appraisal of the war effort in Whitehall. Or what Jordon's wife would say.

He looked out of the window at the roofs of Istanbul and worried at his conscience, wondered if Donaldson and Abrams worried theirs.

The last hour of the night, the darkest hour, when the madman shifts uneasily in the asylum ward, when the night owls call, and the lonely and tormented shift uneasily in their dreams, fending off the demons that come to haunt them.

Daniela was always tormented by the night, she would toss off the bedclothes and rave and mutter words he could not understand. Her dreams were full of men who waited for her in dark rooms and did unspeakable things, dreams of running away and running from, dreams of black shadows and nameless fears and apprehensions.

She said it had been this way as long as she could remember.

Yet sleeping with her, in the literal sense, was one of the things he enjoyed the most. There were not always these terrors. Sometimes she would sleep peacefully and deeply after they had made love, and these were the times he loved, having her nestled under his arm, her leg thrown carelessly across his thigh, the palm of her hand resting neatly in the curls of hair on his chest.

He watched her now as she slept, her naked body dark against the white cotton sheets. Her lips were slightly apart, in the shape of a heart, one arm raised above her head, dark hair trailing across the pillow. She murmured something in her sleep.

He smiled at the pleasure of just watching her, listening to the deep and even sound of her breathing.

Suddenly, unexpectedly, she opened her eyes. 'You're awake,' she murmured.

She licked her lips, and looked around the room, remembering where she was perhaps, who she was with. She stretched her whole body, as languorous as a cat. She let him run his hand along her flank, her breast, and gave him a smile of such delicious promise that he felt himself wanting her again.

'I didn't mean to wake you.'

'Liar.' She rolled towards him and kissed his shoulder. He thought about the night he had woken and she was not beside him in the bed, the night he had been careless and left the cables about Operation Cicero scattered on his desk.

'What's wrong, darling?' she whispered.

He shook his head. 'Nothing.' He stroked her shoulder.

She leaned up on one elbow. 'I feel so safe when you have your arms around me.' When he didn't answer, she looked into his face. 'There is something, isn't there?'

'No, of course not.'

'You can talk to me, Nick.'

'I told you, it's nothing. Just work.'

He rolled away from her and lay on his back, staring at the ceiling. It was steamy hot in the room and he threw off the sheet. Couldn't rest, couldn't sleep. He had to know the truth of this. But how?

He put on a dressing gown and went downstairs to the study. The door was unlocked, as always, and there were

272

papers scattered around on the desk. None of them were important. He never brought EYES ONLY papers home any more. He should never have taken them home that night either.

He went to the drinks cabinet and poured himself a large gin. He didn't want it; it was something to do, something to hold in his hands.

If you were in love with an actress, how could you ever know what was real? he wondered. Every sigh, every kiss, every laugh, every I love you, could be just another performance. Perhaps none of it was real. His desire for her could have been a longing for something that did not exist outside a brilliant disguise.

He looked out of the window. The rain had stopped and wraiths of vapour rose from the cobblestones. The air was breathless and still. He thought about the future, without Daniela Simonici, thought about what he would do when the war ended, thought about the beautiful young woman lying in his bed upstairs, and the shifting sands of the love affair that should never even have begun.

56.

The file on Trojan grew thicker each month. Occasionally there would be one roll of film, sometimes two. The quality of the photographs varied, often the focus would be off, and the results would be unreadable, or the pictures were blurred, where she moved her hand as she was taking the shot.

He gave her documents to copy out, always ensured that they were hurriedly done. There was an art to knowing the quality of information to give to Maier. Some of the information had to be true and verifiable, in order to make the lies seem authentic. They gave up double agents who had betrayed them; they forged coded messages from the SOE in Cairo hinting at an invasion of Greece, a feint for a real invasion being planned elsewhere; there were faked reports of Turkish intransigence towards British interests that, if accepted as genuine, might ease German pressure on Ankara.

Sometimes they met in a coffee house in Sultanahmet where foreigners never went. It was close to the old palace walls, in a cobbled street behind the Sancta Sofia. There were greasy marble-topped tables and chairs, and on the walls were faded photographs of Mustapha Kemal, the great Atatürk, and a copy of Bellini's painting of Mehmet the Conqueror. These pictures were everywhere in

Turkey, homage to the two men who had most shaped the Turkish nation in the last five hundred years.

He sat in a dark corner of their café, the lament of the Turkish music from the radio dulling his senses. He took off his jacket. The back of his shirt was soaked with sweat.

The other customers were working-class Turks with bad teeth and crumpled brown jackets who passed their days smoking hookahs, listening to the monotonous Arab music on the radio and playing endless games of backgammon. Most of them were unshaven, for no working-class Turk could afford a barber every day.

The coffee house might have appeared romantic if one had no sense of smell. But it was high summer and the city baked under the Mediterranean sun. The sour breath of street refuse hung in the air, the heat like a mist, a malevolent vapour that poisoned the lungs and sucked the moisture from the body. Flies swarmed in small black clouds around rotting melon rinds.

A bootblack, crouched by the door, banged his brush on the lid of his box and threw an accusing glance at Nick's muddy shoes. He nodded and the boy came over and crouched at his feet, taking his brushes and cloths and polishes from the wooden box.

As the boy cleaned his shoes, Nick watched two old men puffing away on their *narghiles*, their bad teeth and chalky coughs testament to entire lives spent in such establishments. Pigeons waddled undisturbed and unthreatened between their legs.

A taxi drew up outside and Daniela got out. She wore a jade-green scarf to hide her long dark hair from the stares of the Turkish men. But in a Moslem country a woman is a woman, and as she entered the café, the Turks undressed her with their eyes, their faces hungry and hard.

She sat down and a waiter in a greasy white jacket brought two glasses of apple tea.

They made desultory conversation. She knew straight away that there was something wrong. 'What is it?' she whispered.

He stared moodily into the street.

'What are you thinking?'

The silence went on interminably.

'Are you going to tell me what's wrong or are we just going to sit here like this all afternoon?'

He did not answer her.

'Why won't you tell me?'

'It's nothing.'

'Is it your wife?'

He shook his head.

Those eyes. They looked into his soul and told a million truths and a million lies.

Finally, she reached into her pocket and dropped a roll of film onto the table. 'I shan't stay if you won't talk to me.'

He wanted to say to her: Did you betray me? The words stuck in his throat. She got up and walked away. He did not go after her.

Instead he sat there, weighing the film in his hand, no longer sure of anything, not even his own instincts. How could he ever know the truth of this? How could he ever be sure?

57.

Early morning and Istanbul was coming alive. The roar of the traffic was muted in Donaldson's office. Outside in the courtyard a Turkish servant swept the patio with a broom.

'I wanted to talk to you about Trojan,' Donaldson said.

Nick stared at him. Did Donaldson now suspect her also?

'That last roll of film she supplied us.'

'Sir?'

'It was a gold mine.'

'I'm pleased.'

'The photographs are documents from Maier's recent trip to Germany. They give us the location of two rubber factories and three Messerschmitt assemblies that were recently moved to some abandoned textile plants about fifteen miles outside Vienna. We've passed the information on to Bomber Command in Whitehall. This is excellent work, Davis.'

'Thank you, sir.'

'She's probably our most important agent in Istanbul, perhaps in the Near East. Look after her, Davis.'

'I understand.'

Donaldson leaned forward. 'We have to protect her at all costs. I don't care what you have to do.'

Nick got up and left the room, the ground shifting beneath his feet. She loved him. She had not lied. This was his proof, wasn't it?

Wasn't it?

The mosque courtyard was shaded by plane trees. Pigeons flapped into the air as a latecomer ran across the flag-stones, then descended again to waddle and fuss around the fountain where the men washed their feet before prayer. A cripple crouched in the shade of the cloister sell-ing little trays of bird grain to those infidel visitors who wished to feed them.

He watched her make her way towards him across the baking stones, a jade-green scarf on her head, gold bracelet on her slender wrist. He could not read the language of her eyes.

They did not touch.

She reached up a hand to sweep a stray lock of hair from her forehead and hide it away beneath the scarf so that it would not arouse the lust of a Moslem in his holy devotions. There were fine golden hairs on the back of her wrist. For a moment he glimpsed her bare arm, and remembered how she liked him to kiss her there, his lips gently brushing the smooth, pale skin along her wrist and up to the intimate folds of her inner arm.

'I've missed you,' he said.

'Are you going to tell me what's going on?'

He shook his head. 'I can't.'

The woman he had always dreamed of. Come to prayer, God is great. God is great but what game is God playing here? He had brought him this wonderful woman and He has contrived their destinies so that they might be together, and by some miracle He had made her love him. God is great but He had brought her at the wrong time, while the world was at war and he was married to another woman.

They left their shoes under the cloister and stepped inside the mosque. Hundreds of oil lamps hung suspended from the roof, throwing an amber glow on the faience and into the great dome above.

'I love you,' she whispered. 'I know you don't believe it but the truth is here in my eyes.'

He stared at her. He often stole these moments from her, watching her as she watched others. She never understood why he did this. Sometimes she caught him staring at her as she was dressing, or in the act of brushing her hair, and he knew his gaze made her uneasy. It was not that she was the most beautiful woman in the world; just that she had become the most beautiful woman in the world to him.

'The truth is here in my eyes,' she said again, but when he looked there, he did not see the truth, only his own confusion.

Allahu akbar. God is great. Come to prayer.

BOOK FOUR

58.

Istanbul, November 1943

When Nick heard the voice on the other end of the telephone line, he felt a shiver of apprehension.

'It's Maier,' the voice said. There was no preamble, no banter prefixed with jokes about 'my Englisher friend'.

'Herr Maier. What can I do for you?'

'We must talk,' he said, and Nick thought it must be about Daniela. What can he possibly have to say to me? Nick thought. Is this about Daniela? Is it some kind of trap?

'Where do you want to meet, Herr Maier?' he said.

The *hamam*, the public steam bath, was a social occasion in Turkey, a place to go to relax and chat, the last place you would expect to be followed if you had to organise a clandestine meeting with an enemy intelligence officer.

Maier had named an establishment near the Hippodrome. Nick undressed in one of the cubicles, and wrapped a towel around his waist. An attendant led him to the hot room. Hairy, middle-aged men padded naked through the steam, wiping sweat from their faces. There was a sharp male tang to the place.

He sat down on a bench, feeling the sweat ooze out of his skin. He closed his eyes and allowed himself to relax. He wondered again why Maier had wanted to meet. Is it some new game he is planning? he wondered.

The *hamam* reminded Nick of a chiaroscuro of some classical Italian painter's vision of hell, blurred figures moving like wraiths through the steam, ordinary men with sagging bellies, made monstrous by the heat and vapours.

A figure lumbered towards him and sat himself down on the bench beside him without acknowledgment.

Nick knew Maier's body better than he knew any other man's; he knew, for instance, that he had a birthmark on his left hip and that there was a scar on his chest just below his collarbone. He had learned these things from Daniela and now he found this private knowledge disconcerting.

What else did he know about this intimate enemy? He knew he had a fondness for a glass of vodka before bed, that he slept on his back with his hands folded across his stomach and that he liked black olives. And here was Maier sitting beside him, as if they were total strangers.

He looked remarkably fit, his body hard and well muscled. Nick had imagined, even hoped, that he had run to fat. There was a little grey in his chest hair, but he was powerfully built, a formidable rival.

'My Englisher friend.'

'Herr Maier.'

Maier was changed somehow, his arrogance had gone, as had the gloating smile Nick had come to detest in the foyer of the Athenee Palace Hotel. It had been replaced with something raw and desperate. He wiped a hand across his chest and flicked away the sweat with a casual sweep of his hand.

Nick wondered if Maier had ever made the mistake, as he had done, of falling in love with a girl he was using for his country's purpose.

In a nearby cubicle he heard a masseur pummelling away at soft flesh.

'We have spoken to each other in public before, Herr Maier. Why here?'

'The SD are watching me.' The SD, the Sicherheitdienst, was the overseas branch of the Gestapo. They hated the Abwehr more than all the Allied intelligence services put together.

He kept silent, waited.

'Did you hear the one about Goering? He and his wife give a party. After dinner everyone retires to the drawing room and then Frau Goering realises her husband is missing. She hears this terrible crash from the dining room. She goes in and there is Goering trying to pull the Viennese chandelier off the ceiling. "Hermann!" she shouts. "What are you doing? I told you to leave that alone, you have enough decorations without it!" '

He laughed at his own joke and Nick laughed with him. There were times he found it hard to hate him as much as he would like.

'You don't like the Nazis any more, Herr Maier?'

'I never did,' he said and the smile died on his lips. 'Today I am just a courier, a messenger, Herr Davis. I have very influential friends here and in Berlin. You know this, don't you?'

Nick said nothing.

'What I am about to say is highly sensitive. I will trust you to keep it in your confidence and find someone inside the consulate with whom you can trust this information. My life and the lives of many others depend on it.'

'Of course.'

'Perhaps the lives of millions.'

Millions? Nick wondered where they were headed with this. He supposed they would continue to play their little game with each other: Maier would pretend he did not know that Nick was with SIS; Nick would pretend not to know Maier was a colonel in the Abwehr.

'Naturally, I will treat anything you tell me with the utmost confidence, Herr Maier.'

Maier wiped perspiration from his eyes. 'You know our Führer prides himself on his benevolence. That is the reason Germany took Romania and Bulgaria and Hungary under her protection. Your Churchill didn't understand that.'

'I have a little difficulty myself discerning the difference between protection and invasion.'

Instead of launching into a defence of Nazi policy, Maier surprised him by telling him another joke. 'Hitler, Churchill and Roosevelt are at a peace conference. They have been talking for a long time and they start to get hungry. On the mantelpiece there is a goldfish in a bowl and they talk about how they might catch the fish and eat him. So Churchill makes a noose out of his watch chain and tries to catch the fish, but it doesn't work. So Roosevelt catches a fly and lowers it into the fishbowl on the end of a piece of string as bait, but the little fish ignores it. So finally it's Hitler's turn. He patiently ladles all the water out of the bowl with a teaspoon until the little fish is just lying at the bottom of the bowl gasping and flapping.

' "Well hurry up then, Adolf," Churchill says, "now you fry him!"

' "Oh," Hitler says, "I won't do that unless he asks me to!" '

'You want to talk to me about Hitler?' Nick asked.

'I want to talk to you about peace conferences.'

'Herr Maier?'

'What do you know about Admiral Canaris?'

'I know he is head of the Abwehr. That he is well connected and well bred.'

'And a patriot like myself. Our families know each other well. We love our country but that does not mean we also love the Nazis. That is not the same thing.'

'Why are you telling me this?'

'We are going to lose this war, Herr Davis. Not today, not tomorrow, but we will lose it, there is nothing more certain. And when we do, the Russians will send in their tanks and their commissars and then what will happen to Germany? While I was in Berlin I spoke to a number of well-connected and patriotic Germans who wish to start a dialogue with the Allies. Admiral Canaris himself asked me to make an approach.'

Nick remembered the papers Daniela had stolen from Maier's safe. So they were genuine, after all. He tried to keep the excitement from his voice. 'You are the conduit to Admiral Canaris?'

'Initially, yes.'

'Who else?'

'He has asked me not to furnish you with any further details unless you provide him with proof that someone in the British and US governments is willing to negotiate with him.'

It was hard to sit there with sweat dripping off his nose and remain the cool and composed intelligence officer he was trained to be.

'There seems little point in negotiating with Admiral Canaris if he has no power to change the course of the war.'

'Hitler cannot cling to power in Germany for ever, Herr Davis.'

Nick raised an eyebrow.

'I cannot say more than this.'

'You can try, can't you?'

'We have plans. In order to recruit others, we must have assurances that ridding ourselves of Hitler will have tangible and immediate benefits.'

'All right. I will pass on your message, Herr Maier.'

'Thank you.' Maier hesitated, struggling with what he was about to say. 'You know, I am not a traitor, Herr Davis. I love my country. That is why I am doing this.' Nick saw a mirror image of himself, a man wrestling with his conscience, his duty, his heart. For just a moment he was not a rival, but a fellow penitent.

But the moment passed quickly, to his relief.

Maier stood up. 'I will wait to hear from you.'

As he turned to go, Nick said: 'How is your Romanian mistress?' It was mischievous, and he heard jealousy and anger in his own voice.

A look. Maier gathered himself, reconstructing his fictions so he would not be caught out. By the rules of the game, Nick was not supposed to know that his mistress came to his bed under Maier's bidding; by the same rules, Maier was not supposed to know that Nick was sleeping with her. 'You remember her?'

'From the train.'

'The train,' he said, his face blank. Trying to recollect a lie is much harder than remembering the truth. The etiquette of deception can be demanding. 'I remember now. There was a commotion. I was told you left the train unexpectedly.'

'I got off in Istanbul, as planned.'

'I was misinformed, then.'

'Apparently.' The heat was making him feel faint. He would have to get out of this room very soon. 'You are still with her?'

'Who?'

'The Romanian. What was her name?'

'Daniela. Yes, she is installed in my house in Taksim. She is exhausting. I go home to my wife in Berlin every few months for a rest.'

Maier smiled, taunting him. Nick felt his gut tighten like a fist.

'When the war is over,' Maier said, 'I should not be surprised if we became friends.'

'Perhaps,' Nick answered, his face a mask.

Friends. He would rather cut out his liver with a garden trowel. There was never a time in his life when he so badly hated a man as much he hated Maier just then.

Maier wrapped the towel tighter around his midriff.

'I should like to see this war end,' he said. 'I was never enthusiastic.'

'You seemed enthusiastic enough in Romania.'

'Well, we were winning then. Good luck. I hope you have good news very soon for the Admiral.' And he disappeared into the steam.

59.

Lieutenant General Leonid Feoderev got out of the taxi-cab, and walked past the doorman into the lobby of the hotel. He was watched the whole time, of course, by the Emniyet, the SIS, by his own GRU. But he expected this. He checked into a room at Askatliyan's at the woman's suggestion.

He noted the Turk in the dark brown suit seated in a chair in the foyer, smoking and pretending to read *Cumhurriyet*; then he saw a tall, fair-haired man follow him in off the street and then walk into the dining room, even though it was not yet twelve o'clock. He wondered which of them it was, perhaps both.

He signed his name in the register and went up to the room in a creaking iron lift. The room was shabby and smelled of dust and tobacco. He sat down in a chair by the window to wait. He took out his cigarettes.

She was late.

He heard a tapping at the door and he got up quickly to answer it. There was a woman, dark-haired, beautiful.

'Daniela Simonici?'

She nodded and moved past him into the room. She was holding a black leather briefcase.

'Is that it?' he asked her.

She did not answer. Instead she took off her coat and snapped the locks on the case. 'Shall we start?' she said.

Dear Nick,
I am writing this from Aunt Sarah's house in Newquay. She invited us down to spend the Christmas holidays with her. Life is much quieter here than it was in Surrey. You never hear an air raid siren. There is almost no damage here at all.

Everything is rationed but down here things are easier. In London we were only allowed one egg a week but Aunt Sarah has chickens in the backyard and now we eat as many eggs as we like. It is just heaven . . .

He skimmed the page.

The boys are doing well and send their love. James is shaving now and makes quite a performance of it in the morning—if he cuts himself he wears the nick on his chin like a badge of honour and taunts Richard about it. I am worried that their schooling has suffered through the war; at least they are not yet old enough to be part of it and please God it will be over by the time they are of the age.

You have missed so much of their lives. I try to explain to them what it is you do, but of course I cannot tell them the whole truth, and they think that working in the diplomatic service is not as glamorous as being a fighter pilot.

The war has robbed so many families of so much. There are two women in Aunt Sarah's street who have lost sons to the war, one was in the merchant navy, the

other was a navigator in the air force. I feel guilty hav-
ing two healthy sons of my own. I know that it's silly to
feel that way, but I cannot help it.

I check the newspapers every day for news of what
is happening in Turkey and the Balkans. But most of the
news is about the war in the desert, of course, and the
second front. Is there enough to eat in Istanbul still?

Darling, I know we have had our ups and downs and
sometimes you think me a hard woman but I have always
loved you. I am ready to forgive you. I think we owe this
to ourselves and to Jamie and Richard. Marriage is never
easy, after all. I am prepared to bury the past if you are.

Keep safe. Love, Jennifer

He put down the letter and went for a walk. Winter was
drawing in, the sky overcast, a mist of rain falling. That
England might one day beckon him back seemed an impos-
sibly surreal idea; under the crowding domes of Asia it
seemed a place that existed only in the imagination. He
wanted to stay for ever in Istanbul, as if that other world
did not exist outside of this charmed city.

Above him the mosque of Süleyman loomed over the
old city, the great grey dome flanked by other smaller
domes, like a mother with her brood. The fruit market
spilled into the streets at its feet, between the bazaars of the
old city and the warehouses of the Golden Horn.

Under the arcades professional letter-writers sat at
rickety tables, transcribing letters for their patrons. The
younger men clattered away at big Remington typewriters,
while the older scribes used old-fashioned quills and wrote
in traditional Arabic. They looked careworn and exhausted

by the daily outpouring of human emotions, like priests and doctors. Here was a girl sending a letter to her boyfriend in the army; there, an old father writing to his son in some far-away province.

He imagined how Jennifer might look sitting at one of these tables, relating her letter to an unfaithful husband in some faraway country. He imagined the expression on the scribe's face; theirs would not be a new story to him, or to history.

He could not know how this story would end now for him, or for her.

Insh'allah, any good Moslem would have said.

As God wills.

'I received a coded dispatch from London this morning,' Abrams said.

'About Maier?'

Abrams nodded slowly and Nick knew immediately that it was not good news.

'We are not to pursue any further solicitation from Admiral Canaris's representatives here in Istanbul.'

'Why?'

'Apparently we don't want to upset the Russians.'

He pushed a file across the desk. It was the file on Siegfried Maier and it was as thick as an encyclopaedia. Nick opened it and read the top cable. A coded EYES ONLY dispatch from the Foreign Office in London confirmed what Abrams had just told him.

'Of course, the Russians are going to betray us,' Abrams said.

'I don't understand.'

'There's nothing to understand. They would rather trust Stalin. That's it. They can't see further than the end of the war.' Abrams was white-lipped with anger. It was clear how he felt about this. 'Bow to the greater wisdom, Davis.'

Nick closed the file.

As he got up, Abrams said, 'Tell him I want to meet him.'

'Sir?'

'Maier. I want to meet him. In person. Arrange it.'

'Considering this cable, sir, may I ask why?'

'It's on a need-to-know basis, Davis. And right now you don't need to know.'

Nick hesitated. Abrams's eyes were impenetrable. 'Yes, sir,' he said and left.

60.

He fetched a driver from the car pool and signed out a big Ford. They drove down Istiklal Boulevard, just on evening, the dusk clamorous with the rattle of trolley buses and the cries of *halwa* vendors and newspaper boys. They turned off the main boulevard, and Nick checked to make sure they were not followed. He saw Maier waiting on the corner, as agreed; his driver slowed down and Maier jumped in.

He was nervous and breathing hard. No doubt the surveillance by the SD was playing on his nerves.

'I can tell by your face it is not good news,' he said.

Nick shrugged and shook his head.

'Why?'

'There's nothing I can do about it. My hands are tied.'

Maier rubbed his forehead with his thumb. 'Don't you people want the war to end?'

'Some of us do.'

'Let me guess, Herr Davis. Churchill doesn't want to upset the Russians.'

'I don't know the reason. Over my head.' Even now they maintained these fictions with each other.

Maier closed his eyes and sighed. Nick felt suddenly sorry for him, something he thought he should never do. 'They are drinking mashed acorns at home and calling it coffee. My family has lost their house in Frankfurt to British bombs. My oldest cousin died in the Russian winter.'

Nick remembered that Maier had not been as concerned about the fate of British people suffering under the Luftwaffe's bombs when he had first met him in Bucharest. But that was human nature. People only understand misery when they have experienced it themselves.

'Hitler is a madman. He is going to ruin my country.'

'I agree.'

Their eyes met. They both knew what the other was thinking and it was not about the war. Maier had sent Daniela Simonici to another man to help his beloved country win the war; now the war seemed futile and he thought the sacrifice too great.

'Someone at the consulate would like to meet with you in person.'

Maier looked surprised at that. 'Who is this man?'

'The Chief Passport Officer, Abrams.'

'Of course. He is your boss, Herr Davis?'

'It's on a need-to-know basis. You don't need to know.'

Maier laughed and shook his head. 'What does he wish to discuss that we cannot talk about here?'

'I don't know.'

'Ah, I see. You are also on a need-to-know basis.' He laughed again. 'Very well. You will arrange it?'

'I will arrange it.'

Nick told the driver to turn the car around and they headed back along Cumhurriyet Caddesi into Taksim. Maier made some desultory comments about the weather. Nick told him again he would be in touch and that he was sorry he had not been of more use to him and his friends in Berlin.

Maier jumped out of the car in a quiet street near the casino and the war went on.

61.

Nick drove slowly down the cobbled *soguk*, the Street of the Lady. Maier appeared from the shadows of a doorway and jumped in the back next to Abrams.

'Drive,' Abrams said.

Nick coasted to the foot of the street and then turned right towards Taksim. At this time of the night there was little traffic and he checked in the mirror that he was not being followed. He drove across the Galata Bridge and headed towards Seraglio Point.

He eventually parked the Humber in a quiet street below the Sancta Sofia.

'Enjoy your walk,' Abrams said.

Nick got out of the car. He went back up the hill, following the walls to the gateway of the old palace. A cool night, but fine, a crescent moon scurrying across the sky between ink-black clouds. He saw the glow of cigarettes in the back of the Humber as the two men talked. He wondered what the hell this was about.

He enjoyed his own secrets; he did not enjoy the secrets of others.

Looking up, he saw the niches high in the old palace walls where the Sultans had left the heads of traitors to blacken and rot in the sun. They knew how to deal with malcontents then.

He smoked a cigarette, then another. He looked at his watch. Twenty minutes.

One blast on the car horn. His signal that they were finished.

He went back to the car and got in behind the wheel. He glanced in the rear vision mirror, adjusted it so that he could get a look at Maier's face but the German was inscrutable. They drove in silence back across the bridge. Nick stopped the car in the Street of the Lady and Maier jumped out. They drove back to the consulate.

'Everything okay?' he asked Abrams.

'Everything went swimmingly,' Abrams said. When they got back to the consulate, instead of going home Abrams went back to his office. Christ. It was past midnight.

Nick returned the car and took a taxicab home.

Donaldson did not look fit. He was short and round, a pot belly sagged over the waistband of his shorts, and when he appeared on the mildewed squash court the consulate maintained for its staff in the basement, Nick almost laughed. But when they started playing, he quickly realised he had underestimated him. After fifteen minutes Nick was doubled over and labouring for breath, while Donaldson had barely broken sweat. He had taken up residence on the apex of the T and mercilessly ran Nick from one side of the court to the other.

While Nick caught his breath, Donaldson good-naturedly bounced the squash ball on his racquet. 'How are things, Davis?'

'Good, sir.'

'Happy with your work?'

'Yes, sir.'

'Get on with Abrams?'

'Absolutely.'

He had thought it just another innocent enquiry until he saw the expression on Donaldson's face.

'Bit of a queer fish, though, isn't he?' Donaldson said.

Nick did not know how to answer.

'Jewish.'

'A man's religion is his own affair, sir.'

'Nonsense. Be careful of him, Davis.'

'Sir?'

'Just be careful. He has some unfortunate friends.'

'How do you mean, sir?'

Donaldson handed him the ball. 'Your serve, I think. I was lucky those first two games. I think you've got my measure now.'

But Donaldson thrashed him again, fifteen to three, then shook his hand and they walked off the court. Nothing else was said.

62.

Ten miles east of Moscow

Lieutenant General Leonid Feoderev stood at the window of his study and stared at the birch trees, lost to his own thoughts. It was cold in the house, he had not lit the fire since his return from the front, and he could see his breath misting on the air. There was a thin film of ice on the inside of the windows.

But personal comforts no longer concerned him. He was accustomed to the cold. Much worse than this at Stalingrad; cold, hunger and exhaustion had been such a part of his life that he almost missed them now.

It was different when his wife was still alive. He had enjoyed his ease then. But since Natasha had died he found he had reverted to living like a soldier even when he was away from the battle lines. Hard to really care about anything any more.

The dacha had been empty for months, there was dust on everything. He had dismissed the servants after the funeral.

The curtains to the living room were drawn. He patrolled the room for a while, seeking out its ghosts. There was an upright pianoforte and he lifted the lid and touched several notes. He could not play; that was Natasha. He had loved to listen to her. Even now, when he closed his eyes, he could hear the haunting sounds of *Für Elise* and see her lips pursed in concentration as she read the sheet music, her long sensitive fingers dancing over the yellowed ivory keys.

There was a wind-up gramophone in a corner of the room. He touched the needle to the record, a Bach étude.

As he stared at the detritus of his former life, he rehearsed how he was going to kill Joseph Stalin.

His battered leather briefcase lay on the study table. Another, exactly the same, lay beside it. It contained a time bomb and explosives. At the next war cabinet meeting he attended in the Kremlin, he would place the briefcase beside his chair and when it exploded he would certainly die but Comrade Stalin would die with him.

When they searched the dacha, the NKVD – Stalin's Gestapo – would find, in his desk among his papers, a telephone number for the British Consulate in Istanbul and the name of an Istanbul restaurant that was a favourite haunt of members of the British Secret Intelligence Service. They would discover also that he had been in Sebastopol the previous week and that he had met with the captain of a Turkish merchantman, and they would then discover that the merchantman was out of Istanbul. When they looked for the captain, they would find that he was in the employ of British intelligence in Istanbul.

There would be only one inescapable conclusion.

Feoderev winced and clutched at his side. The cancer the doctor had diagnosed was bothering him more each day. Soon the pain would become so severe that he would need drugs. He would be dead long before then. He would not let the cancer do to him what it did to Natasha.

He was a soldier, not a politician. Fighting the Germans was his duty, but he had always despised Comrade Stalin.

The man was a butcher. He had no choice but to do what he was about to do, but he could not deny there would be little satisfaction in ending it this way.

Nick was not told the visitor's name, or his diplomatic rank. He guessed he was from the Foreign Office in Whitehall.

'I'd like you to meet someone, Davis,' Donaldson said to him, after his secretary showed him into his office. The other man rose languidly to his feet. 'This is Nicholas Davis. Trojan was his protégé. Quite a feather in his cap.'

'Splendid to meet you.' A limp and rather damp handshake. He was a tall man running to fat, with thinning fair hair swept back from his forehead and a city banker's pink-flush to his cheeks. He was jovial, of course, and smiled like the devil himself.

Abrams joined them and they all sat in Donaldson's office drinking the orange tea that the secretary had brought, while the man from Whitehall warmed his ample backside on the central heating and chided them gently about the weather, which he thought would be warmer. It displayed a charming ignorance of world geography and climate that was entirely feigned, in Nick's opinion.

The cold grey eyes were like flint.

'Now then,' their visitor said finally, 'I wanted to talk to you fellows about Trojan.'

Something in his tone made Nick uneasy.

'How much do we know about this agent?'

Nick took a deep breath. He wondered where this was leading.

'Trojan was recruited in Bucharest,' Abrams said.

'How much are we paying him?'

Donaldson glanced at Abrams and nodded. The identity of every agent was protected by the use of code names and a control might only reveal the true identity to very superior officers of the Service.

'It's a she,' Abrams said. 'She's the mistress of the Abwehr head of station here in Istanbul.'

'Very impressive.'

'She is considered something of a coup.'

'I imagine she is. Almost too good to be true, really.'

Silence.

'Expensive?' he asked.

'She's not working for us for the money,' Nick said.

'Why *is* she working for us?'

'She's Romanian. Her father was ruined by the fascists and we think her brother was murdered by the Iron Guard. She hates the Germans.'

'Good story. Sounds plausible enough. But I've looked through the file we have in London. Most of the information she has given us has been vague and inconclusive and on several occasions it has been highly inaccurate. For months we were led to believe that the German Ambassador in Ankara had come to an accommodation with the Turks, and on the basis of this information we almost took precipitate action that would have been disastrous. In fact, we wonder now if your enthusiasm for this source is misplaced.'

Nick thought about Dobruja. He thought about Dobruja all the time. The man from Whitehall put his hands behind his back, regarded them in the manner of an officer inspecting his troops.

'RAF and US bombers are flying sorties every day over Germany. The High Command are looking for reliable targets. Jerry's factories, rubber, oil, gasoline, aircraft and ball bearings are top of the list. That's why we sat up and took notice when we saw this last relay from Trojan, about the Messerschmitt factories near Vienna. Harris is eager to go after them. But what if this information is wrong? It could be a trap and a lot of our young flyers will pay for our mistakes with their lives. You see what I'm getting at?'

'We broke up a major spy ring in Iraq based on the information we got from Trojan,' Abrams said.

'Well, we don't know how effective those Iraqis were. It's good practice to spice lies with truth. You give up a little to get a lot. We all know those games.'

'What are you saying, sir? Do you think Nick here is wrong about his agent's reliability?' *His* agent. Already Abrams was distancing himself.

'Why would Maier have so much sensitive information from outside the Balkans in his possession? That's the question.'

Donaldson's secretary knocked on the door. The Consul General was free to see the visitor now. 'To be continued,' the man from Whitehall said. 'Perhaps you chaps would like to think about what I've just said.' He nodded cheerfully and breezed from the room.

After he had gone, there was a long silence. Abrams and Donaldson looked at each other. 'I hope this isn't going to turn into a fiasco,' Donaldson said.

'I trust her,' Nick said.

'Yes, but can Bomber Command trust her?' Abrams said. Nick knew it wasn't the bomber crews he was thinking about. It was his career.

'What about the document she stole from Maier's safe? We know that was genuine now.'

Abrams shrugged. Donaldson just looked away.

That night he stood at the window of his study looking out at the little garden with its lonely Judas tree, the secret court by which she often came to the house. The drizzle had turned into a heavy soaking downpour and rain dripped steadily from the eaves. He imagined her down there in the dark garden, conjured an image of her as she moved through the night like the shadow of a cloud upon the sea, a ghost upon the stairs. He would not believe she had betrayed him; but then he could not afford to, not now. And that, he supposed, was the problem. He had too much invested in his own version of the truth to ever believe that he might be wrong.

63.

Ten miles west of Moscow

Feoderev stared out of the window of the Zil limousine at the tall stands of birches, the branches dusted with white. The ground was diamond hard and frost glittered on the brown earth. He kept his hand on the leather briefcase at his side, the numbness that he had felt since Natasha died finally replaced with fear. He was dying anyway, of course; he had steeled himself for his choices this morning but he had not thought it would be quite as hard as this.

The limousine raced along Kuzotovskiy Prospekt and the grim sweep of the western suburbs of the capital. They crossed the Moskva River at the Borodinskiy Bridge and headed towards the Kremlin.

He supposed by this time tomorrow his name would be broadcast on radio stations all around the world. He had never desired fame or glory for himself; he supposed neither were on offer, just the kind of notoriety all assassins of famous people achieve after their death.

His chauffeur went through a barred gate on the other side of Red Square, and drove across the cobbles to a small court-yard with a private entrance. The man opened the door for him. He hesitated for just a moment, to catch his breath. He wondered if Natasha would be proud of him today.

He went in the usual way, to his office overlooking the armoury. The war cabinet meeting was not for another forty-five minutes. He planned to have a large shot of vodka in his office before he went to the meeting.

He got into a cage lift and wrenched the gate closed. The lift rattled and groaned as it ascended to the third floor. He got out and strode down the carpeted hallway towards his office.

He stopped. There were half a dozen NKVD officers standing outside the door, holding automatic weapons. He turned around. Behind him was Beria himself, surrounded by three more uniformed NKVD guards.

So, he had been betrayed.

He knew what he had to do. He reached into his pocket, and the guards shouted a warning. Well, let them shoot me.

The safety was off. He brought the pistol straight to his mouth and placed the muzzle against the palate. He knew all along it might come to this.

He pulled the trigger.

From her window, Daniela watched the *hamals* trudging through the rain. Donkeys clipped past with wicker panniers of oranges and grapes, steam clinging to their flanks. Black anvils of cloud rose over the Marmara Sea.

In her hands she held a framed photograph of her mother, the only likeness she still owned. With her finger she traced the contours of her mother's face, as tenderly as if she was living flesh and blood.

'I wonder what you think of me now,' she murmured.

Outside, the rain beat on the roof like a barrage of nails.

'What am I going to do? You must be so ashamed of me. But what else can I do? I was always a disappointment, wasn't I? I'm just putting these bad instincts to good use.' A tear coursed down her cheek. She rubbed it away angrily. She had no cause to feel sorry for herself.

She stood up and paced the room.

'What am I going to do about this Englishman? I love him. He talks to my soul. But he's married, mama. Why does it have to be like this? Why can't it be easy? Why does it always have to be wrong for me?'

She went back to the window and stared at the lights of Taksim and wondered where her life would take her now. The night's black and silent gate closed on the city. She looked for a light in the sky but there was none.

64.

Walking through the massive armoured doors of the spice market was like walking into a fortress. The bazaar was an assault on the senses: the rich fog of smells, the shouts of merchants hawking to their customers, the dazzle of mounds of yellow turmeric and golden cinnamon and pink saffron.

He was carried along in the crush of people, escaped up some worn stone steps by one of the gates. The steps led to a barred wooden door. His knock was answered by a robed Turkish servant who led the way to Maier's office.

He felt a blast of heat as he entered, the room warmed by two charcoal burners. It was opulent; thick green and russet-brown Anatolian rugs on the floor, tiles of blue Izmir faience on one wall. A fretted window looked down into the bazaar. Impressive.

'My Englisher friend,' Maier said, rising to his feet from behind a heavy walnut desk. There was no smile. He looked haggard.

'Herr Maier.'

Maier indicated a chair on the other side of the desk. He reached into his drawer and brought out a bottle of *raki* and two glasses. 'It's a little early in the morning,' he said.

'I could do with one.'

'Good,' he said. 'So could I.'

He pushed the glass across the desk. Nick added a little water, turning the clear liquid the colour of milk. It tasted of aniseed.

'You wanted to see me.'

Maier lit a cigarette and leaned back in his chair. He seemed relaxed, but the hand that held the cigarette was shaking. 'You know who I am, don't you?'

So, at last, Nick thought. We are not fencing any more. 'Tell me.'

'I am a colonel in the Abwehr. I am sure you know this.'

'You invited me here to tell me this?'

'You know I did not.'

'What is it you want?'

'I want to get away from this war.'

'You want to defect?'

He ran a hand across his face. 'They have left me no choice.'

The defection of an Abwehr colonel would be a stunning coup. Nick found it hard to contain his excitement. 'When?'

'That is yet to be decided.'

Nick wondered if this was another game. He drank some of the *raki* and considered. 'Should we agree, you will of course be expected to share with us everything you know.'

'It makes no difference now. The war is lost.' In fact, Maier looked defeated also. Or was it all just an act? 'I shall need time to get my family out of Germany.'

'Is that possible?'

'Everything is possible.'

'What about your mistress?'

His eyes were suddenly hard and very bright. 'What about her?'

'Would you expect sanctuary for her as well?'

Maier smiled, finally prepared to abandon the game. 'That would largely depend on you, Herr Davis.'

His chest was tight and it was hard to breathe. 'On me?'

'Of course. We both know the reason.'

Their eyes locked. Maier's were ice blue and impossible to read.

'You have taken me by surprise,' Nick said.

'I should hate to be predictable.'

'I will have to talk to my superiors.'

'Of course you will. And your superiors will fall over themselves to help me.'

He was right. To have the head of the Abwehr's Istanbul section defect would be a body blow to the Germans.

Nick finished his *raki* and stood up. 'I'll be in touch.'

Maier offered his hand. Nick hesitated, then shook it. It was the first time they had ever touched each other.

'There is something you should know, Herr Davis. There is someone inside your consulate working for the Russians.'

Nick stared at him. 'How do you know this?'

'Recently we captured one of the top NKVD agents here in the Balkans. I have seen the transcripts of the interrogation.' He handed Nick a brown manila envelope. 'These are copies. But you should be careful who sees them. Take them straight to Herr Abrams.'

'How do I know these are genuine?'

'You don't. But Abrams will.'

'Good day, Herr Maier.'

'*Wiedersehen*.'

Maier's servant showed him to the door and he descended once more into the bedlam of the market. He did not return to his car immediately, instead he wandered the bazaar aimlessly for almost an hour. He ignored the imprecations of beggars and hawkers, sorting the pieces of the puzzle in his mind, planning his future with Siegfried Maier's former mistress.

Abrams was a different man outside the consulate. At work he was austere, almost bloodless. Away from the authority lent him by his office, he appeared surprisingly ill at ease.

He lived in a vast and well-ordered house of dark mahogany furniture and book-lined shelves, in the old quarter of Istanbul. The windows looked out over the Sea of Marmara. It was a house of order and distinction; the parquet floor shone like glass and there was a pianoforte in the bow window. Nick wondered if it had ever been played.

The invitation to dine alone with him had taken Nick by surprise and it was one he could not readily refuse. The dinner conversation had been stilted and painful; they had kept to well-worn parameters of work, war and politics.

It was after they had withdrawn to the drawing room and a servant had brought them coffee that Abrams finally raised the subject of Maier's recent allegations about a Russian spy inside the embassy.

'Do you believe him?' Nick asked.

'It's feasible.'

'Did you read the documents he gave me?'

'Impossible to verify them. Of course the contents disturb me. I am more concerned these days about our Russian friends than our German enemies.'

'They wouldn't want to hear that in Whitehall.'

'That's why they sent me to Istanbul.' His face changed, suddenly there was a petulant crease between his eyebrows that signalled the onset of one of Abrams's fits of pique.

'Your Mr Arazi from the Haganah once quoted me an Arab proverb, "the enemy of my enemy is my friend". But he's wrong, Davis. When this war is over you'll see. No-one takes any notice of us now, but Stalin's more of a threat to us than Hitler ever was. No-one in Whitehall or Washington will listen.'

He had made himself too angry to sit still. He got to his feet and went to the sideboard, opened a silver cigarette case and took out one of the strong Turkish cigarettes he favoured. 'Germany's not our enemy; Hitler is. If we could help the Germans throw him out, it would all be over. We need a strong Germany to keep the Russians out of Europe.'

Nick had heard this rant before and there was nothing he could think of to say. While Abrams droned on, Nick looked around the room, tried not to appear too distracted. He noticed that the leather-bound books on the bookshelves had been arranged in alphabetical order by the author's surname and he smiled. Typically Abrams. There was a gold-framed portrait of King George V on the wall and several stern-faced photographs of a man and woman who were perhaps Abrams's parents. He also saw something he had not expected, a sepia photograph of a young woman. It was yellowed with age and the features were indistinct. It had been posed in a photographer's studio, with a pastoral scene painted on the backdrop.

Abrams had lapsed into brooding silence. Nick decided to distract him by asking him about the photograph. 'Your sister?' he asked him.

Abrams drew on his cigarette. 'She was my fiancée.'

'Your fiancée?'

'She broke it off two days before the wedding. Never saw her again.'

Nick was unable to hide his surprise. He had often wondered about Abrams, about his past and his private life

313

outside the embassy. He sometimes wondered if he had any internal life at all.

'How long ago did this happen?'

'Long time ago, Davis,' he said with a flash of irritation, bringing the subject to a close. But then he added, unexpectedly: 'I knew I could not feel the same affection for a woman again. So what is one to do?'

What is one to do, indeed? Passion sounded quaint when it was couched in the formal language of the diplomat. So, the cold fish had a heart, after all. He still grieved for one lost love affair.

Abrams sat down and continued his diatribe on the evils of communism, and the woman in the photograph was forgotten. Nick did not raise the subject again.

What is one to do?

He never ever found out her name.

65.

Nick had been to lunch with Donaldson and the United States military attaché at a restaurant on Son of the Slave Street and they were walking back along Istiklal. Nick turned up the collar of his coat against the biting wind. He stopped to light a cigarette and let Donaldson and the attaché go ahead. When he looked up, he saw a well-dressed Turk heading towards them from the opposite direction, holding a large briefcase.

There was something about the man that troubled him, something he could not define. He remembered Jordon, that sixth sense he'd spoken of.

He heard someone frantically shouting his name from the other side of the street and turned around. He saw Daniela waving desperately to him from outside the bank on the far side of the boulevard. He called to Donaldson but he and the attaché were already fifty yards ahead. He would catch them up.

The man with the briefcase had stopped.

'Nick!' Daniela screamed at him. 'Nick, please!'

He turned towards her, fought his way through the chaos of trams and cars on Istiklal. 'Daniela?'

The expression on her face made his blood cold.

'What's wrong?'

There was a deafening explosion and the world went black.

He was astonished to find himself lying on his back on the cobblestones. He sat up, his ears ringing, and stared down at his body in panic, feeling his legs and arms. He seemed to be uninjured. There was blood but he couldn't find a wound.

'Daniela?'

She lay beside him on the ground, face down. God, no. Please God, no. He rolled her over, thinking the blood came from her, and searched desperately for a wound. He prayed to a deity he did not believe in, and in his head he promised Him any bargain if only she could be unhurt.

'Daniela!'

Her eyes flickered open.

'Are you all right?' His voice sounded as if it was coming from a long way away. He put a hand to his face, found blood leaking from his ear.

Daniela threw her arms around his neck and clung to him.

'Are you hurt?' he said.

She shook her head.

The man with the briefcase had disappeared, there was just a stain on the ground where he had been. A human hand lay in the middle of the street, on the tram lines.

Donaldson and the attaché were just bundles of bloody rags on the pavement. He realised that if it were not for Daniela, he would be dead too.

She had her face pressed into his shoulder and her voice was muffled, he could hardly hear her, could hardly hear anything. 'I thought I was too late.'

'You knew,' he said.

'I can't lose you,' Daniela said.

He held her away from him, looked again for wounds. 'You're not hurt?'

She shook her head.

He staggered to his feet, helped her up from the ground. He felt nauseous, and his balance was gone. As his head cleared, he started to think again like a professional. 'You have to get out of here,' he said to her.

The questions could come later. She had to get away before the police arrived.

'Run,' he said and pushed her away. She staggered, then hurried away towards Son of the Slave Street. She looked back once, then was gone.

In the distance he heard the clang of a bell as the first police car headed down Istiklal Boulevard.

66.

Abrams poured three fingers of whisky into a glass and placed it on his desk in front of Nick. 'You look like you need it,' he said.

'Maier,' Nick said.

'What was that?'

'Maier planted that bomb. He had Donaldson murdered.'

There was a constant ringing in Nick's right ear. The doctor said the explosion had ruptured an ear drum. That was where the blood on his shirt had come from.

Abrams sat down, crossed his hands over his stomach and considered. 'Murder's rather a strong word to use when men are getting slaughtered in their thousands in Italy and North Africa.'

'If it wasn't for Trojan, I would be dead now.'

'Trojan?'

'I saw her there just before the bomb went off. She saved my life.'

'I was supposed to join the three of you for lunch. If it wasn't for an urgent call from the Australian Ambassador's office, I'd be dead too. Asked you to come with me, if you remember. Just fate, old boy.'

'The only way she could have known is if Maier told her.'

Abrams sighed. He leaned forward, pushed the brown manila envelope that Maier had given him across the desk. 'The transcripts of the interrogation of the NKVD agent the Abwehr captured in Sofia. He didn't just claim that there was a Russian agent inside this consulate. He gave him a name.'

'And?'

'Donaldson.'

'Donaldson?'

'Here's something else for you to think about. Four days ago there was an attempt on Stalin's life.'

'What?'

'A Russian lieutenant general by the name of Feoderev tried to smuggle a briefcase loaded with explosives into the Kremlin. The NKVD were tipped off and were about to arrest him when he shot himself in the head. At this stage, we think Feoderev was part of an Abwehr plot. If Stalin was dead and Russia withdrew from the alliance, Canaris would have a better chance to negotiate a separate peace.'

'Who was Feoderev?'

'He was one of the chiefs of staff at Stalingrad. He had been decorated three times and made a hero of the Soviet Union by Stalin himself. Apparently his son was captured by the Germans and they may have used that as a lever. Who knows? Or perhaps he just saw himself as a patriot.'

'What about Donaldson?'

'If he was working for the Russians, then the Abwehr needed to get rid of him. Who knows what damage he's done while he's been here.'

'This is going to cause a furore in Whitehall.'

'Only if it gets out.'

They looked at each other.

'Both our careers would be finished. We'd be tainted with this for the rest of our lives.'

'It must come out eventually.'

319

'Why?'

Nick thought about this: Abrams was right. Why?

'Whitehall will want to know why Donaldson was murdered.'

'Perhaps someone wanted to kill the American military attaché. Perhaps it was a mistake. People will be blowing smoke in their eyes from every direction, Davis.'

Nick was silent a moment, thinking this through. 'Could Donaldson have tipped the Russians off about the assassination plot?'

'Possibly. If he had someone working for him inside the Abwehr. The question is, who?'

'Maier may be able to tell us that.'

'If he comes over.'

'He will.'

'The fact is, I shan't miss Donaldson. Anyone on the payroll of the NKVD probably isn't cut out for His Majesty's diplomatic service.'

'Do we know the identity of the bomber?'

'The Emniyet are working on it. But it's going to prove rather difficult, I imagine. They found a part of his forehead on a balcony about twenty yards from the explosion. Apparently he had a wart over his right eyebrow. It's not much to go on.'

'And the bomb?'

'We suspect it was set off by remote control. No doubt the bomber had been told he would have time to get away. They lied to him. Terrible thing, lies.'

Nick finished the whisky. 'What's going to happen now?'

'The war will go on. Business as usual. That's it, Nick. That's what's going to happen. Take the day off. Go home. Get some sleep. You look awful.'

Nick did not go home. He walked down to the Galata Bridge, tried to think things through. He thought he could

320

not trust Daniela, but she had saved his life; Maier was his enemy, but he wanted to be his friend; Donaldson was his chief, but he had been working for the Russians. He did not know what to believe any more. He did not know if he even believed in belief.

She had come in the evening, had rung him at the embassy to assure herself again that he was all right and to say she had to see him. They made slow love by the light of a single candle on the bedside table. They were both bruised and shaken, and their lovemaking was tentative.

Afterwards they lay in each other's arms, the warmth of each other's bodies making life seem even more precious. 'How did you know?' he whispered.

'I heard Maier talking. On the telephone.'

'Who was he talking to?'

'I don't know.'

'What else did he say?'

'Just that there would be a bomb. I knew that you worked for Donaldson. I had to be sure you weren't with him.'

'When did this happen?'

'This morning. No more than an hour before it happened. I thought I would be too late. I made up some excuse to get out of the house.'

It is true, he thought, that death is an aphrodisiac. Soon he had to make love to her again, finding an affirmation of life in loving. He took her in his arms and she surrendered to him again, throwing back her head for his lips to follow the long smooth line of her throat and shoulder. Charcoal burners glowed in the corners of the room and rain beat against the windows.

Their breathless murmuring was drowned by distant thunder that rattled the glass in the windowpanes. Daniela gasped and arched her back with him as the storm broke over the city, icy rain like gravel thrown at the windows, the old house moaning in the wind.

She slept in the crook of his arm and he listened to the deep, even rhythm of her breathing. After a while she rolled away from him and he turned on his side to watch her, her hair fanned out on the pillow, her lips open, in the shape of a heart.

She slept for perhaps an hour, her right arm tossed carelessly over her head. She was a bad sleeper, and lately her bad dreams had become more frequent. Once, in her sleep, she had taken his pillow from under his head and hurled it across the room. But tonight at least she slept as peacefully as a child, her breath sighing deep in her chest.

Then she rolled onto her side, and her eyes opened. She was blearily beautiful from sleep but what could be poignant in marriage becomes painful in the affair.

Hours yet before she had to go home; instead he could think only of the days and weeks that she would sleep somewhere else.

'Marry me,' he whispered.

A shadow passed across her face. 'You're already married, Nick.'

'I want you to leave him,' he said, confident that his logic would defeat her. 'You can't put yourself in any more danger. The Germans are losing this war. Let me protect you now.'

She smiled and reached up a hand to stroke his face.

'I can get a posting to Rome or Paris when all this is

over. I can arrange a British passport. I've already spoken to Abrams.'

'You have a family, Nick.'

'It's you I love.'

'And your wife loves you. So do your boys. After the war you have to go back to them.'

She tried to bring his mouth towards her, the kiss he ached for whenever they were apart. But now he pulled away, trading the moment to contend with her.

'I'm not going back.'

'I don't want you to leave her.'

'It's my decision.'

'I can't take you away from your family.'

She tried to roll away but he caught her shoulder and pulled her back to him. The rain drummed harder on the roof.

'What if Maier wasn't around? What would you do?'

'Do you think Siggi will leave me?' she asked him.

'It was just a question.'

'I don't know.'

'You must have thought about it.'

An eloquent shrug of the shoulders.

'Why won't you come and stay here?'

'Let's not do this now,' she said.

'Stay here tonight.'

Her face twisted; he did not know if she was about to cry or to rage. 'I can't,' she said and she put her face in her pillow, beat it with her fist as ineffectually as a child.

Outside, the storm had passed, was no more than a distant rumbling over the Sea of Marmara. The sound of a thousand gutters leaking water onto the cobblestones, everything cold and shining wet.

He took her hand, squeezed it, as if he could force her to see things his way. 'How can you live this way?'

'You don't understand. It's so easy for you.'

'Easy? How can you say that?'

She took his hand and placed it on her breast. 'You'll always be here, Nick. In my heart. Even if we're far away from each other, you'll still have a place right here inside me.'

He wanted to rage at her: What good is that to me? How can I take succour and comfort from something I cannot see? At school the Bible teacher had told them about the love of God, and it meant nothing to him when he was lonely or frightened or in despair. That kind of love was the refuge of those too afraid to love what was real. He never found any hope or salvation in what was invisible.

It was at times like this that he wanted to end it. It was no longer an affair; he felt Maier was the interloper, not him, and he just wanted to end the game they were playing, get her away from him and out of danger. He wanted peace from this endless longing, the grinding jealousy he felt watching her dress to go to the bed of another man, the waiting for the next time, never knowing when the end might be.

67.

As far as the Nazis were concerned, the Abwehr had more unreliable people than the French Resistance. Himmler, the head of the SD, thought the Abwehr a greater threat to security than the SOE.

Abrams was convinced that Maier would have to make his move soon. He wanted Nick to meet with him again, push him towards that final irrevocable step.

At his urging, Nick telephoned Maier and arranged a meeting in a coffee shop in the old city.

The inevitable portrait of Mehmet the Conqueror gazed down from the wall with malevolent wisdom. The waiter brought coffee in a tiny cup. Tendrils of steam rose from it. As usual it had the consistency of boiling mud, but it revived him. Turkish coffee hits the heart like an electric shock, dark and bitter and very, very strong.

Hammering from the blacksmith next door all but drowned out the wail of music from the radio. Tinkers went past on bicycles, wheels slipping on the ice. Here was the city of the ordinary Turk, a few old men in frayed brown suits smoking water pipes and sipping from little glasses of tea and playing backgammon, watching the foreigner with wary eyes.

He looked at his watch. Maier was late and he started to grow uneasy.

But suddenly he appeared, fedora pulled down over his eyes against the wind, the collar of his grey overcoat turned up around his chin.

He sat down beside Nick. There were no formalities.

'How's the spice business?' Nick said.

'I know nothing about the spice business. I care less.'

Nick ordered more coffee.

Maier lit a cigarette. Three attempts to light the match. 'You know Kaltenbrunner has written to Hitler?' Maier said. Kaltenbrunner was Himmler's deputy in the SD. 'I saw a copy of the letter. It was smuggled out of the Reichstag by one of our own people. Kaltenbrunner said the Abwehr operation here in Istanbul was a viper's nest. A fine testimonial after we have served our country so faithfully, don't you think?'

'Why are you telling me this?'

Maier exhaled a long stream of smoke. 'I do not wish to see Germany destroyed by the Nazis.'

'You have decided to defect?'

'Defect is such an ugly word. But yes, you are right. I do not wish to be a traitor to my friends and colleagues but I cannot continue to serve the Nazis. That is the truth of it.'

'What do you want, Herr Maier?'

'If you help me I will tell you everything I know about our Istanbul operation.'

'Will you tell us what you know about Donaldson?'

What was that look in his eyes? It was there for a moment, and then it was gone. 'Of course. I must have sanctuary for my family also.'

'Where are they now?'

'They are still in Berlin. Some friends of mine are arranging visas for Turkey.'

'You should not leave it too long.'

Maier was smiling but the strain told in his eyes. Defection was not the only thing on his mind.

'What about your mistress?'

'What about her?'

'Will you require a visa for her also?'

'I'm afraid that will not be possible. Frau Maier may not appreciate it.' He leaned towards him. Nick smelled tobacco and expensive eau de cologne. 'You don't seem such a bad fellow, my Englisher friend. There have been times, of course, when I would have liked to have cut your throat. But there it is.'

And I would have liked to have cut yours, Nick thought. But you sent her to me; it was your doing. Still, it was gratifying to know that he had disturbed Maier's rest as much as he had disturbed his.

'So it is agreed?'

'As soon as you're ready, call me on the telephone at the consulate. Or at home. Here is my number.' He pushed a slip of paper across the table.

Maier pocketed it, finished his coffee. He got up to leave. 'Now I must be off to buy more cinnamon.'

'Good luck with it. I believe it's a seller's market these days.'

Maier hesitated; it was impossible to tell if he was angry or sad. 'She is a remarkable woman. But you know that.'

'Yes, I do,' Nick said.

'You'll never have her, you know.' And with that he walked away.

'God put your dick on the outside and your heart on the inside and He did it for a reason, old boy. Only one way to

327

get attached to women, sport, and that's through the carnal organs. The heart's for keeping, it stays on the inside and it's not meant to get attached to anything. All right?'

They were in a dark bar near Taksim. Max's mistress, Adrienne Varga, was singing a sad Hungarian ballad on the tiny stage, accompanied by a Turkish *baglama* player.

There was a patina of sweat on Max's high forehead, and it gleamed in the reflection of the stage lights. It lent him a look of crazed desperation.

'Take me and Varga. Nice girl. Acrobat, if you understand my meaning. Easy on the eye. Secret is not to get too attached. Just a woman. Half the world are women. Got to remember that, sport.'

'I'll try.'

Varga was indeed beautiful, Slavic blonde, snake-hipped, and with a torchy voice that had every man in the bar devouring her with his eyes.

'I shouldn't have told you,' Nick said. 'I knew you wouldn't understand.'

'Understand perfectly. Intent on fucking up your life over a woman. Been done before. Wish you all the best with it.'

'I love her, Max.'

'Men don't fall in love, sport, they get hard-ons.'

'You're a cynic.'

'Of course I am, I'm a journalist.'

Varga had finished her ballad, and had moved on to another slow and plaintive love song to tumultuous applause from a group of Turkish men sitting right at her feet below the stage.

'I want to marry her,' Nick said.

'Why ruin a good thing? Don't understand you, old man. Ever met a happily married man?' His voice rose to a theatrical whisper. 'Between you and me, Varga wants to get married too.'

'You don't?'

'Don't believe in it. Once is enough. Told her no.'

Max finished his whisky and ordered another. Drinking too much. Getting beyond help. Nick looked at Varga and wondered if any woman could reform him.

He doubted it.

68.

They stood side by side on the Galata Bridge, staring into the cold black waters, buffeted by the wind. Not many fishermen out here today, the wind raising whitecaps on the Horn and the little ferries bucking like horses on the churning waves.

As always she asked if he had heard from Jennifer. He felt she was always trying to put the two of them back together. But he told her the truth: that Jennifer had written three times that month, that she was well and back in London and the boys were back at school, Jamie in his final year.

'They'll be looking forward to seeing you again.'

'That may not be for a while yet.'

'When this war finishes, you must go back to your family.'

'I'll never go back to Jennifer. Not now.'

'Then you'll find someone else.'

'I want you.'

'I'm not good for you. You have to find some woman who can make you happy.'

'I have found her. You're the one I want.'

'There'll be other women who will make you happy.' There can be no worse torment, he thought, than the woman you love wishing you happiness with someone else, pushing you into someone else's arms. Could there be anything quite as exquisitely cruel, or painful? It was said in kindness, of course, for he believed she truly did wish him to be happy. Instead he wanted her to feel as jealous and possessive of him as he did of her.

She reached for his hand. 'I wish it could be you and I.'

'It could be, if that's what you want.' His anger and frustration made him do something he never thought he'd do; he betrayed a military secret to her. 'He's bringing his wife and son to Istanbul. Did you know that? He's coming over to our side, Daniela. Where will that leave you?'

There was a look of ineffable sadness on her face. He realised she already knew.

'I can look after you,' he said.

'If it's meant to be, it will happen for us,' she said.

'It's people who decide whether something is meant to be.'

'You can't fight fate, Nick.'

He did not understand this fatalism she clung to. It was as if she had decided that she had been born under a dark star and there was nothing anyone could do for her, that she had no control over her own life. He had never believed in fate. People believed in destiny when they did not want to take responsibility for their own choices.

At times like these he wanted to rage at her, shake her, but he knew it would do no good. She seemed as determined to be unhappy as others were greedy for money or for sex or for power, clung to it with blind devotion.

'I love you,' he said. 'Why do you keep pushing me away?'

'You can't keep doing this to yourself,' she said, all business now. 'I've given you everything I can and you still want more. What's wrong with you? Perhaps we should stop seeing each other.'

He had been sure that one day he would get through to her, by sheer force of will. But now he realised that he might really lose her.

331

'I can't do this any more,' she said. 'I can't keep hurting you this way. I'm sorry, Nick.'

'But what are you going to do?'

It was a sad smile, a tired smile. 'I'll survive. I always do.'

Their affair had lasted through three years of separation and danger and doubt, yet now that she no longer needed to stay with Maier, she was going to walk away from him. It could only be that she did not love him, had never loved him.

He was tired, tired to his bones, and there was no fight left in him to continue.

He let her walk away from him across the bridge, towards Beyoglu. The world was grey and cold. The boom of a freighter's siren echoed mournfully across the water.

Wooden houses swayed over the street. Above the roofs he caught a glimpse of the Marmara Sea, caiques beetling among the anchored warships. A muezzin called the faithful to noon prayer, his voice joined by another and then another, their chants echoing over the city in discordant holy song.

Something made Nick look up. He saw a woman's face appear for a moment, peering down from a half-shuttered window, through the jalousie. They understood desire, these sons of Mohammed, but in keeping their women sequestered they showed more of a man's nature than they did of a woman's.

One of Mohammed's nephews had once remarked that there were ten parts of desire and women possessed nine of them; but it is the soul that desires, Nick thought, not just the body. It is the soul that loves and loves truly, he thought; men love with the eyes, women with the heart.

He stopped at the end of the street and looked back to satisfy himself that he had not been followed. All he saw was a single movement behind the jalousie of a house halfway along the street, a woman watching him, another soul like himself, trapped in a fretted cage.

Omar's house dated from the Ottoman Empire of the seventeenth century. It had been grand once, but now it was long past its faded glory, the wooden casements and loggias grey with age, paint peeling in strips from the front door like charred skin.

Nick opened the side gate and made his way through the sparse garden. He rapped on the door and waited. He was about to knock again when he heard a key turn in the lock and the door edged open.

A smell of must and something else, something sweet and sickly, came from inside. Omar's wife peered at him from the gloom, her head wrapped in a heavy scarf. Her black eyes regarded him with dread. A foreigner coming into the house could only bring her husband bad luck.

Nick slipped off his shoes and went in. It was dark and cold. He looked around. The house had once been full of heavy mahogany furniture, and there had been layers of Bokhara carpets on the floors. Now it was almost bare, just a few kilims hanging from the walls; the rest had been sold off to meet Omar's craving.

The woman led him to a bedroom at the back of the house.

Omar lay on a carpet in a corner of the room, on his left side. The room was dark, and thick with sweet-smelling smoke. Nick sat down cross-legged beside him on the floor and waited.

He watched Omar take a ball of sticky black opium on the end of a needle and tamp it into the bowl of his pipe. He lit it with a taper and inhaled the thick smoke, his eyes dreamy and unfocused. Nick could not be sure that he knew he was even there. The heady sweet scent of opium drifted in the room.

Just when Nick thought he was lost to his dreams, Omar beckoned him closer.

'*Effendim*,' he murmured. 'A long time since I have seen you.'

'*Günaydin*, Omar Bey. May your day be bright.'

'How goes it with you?'

'I am well, Omar. God be praised.'

'I have heard you have problems with a woman,' Omar said.

'People like to gossip.'

'I understand, *effendim*. The only men who do not have problems with women are dead.'

He grinned, and inhaled more of the sweet smoke.

'Popescu Bey wants to arrange a meeting. Here in Istanbul. He is sending his own envoy, from the Ministry. It is his son-in-law, an army officer, the son of one of Popescu's closest friends. His name is . . . it is . . .'

Omar had drifted away from him again, into the soothing arms of the opium. Nick stood up, disgusted, and hurried from the house.

When he got outside, he thought he was going to be sick. The opium smoke had nauseated him and he had to cling to the wall for support.

He made his way back down to the Galata Bridge, where just that morning Daniela had walked away from him for the last time.

He had intended to catch a taxicab from there to the consulate but instead he went down the steps to the pontoon in the shade of the bridge. He felt the timbers lurch and sway beneath his feet as a trolley bus thundered overhead.

Out on the harbour small clouds of gulls hovered and shrieked around the stern of a fishing boat. The Turks called them the lost souls of the Bosphorus, the ghosts of those who had died in its black waters, the discarded harem girls and the strangled courtiers. So many lost souls in the world, he thought; he sometimes thought he might be one of them, Daniela too.

Am I so different from Omar? he wondered, addicted to the sweet black resin of my desire? They said that once you were a slave to opium, the only way out was from the Galata Bridge. He stared into the water and imagined he saw his own face staring back, gaunt, haunted.

'It's not desire,' the face told him. 'You know it's more. You know you love her.'

'I can't love her,' he said, 'I'm supposed to love someone else, for Christ's sake.'

But it was too late. The man he had lived with all his life had slipped away from him. The reflection in the deep and swirling waters was a different face than the one he had once known. That private and secretive man had let slip his guard and a stranger had usurped his identity, stolen his passport and the key to his house, and taken over his life.

He knew that whatever happened with Daniela, he could not go back.

Would anyone understand this, his friends, his family, his boys? He turned away from the bridge, saw a *hamal* labouring up the gangway of one of the ferries moored at the docks, bowed under massive sacks of rice. As the load was lifted from his back by two deckhands, Nick saw the look of relief on the man's face, the elemental pleasure of shedding a terrible burden.

He thought he knew how he felt.

69.

One night the rain and snow disappeared. Daniela woke to a bright clear day, the sky washed blue. She opened the window, heard the shouts of hawkers in the street, and the loud insistent braying of a donkey.

She had slept badly again, her dreams disturbed and fraught. She woke thinking about him.

What was she to do? He had touched her soul. The times they had had together had been some of the most wonderful moments of her life, but he always wanted more, he could never take just the moment, there was so much he didn't understand, couldn't leave alone.

Did he think she had not lived a moment before she came into his life? Did he never wonder about how she had survived and not the rest of her family, did he never think how the guilt of surviving had hurt her? He wanted to threaten or cajole her into doing as he wanted, as if he had some claim on her, when he was still a married man with two sons in England. Did he understand nothing of her heart?

She had given him all she had been able to give. Why did he always want more?

And yet she missed him. She knew she had to see him again, just one more time.

Dear Nick,
This is the hardest letter I have ever had to write. I really don't know where to begin.

I have always tried to be a good wife to you. What happened to us recently was not of my doing or my design. I was prepared to forgive you and move on with our lives, if that was what you wanted.

But it was clear to me the last time you came back to England that you had no desire to do that. And from your recent letters, I know your heart and your mind are elsewhere.

As you know, for two years I have been seeing a major from the local air force base. He lost his wife in the Blitz and we have been friends; I think I have been a comfort to him and he has been of some comfort to me. We have never strayed beyond the bounds of propriety. You know I would not do that to you, Nick, I have always been a good and faithful wife.

However, in the last weeks things have changed. I am not proud of this. I am a woman, Nick, and I cannot wait for ever for you to make up your mind. He has asked me to make a new life with him, and this is what I now intend to do.

I am sorry. But it was you that brought another woman into our marriage and I have waited long enough.

I hope you will see this is for the best. I have seen a solicitor to organise the papers. I assume you will have no objection.
Jennifer

Nick paced the room, the letter clenched in his right fist. He did not regret a thing he had done, but now, curiously, he felt an acute sense of loss, even though he knew that what he felt was grief for something lost in the past. In the space of a week he had lost the woman he had loved for almost twenty years and the woman he loved more than any other in his life.

Yet it was what he had expected would happen all along.

70.

The Park was a drab stucco hotel set back from the broad avenue of the Ayas Pasha Boulevard, across the road from the German Consulate, with its huge red and black Nazi flag. There was a circular driveway, for ever crowded with German and French limousines, and at its centre were a few forlorn flowerbeds.

It was the unofficial fascist headquarters of Istanbul. They congregated in its bars and restaurants: Germans, Hungarians, Austrians, even Arabs and Japanese. On his way to the lift, Nick saw an Iraqi diplomat in furtive conversation with a German journalist in the foyer and filed that away for future reference. He had a watching brief for every Nazi and fascist sympathiser who went in and out of Istanbul; they all appeared at the Park sooner or later. But tonight he had business of his own and the best place to do it was under the noses of the Abwehr.

He rode the elevator to the fifth floor alone and when he got out he checked that the corridor was empty. He walked quickly to suite 505 and knocked on the door. A gorilla in a badly fitted suit threw open the door and ushered him inside. He was about to pat Nick down but Popescu waved him away.

The two men shook hands and Popescu led Nick to the

window and two red upholstered leather armchairs. He offered him *raki*. The gorilla brought the drinks.

Popescu was urbane, dressed in the manner of a cavalry officer, with a cravat and dark suit, and had the air of dissipation and education affected by men of breeding in Romania. He was the leader of the liberal opposition and his family had been involved in Romanian politics for seventy years, the voice of reason among a coterie of racketeers, industrialists and police chiefs. Even now he still had Antonescu's ear.

'So, at last we meet. I trust I have been of some assistance to you.'

'Indeed.'

'I have done what I can. I have no love for the Germans, Monsieur Davis. But matters of political expediency have constrained me.'

'How are things in Bucharest?'

'Not good. You know our boys were fighting in Stalingrad? We had one hundred and fifty thousand casualties. In other words, Romania no longer has an army.'

'It's a lot of men to lose.'

'I believe it was a policy decision by the German High Command. They wanted to destroy our army in case we ever decided to fight them. It was a way of disarming us.'

'And a very effective one.'

'One hundred and fifty thousand men, and still we do not have our lost provinces returned to us. But then, you warned us about Monsieur Hitler.'

'In the circumstances, there was little you could have done.'

'I am glad you see it that way. But it doesn't help my son. He was an officer in the artillery. He lost both his legs at Kiev.'

Popescu finished his *raki* and now he was no longer smiling.

'Why did you want to see me?' Nick asked.

340

'There are some of us in Romania who have always been sympathetic to the Allied cause, you understand that?'

'I think so.'

'We believe it is important that discussions between your government and ours continue. You cannot allow the Russians to march into Bucharest. It is not in your interests and it is certainly not in ours.'

'They are our allies.'

'Allies? Your Churchill and Roosevelt are letting Stalin do as he pleases.'

'I will do everything I can, believe me.'

'I hope so.'

'Tell your government they still have friends in Bucharest.'

'You'll always have an ear to London through me,' Nick promised.

'I am delighted to hear this. Now, let us talk about our common ground and how we might save Romania from this disaster. You never know, we may need each other one day.'

Nick smiled politely. He could see that one day Popescu might well need him, but he did not see how it could ever be the other way.

71.

Music drifted from the hotels around Taksim Square. Nick walked arm in arm with Daniela through the Saturday night crowds, laughter spilling from the sidewalk coffee houses of Istiklal Boulevard.

They had dinner at the Taksim casino. There was a floor show, a Hungarian girl singing slow, Romanic ballads. She was a refugee, like so many in the wartime city, and luckier than most, for she was tall and blonde and had great legs. She drew an appreciative crowd of admirers, Americans mostly. Even the ambassador when he was in town. It was said he was having an affair with her.

Nick ordered champagne and they sat at one of the front tables. The men in the audience couldn't get enough of the blonde, but for himself Nick couldn't take his eyes off Daniela. She was looking up at the stage but her eyes had that unnerving thousand-yard stare of someone who has just seen a terrible death. Her knuckles were white as she gripped the edge of the table. Her foot was tapping to a faster beat than the music.

He had always been bewildered by her moods. He tried to make desultory conversation, without success. He loved this mysterious, enigmatic woman but there was a barrier between them he could not penetrate.

She had walked away from him on the Galata Bridge; then tonight she had called and asked to meet him. But then she had hardly spoken a word all night, consumed by her own thoughts.

'I'm not very good company tonight,' she said. 'Perhaps we should go home.'

'Why did you call me, then?'

'Please,' she said. 'I can't do this now.'

He shrugged, then called for the bill and went to get their coats from the cloakroom. He was tired of all this, told himself he just wanted to be free of her now, that he should accept his own foolishness and leave her behind, have done with it. Yet he knew he couldn't do that. She was in his blood.

She did not wait for him, went ahead into the street.

He had just collected their coats and was walking across the lobby when he heard a commotion outside. There was a black Mercedes saloon stopped in front of the casino and he saw a woman's legs kicking frantically from the open back door. The doorman ran down the steps to help her, but a burly man in a dark suit came out of the shadows and hit him with his closed fist, knocking him down, with the casual ease of a professional. The doorman did not get up.

His assailant jumped into the back of the saloon. There was a growl from the Mercedes's exhaust as the driver gunned the engine and drove off, tyres slewing on the cobblestones, the back door swinging open.

'Daniela!'

The saloon bounced on its suspension as if there was a violent struggle taking place in the back seat. Nick saw the brake lights blink on and off several times as it veered through the traffic.

The Opel he had signed out of the car pool earlier that evening was parked fifty yards away up the street. He

343

pulled the driver out from behind the wheel – he had been asleep with his head over the back of the seat, snoring – and jumped in. He started the engine and crunched the gears into drive. The car fishtailed as it took off, leaving the driver standing there in the street, bewildered and still half asleep.

The car rocked to the right as he swerved through the traffic, chasing up through the gears. His hands shook on the wheel, body flooded with dread and panic.

Taksim Square was crowded, neon-lit and noisy, and he punched the horn in frustration, dodging pedestrians, trams and buses. He followed the Mercedes through the cobbled streets of Cumhurriyet Caddesi, past banks and offices and warehouses, then into the suburbs, past locked-down shops and garages lit even at this time of night by kerosene lamps. Soon he had left the lights of Beyöglü behind. The roads became narrower and filled with potholes.

He leaned across the front seat and found the Webley revolver he had put in the glove compartment as insurance. It was reassuringly heavy in his hand. He laid it on the seat beside him.

He was shouting at the top of his lungs, swearing at the car, and at himself for being so careless. Soon he was out of Istanbul and into the rolling hill country of Thrace. He was driving too fast, narrowly missed an old farmer on a donkey who appeared suddenly in the glare of the head-lights. It was a bad road, a boneshaker, jarring every joint in his back. Who had done this? Where were they taking her? And why?

He kept the accelerator pedal pressed hard on the floor.

The engine was at a constant, high-pitched scream, the needle flickering dangerously high on the revolution counter.

The headlights bounced, a narrow white tunnel leading him through the scarred hills. He had lost sight of the Mercedes now but dust still hung on the bends, so he knew he was close, and every few minutes he caught a brief glimpse of the red tail lights.

Why Daniela?

A crest in the road. Blackness ahead, then a sudden blaze of headlights, blinding him.

He swerved instinctively, pulled the wheel hard to the right as his foot slammed on the brake. The car spun around, the wheels losing traction on the road. He fought the wheel. The Opel slid sideways into a ditch, throwing him across the front seats, and he blacked out.

When he regained consciousness, the car was facing back up towards the road, headlights skewed upwards at the sky by the slope of the bank. He remembered his revolver and scrambled desperately for it on the seat and the floor well, but it was gone.

72.

He heard men running towards the car and the door flew open. A trap. He realised with sickening clarity that it was him they had been after, not Daniela.

He was hauled out of the car. He felt a heavy blow to the side of the head and his arms were pulled behind his back. He tried to struggle free and his resistance earned him another blow to the head. The strength went out of him and he sagged forward.

He was aware of the sharp bite of rope on his wrists.

They dragged him away from the car. Even half conscious, a part of his brain was still calculating. They had used Daniela to get to him. But what could he have done? Even if he had known, he would have gone after her.

By now his driver would have reported to Abrams, and Abrams would have made a call to the Emniyet. But it would be morning before anyone found the wreck of the Opel. By then it would be much too late.

They dumped him in the back of the Mercedes. He raised his head to look for Daniela. What had the bastards done to her? But then a boot slammed down on his neck, pinning his head to the floor. The door slammed shut and they bumped away again over the potholes.

He could not see his captors' faces in the darkness and no-one in the car spoke a word.

Daniela! Jesus. He had let her down.

The Mercedes lurched to a stop. The door was thrown open and Nick heard the gentle rolling of the sea. They dragged him out of the car and dumped him on the ground. He heard Daniela screaming and he called out to her, though what solace he could have given her right then, he could not afterwards imagine.

One of the men kicked him in the ribs for his trouble.

The sudden pain made him angry. He rolled onto his back and lashed out with his foot, and the toecap of his shoe caught his tormentor in the groin. The man screamed and doubled over. But Nick did not have time to enjoy his small victory. He did not feel the blow to the back of his head, administered by the man's colleague, but it was professionally delivered, with a minimum of fuss, and it was the last thing he remembered for hours.

He woke up with the stink of diesel in his nostrils. He vomited. He thought it was because of the blow to his head but then he realised he was on a boat, battling heavy seas. His hands and feet were tied and he was trussed in the hold, rust-coloured bilge lapping around his feet. Fuel cans, rope, and a spare anchor lay around him.

The stink of fish made him vomit again. He rolled away

from the bilge, still gagging. Through the open hatch-way above his head he saw a grey, cold sky, streaked with the last fading rose of dawn. He heard guttural German voices from the wheelhouse.

He tried to move but it only brought on another wave of nausea. He called out for Daniela. There was no answer.

He guessed they were somewhere on the Black Sea head-ing north. Fishing boats migrated up and down the coast, despite the war, evading the patrol boats. He used such boats himself to smuggle agents in and out of Greece and Romania.

The pitch and roll of the boat brought on another wave of nausea, and he closed his eyes, tried to control it. He wondered how long this torture would continue and when the real torture would commence.

They said the waiting was the worst.

73.

He did not know how long they were at sea. He guessed it was early afternoon when the hum of the engines changed pitch. The boat stopped rolling and they entered calmer waters. He heard shouts as they manoeuvred through shallow waters and the boat jarred against the pilings of a jetty.

Three men came down the ladder, picked him up and dragged him towards the companionway. It was bitterly cold on the deck, a lowering sky. He was hauled down a gangway and for a moment he was afforded a glimpse of the fishing boat that had brought him here, a paint-blistered wheelhouse and rust leaking down the hull. He twisted his head around and saw a handful of fishermen's shacks and a knot of soldiers in grey uniforms, watching his arrival with contempt and with fear.

He was thrown in the back of a van.

He guessed he was inside Romania. As he lay on the cold metal floor, his hands numb from the ropes on his wrists, he waited for the doors to open again, for Daniela to be thrown in beside him. But instead the van's engine roared to life and they bumped away, over rough ground.

Where was she? What had they done to her? She had to

be alive. Yet a part of him did not want her to be alive, not any more, for he did not want to contemplate her sharing this same fate.

He lay on his side with the cold metal floor of the van pressed against his cheek and his arms on fire with pain.

Just twelve hours ago he had been sitting in the Taksim casino with a glass of champagne and a beautiful woman; his best charcoal double-breasted suit was not smeared with unidentifiable filth from the hold of a fishing boat and there was no dried blood crusted onto his face. He could not then have imagined the simple torture of having his arms tied behind his back for twelve hours, how his shoulder and elbow joints would feel as if they were on fire, how he would want to scream not from the intensity of the pain, which was never severe, but because he could not find a way to relieve his discomfort even for a single moment.

The van stopped and the doors were thrown open. He saw a quadrangle, surrounded by two-storey brick barracks. Several dull grey army trucks were parked around the perimeter. A Romanian flag hung limp on a flagpole in the centre of the parade ground.

Two men hauled him out of the back of the van, and dragged him across the frozen ground towards a low brick building. He twisted his head around, looking for Daniela.

But he was alone.

Three guards in the uniform of the Romanian military were watching from the entrance. There was another man in a knee-length black leather coat, wearing the insignia of an officer in the SD.

His mouth was dry, he could hardly breathe. He tried to stand but his knees buckled underneath him.

He knew what would happen now.

74.

He was in his late fifties, with short greying hair. His English was cultured, with an Oxbridge accent. His voice was softly cadenced, a man of education and refinement. He sat on the other side of a wooden trestle table, two Romanian soldiers guarding the door behind him. Apart from the wooden trestle table, the room was bare. There was a high barred window and bare brick walls.

He said his name was Overath, and that he was a major in the Sicherheitdienst. He had the manner of a doctor with a patient whose condition was delicate and possibly terminal, and it had fallen on him to break the bad news to the family.

Nick realised he was powerless. His bowels felt as if they had turned to water. He thought about Jennifer and the boys, how he yet wanted to make them proud of him. He thought, too, about redemption and about Daniela, and tried to persuade himself that she was somehow still alive.

His mind searched for a way out.

They had taken the ropes off his wrists but his hands lay useless in his lap and raising them was like lifting sandbags. Both wrists were swollen and bloody from where the ropes had cut into the flesh.

'I imagine you know why you are here,' Overath said.

'I am assistant military attaché to the British Consulate

in Istanbul and you have violated the terms of the diplomatic code.'

'You are a major in British Intelligence, and you control a number of agents who spy on the Abwehr and friends and allies of the Reich.'

Nick wondered if he knew Daniela was one of their agents. He wondered if they meant to interrogate her as well, find out how much she had told them about Maier.

The SD would not have gone to this trouble, of course, if they were not certain of his identity. He knew what he had to do; he must limit what he eventually told them, give them false information, play the game as long as he could.

'What happened to my friend?'

Overath smiled and did not answer. Instead he pushed a piece of paper across the desk. 'Write down the names of your agents in Istanbul, please.'

'I can't.'

'You will not co-operate?'

'I mean I can't pick up the pen. Your assistants were a little too enthusiastic.' He showed him his wrists.

'Then you can tell me the names,' Overath said, 'and I'll write them down.' He pulled the pen and the piece of paper towards him.

It was all part of the game and Nick went along with it. He made up some names and addresses, stalling for time. He included the name of a known Abwehr double agent to add to the confusion.

When he finished, he looked up at Overath. The major's eyes were black and cold and the gentleman's smile was gone.

353

His new home was a small dank cell with an iron bunk and a hole in the cement floor for the toilet. During the night a stale hunk of black bread and a pannikin of evil-smelling water were pushed through a small hatch at the bottom of the grey steel door. Dinner.

He froze under a thin and louse-ridden blanket, heard rats scuttling across the floor in the darkness. He imagined they got in through that same terrible hole in the floor that had been provided for his sanitary needs.

He thought he heard a scream somewhere in the night and sat suddenly upright, a cold grease of sweat over his body. They were torturing her. He sat there with his heart bounding in his chest, waiting.

Just silence. He had imagined it.

He lay down again and tried to make sense of what had happened. Was Maier behind this? He didn't think so; this was an SD operation, and they had used Daniela as bait.

Of course, there was another, more terrible, possibility but he refused to entertain it.

Finally, from sheer exhaustion, he fell into a black and dreamless sleep.

He was woken suddenly by the sound of heavy boots in the corridor outside. The metal door slammed open, voices shouted at him in German and a bright light was shoved into his face. Two guards hauled him to his feet and dragged him out of the cell and down the corridor.

It didn't help that he knew what they were doing, that he had expected it, that he knew this was when most interrogations were carried out, the mind and spirit weakest in the middle of the night. His body was ready to betray him, begging only to be allowed to rest, to sleep.

He was dragged into the room where he had first been interrogated that afternoon, and thrown roughly into a chair.

'You are playing a game with us,' Overath said.

'I told you what you wanted to know.'

Overath picked up a pack of cigarettes from the table and shook one into his hand. He offered one to Nick, who shook his head.

Overath put the cigarette in his mouth and picked up the gold lighter that lay beside the pack. He lit it, drawing the smoke deep into his lungs. He smiled through the wreath of smoke, the smile of a patient man with plenty of time.

'We know you used a Romanian girl called Daniela Simonici to spy on an Abwehr colonel called Siegfried Maier.'

Nick flinched at the mention of her name. 'Where is she?'

'That is not a concern of yours.'

They knew too much, he realised, his denial wouldn't help her. 'She's not a spy. We were using her for disinformation, that's all. Look, we let her see various documents and we knew she was copying them and taking them back to Maier. She was not our agent. She didn't even know what we were doing.'

Overath gave him a look of supreme forbearance. 'We will find the truth from her, in due course.' He must have seen the look of panic on Nick's face because he added, 'Unless you want to spare her that.'

What could he do to save her? At that moment there was nothing he could do to save himself. 'I told you. We gave her certain information we wanted Maier to have and she pretended to him that it was stolen.'

'You are telling us nothing we do not already know.'

'Then you don't need to question her, do you?'

'Perhaps we are saving her interrogation for you.'

Nick couldn't breathe. He had prepared himself for his own ordeal; but if they brought Daniela in and brutalised her in front of him, he would have to tell them everything. Overath saw the look on his face.

'We want to know the names of your agents in Istanbul,' he said.

'I gave you their names.'

'And we shall check them all. You see, you pretend to be afraid of us, but that is just your training, correct? Give us a lot of names, pretend to co-operate, give us facts that are difficult to verify. You are told to stall for time, while your colleagues work out what you know and what you might tell us and react before we can move against you. Is that not true?'

'I'm not a brave man, Major Overath, I know my limitations. You're making a big mistake here. I'm not as senior as you seem to think.'

'Let me be blunt. The Abwehr has failed the Führer and the German people here in the Balkans. They have allowed themselves to be compromised. Now we wish to redress the balance.'

There is no way out of this, Nick thought. I am going to die in this place.

'Tell us what you know about Admiral Canaris.'

'What?'

'We believe certain influential men are plotting against the Führer and against Germany. You know this.'

Nick thought about the papers Daniela had stolen from Maier's safe two years before. Is that why they had taken him? 'Actually, I don't.'

Another smile, this one twisted with regret. Overath's eyes flickered to the guards and he nodded in silent command.

The guards lifted Nick by the elbows and pulled him out of the chair. They ran him backwards down the corridor, his arms wrenched behind him.

This room was empty except for a single wooden stool. A thick iron bar was cemented into the wall near the ceiling with two strong ropes attached to it, each ending in a slip-knot. He was hauled onto the stool and a noose was pulled over each wrist.

Another guard entered the room holding a rubber truncheon. His appearance was terrifying, as Nick supposed it was meant to be: a Cro-Magnon with a bullet-shaped head and lips like raw liver. The stool was kicked out from under his feet and he swung in the air, helpless. He grunted as his shoulders took the strain of his entire weight.

Overath walked into the room.

'Begin,' he said.

The man with the truncheon stepped forward and swung the bat into Nick's kidneys. The result was startling. Nick gasped at the sudden pain. It was like an electric shock. For a moment he could not breathe.

His whole body went into spasm. He felt himself jerking and twitching at the end of the ropes like a puppet.

Overath stepped in front of him. His tone was conversational, his manner utterly relaxed. He had his hands in his pockets. 'Now. Do you see the position you are in? Do you understand now?'

It was cold in the room but there was a slick of sweat over Nick's entire body. He closed his eyes, tried to breathe through the pain.

Overath sighed and lit another cigarette with the gold

lighter. 'Can we get this business over with? Do you wish to co-operate?'

'I've told you . . . what I know.'

'If you are going to be difficult, you leave me no choice,' he said and the beating began in earnest.

Nick lost track of time. Each second was an eternity; but perhaps the whole ordeal lasted just a few minutes. He remembered screaming so loudly near the end that it hurt his throat.

Finally, he passed out.

When he came around, he was lying on the cold cement floor. Overath leaned over him. 'It won't do any good, these heroics. We have all the time in the world.'

Nick tried to sit up but even the slightest movement sent a shock of agony through his body. He couldn't even speak. And they had only just started.

He knew if they even threatened to do this to Daniela he would tell them anything they wanted. The world was a black and infernal place. There was no way out.

75.

Nick was taken back to his cell and thrown on the iron bunk. He was passing blood, couldn't even drag himself to the hole in the floor to urinate. He didn't care.

He lay in the darkness, trembling from shock, unable to move, unable to sleep because of the pain. He shivered in the cold. He thought about Jennifer. He thought about his boys.

But mostly he thought about Daniela.

If they did not bring her in for his interrogation, it meant she was dead. If they did, he must betray his country and his friends. There was no comfort anywhere in the shrieking, silent darkness.

He heard the sound of boots coming down the corridor. He couldn't breathe, the fear of what was about to happen almost suffocating him. The door swung open and two Romanian soldiers hauled him to his feet. He cried aloud at the pain.

They held him upright between them and dragged him down the corridor. He tried to prepare himself for the onslaught, determined to hold them off as long as he could. It was what he had been trained to do.

The same room, the same SD major. But this time Overath was not alone. There were two other men in dark suits arguing with him in German. He recognised one of them; it was Popescu.

When he saw Nick, Popescu's face twisted in shock and disgust. Must look a sight, Nick thought. He was covered in filth from the cell and his clothes were stained with blood. He imagined he did not look quite as dashing as when Popescu last saw him at the Park Hotel.

The argument recommenced, voices raised even louder now. Eventually Popescu walked across the room and whispered: 'You are coming with us.'

'What's happening?'

'You are a guest of the Romanian Government and you have been treated abominably.'

Popescu snapped an order and the same Romanian guards who had hauled Nick to the torture chamber now guided him gently down the corridor, murmuring words of encouragement, so solicitous he might have been a relative. Popescu and his colleague walked ahead of him. As they stepped outside, Nick felt a startling dash of rain on his face.

He wondered if this was part of the strategy. In a moment he would be dragged away to another cell, another torment. He did not allow himself to hope that it was over.

He was helped into a waiting black saloon, and Popescu jumped in beside him. His colleague sat in front. A uniformed Romanian officer got in behind the wheel. They drove across the muddy yard and out through the gates.

At any moment he expected they would turn around and drive back into the barracks. Overath would be waiting, smiling, and he would be taken back to the cell and it would all begin again.

'You need a doctor,' Popescu said.

'What's happening?'

'We are getting you out of here.'

'Why?'

He seemed surprised that Nick should ask him such a question. 'The Germans are going to lose this war. They don't seem to understand that.'

The car hit a pothole. Nick cried aloud at the sudden pain in his kidneys. Popescu shouted angrily at the driver. He slowed down.

'We want you to talk to your government,' Popescu said. 'We want to negotiate a truce.'

'When you do, you have to remember that it was us who saved you,' the other man said in heavily accented English.

'Tell your people that we want the Germans out of our country. We don't want the Russians marching in here.'

It was hard to concentrate. His head sagged onto his chest.

So, it was not a trick. The driver would not turn the car around, he was not going back to the prison, there would be no more beatings.

'Are you very badly hurt?' Popescu said.

'I'll be all right,' he said but every jolt of the car felt as if someone had touched an electric wire to his kidneys.

'Where's Daniela?'

'Who?'

'There was a woman kidnapped with me. Her name is Daniela Simonici. They think she's an English agent. We have to go back for her.'

'There are no other prisoners,' Popescu said.

'They're holding her in the barracks.'

'No, you are the only one.'

So, she was dead. They had murdered her and tossed her from the boat into the Black Sea.

361

All the way to the border, Popescu talked to him about how a deal might be brokered between his faction and the Allies, how an envoy might be sent to Istanbul and how negotiations might be opened. Nick saw Popescu's lips moving and he heard the words, but grief and pain numbed him and later he could barely remember a word that was said.

They were waved through a German checkpoint, past a column of German infantry travelling on open trucks, boys most of them. No doubt their faces looked like his own: they could not believe the future had turned out the way it had, when once it had looked so assured.

76.

The sheets were cold, soaked with sweat, and they stuck to his body. He tried to kick them off. He heard a woman's voice and his eyes blinked open.

A nurse took his pulse, her fingers pressed to the carotid artery in his neck, counting out the beats on the watch pinned on her uniform. Both his wrists were heavily bandaged, where they had been lacerated by the ropes.

He tried to remember where he was. It was like peering through fog. He remembered Popescu walking him to a border post, and two Turkish police half carrying him to an army jeep.

'Where am I?' he said. His throat was dry as bone, and his voice came out as a hoarse whisper.

'You're in the American hospital,' the nurse said with a heavy French accent.

'I'm in Istanbul?' A part of him still suspected some kind of trick.

'Of course.'

There were other fragments: he remembered a tortuous drive from the Turkish border across badly made roads, a blur of pain, stopping frequently to pass blood. Perhaps he fainted, for he had no recollection of arriving in Istanbul.

'Can I have . . . some water?'

She poured a little water from a jug beside the bed into a glass. She supported his head and held the glass to his lips. He had never been an enthusiast for water, but it tasted better to him right then than a cocktail at the American Bar.

'What time is it?'

'It is five o'clock.'

'In the afternoon? How long . . . have I been here?'

'You were brought here last night. You were in pain. The doctor gave you something to help you sleep.'

His body felt curiously light. They had given him morphine, perhaps. His unshaven cheeks prickled against the sheets. More details came back: an empty border crossing, rolls of barbed wire and guards with machine guns slung over their shoulders. It could have been years ago.

The door opened and a white-jacketed doctor walked in, Abrams with him.

'Mr Davis. You are looking better,' the doctor said.

'Am I okay?'

'You have severe bruising to your kidneys. There was some internal bleeding. I feared at first that you had suffered serious damage but fortunately that is not the case. I have to warn you, you will continue to be in pain for some time. But your stay here will not be too long.' He checked the chart at the end of the bed and nodded, satisfied. 'I shall leave you alone with your colleague.'

He walked out.

Abrams's face swam into his vision. 'How are you feeling?' He sat down on the chair next to the bed. 'Well. What a pickle.'

A pickle. Nick started to laugh, then winced at the pain. A pickle.

'The night you disappeared there was hell to pay. We didn't find your car until next morning. By then it was too late to do anything. We followed the tyre tracks to a disused pier. We guessed what had happened.'

'What about Daniela?'

Abrams frowned.

'Trojan. She was with me at the casino.' Nick nursed one last vain hope that she had been spared, left behind on the beach.

Abrams shook his head. 'No sign of her.'

A blackness settled on him and he wished now only for the warm gelatin embrace of the morphine to enfold him completely, to never have to return to his cold life.

'Tell me what happened,' Abrams said.

In a monotone he recounted everything that happened from the moment they left the casino. He told him what he had told Overath during the interrogation; almost all of it had been false. He had not been particularly brave. They had not had enough time to work on him; he knew he would have told them everything in the end.

Abrams seemed satisfied. 'You have great fortitude,' he said. 'This could have been disastrous.'

'You mean it wasn't?'

'You're alive. We got you back,' he said, as if he himself deserved some credit for it.

The nurse came back into the room. 'You should leave now, *monsieur*. He needs to rest.'

Abrams stopped at the door. 'We have to get Maier out,' he said and then left.

77.

Grief and guilt were his constant companions. They sat gloomily by the bed when he woke in the mornings. He would open his eyes and for a few sweet moments the day might hold promise, but then he would remember and he would close his eyes again and wish once more for the merciful refuge of sleep.

When he should have grieved for the loss of his marriage, he grieved instead for her. There was nothing in his life that consoled him or gave him reason to continue; not his sons, not his duty. Human beings survive on oxygen and on hope. If contentment is not present in their lives, there must be the promise of it. But it seemed to him now that all hope was gone.

A thousand ways she could have died on that boat. He had witnessed them all in his mind. He had failed; he had let her down.

He found himself longing for the obliteration that Overath might have given him in the end. He could have given up his secrets and then they would have shot him, and this wretched struggling with himself would have been over. Did any of it really matter in the end? A few names added to Overath's file would have made no difference to the outcome of the war; his heroism or lack of it would have counted for nothing.

A few weeks later he saw Maier in the bar of the Pera Palas. He looked grey, his cheeks gaunt. The SD were watching him night and day. So far he had been unable to get his wife and son out of Berlin and the pressure was telling.

They spoke on the telephone; Nick gave up all pretence and asked him what had happened to Daniela.

'I don't know,' Maier said, his voice flat. 'She went out one night and never came back. Do you know perhaps?'

There was nothing Nick could tell him.

He woke to the clamour of the telephone beside the bed. In his dream, he had been running through sand, hunted by faceless men. He was soaked in sweat.

He fumbled for the telephone in the darkness.

'Davis?'

'Who is this?'

'It's Abrams.'

'What's happened?'

'The SD are arresting Abwehr officers all over the city.'

Nick turned on the lamp beside the bed and looked at his wristwatch. A quarter to three in the morning.

'We have to get Maier out now. I'm sending a car round. Do what you can.'

He hung up.

Nick swung his legs out of the bed and dialled Maier's number. Maier picked up the telephone on the first ring. 'Where are you?' he said.

'At home. I just heard. The SD have started making arrests.'

'Yes, there's two of them standing in my living room right now.'

'Stall them,' he shouted into the telephone. 'I'll be there.'

He pulled on a shirt and a pair of trousers. As he ran down the stairs, he heard a car pull up in the street outside. He was still pulling on his jacket and buttoning his shirt when he jumped in. 'Hurry!' he shouted to the driver.

They drove across the bridge and up the steep hills to Pera, through dark, cobbled streets. It took seventeen minutes by his watch to reach Maier's apartment in Taksim. As they pulled up outside, he saw a light burning at a second-floor window. There was a Horch limousine parked in front of the building near Maier's Mercedes. Two stiff little Nazi flags framed the radiator.

Nick's driver punched the horn.

Maier must have been at the window, watching. He told Nick later that the two SD men had been quite civil, had merely told him he was being sent back to Berlin, and gave him time to pack his suitcase. When Maier saw the consulate limousine, he simply dropped the case and dashed out of the door.

Nick saw him running out of the apartment. He threw open the rear passenger door and Maier jumped in.

As they drove off, Nick looked out of the rear window and saw two SD agents running towards the Horch. But by then they were already turning into Istiklal, speeding away towards the British Consulate with their prize.

78.

A cold blue dawn in Istanbul. Maier sat in Abrams's office, eating scrambled eggs and bacon. He had a good appetite and he was getting better hospitality here than he would have got from Himmler.

Maier finished his breakfast and pushed his plate away. 'Bastards,' he said, lighting a cigarette.

Abrams sat down in an armchair close to the window and sipped his tea. 'The German Embassy has told the Turkish police that you've been kidnapped and have asked them to look for you.'

'Will they?' Maier said.

'They'll leave not a piece of paper on their desks unturned. But I doubt very much that you'll show up.' He leaned forward. 'So, Colonel Maier, what do you have to tell us?'

Abrams's secretary was sitting unobtrusively in a corner of the room with a shorthand pad open on her lap. She picked up her pencil.

Maier sat back and wiped his mouth with a napkin. He shook his head. 'They will call me a traitor at home.'

'We have an arrangement. It's too late for negotiation.'

'Hitler is a madman. I always said so.'

'I'm sorry, colonel, but we're not here to discuss philosophy, just facts.'

Maier looked grey. He was safe, but someone in Germany would ensure that his wife and son were punished for his betrayal. Even now the SD would be knocking down the door of their Berlin house. But he had no choice; he had waited until the last moment to try to get them out, and there was nothing more he could have done for them.

He closed his eyes and began to talk.

He talked for five hours, gave them the names of Nazi sympathisers and Abwehr couriers and agents · in Palestine, Syria, Iraq and Egypt; told them what he knew about Allied operations inside Bulgaria, Hungary and Romania, what the Abwehr had learned of British and American intelligence inside Turkey, and, with rather more satisfaction, everything he knew about SD activities as well.

When Maier had finished, Abrams's secretary had filled one notebook and was halfway through a second. It was a major coup; Abrams's immediate career was assured.

The ashtray in front of Maier was full to overflowing and the atmosphere in the room, a heady fug of sweat and tobacco smoke, made Nick nauseous. Maier's hands were shaking; too many cups of strong Turkish coffee, perhaps.

'What about Donaldson?' Nick asked him.

Maier looked at Abrams and there was a moment's hesitation. 'I don't know anything about that.'

'Daniela did. She warned me.'

He shook his head. 'She lied to you.'

'She said she overheard you discussing a bomb on the telephone.'

'She was always a very good liar,' Maier said. He looked at Abrams for support.

'He's right, Davis. I don't think Trojan was everything she appeared to be.'

Nick sat back, a knot of dread in his stomach. He knew what was coming next.

'What about Daniela Simonici?' Abrams asked.

Ever since he began talking, Maier's voice had not risen above a monotone, but now Nick read something else in it, a note of triumph, perhaps. 'Ah, yes, Daniela Simonici,' he said and gave Nick a look that he could not fathom.

'You asked her to seduce a man named Grigoriev,' Nick said, businesslike in front of Abrams. 'He worked for the NKVD.'

'I asked her to do many things for me. But yes, I had her seduce him. She lured him to a quiet hotel in Taksim where some of my agents were waiting. He was drugged and smuggled across the border into Bulgaria so that he could be interrogated properly.'

Abrams leaned forward, his elbows resting on his knees. 'Was this the same plan you used to get Davis here out of Istanbul?'

Nick felt as if his heart had stopped.

'I asked her to spy on Major Davis a long time ago.'

'I know this,' Nick said, eager to wipe the smirk from his face. 'She told me on our first meeting in Istanbul.'

'As I asked her to do.'

A long silence in the room as the two Englishmen considered the implications of this remark.

'What do you mean?' Abrams said.

Nick felt numb. 'She was double-crossing us?'

'I judged that it would be more valuable to us to have her feed you disinformation than try to obtain legitimate documents. I assumed, correctly, that you would only bring paperwork home on very rare occasions and that it would be impossible for Miss Simonici to gain consular access no matter how deeply you fell for her charms.'

'Everything she gave us was false?' Abrams said.

'I made it appear that she was taking these photographs herself by making them as amateurish as possible. And I salted the prize with a few tokens, expendable items.'

Nick closed his eyes. Christ.

'The second benefit Miss Simonici afforded us was that I knew almost everything she brought *me* was disinformation. Although it was not useful in itself, it allowed us to make the correct interpretation of other intelligence we gathered.'

Abrams sighed heavily.

'And then there was the capture of Major Davis here. I disagreed with such ungentlemanly behaviour, but the SD insisted, and at the time I was trying to curry favour there, hoping to buy myself more time to plan my defection. It didn't work, obviously.'

Nick thought for a moment he was going to be physically sick.

'She knew?'

'That you were to be captured and tortured? Yes, she knew.' Nick felt as if he had been plunged into ice. 'Major, for a long time I was under the illusion that she loved me, also. Like you, I found it difficult to separate my professional activities from my feelings for this girl. But finally I came to understand that she was totally mercenary, without scruple of any kind. It is a pity you did not understand this also.'

'What happened to her?' Abrams asked.

Maier shrugged. 'I think she is living in Bucharest. With a major in the Siecherheitdienst. Overath, I think his name is.'

Nick went to the window, threw it open. He took deep lungfuls of cold air, his knuckles white as he clutched the windowsill. He looked down into the garden; there were buds appearing again on the branches of the Judas trees.

'She lied to me.' He said the words aloud so they might make some kind of sense.

She lied to me.

She told him that she loved him, yet she had deceived him for three years, and then she lured him into a trap. He had been tortured and would have certainly been murdered if not for Popescu's intervention.

He imagined he saw her face beneath him on a moonlit pillow. *Baby, baby.*

He tried to mount a defence for her, persuade himself that she might yet be innocent. But he knew he had been a fool. He cursed the moment he had ever laid eyes on her, let the cold spring day wash over him, the cold wind making his cheeks burn with shame and with hate.

The fine spring morning had turned foul. Filthy clouds rushed in from the north, and it started to drizzle. He closed his eyes. He felt as if he had been eviscerated with a blunt spoon.

Max King had always told him never to get too involved with a woman. He had a wife at home and Adrienne Varga in his bed in his Istanbul apartment. It was just a casual affair, he had said. She means nothing to me.

On the night Nick was rescuing Maier from the SD, Adrienne Varga told Max that she had met and fallen in love with another man, an Italian diplomat. She was leaving him.

That night a Turkish cigarette vendor, on his way home from Taksim Square, saw Max fall from the Galata Bridge into the swirling waters of the Horn below. The man said Max was drunk and fell by accident but Nick supposed no-one would ever know the truth of that. He supposed Max would have loved the irony; after a lifetime of alcohol it was too much water that killed him.

If Max had been around, Nick could have talked to him about the betrayal, and perhaps he would have talked some sense into him. You should never go overboard over a woman, Max had said. But perhaps in the end he couldn't keep his own golden rule. Or perhaps he never believed it himself; as he said many times, he was just a journalist, and one should believe only half of what he said and none of what he wrote.

79.

He kept his Webley .38 revolver in a drawer in his study, a replacement issued by the Service for the gun lost the night he was kidnapped. He took it out of its hiding place to clean it and re-familiarise himself with its mechanism.

He felt broken inside. It is why we fear to love too much, he thought. Leaves us defenceless, old chum, he heard Max say. Always hold something in reserve, that's the thing.

We retreat from the basic truth that love has the power to strip us naked as much as to heal. So we choose comfort over passion, security over the terrifying freefall of the heart.

There was a small box of ammunition in the drawer and he took out one of the bullets and placed it with great care in the revolving chamber, spun the mechanism several times and then snapped it shut.

There were many advocates for the defence: his sons, of course, for it was not a lesson any father wished to teach his children; Jennifer, also, who kept a light burning in his past, would still grieve for him, though he had given her good cause to hate him; most of all there was Daniela Simonici, a wraith, perhaps one of the lost souls of the

Bosphorus now, telling him that Maier had lied, that she had never betrayed him, not once.

He was not a religious man but an omnipresent God was there also, frowning in silent admonition, for by such an act he was damned, if his schoolboy Bible was to be believed; and there was that most terrible Judas, hope, whispering that tomorrow might be better if only he would endeavour to live another day. Hope is just despair deferred, someone once said.

For now he would leave it to chance to decide.

He was not an especially brave man and it took great courage to hold a gun to his own head and pull the trigger. But he had also never felt as abandoned of all human emotion as he did at that moment.

The hammer snapped back and the chamber turned in the revolver. One chance in six, good odds for a merciful deity, if there was such a thing, or for fate, if that was all it was. For the first time in months, perhaps years, he felt a sense of elation, for his future was finally to be decided and he was free of all responsibility for it.

BOOK FIVE

80.

Bucharest, August 1944

A nd chance decided.
Three months later chance brought him to another
day in August, a blue and hot morning, and to an RAF
de Havilland that flew him and Abrams from Istanbul to
Bucharest. As the plane approached the airstrip on the
southern fringe, Nick saw a pall of smoke hanging low
over the city. Once again Romania had been betrayed.

The Soviet offensive had begun on August 20 and the
German and Romanian positions had collapsed rapidly.
Carol's son, King Michael, had staged a coup with the help
of the army and had Antonescu arrested, then replaced his
government with Popescu's National Democratic Block.
The King immediately announced that his country would
join forces with the Allies against the Axis powers.

That night the German commander was received at the
palace and, after a brief discussion with the King, had
undertaken to leave Bucharest immediately. He kept his
word; but as soon as he was gone he ordered the Luftwaffe
to bomb the city. The raids had continued unabated for the
last three days.

They touched down at the Baneasa airfield, taxied past the wreckage of German Heinkels caught in a Russian bombing raid a few weeks before. They bumped across the grass towards the hangars at the edge of the aerodrome.

Bucharest, once more. She was out there, somewhere.

Nick looked at Abrams in the seat beside him, wondered what he was thinking. Two weeks before, a field marshall and four generals had been executed for their part in the plot to kill Hitler. Canaris himself was strangled with piano wire. Abrams was on the winning side but in many ways he had lost the war.

His face was a mask. He would have to make the best of this. The Soviets would be arriving soon and his brief was to liaise with their new allies; Abrams had come to meet the Devil.

There was a black Opel saloon waiting outside the customs shed. As Nick climbed out of the de Havilland, Popescu ran across the grass to greet him.

'Welcome to Romania!' he shouted over the roar of the engines. 'I hope you enjoy this visit more than your last.'

A grim joke and Nick didn't answer. Popescu kissed him on each cheek in the Romanian manner. Abrams held out his hand for a more formal introduction. Popescu led the way to the car.

If the Romanians had listened to Popescu and had negotiated with us sooner, Nick thought, perhaps they would not be in the predicament they now find themselves. But their fate had been sealed three months before when Churchill and Roosevelt had agreed on the military operational zones in south Eastern Europe; by terms of the agreement the Allies got Greece, the Russians got Romania.

It was too late to do anything about that now. The Red Army were closing in on the city.

As they drove in from the aerodrome, Nick heard the rumble of artillery in the distance. The Russians were just a few miles away, wiping out the remaining pockets of German resistance.

The roads shimmered with mirage. They passed through dismal suburbs, past wooden shacks, tethered horses and goats, then concrete blocks of flats, surrounded by wasteland or peasant fields.

Finally, they reached the city itself, still ravaged by the earthquake and the civil war over three years before. Many of the buildings that survived had now been reduced to rubble by the Luftwaffe.

He remembered Bucharest when he first arrived in 1939, more decadent than Paris, they said, and cheap, too: Black Sea caviar sold by the pound, and lunches that lasted from noon until five; there were Parisian perfumes and Parisian fashion in the shops along the Chaussée; the city's public gardens were lush with flowers and its streets were swept daily by an army of peasant women with stick brooms.

But that was then.

Now the streets were deserted; the few stragglers they saw were empty-eyed and dressed in rags. Much of the city lay in ruins, and the boulevards were cratered from German bombing raids. The shops along the Chaussée were boarded up, and almost all the lime trees were gone.

There was one ruin he was pleased to witness: a mob had burned down the German Bureau. It was gratifying to see it gutted and smouldering.

Sirens began to wail around the city. Those caught in the open started to run. Nick heard the terrifying banshee scream of Stukas in the sky. Popescu shouted at the driver to get off the street.

They jolted to a stop in front of the National Bank. Popescu threw open the door and herded them towards the building. 'This way, this way!'

They took refuge inside one of the vaults. Nick felt the ground shudder above their heads as the German bombers once again took extended leave of their former allies.

So long and thanks for all the oil.

81.

It stank inside the prison, stank of fear and sweat. A guard led the way to the warden's office. The grey brick walls and the keys on the guard's belt reminded Nick of his own brief tenure as a prisoner inside a place very much like this. Unspeakable things had been done here and even though he had one of Popescu's confederates with him, a bespectacled functionary by the name of Emile, he could not help a shudder of apprehension when he heard the steel door slam shut behind him.

The mention of Popescu's name brought the warden snapping to attention. He was a self-important little man in a brown uniform. Nick looked around his office: a grim room with a steel desk, a grey steel filing cabinet and a barred, grimy window that looked out onto a cement exercise yard.

Emile dismissed the warden's unctuous offer of *tsuica* with a wave of his hand. 'We are looking for two prisoners who were brought here at the start of the war,' Emile told him. 'This gentleman is the assistant military attaché from the British Consulate in Istanbul and he has a special interest in knowing their fate.'

'Of course,' the warden said. 'What were their names?'

'Simonici,' Emile said. 'One was named Simon. He was

arrested in June 1940. The other was his brother, Amos. He was still at liberty in December, 1941. That's all I know.'

'A moment please,' the warden said and he hurried outside to the clerk's office to check the files himself.

While he was gone, Nick asked himself again why he was doing this. She had betrayed him, he owed her nothing. And yet a part of him still wanted to believe that Maier had lied. Besides, if he found one of her brothers, he might yet find some answers. It was six months now and he still thought about her every day.

They might even lead him to her.

The warden returned a few minutes later with a dusty cardboard folder. He laid it on the desk in front of him. 'I have found the records. Amos Simonici was arrested on March 28, 1942. Age twenty-four. A banker. A Jew,' he said with a sneer. 'He died while trying to escape. Fell from a third-storey window.'

Emile turned to Nick and explained what had just been said. Nick shrugged; he had supposed it was a fool's errand, had not really expected to find either man alive after so long.

'He is the only Simonici on file. There is a file note here. It seems there is another member of the family, but his name was Kransky, Simon Kransky. He was taken from here in November 1940 by the Abwehr and transferred to another prison. I remember him. He was returned here only recently, in March.'

'He's here?' Emile said.

'Yes. You wish to see him?'

Emile turned to Nick. 'The one called Simon is still in this prison. You wish to see him?'

Nick had not expected this. 'Yes. Yes, of course,' he said, and suddenly he felt hollow inside.

He was emaciated after four years in a Nazi prison. His hands were chained in front of him and Nick could make out the bones in his wrist. His eyes were sunken in his head, yellow with jaundice, and his skull was shaved for lice.

The ring finger of his left hand was missing.

He sat in the chair on the other side of the desk – Emile had commandeered the warden's office for the interview – and stared at them with a mixture of fear and suspicion. It appeared he spoke no French, so Emile again translated for Nick.

'Tell him, please, who I am,' Nick said to Emile, 'and that I'm from the British Consulate in Istanbul. Tell him we're here to help him.'

There was a quick exchange, which seemed to impress the other man not at all. He answered with a few sullen words and looked away.

'He wants to know how you can possibly help him,' Emile said.

'Does he know the Germans have left Bucharest?'

'He knows. He doesn't seem to think it's going to make any difference.'

'Tell him who you are. Tell him you can get him out of here.'

Another swift exchange. For the first time Nick saw hope in the man's eyes, grudging and fearful though it was.

'Ask him if he knows a woman called Daniela Simonici.'

Emile translated and seemed surprised by the answer he received.

'Is he her brother?'

A murmured exchange. Emile shook his head. 'He says no, he's not her brother. He's her husband.'

385

Popescu had arranged the loan of a car and a driver for him. Nick directed his chauffeur to the old Jewish Quarter. He remembered how one cold night he had walked Daniela through these ancient cobbled streets. All that was left now was scorched walls and mountains of rubble.

He wondered what had happened to the thousands of people who had once lived there; perhaps some had sailed on the *Struma*.

His driver parked in the square. Nick knew the way from there.

The apartment where she had lived was gone. The whole block had been obliterated, just a few walls teetering dangerously above the street.

What was he looking for? He was a fool to still be in love with a woman who had betrayed him this way. Yet whatever she had done, it did not matter to him now. He loved her, that was the heart of it. He could choose to turn that love into hate, if that made it easier to bear, it was his choice. But she had touched something in him, and he had loved and loved well perhaps for the first time.

She had been his philosopher's stone. Time alone would tell if he would ever make use of this alchemy.

He knew he would never see her again. He crouched down among the rubble of bricks and charred wood and said a prayer for her, wherever she was.

82.

But he did see her again.

He saw her again in the only place she could possibly be. At the Athenee Palace.

The garden had been hit by Allied bombs in an air raid and was just rubble now. All evidence of her former guests and masters had been erased. The huge red and black swastika was gone, revealing a crack in the facade, left by the earthquake of 1940. The gloom of the lobby with its pairs of yellow marble pillars like a tomb.

The fox-furred princesses, the effete South American diplomats, and the Nazi functionaries had seen out their time. The city's former masters were now departed and the plush cherry sofas and Louis XV chairs awaited the arrival of the new commissars. Or perhaps the cadres of the Workers Soviet would disdain the luxuries of the grand old hotel.

Somehow he seriously doubted it.

He remembered where she had sat that night. He had almost stumbled over her in the darkness.

I'm a good actress. I always have been.

Regret and grief almost choked him. Instead of going up to the room Popescu had arranged for him, he sat where he had sat that night, and summoned her from memory.

And then she walked through the revolving door with a man in the uniform of a senior Romanian army officer. His beautiful survivor, arm in arm with another lifeline.

She saw him and stopped.

She was a good actress – *always had been* – but in that moment her talents deserted her.

'Daniela!'

She turned and walked quickly away. The army officer stared after her in bewilderment. Nick brushed past him and followed her out of the door.

It was breathless hot outside and the bright sunlight hurt his eyes. She looked over her shoulder and when she saw him following, she started to run. She stopped once to take off her high-heeled shoes, as she did that day they ran from the Guardists. He could feel the candescent heat of the cobblestones even through the soles of his shoes. She must have been scalding the soles of her feet through her stockings.

He chased her across the square. She could not run very fast in her narrow skirt and he gained on her quickly. She dodged into the Cretulescu church. He followed.

Burnished icons, bearded and sombre, gazed down from the age-blackened walls. Gold gleamed from the altar in the visceral darkness.

A strange place for a Jew to look for sanctuary.

He waited for his eyes to adjust to the gloom; then he saw her, kneeling beside an icon of Saint Antony. She was still trying to catch her breath. Her face was streaked with tears.

'What are you doing here?' she whispered.

'I thought you were dead.'

'What do you want?'

The moment seemed unreal. For months he had battled in his memory with what Maier had told him, like a detective searching for clues, a lawyer searching among reams of testimony for evidence to support his case, for indictments against her. A part of him had thought she was dead and he had mourned her. Now here she was, his beautiful Daniela, a memory returned to life.

He did not know whether he wanted to kill her or kiss her.

She was shaking, as if there were small electric shocks running through her.

'I thought you were dead,' he repeated.

'I thought you were.' She looked up at him and the look in her eyes melted him. She wailed and collapsed into his arms, sobbing like a child.

I should hate her, he thought; why can't I hate her?

'Baby,' he whispered.

'I know what they did to you. Oh God, Nick. Oh God, how can you ever forgive me?' Her tears had stained his shirt. She tried to rub off the mascara and only made it worse.

'What happened? Daniela, for God's sake, what happened that night?'

It came out in a rush. 'I don't know, there were two men, they put a cloth on my face, some sort of chemical and I couldn't breathe, I think I passed out, when I woke up I was on a boat, I heard them talking about you, where they were taking you, what they were going to do. Oh God, I thought you were dead.' She traced his lips with her fingertips.

'How did you get away?'

'They left me tied up on the boat for hours and then they put me in a van and drove me to a prison, I thought they were going to kill me, they kept me there for weeks and then one day they just let me go. I don't know why.'

He thought about what Maier had told him. He could have been lying: he had good reason to. It might have been sheer malevolence, a desire for revenge, or perhaps he just thought, well, if I can't have her, neither will he. Could anyone ever really prove what had happened?

'What did they do to you?' she whispered.

He looked into those wonderful golden eyes, searching for a reason to believe. 'It's all right,' he said and with three words he dismissed the hell she had led him to. 'Are you okay?'

'I'm alive.'

He smelled perfume, and there were silk stockings on those beautifully sculpted legs. No doubt there was a German officer in a staff car on his way out of Romania with fond memories of Bucharest. Major Overath? No, surely not.

He wondered if the Russians would be as generous.

'You haven't asked me about Maier,' he said.

He heard footsteps echoing in the nave, saw a priest enter from the sacristy. Daniela pushed herself away from him.

'I'm sure he's fine.'

'He came over to our side.'

'You said he would.' She looked up at him, and as quickly looked away again. 'He told you?'

'Of course. He took great pleasure in it.'

'You must hate me.'

'I should, but I don't.' He had expected to hate her. He had spent six months trying to stir enough venom in himself so that he would hate her. But it was impossible. 'Where are you living now?'

'I'll take you there,' she said.

They stood up and walked outside. Heat like a furnace after the cool of the church. She came to stand beside him on the steps, then reached up and touched his face as she had done a hundred times before.

'I always loved you,' she said.

It was six blocks from the hotel, a street with barely a building left standing. She led him up two flights of cement stairs, the landings piled with rubbish; there was a stench impossible to describe. She pushed open the door to a third-storey apartment.

He followed her in. She lit a candle. There was a dingy living room with an ancient table and two chairs, a single bedroom with a narrow bed, and a dark kitchen, the sink stained with rust from the taps. He sniffed at the smell of boiling cabbage from the flat below.

She was gazing at him with that look of longing he had come to know well during their long affair. 'I can't believe it's you,' she said.

'Why did you run away earlier?'

'I was afraid.'

'Of what?'

'Of you. I saw it in your face. You knew what I did. I didn't think you would ever forgive me.'

'Maier said that you knew the SD were going to kidnap me. He said you were in on it.'

She turned pale and reached out to the table for support. 'Tell me you don't believe that.'

'What is the truth?'

'I could never do that to you. I always loved you. I never lied about that.'

'You lied about a lot of other things.'

'I had to.'

'Why did you do it?'

'Does it matter now?'

'Yes.'

'He took care of me. He was kind. And you were married, Nick.'

'So was he.'

'But he didn't want anything else.' She shook her head. 'I know you don't believe me but I just wanted you to love me.'

He reached into his jacket. 'Do you need money?' he said and he took out his wallet and pushed a fistful of *lei* into her hand. She stared at the banknotes and her expression was unreadable.

'Jennifer and I are getting a divorce.'

'She won't do that. She loves you too much.'

He shrugged. 'People get tired of waiting. And there was nothing to wait for, in the end.'

'Do you want to stay with me tonight?'

'Here?'

'Anywhere.'

'No.'

She looked disappointed but not surprised. 'I understand.'

'No, you don't,' he said and let himself out, and as he made his way back down the darkened stairwell, he felt as if there was a stone in his throat. He had mourned her once; now he would have to do it all over again.

83.

Simon had been shaved and washed, at Popescu's orders. Nick picked him up from the Prefecture in an Opel saloon. Simon sat stiffly in the back in a suit Popescu had arranged for him. It was two sizes too large and sat on his bony frame like a sack. As they turned into Strada Lipscani, Simon's expression was frozen between fear and bewilderment.

They stopped outside a crumbling apartment in a bombed-out street; Nick got out and indicated that Simon should follow. The younger man looked scared. Perhaps he thinks I've brought him here for execution.

Nick led the way up the concrete stairs. He was breathing hard when he got to the landing at the third floor but it had nothing to do with the climb. His throat had closed over. Here it was: he had lost everything. Perhaps it was all he deserved.

He knocked on the door. He had sent a courier to her apartment that morning to arrange the meeting.

She opened the door, and Nick wondered if this would be the last time he would see her.

Her face creased into a smile. Those golden eyes. She was wonderful. His heart broke.

'There's someone to see you,' he said and stood aside.

She looked over his shoulder at Simon and for a moment there was only confusion. Then she recognised him. Nick heard a choking sob. Simon stepped forward and threw his arms around her. She clung to him as he wept. Their eyes met over Simon's shoulder and, as she had said to him in Instanbul, the truth was there in her eyes.

He walked into the flat and threw some papers onto the table. 'These are safe conduct passes,' he said. 'I pulled some strings. There's a little money also. It will get you both as far as Istanbul. From there I can arrange British passports.'

She broke away and stared at Nick. 'Why have you done this?'

'You don't have to ask me that.'

Simon was sinking slowly to his knees, God alone knew what four years of brutality and incarceration can do to a man. But then the war had taken all of them places they did not think they would ever go.

The man was crying into her skirt.

No goodbyes. Nick hurried downstairs to the street. His driver was waiting in the Opel. As he got in, he heard a shout and he turned around to see her running towards him.

'Wait!'

She tried to put her arms around him but he stopped her. He needed all his self-control now. He would do this with dignity, at least.

'You don't have to explain,' he said.

'I owe you at least that much.'

He shook his head. 'No. You loved me. That's enough. I'm sorry, I'm sorry I ever doubted that.'

And he got in the car.

'Let's just get out of here please,' he said to Popescu.

He is so thin, Daniela thought. What have they done to him?

She cooked a little food. Her Romanian officer had brought her some meat and she had a little polenta and bread. His eyes went wide at the smell of the meat cooking in the pan and when she put the food in front of him, he gulped it down like an animal and did not look up once, barely drew breath.

Afterwards she fetched him some *tsuica* and they stared at each other across the table.

'Who was he?' Simon asked her.

'The Englishman? He was . . . I met him in Istanbul. He helped me.'

'Was he your lover?'

'No,' she lied.

'I could see it in his eyes. He loves you.' He shook his head. 'It doesn't matter. I don't want to know.'

If he did not want to know, how could she ever tell him? How would he ever know what she had done? And if he did not know what she had done, he could never know her at all, know her truly for who she was. If he did not know, how could he ever forgive her?

In the three years of their marriage before the war began, she had never felt for Simon what she had felt for Nick. Perhaps, she wondered, Nick had experienced this same dilemma with his wife. Perhaps he had not lied to her, perhaps he had never intended to go back to Jennifer, after all.

'I wrote to you every month,' he said. 'Did you get the letters?'

Of course, she had got the letters. The letters were his lifeline, and she had read them all, and kept them in her battered brown suitcase along with the photograph of her mother and her best clothes and her silk stockings, all she had in the world.

His first letter was an appeal to her to help him, written under the eyes of his Nazi gaolers; later he had written about life in the prison and his words had filled her with horror. After a year or so, the letters became remote and disjointed, he spoke more of the past and schooldays and growing up together and nothing of his privations.

She had never been allowed to write back to him.

The letters were tied with string, in a large bundle, in the bottom of her suitcase; her only link with him, and with the life she had once cherished, with her marriage, and her father and mother. But the past was gone now. This man was a ghost.

'Do you want to tell me about prison, about what happened?'

'I don't want to talk about it.'

'Did they beat you?'

'The Guardists beat me every day. Then the Germans came and took me away and they did this.' He held up his hand, showed her his mutilated left hand where they had cut off his third finger. 'But after that they treated me all right. They only beat me when they felt like it and they made sure I got a meal every day.' He looked around the room. His eyes were haunted and she knew in his head he still heard the slamming of cell doors and the screams of other prisoners.

'What about you? How was your war?'

What could she say? It had all been done for him, but how much could she tell him?

She stroked his hair and let him lay his head on her breast. If not for the war, they would have been content enough, she supposed, but now she had found a man whose heart had sung to hers, and the knowledge of it would haunt her always.

She loved her husband in her own way. Simon had been kind to her, he had loved her when no-one else would and she would always be grateful to him for that.

'I'll look after you now,' she whispered and held him in her arms like a child. She had carried him like a burden now for four years, she had kept him alive, he was hers. But inside her there was a tiny voice that whispered to her, Oh how I wish he had died and then I could be free.

'Come here,' she whispered.

She took him into the bedroom. She helped him take off his clothes, was shocked at how thin he was. He reached hungrily for her, squeezed her breasts and ripped at her clothes. She let him lay her on the bed; he lifted up her skirt and tried to enter her too soon. She guided him inside her and it was over very quickly; he cried as he came.

Afterwards she held him and stroked his back.

He slept badly, he moaned and shouted in his sleep. She held him in her arms and gentled him. She did not sleep at all. Instead she thought about Nick; she wondered where he was tonight and wanted him more than she ever had.

84.

The next day an envelope was delivered to Nick's room. It had been left at reception that morning. It was addressed: 'Nicholas Davis, C/- Athenee Palace Hotel, Room 412. Please deliver.'

He sat on the bed and stared at it for a long time. Finally, he found the courage to open it.

As he did, he remembered again when he had met her in those summer days of 1940; it had been a different city then, and he had been a different man.

He tore open the envelope and let it slip to the floor. He did not read the letter word for word the first time. The second time, he read it more slowly, and read it many more times before he finally set it aside:

> Sweetheart, you have to know that I love you, here, today, right now. Now you know my little secret but you do not know everything. So I will tell you. I owe you at least that much.
>
> I imagine Siggi took great delight in telling you what I did for him. I wonder if he told you why.
>
> When I was sixteen I was courted by a boy called Ilie, a Romanian, he was an Orthodox Christian. I did this over the objections of my family, went on seeing him

after they forbade it, because I thought he loved me. I became pregnant to him, and when he found out, he abandoned me. I was disgraced. My mother stood by me; if not for her, my father would have thrown me out on the street.

I lost the baby, a boy, in childbirth. The doctor says I cannot have children now.

I did not think any boy would want me after Ilie. But then Simon came into my life. Simon had known me since schooldays, he said he had always loved me, and he married me despite everything.

You know what happened to the Jews here when the war came. My mother died just before it started, and I thank God for that, for she did not have to suffer through it. My father was arrested by the fascists and our bank was taken over by a German financier; we lost the apartment and the servants, everything.

Simon and I hid in the apartment in the Strada Lipscani. You know what I did to help keep us alive.

This is where we were going that afternoon Simon was arrested by the police. Why did I not tell you then that he was my husband? Because I knew I might need your help and I thought you would not give it as readily if you knew the truth. Men always want something in exchange.

Although now I know I was wrong about you.

Simon was one of the few in the Prefecture still alive when Antonescu put down the revolt. Soon after he fell into the hands of the SD. I asked Siggi to help me get him out. Instead he used Simon to make me one of his agents.

The first thing the SD did was send me one of Simon's fingers, with the wedding ring still attached so there could be no doubt. The SD did this, not Siggi. He is not one for brutal methods, though he was never reluctant to use those who are. He told me Simon would come to no further harm if I did as he asked. He made it sound as if he was my protector, not my tormentor. What could I do? The Germans ruled the world and the British were leaving. So you see, I didn't do it for the money. I didn't want his money and I didn't want yours.

Simon was allowed to write to me on the first day of each calendar month. I lived on my nerves until that letter arrived. But Siggi promised me Simon would be all right as long as I complied.

I did love you in Bucharest, Nick, even though I knew it was wrong. I did not have to force myself to like you. That part was not staged.

It was Siggi's idea for me to approach you on the train, it was planned days in advance. The farce with the Bulgarian border police was to persuade you to trust me.

All the while I was pretending to spy for you, Siggi was pulling the strings. Did it matter in the end? Did you lose the war because I tried to keep my husband alive?

I did many things that I am not proud of. But I did not know about the kidnapping. I swear to you I knew nothing about that. Yes, one of the SD found me, wanted me to lead you into a trap so they could capture you, told me that if I refused, Simon would be killed. But I wouldn't do it, I couldn't do that. But they used me anyway. I suppose they really didn't need my co-operation. They did it without my knowledge. You have to believe that. When I found out what they did to you, I just wanted to die.

Do you think Siggi would have let the SD capture you? You knew he was about to defect, you told me yourself. What if you had told them what you knew about him? It would have been his death warrant. He made up lies about me later, when he was safe, and he did it out of spite.

400

I know you won't believe me but I did fall in love with you. I loved you then and I still love you now. If you had not been married, I would have stayed with you for ever.

But you had a family, Nick, and a wife. What could I do? And I still have a husband. He has first claim on my duty now, if not my heart.

I meant every word I said to you. I love you, Nick, I love you more than words can ever say.

I wish there had been another ending for us; I wish there had been another time. I will always hold my memories of you safe with me. I hope you will not renounce yours.

Once, you told me: if it is not madness, it is not love. Well then, you have been mad for me. For my own part, I did what was right in trying to save my husband's life. I gave you my love and I thought that would be enough for you.

It's getting late now and soon it will be too dark to write. Go home, my darling Nick, and forget me and forget everything that happened here.

Goodbye. I love you. D

That afternoon Nick stood on the balcony of his hotel room and watched Russian tanks roll through the boulevards of Bucharest, as the German tanks had before them. He should have cheered, of course. The Russians were their allies. But he did not feel like cheering.

Abrams turned to him. 'If you invite a wolf into your house, don't be surprised if he doesn't want to leave.'

'Is that a proverb?'

'I don't know. It sounds like it should be.'

'My mother used to say that no matter how bad things get, the sun will still come up again in the morning.'

'Will it? Only if Stalin says it can. Well, shall we go downstairs and greet our new friends?'

Simon was sitting on the windowsill looking down into the street. The day was grey and oppressive. He had been silent all day, brooding with his thoughts. She imagined he was still in prison.

'Won't you talk to me about what happened?' she said.

'I don't want to.'

'We have to talk.'

'Not about prison. I want to pretend it never happened.'

She took a breath. 'Well, I have things to tell you.'

'It's best left in the past, where it can't hurt us.'

And he turned back to the window. She saw his reflection in the glass, his face sallow and pale.

But the past can always hurt you, she thought.

She remembered how terrified she was each month that his letter would not come and how she had imagined this reunion. She thought she would feel again what she had felt before. She thought about how it had been once, the lunches at Capsa's, the dinner parties at the apartment on the Boulevard Bratianu, the walks together through Cismigiu Park.

Why couldn't she feel that way again?

Nick had shown her a different kind of loving. Now she knew what it was like for a man to show her real passion. Wasn't it enough that Simon had been kind and still loved her, would always love her no matter what?

402

That night he pulled her towards him in the narrow bed and made love to her again more gently, but as she closed her eyes it was not Simon above her, it was Nick. Her heart betrayed her when she wanted so much to be her husband's wife again.

85.

Our new friends.

At first Molotov, the Russian Foreign Minister, demanded that the Soviet High Command alone supervise the armistice with the Romanians. Only considerable pressure from Churchill and Roosevelt made him agree to an Allied Control Commission, that included American and British representatives. But Stalin insisted the Soviet High Command reserve all the important decisions for itself. Further, the Allies would not be allowed to deal directly with the Romanian Government, but would have to use the Soviet authorities as intermediaries.

So, Nick thought, no more intimate conversations with my friend Popescu.

Things in Bucharest were changing rapidly. He and Abrams had been ordered to co-operate fully with their new allies, but it seemed the Russians did not want to co-operate fully with them.

An army of Soviet bureaucrats and cadres had taken over the Interior Ministry. And while they awaited their largesse, Abrams fumed in his hotel room, pacing the floor. 'I told them this would happen,' he raged. 'All along I warned them, but they would not listen. Now let's see how far we can trust our working-class comrades!'

Nick and Abrams cooled their heels in the Athenee Palace for three days before the new masters of Romania agreed to meet with them. At five o'clock one evening, they presented themselves on the third floor of the Interior Ministry. They were met by a man in an olive uniform with red shoulder tabs, who introduced himself in halting English as General Demischenko. He was balding, and had moustaches and a beard that reminded Nick a little of photographs he had seen of Leon Trotsky. He wore cheap spectacles and a querulous expression.

They were treated more like prisoners of war than allies. Two Russian soldiers escorted them into Demischenko's office and their credentials were examined minutely before he offered them both a seat. A thick-set man with cropped blond hair and a face like a bullet stood behind his chair, a silent and menacing presence.

The meeting had been arranged so that they might share intelligence on agents and allies in Bucharest. But as the meeting progressed it seemed to Nick that they were sharing much more with Demischenko than he was sharing with them. He could see that Abrams was unable to contain his anger; the blood had drained from his face and he could barely articulate a sentence. He left much of the talking to Nick.

It was only at the end of the meeting, just as they were about to leave, that Demischenko pushed a file across the desk and asked them if they might care to examine it.

'What is this?' Abrams asked.

'This file is about a female subject . . .' He read from his notes and then peered up at them over the top of his spectacles. '. . . Daniela Simonici. Do you know of this woman? She was the mistress of an Abwehr colonel in Istanbul.'

'We know of her,' Abrams said.

'She was used to lure one of our agents into a trap. He allowed himself to be seduced by her.'

405

'Yes. His name was Grigoriev.'

'So you know of this? Did you also know that because of her, he was captured by the German Sicherheitdienst. She lured him to a house in the Galata area and he was kidnapped and smuggled out of Turkey into Bulgaria. He was one of our best agents and knew a great deal. They made him talk. Because of her, we lost one of our most dedicated cadres here in Romania, a committed Bolshevik and comrade, by the name of Jan Romanescu.'

So, Nick thought. She didn't betray me. It was not my fault that Jordon and the others died.

'Did you know she was having an affair with someone inside your consulate and that she was passing along false information? She was a double agent.'

This little performance is intended not as a candid exchange but to embarrass us, Nick thought.

'She is once more living here in Bucharest,' Demischenko said. 'I have just discovered she has been having an affair with an artillery captain.'

'What will happen to her?' Nick said.

Demischenko's expression was contemptuous. 'She is an enemy of the people. No doubt she will be arrested and brought to justice.' He stopped and removed his glasses. 'Perhaps.'

'Perhaps?'

'Grigoriev had a brother. His name is Alexei and he works for the NKVD. This is him, standing behind me. He may wish to take matters into his own hands.'

When they finally walked out into the dusk, Abrams brushed imaginary dirt from his clothes. 'Well, there's our new allies,' he said. 'Good-oh. No doubt they'll throw us out of Bucharest quicker than the Germans.'

The grass in the park was withered and the leaves on the remaining lime trees curled to brown and rattled like dried paper in the furnace breath of the wind.

Abrams loosened his tie, then picked up a soda bottle that he found in the grass and tossed it petulantly into the lake. Nick had never seen him lose his temper before.

'Communist bastards.'

The shallows of the lake were crusted with a detritus of rubbish: bottles, orange peel, paper bags. The hawkers who sold sesame cake and *lokum* wandered aimlessly, without customers. The nearby café was empty, its broken chairs and grey weathered timbers reflecting the sad demise of a city too exhausted to care for itself.

'Well, they were wrong about Grigoriev anyway,' Abrams said.

'Sir?'

'Maier told me Grigoriev didn't tell them anything about Romanescu and his group.'

'So who did betray us to the Germans?'

'I did, Davis. Me.'

Nick was too astonished to speak.

'I was right about the Russians, wasn't I? You've seen for yourself what these bastards are like. Every one of them's a little Hitler in the making.'

'But Romanescu – they were on our side.'

'They were fighting the Germans, but they weren't on our side any more than these damned Russians. As soon as the Germans were gone, they would have been fighting us. I let Jerry do the job for us. It was only a small contribution but I hope one day somebody appreciates it.'

Nick felt a thick droplet of sweat trickle down the back of his shirt. 'But it wasn't just Romanescu you betrayed. You betrayed Jordon. You betrayed me.'

'Sorry, bigger picture and all that. Shame about Jordon, of course, probably a fine chap. But sacrifices have to be made for the greater cause. Even Romanescu would have agreed with me there.'

'Jesus Christ.'

'Come on, Davis, it's what we do. Spilt milk and all that.' He put his hands in his pockets and looked out over the lake. 'I don't act alone, Davis. There is a group of us, we went to Oxford together, we believe in the same things. It's known as the Aylesbury Club. Rather fanciful name, I suppose, because we never meet, not as a group, but we all work inside the intelligence community and we're all committed to the same ideals.'

'Betraying your friends?'

'I'll forget you said that for now. Jordon wasn't a friend of mine and neither are you. We're colleagues. There's a difference.'

'Betraying your country, then?'

'On the contrary. It's those fools in Whitehall who have betrayed us. They've delayed the end of this war and cost hundreds of thousands of Allied lives because they don't want to upset Stalin. If we'd helped Canaris, and come to an accommodation with the Germans, would that really have been so bad? Better than turning Europe red.'

'What did you say to Maier that night outside the Sancta Sofia?'

'He had a plan to assassinate Stalin. He had a very high placed contact called Feoderev. He had your friend Daniela take him a specially designed briefcase, it was actually a bomb. I helped him with some other arrangements.'

'What other arrangements?'

'The attempt to assassinate Stalin was an Abwehr operation. But there was no point to it unless it looked like it originated with us. I helped him a little with that.'

'Helped him?'

'The alliance between the Allies and the Soviet Union would have been destroyed if there was any suspicion of British involvement in Stalin's assassination. I ensured that the connection would seem authentic.'

'But Donaldson found out?'

'Still don't know how. He was spying on me. Can you imagine, Davis. Nerve of the fellow.'

'So the Abwehr assassinated him. And you knew about it?'

'Of course.'

'I could have died that day, too.'

'Tried to get you to come to lunch with me, remember? Did my best. Could hardly tell you why I thought you shouldn't go to lunch with Donaldson. Would have given the game away.'

Nick could hardly credit this, except that it made perfect sense, so he knew Abrams was finally telling him the truth. Abrams had hidden his fanaticism beneath a veneer of refinement that was quite illusory.

'This goes all the way back to Bucharest, doesn't it? It was you who betrayed Bendix. You fingered Clive Allen for it.'

'Without the oil, Hitler might not have attacked Russia. We wanted him to have the oil. We thought they'd destroy each other. In the end it broke Hitler, but not Stalin. Too many of those Russian bastards to kill.'

'You're insane.'

'I like to think of myself as a visionary,' Abrams said. 'Keep your own counsel, Nick. You'll never be able to prove a thing and after the Trojan fiasco you'll be lucky if you get another posting again. You may need me in the future.'

'Jordon had a family. He had daughters.'

'You don't volunteer to go behind enemy lines unless you have a death wish.'

Abrams threw another bottle in the lake.

'And Constantin? Bendix? Me?'

'All for the common good, Davis.'

It was getting towards twilight. The sky was stained a dusty violet, the first stars appearing in a deepening sky. He could not bear to look at Abrams a moment longer. He turned to go. There was one good thing left for him to do.

'Where are you going, Davis?'

'There's one life I can save. You make me sick, Abrams.'

'You're breaking my heart, dear.'

Nick spat on the ground. Abrams just laughed.

86.

In other circumstances he should have been wary of venturing into the ruins of Bucharest after sunset. Six blocks from the hotel the city was a world of darkness and monstrous shadow, lit only by the blue flames of spirit stoves, refugees huddled in the wreckage of ruined apartment blocks.

Soon he was lost. He swore heavily under his breath. Christ. Even with the heavy revolver in his jacket pocket he was nervous. There were scavengers and deserters all over the city.

He turned a corner and bumped heavily into another man. It startled him and he reeled back, ready for an attack. But the man ignored him and walked on.

He was about to walk on, too, but some instinct made him turn around and follow the man. He moved out of the shadows and he saw him for just a moment, silhouetted in the moonlight: a broad and square face, flat and hard as a shovel, hair shaved short to his skull. He knew this was the man he had seen that afternoon, in Demischenko's office, standing expressionless behind his chief.

The man turned into an apartment block at the end of the street and went inside. This was it, this was her apartment.

He took out the revolver. He had practised on a shooting range but he had never fired in anger or in darkness or in a confined space. He heard the Russian's footsteps echo on the stairwell above him. He started to run up the stairs.

In the darkness, he tripped on some rubbish and fell headlong. His shinbone cracked on the concrete. He swore at the pain.

Already the Russian was kicking in the door. He shouted a warning, hoping to distract him, and ran blindly up the stairs.

The door to the apartment lay on the floor, ripped off its hinges.

A single candle burned on a table in the middle of the room. He called Daniela's name but there was no answer.

The train pulled out of the station, arc lights revealing a few homeless souls crouched around spirit stoves. An unshaven man in a balaclava, sitting beside the tracks, stared up at them and the look on his face made her shudder. She was relieved to be finally leaving this terrible city behind. She did not know Bucharest any more.

Simon took her hand and squeezed it, reassuring her. Hard not to love a man who was kind. He had his cap drawn down over his eyes, and she couldn't see his face, but she put her head on his shoulder, felt the rough wool of his jacket against her cheek. He still was just bones underneath.

She promised herself that soon there would be a new life and she would be happy again. She hoped it was true.

There were few places to hide and he had only a few seconds to decide. He could not wait there in the doorway. Holding the revolver in front of him, two-handed, he ran into the kitchen.

Empty.

'Daniela!'

He has to come for me first. I can't let anything happen to her.

He heard a noise behind him, from the bedroom. He turned, saw a silhouette in the doorway in the candlelight. He saw the pistol raised towards him and he felt very calm. There was a sense of sudden and blissful peace. It was over. He knew what would happen and he took a split second to correct his aim, knowing it might make every difference to her, if not to him.

The pistol shot sounded like cannon fire in that confined space. He fired his own weapon at the same time. He did not feel the bullet. He did not even know he was hit. He concentrated on his aim, as if he was back on the practice range, and squeezed off two more shots before he went down. There was no pain.

87.

They found an old boarding house near the docks while they waited for a ship to take them to England. That first night they slept on a cot barely wide enough for one. The room stank of stale sweat and boiled greens.

As Simon undressed, she saw his ribs through his pale skin, and the fading cicatrices of scars on his back.

She took a deep breath. She had been waiting for the right time. Would there ever be one? 'There's something I have to tell you.'

He sighed, puffed out his cheeks. 'Let's not do this now.'

'I have to tell you about the Englishman.'

'It doesn't matter. That's all in the past.'

'It does matter. I loved him, Simon. I still love him.'

He was silent.

'We were lovers for three years.' She waited to see what he would do. She hoped he would hit her. She would deserve it.

But he didn't hit her, because then she would have been free to walk away. Instead the look on his face broke her heart. 'I told you, it doesn't matter.'

With those few words, it was as if the last four years did not exist. And if they were to survive, that other time could not exist, because then they could never go on.

'I forgive you, Daniela.'

She had not asked for his forgiveness but she accepted it. She hated herself for her weakness with him, weakness she had never had all those years on her own. She was his wife and she knew he would never let her go.

The heat was relentless. Daniela and Simon sat in a tea house above the docks staring at the crowds moving about the quay, the dispossessed and the desperate, all looking for another home and another chance.

A passenger ship had just docked in the Horn and passengers spilled into Tophane Square from the customs and shipping offices: turbaned dark-skinned men loaded down with chickens and hessian sacks, well-to-do Turks with porters scurrying behind them with their portmanteaux.

Daniela studied Simon's face, tried to find something that would make her heart move, but there was nothing, nothing but gratitude that he had treated her well, that he had saved her. She wished she could have loved him more. It would have been so much easier.

They had with them the tickets they had bought with the money Nick had given them, and the passports, as he had promised. All their possessions were in the two cardboard suitcases at their feet. They had left the flat and just walked out, caught the first train to Constanza and a boat to Istanbul. She had wanted to say goodbye to Nick one last time but how many times can you say goodbye?

Simon had been gentle with her these last weeks, had shown her more tenderness and understanding than perhaps she deserved. She had waited for the love to flood back, as she had expected it to do. She waited to feel with him as she had with Nick. But as the weeks of their exile went by, she only grew increasingly frustrated and did not know if it was because of her own shortcomings or his.

He seemed withdrawn, and she imagined that this was because of his imprisonment; of course it would be this way. But then she remembered he had always been like this, even in their best times. It was the way he was.

She knew it could never be the same between them, not ever again.

It seemed as if she had carried this baggage all her life. The memory of Ilie's betrayal was as fresh as if it had happened yesterday. When her father had discovered the relationship, he had forbidden her from seeing him, but she had gone behind his back. She had let Ilie do it just that one time, she had wanted to please him, and afterwards he had told her it was just their secret and she kept that secret until she discovered she was pregnant and it was impossible to keep it any longer.

She thought he loved her but afterwards she realised he had used her and she never forgot his betrayal, for she had risked everything for him. When she had the baby, she had to endure the shame of it alone.

To his Romanian friends, Ilie was a hero and she was just a Jewish whore.

She told herself she would never trust any man again. But when Simon showed interest in her, asked her father if she would marry him, even though he knew her shame, she had been overcome with gratitude.

He had demanded little of her but to be his wife. She had not known he had longed for her all that time; and she owed him so much for rescuing her when no-one else would. How could she let him down now?

And yet.

She watched him as he stared down at the Horn, one fingertip absently tracing the fine scar on his jaw where the

Guardists had beaten him. She thought of him as he used to be, when there was flesh on his bones, a good-looking boy who could have had any woman he wanted. Why did he choose her? One day soon he would be attractive again. He was still young, and he had survived, when so many had died.

She took a deep breath. 'I'm not coming with you,' she said.

'What?'

'I said I'm not coming with you.'

'What are you talking about?'

'I can't.'

He laughed, then frowned, not knowing what to say to her. 'I don't understand.'

'I just can't do it.'

'You don't want to go to England? Where do you want to go?'

'I don't want to go with you,' she said. She could not believe she had heard herself say the words.

'You're not serious.'

'You never asked what happened to me during all those years you were in prison. Don't you care?'

'I don't want to know. That was our agreement.'

And this was how he defeated her, always. This was how it was when they were first married. By not contending with her, he left her always feeling that she was wrong, that she was always complaining and he was the patient one.

But this time she pressed on. The only power she had in the world was the truth; the truth was her freedom. 'I lived with a German Abwehr colonel as his mistress and I did anything he asked of me in order to keep you alive, Simon. I slept with him and I spied for him. And I fell in love with the Englishman. I slept with him and I fell in love with him.'

417

The look of naked pain on his face cut her like a knife.

'Are you asking me to forgive you? Because I have. We don't have to talk about it any more. It's all in the past now.'

'It's not in the past. I'm in love with him still.'

'There's no point in talking about this. You're my wife. Whatever happened in the past is best left there.'

'This isn't the past, Simon. This is the present. I feel this way now.'

He winced. God, every look, every shadow in his eyes; she did not know if she could go through with this.

'You can't abandon me now. Not after everything.'

'Simon, I'm sorry.'

'You have to forget about this. We'll go to England and you'll forget about what happened in Istanbul and we can get on with our lives.'

'I love him,' she said.

There are moments in every life around which the future turns. She knew this was the moment she could take her freedom back, if she was strong enough, if she had courage enough. But inside she was still the stupid girl who had got herself pregnant and who no-one could love. Anyway, she deserved to be punished for taking Nick from his wife and family.

She heard herself say: 'Please let me go.' If he saw her desperation, how much she needed her freedom again, he would relent.

'I can't live without you,' he said. 'Not after all I've been through.'

'I've been through a lot, too.'

There was such a look of desperation on his face. She just wanted to run away.

'Do you know what it's like to be beaten until you pass out?'

'Do you know what it's like to be another man's whore?'

'I didn't survive three years in that Nazi prison just to have you leave me.'

'You wouldn't have survived three days without me!' she screamed at him.

'How can you do this?'

A look of panic on his face. He looked like a little boy and all she wanted to do right then was hug him and tell him everything would be all right.

'You can't do this to me. Not now,' he said.

'I'm still in love with him,' she said, knowing the truth was all that would keep her from the boat and a future she no longer wanted.

'I can't live without you.'

She knew he was right. Three years in prison had robbed him of all resources. But how much did she owe him? How long before she paid off her debt?

She could feel her resolve slipping away. She had once promised herself she would never live her life for another man, but she now found she still owed him interest for what he had once given her. Would the debt keep compounding for ever?

'How can you do this, after I married you, when no-one else would? Have you forgotten that?'

And there it was, it was said. Would she abandon her husband now, when he was begging her to stay?

Everything she had done these last three years had been for him. How could she let him go now? There was so much of her invested in his survival.

He started to cry. And with the tears, she felt her resolve slip away.

'Don't cry,' she said and held his head against her breast and stroked his hair. 'It's going to be all right. Don't cry.'

'Look, we've both been through a lot,' he said. 'We'll talk about this on the way to England. All right?'

88.

Nick first saw Daniela Simonici in the American Bar of the Athenee Palace Hotel in Bucharest in the June of 1940. He couldn't take his eyes off her. Hard to say what makes a man lose his head over a woman. The city was full of beautiful women, penniless countesses and fox-furred demimondaines looking to be rescued. Until that moment he had spared them only an appreciative glance, as a man does. But on Daniela Simonici his eyes rested and stayed.

Four years later, in the September of 1944, with the Russians in Bucharest and the Allies in Brussels, he sat on the balcony of the American Hospital in Istanbul in a wicker chair, staring at the slick waters of the Bosphorus, and wondered at his misfortune at being alive. You would think you could trust a professional assassin to find his target, even in the candlelit gloom of a tiny apartment. A collapsed lung, the loss of almost three pints of blood, it might have killed other men, the doctors had said to him before they transferred him to Instanbul to convalesce. You have a great will to live.

Where had that come from? he wondered.

He watched a freighter pull away from the quay and make its way towards Seraglio Point. He knew Daniela Simonici was on board.

He saw Max walking across the lawn towards him. Another ghost, another spectre from the past.

Is it right to break the bonds you have made in the past to pursue the happiness you find in the present? Daniela thought not and he accepted her judgment. Until then he believed he had a right to such happiness. Now she was gone he no longer cared about the answer.

He knew what he had done those three years in Istanbul was madness; but if it was madness, then it must have been love.

Max sat down, watched the ship moving out of the harbour. 'Is she on board?' he said.

Nick did not speak, could not find his voice.

'She'll be back,' Max said. 'Girl like that. She'll be back.'

But if she never did come back, he wondered what he would do. She had been in his life for so long, it was impossible to imagine living without her now. The horizons of his future stretched ahead of him, without pity. When you have been in love, as when you have known true madness, you are changed forever. It is impossible to come back.

Acknowledgments

My thanks once again to Kim Swivel, my brilliant editor at Random who worked with me on *My Beautiful Spy*, from its broadest canvas to the fine details. I am indebted to Jude McGee, my publisher from heaven for her support for me and this book. I would also like to thank Zoe Walton for her patience with me in supervising the realisation of this book.

My thanks, too, to Carol Davidson, Caitlin Spencer, Karen Reid, Lisa Bardetta and, of course, Fiona Henderson for their ongoing support. And to Peta Levett and all at The Shire.

Finally, my thanks to my agent and good mate Tim Curnow who helped me pull this book into shape when I wanted to toss it away. And finally to Daniela herself, without whose enthusiasm and encouragement there would have been no Beautiful Spy.

Also by Colin Falconer

ANASTASIA

Some men don't fall in love; they get lost. I was lost from the moment I saw Anastasia Romanov in the taxi club that first night . . .

When American journalist Michael Sheridan jumps into the Whangpoa River to save a woman he met in one of Shanghai's taxi clubs, his life is changed irrevocably. A Russian refugee, Anastasia Romanov bears an extraordinary resemblance to the princess said to have survived the brutal murder of her family at the hands of Bolshevik revolutionaries, but she is suffering from amnesia and remembers little of her life before Shanghai.

Unravelling the mystery of Anastasia's identity and past takes them both from Berlin to the pre-war London of the 1920s, from Bolshevik Russia to New York just before the Wall Street crash. Spanning the turbulent and romantic decade of the twenties, *Anastasia* is a tale of murder and betrayal, royal scandal and financial intrigue.

'Falconer weaves a pacy story of obsession, love, greed and corruption . . .[He] writes with skill and grace . . . really well done.'
Sydney Morning Herald

'A beauty . . . Falconer's grasp of his period and places is almost flawless . . . He's my kind of writer.'
The Australian

Also by Colin Falconer

AZTEC

A spectacular tale of the legendary woman who brought Montezuma's empire to its knees . . .

Sold into slavery as a child by the Spanish adventurer Cortes, the life of Aztec princess Malinali is one of the most fascinating and enduring legends of Mexico. Reviled as a traitor responsible for the destruction of the native people, yet honoured as a heroine and symbolic mother of the nation, her extraordinary and passionate story has never before been so evocatively told.

WHEN WE WERE GODS

A vivid portrait of an unforgettable woman who thrived and triumphed in a world ruled by men.

Arrestingly beautiful and fiercely intelligent, Cleopatra VII of Egypt was barely more than a teenager when she inherited the richest empire in the world. Imperilled at every turn by court conspiracies and Roman treachery, Cleopatra brazenly sought a partnership with the only man who could secure Egypt's safety: Julius Caesar, a wily politician and battle-hardened general with a weakness for women. The result was a passionate love affair that scandalised Rome and thrust Cleopatra into the glittering but deadly world of imperial intrigue and warfare – a world that she mesmerised and manipulated even after Caesar was gone.